Dugger was in it now. There was no more room for doubt. Something had happened at Regensburg; his would-be killer had slipped when he said that. And it related somehow to the deaths of his former agents.

Dugger realized that he would be dead now too if he had not had the luxury of almost accidental warning.

He had been lucky.

He intended to give the others who remained alive the same chance.

He didn't know how hard that would be. . . .

The Regensburg Legacy

Jack M. Bickham

TOR

A TOM DOHERTY ASSOCIATES BOOK

With special thanks to
Dr. Jess McKenzie,
Harold Kuebler,
and—of course—Bumpers.

THE REGENSBURG LEGACY

Copyright © 1980 by Jack M. Bickham

A Tor Book

Published by Tom Doherty Associates, 8-10 W. 36th St., New York City, N. Y. 10018

First printing, April 1983

ISBN: 0-523-48062-8

Printed in the United States of America

Distributed by Pinnacle Books, 1430 Broadway, New York, N. Y. 10018

This one is for Momma

The danger for all rulers is that they begin to believe that history is the result of great generalities instead of the sum of millions of small particulars; that a proud man without shoes may starve before he presents himself at a place of employment unshod; that a petty, brutal bureaucrat may spark a revolution; that high blood pressure may plunge a great man, even a pope, into melancholy and despair; that a woman may sell herself to many men for money because she cannot give herself to any single man for love.

—*Morris West*

The Regensburg Legacy

PROLOGUE

Regensburg, West Germany: November 10

It was a typical German snowfall, quiet and vast, sifting out of a metallic sky. It seemed harmless and eternal, but already the roads were thickly coated, the rolling fields pure white, the great firs on the hillsides bent low by the weight on their shoulders.

On the outskirts of Regensburg, smoke drifted from the chimneys of the gaunt gray barracks buildings that had once housed Nazi storm troopers. Kendall Barracks, it was called now, home of a United States armored battalion on the Danube some seventy-five kilometers from the Czech border.

The temperature was $-6°$ Centigrade, and in the sprawling central assembly yard the work detail of American GIs looked miserable. There were eleven of them. The snow coated their heads and shoulders, and they stomped their feet on the frozen cobblestones to maintain circulation. The ragged ditch they had been tearing in the pavement was momentarily abandoned, shovels tossed down, air hammers laid aside, the big olive drab backhoe machine shut down. Ten-minute break.

Everything seemed to be timed in ten-minute intervals at Kendall. It was considered forward duty, and everything was taken very seriously. Combat readiness time, day or night, was ten minutes, too. Back home, people said the other side would never attack. Suicidal for both sides, people said. It was easier to believe that back home. Here, when you arrived, they took you for a border tour and you saw the wall for yourself. It made a believer of you, and you began to believe what the Europeans had always believed, that the next war would be a tank war. Fought right here.

Here the combat readiness time did not seem unreasonable.

The work detail seemed unreasonable.

"Dogfaces," a GI named Cornwell said, peering through icy eyelashes at the rock walls of the German-built barracks surrounding the yard.

"What?" The man next to him, named Herbert, was startled.

"Dogfaces," Cornwell repeated bitterly. "That's what they used to call GIs all the time. I see why. You change the name, you don't change the status any."

"The sewer pipe has to be dug up," Herbert pointed out.

"It's Sunday."

"People shit on Sunday just like every other day."

"Yeah, man," another GI, named Sanders, said, grinning. "You want that shit backed up all the way to *your* bunk?"

The leader of the detail, a sergeant named Maxwell, had been squatting nearby. Now he stood and tossed his cigarette into the raw wet earth already dug out of the growing ditch. "All right, men. Back to work."

With considerable grousing and unnecessary motion, the GIs went back at it. Three of them went back to the air hammers. The compressor motors were cranked, their chuffing loud in the snowfall. The hammers were dragged to pavement edges and turned on, racketing deafeningly. As pieces of the pavement were broken, other men shoveled out the cobbles and dirt.

Nearer the far end of the long ditch, the backhoe operator started his diesel, adding its throaty engine noise. His job, after the pavement had been broken and the cobbles laid aside, was to deepen the trench to uncover the sewer pipe which had collapsed and caused all the trouble. With delicacy that could have handled crystal, he positioned the narrow scoop in the trench and lifted out three hundred pounds of wet German clay.

Watching the work progress, Sergeant Maxwell allowed himself the luxury of speculating about how long it had been since this earth had been disturbed. He was something of a romantic, and knew more of the history of this place than any of his men. It had been Kendall Barracks for more than thirty years now, but it had been a German *Panzer Kaserne* long before that, back to 1938. Standing here with his hands and feet numb from the cold, Sergeant Maxwell amused himself by imagining how the German soldiers had probably bitched just like this when they laid down the pavement in the first place.

They had done a hell of a job: three inches of gravel, four inches of concrete, an overlay of gray cobbles in perfectly symmetrical archway patterns. Germans built things to last. The only thing they had overlooked was the possibility of the pipes finally caving in under all the paving.

Of course they hadn't counted on Patton, either.

It had been elements of Patton's 4th Armored that took Regensburg that May so long ago. The Breakthrough Division, news flacks had called them, and they had lived up to their name that day. Regensburg had fallen on a day when elements of the 4th covered more than twenty-five miles, hell-bent for Prague, thinking maybe they could get *there* before the diplomats ordered them to stop and wait for their brave Soviet allies to slog in from the other direction.

Army intelligence had placed an entire division of the German 5th Panzer Army in the Regensburg area, but it had fallen after surprisingly light resistance. Parts of the *Kaserne* had been blown up by Nazi demolition teams, and several tanks had tried to escape to the north, a fatal mistake that got them chopped up near Amberg. Most of the expected German tanks had never been found at all.

One story said the Germans had been engaged in secret research at Regensburg and the demolition crews had done their work to bury all sign of it forever. Another story said there had been huge underground garages and everything was still buried down there someplace. Sergeant Maxwell liked the idea, but didn't give it much credence because he had heard the same yarns about Patch Barracks, near Stuttgart, and McGraw in Munich.

The work continued. So did the snow. Evening was coming on soon and they would have to knock it off. Sergeant Maxwell wondered whether his captain would chew his ass for not completing the job. It was getting colder.

"Hey, Sarge," one of the men panted, "how about another break, man?"

"Later."

The work went on.

In a little while there was a diversion. The backhoe stopped working abruptly, its engine note changing to a growl. Sergeant Maxwell saw the operator stick his head out the cab window and wave at him. A couple of the GIs nearest the machine put down their shovels and jogged over to the ditch where the backhoe arm was fully extended downward. Sergeant Maxwell saw the operator working his toggles. The machine bucked and smoke gushed from the stack, but the scoop did not retract.

Sergeant Maxwell strode down the ragged trench. As he reached the site, the backhoe operator shifted to neutral and idled the engine. He joined the other in looking into the ditch where the scoop seemed to be stuck.

The scoop was at the bottom of the hole, filled with yellow German dirt. But more loose dirt and gravel were sifting down the sides of the trench, rushing *past* the scoop —falling in somewhere deeper.

Which didn't make sense.

"That mother caved in!" one of Sergeant Maxwell's men said.

"Caved in to *where?*" the other asked.

"How do I know, man?"

The hairs on the back of Sergeant Maxwell's neck bristled. The other men were coming over.

"Pugsley, what did you do, man? Go through to China?"

Pugsley, the operator, climbed down and joined Sergeant Maxwell in inspecting the situation. The loose earth had stopped sifting down, and there was—clearly—a two-foot hole in the bottom of the trench beside the scoop blade. It was black and it looked deep.

"You want me to try again to retract the scoop?" Pugsley asked. "It's caught on the edge of the pipe where it rusted out and fell clean through into that, uh, what-ever-it-is down there."

"Leave it as it is," Sergeant Maxwell said. His heart was beating fast. "Slater. I want a couple of flashlights and a ladder, fast."

The GI named Slater went running. They stood silent, looking down into the ditch, and he was back inside three minutes. He had two flashlights, and was dragging a ten-foot section of aluminum extension ladder.

"We're going to hang the ladder down over the side and into that hole," Sergeant Maxwell explained. "You guys are going to hold it and I'm going to climb down there and have a look-see."

"You have all the fun," Pugsley said as the ladder was placed in the ditch.

"You want to go down first?"

"Shit no!"

Sergeant Maxwell put one of the flashlights in the pocket of his jacket, got a leg over the ladder, and climbed down. The ladder trembled, and dirt tumbled down around him as he reached the bottom. Hanging on with one hand, he bent over awkwardly and tried shining the flashlight into the hole. He couldn't see a thing. Dank, stale air was pouring up out of the hole.

Sergeant Maxwell knew he could be smart, climb back up top, and go report to the general—or he could go on down through the opening as far as the end of the ladder. If he was half smart, he would go report.

Well, forget being smart.

Moving very carefully, Sergeant Maxwell climbed down, putting first his feet and then his legs down through the opening. His feet found the bottom rung of the ladder as his shoulders were at the level of the opening. Taking a deep breath, he twisted his body around so he could duck entirely down through.

He swung the beam of the flashlight below. There was a metal object about two feet below the end of the ladder. There was black paint speckled with bright orange rust . . . a circular chamber of some kind with a . . . a lid in it . . . and out in front—he swung the beam—a long steel tube of some kind. . . .

"Jesus Christ," he said in recognition.

"Hey, Sarge!" Pugsley called from above. "You okay?"

Sergeant Maxwell licked his dry lips. "I'm okay. Listen! I'm going to get off the ladder. As soon as you feel my weight off the ladder, you come down. You understand?"

"Yo," Pugsley called. He did not sound happy.

"Slater?"

"Yo?"

"Go get the CO."

"You mean—"

"I mean the general, *yes*. Right now!"

"Yo!" Dirt tumbled down around Sergeant Maxwell's shoulders.

Judging his distance carefully, Sergeant Maxwell swung off the ladder to the metal deck below. He climbed on down off the deck and in a moment was standing on a paved floor. Daylight shone in through the hole above, revealing a shower of dirt as Pugsley climbed down. Sergeant Maxwell swung his beam in all directions. He could not believe this.

Pugsley came through the hole. "Holy shit!"

"Climb down. Be careful."

Pugsley complied. Moments later they were standing side by side, shining their flashlight beams this way and that.

The underground area was full of tanks. They were arranged in neat rows, nose to tail, turrets depressed and hatches open, ready to roll. The tank they had climbed down upon was a great old Tiger, eighty tons on fourteen tracked wheels. There was a layer of bright rust on the treads and an occasional corner, but most of it seemed in mint condition, gleaming under a dusty layer of black paint, German cross, and other insignia intact on its flanks.

There were rows of Panthers, too, the finest German tank of World War II, at least two dozen of them and probably more. And in other neat lines across the huge expanse of the cavern were other vehicles: Mark IVs with mesh over the running gear to frustrate attack . . . heavy trucks . . . staff cars, light vehicles like jeeps. But mostly it was tanks, row after row of them, lined up farther than the light of the flashlights would carry.

Sergeant Maxwell was conscious of his heartbeat. He smelled the faint odors of gasoline, diesel fuel, and lubricants. Somewhere there had been massive ramps leading to the surface, and huge doors. He could imagine the blaring of the klaxons, the lights coming on, the engines roaring to life.

"How big *is* this place?" Pugsley asked.

"You want to explore?" Sergeant Maxwell asked.

"Maybe we ought to wait, Sarge, and let the CO come down."

"Right," Sergeant Maxwell said. "And then we can climb back out and let him and the other big shots take over."

"Shit," Pugsley said, and started walking east, around a Panther.

Sergeant Maxwell followed. They moved between rows of tanks, past a steel worktable where technicians had been overhauling parts of an engine right beside the tank with the problem. They kept moving, leaving the tanks behind and crossing a dusty space filled with other wheeled worktables, carts, storage bins. At last they reached an interior wall, granite, with pipes studding its surface and a single steel door. A small booth stood empty beside the door, proof that it once had been under continuous guard.

Pugsley stepped forward to spray his light over a metal sign on the door.

"What's it say?" Sergeant Maxwell asked.

"Entry *verboten* except special authorized personnel," Pugsley translated.

"Is it locked?"

The door creaked. "Nope. Shall we go in?"

"Why not?"

They entered a tunnel with walls like gypsum that streamed water. Doors led off the tunnel. Some were locked. Shining their lights through small glass windows in some of the doors, Sergeant Maxwell and Pugsley saw worktables, racks of glass bottles, sinks, coils of tubing.

At the far end of the tunnel they reached another door and opened it. They went into this area, their flashlights shining around at random. Sergeant Maxwell began to feel distinctly uneasy.

It was Pugsley who put Sergeant Maxwell's own question into words.

"Sarge," he said huskily, "what *is* all this stuff?"

1

Burghausen, West Germany

The summer so far had been a disappointment.

Now it was late June, but still cold in the area around Burghausen, at a once strategic bend in the Salzach River on the Austrian border.

It was just nightfall. Cool fog drifted up from the river, through trees and narrow streets and around the crumbling battlements of the huge, brooding castle on the high ground. A steady drizzle fell. Woodsmoke wafted from chimneys of rows of small stone houses, tendrils curling backward over gleaming red tile roofs. Here and there lights shone warmly behind steamy windows, but the village seemed still as a graveyard.

Not far from the river, where the main highway twisted through the town, the gloomy silence was broken by the sound of an automobile engine. A Fiat 127, headlights glowing, slowed at a road sign intersection near a vacant-looking *Gasthaus*, then turned left onto the side street. Passing small houses with tiny front yards protected by hedges and rock walls, it proceeded about a block, then slowed and pulled to the side. The driver could be seen, peering through the front windshield to verify the number of the house he had selected. After a moment the windshield wipers stopped slapping and the lights, then the engine, were turned off. The driver got out of his car and went hurriedly through the wooden gate on the way to the front door of the house, which had no lights showing in its windows.

The man was tall, very thin, wearing a rumpled business suit too light for the unseasonably cold weather. He had no hat. His hair was thin and was now more gray than blond. He had a bulky leather briefcase under his left arm.

After glancing up and down the deserted street, he rapped on the door. After a little while a light flashed on in one of the downstairs windows and the door opened.

The man inside the house was about the same age, somewhat heavier, with wide shoulders. He was wearing faded Levi's, a flannel shirt, and comfortable old work boots. His dark hair, flecked by gray, was cut quite short. For a moment there was no recognition in his wide-spaced gray eyes.

"Joe Dugger?" the visitor said, extending his right hand. "Remember me? Charlie McCoy?"

Joe Dugger's craggy face relaxed in a puzzled grin. "Charlie? What are you doing out in this Godforsaken part of the world? Get in here! You never did know enough to come in out of the rain!"

The two Americans exchanged warm handshakes, and McCoy went inside. Dugger led him through a dimly lighted hallway to a small living room packed with old furniture and books. A fire burned smokily in a stone fireplace. Dugger moved between chairs and stacks of books with the natural grace of a woodsman, turning on two lamps and moving some stacks of magazines so there would be places to sit facing in front of the fire.

"What the hell brings you to Burghausen, Charlie?"

"A little business, a little pleasure."

"Which am I?"

McCoy was a quiet man with a lazy smile. He held the smile now. "Maybe a little of both."

"Are you hungry?"

"I ate back down the road about an hour ago, thanks."

"How about a drink?"

"Thought you'd never ask."

"Sit there."

McCoy sank gratefully into one of the overstuffed armchairs flanking the fire, and Dugger vanished briefly into the kitchen, returning with a bottle of Chivas Regal and two tumblers. He placed them on the coffee table. "You want rocks?"

"Why dilute good liquor?"

Dugger sat facing McCoy, uncapped the bottle, and poured three fingers into each glass. McCoy, still holding his briefcase under his arm, extended wet shoes to the edge of the hearth. Dugger handed him his glass. They looked at each other a moment.

"To your good health," McCoy said, raising his glass.

"Cheers."

A log broke in the fireplace, showering sparks.

"Well, you've got a nice place here," McCoy observed.

"It serves," Dugger said.

"But why here? Why in Germany?"

Dugger held his smile, but his eyes were not amused. "Why not Germany?"

"God, I hate it," McCoy said with feeling.

"Germany?"

"I'm in Stuttgart now. I've got two years to go before reassignment. I think I would take anything to get out earlier. I would consider Guatemala, even."

"Bad boss?"

"No, I've got a good boss right now, as a matter of fact. And it's not quite so unfashionable to work for the Agency. That's just another thing about the seventies I'm glad we've got behind us." McCoy either grimaced or smiled; sometimes it was hard to differentiate. "And God knows we've got enough work: spies and counterspies, double agents, triple agents—"

"You're breaking my heart," Dugger told him, "but you're not explaining why you hate Stuttgart."

"Because it's in Germany. Christ, I hate Germany. The rude fucking people, their authoritarianism. They didn't learn any manners in World War One and they didn't learn any in World War Two and they haven't learned any since then. The Goddamned arrogant bastards *still* think they're the greatest in the world. How can you stand to live here among them by choice?"

"I like them," Dugger said.

"Shit," McCoy said.

"No. I do. And I love their country. I love Germany."

"Since you got out of the Agency you've had three or four novels published. You've got your retirement, too. You could live anywhere."

Dugger put his glass on the table. "Look, Charlie. You didn't come here to talk about where I live."

"No. I didn't."

"Are you still operational?"

McCoy hesitated an instant. "Not ordinarily."

"Are you operational at the moment?"

"Well, I'm looking into something."

Dugger leaned back. He was not surprised. The surprise had come in finding McCoy on his doorstep. "What's it all about?"

"I guess you're still writing?" McCoy countered.

"Yes. You don't live in Germany today on a CIA pension."

"What's the current project?"

"An adventure yarn. Like the others."

"Did you ever consider writing about your CIA days?"

"No."

"Why?"

"You know the answer to that, Charlie. I'm a professional."

McCoy sighed and propped the briefcase on his knees. Unsnapping catches, he removed a thin sheaf of what appeared to be the Xeroxed pages of a manuscript. He handed them across the table to Dugger. "We've got a problem."

Dugger glanced at the title page:

DECADES OF TREACHERY: THE OSS AND CIA
Reports From the Inside by Ten
Who Once Worked Within and For
The World's Most Infamous
Secret Organization
As Compiled and Written by
ALAN LECLERC

"Pen name, I suppose," Dugger said.

"It comes from a Le Carré novel."

"Clever people, these mudslingers."

"It's mostly a rehash," McCoy told him, "reminiscent of the stuff that came out in the seventies. Chile, Italy, Southeast Asia. Here. Look at this page."

Dugger complied, scanning the first few lines.

> Paradigmatic of CIA activity throughout this period was the operation at Essen in 1977. This operation was countenanced by highest authority and hopefully was undertaken without awareness or approbation by echelons within the White House, in view of the sinister guidelines mandated in the field.
>
> Essen, at the point of time under examination here, became a veritable battleground for freedom. The goal of U.S. agents was nothing less than the extermination of all free-thinking youthful critics of the Bonn government. . . .

Dugger had read enough. He looked up again at McCoy. "Well?"

"Essen was your operation, wasn't it?"

"Yes, it was."

"Joe, did you write this stuff?"

"Did I—" Dugger broke off more in astonishment than anger. "Have you ever read any of my books?"

"Sure. The one about the fishing expedition—"

"Then how do you think I could write *this?*"

"Calm down, man."

"No." Dugger slapped the pages with the back of his hand. "This is crap. Is there anything in my work to indicate I could write this badly? Is there anything in my record to indicate I would do something like this? Are your language and syntax analysis people so dense they couldn't eliminate me as a suspect by running copy through a computer comparison program?"

"All right, all right." McCoy held up his hands. "I had to ask."

"Shit, you had to ask!" Dugger was fuming. "If you want to know who wrote this garbage, go to the publisher and ask."

"It's not quite that simple. This is a small British house and they think they have a hot item. Their security is pretty good. We haven't gotten to first base in trying to learn the real identity of the author."

"How did you get these pages, then?"

"We got them," McCoy replied grimly.

"And you figured I wrote them."

"Joe, we had to *ask*. There's some new stuff in here about the Essen job. You were on that. There is also a lot of detail about Joseph Obutu, back when you worked with him at Geneva and the revolution in Marandaya was just getting going good."

Dugger felt a distinct chill. Joseph Obutu was now president of the African nation of Marandaya, a country generally friendly to the United States and its Western allies. Seven years ago the situation had been far different. Marandaya, newly freed of colonial rule by the French, had been in the control of a small military junta, and leaning left. Joseph Obutu had been the leader of a group of Marandayan patriots at the mission in Geneva plotting the overthrow of the junta and restoration of democratic rule. It had taken more than a year. In the end, Marandaya had been freed and Joseph Obutu elected its first president.

But only a handful of people in the entire world knew of Obutu's old ties to Dugger and the CIA. There was new unrest in Marandaya today, a leftist guerrilla group operating in the country's western provinces.

Information such as was contained in the manuscript could fan the flames.

"Can you stop publication?" Dugger asked.

"Go to court?"

"Yes."

"No. That would only draw more attention to the thing."

"Where did the information come from?"

McCoy's smile was mirthless. "Precisely the question I wanted to ask you."

Dugger thought about it. "I knew his real identity.

Helmut Schraeder knew. Heidigger knew. Frank Bauer.
LaFontaine. Rudi Wetzel. No one else.''

"All your agents," McCoy pointed out.

"They had to know. If you remember the operation—"

"I know, I know."

"If your files in Washington haven't been compromised, this leak had to come from one of those I just mentioned."

"Any guesses?"

Dugger gave his old associate a bitter, knowing smile
and said nothing. It was axiomatic that a case officer was
not supposed to get emotionally involved with the nationals he employed as agents. Liking an agent made it
messy when you asked him to risk his career or even his
life. Some case officers were able to maintain textbook ob-
jectivity, but most didn't. Dugger remembered most of
his agents with something almost like love. He still cared
about them. The idea that one could now be a traitor was
too repugnant to comment on, even though intellect told
him it was wholly possible.

Charlie McCoy sipped from his glass. "All right, then.
There's something else."

"About the leak?"

"About the guys who used to work for you."

"That being?"

"Heidigger."

"What about him?"

"Heidigger is dead."

The news hurt. "When? How?"

"He fell down some steps last week. He was living in
Hof. The landlady found him."

"Was it an accident?"

"It certainly looked like an accident. But Heidigger was
not a clumsy man and he was not a drinker. And what
happened to Schraeder makes it a lot less likely that it was
an accident."

"Helmut? Something has happend to Helmut?"

The corners of McCoy's mouth turned down. "He's
dead, too."

"Jesus Christ. When?"

"Also last week. In Cologne."

"How?"

"He was found drowned in his bathtub."

Dugger stood and walked to the window. He looked out at the rain, which was coming harder now. "Any theories?"

"Not yet." McCoy's voice was flat. "The obvious conclusion is that the book is part of a new drive to undermine Joseph Obutu. Maybe Heidigger and Schraeder died accidentally. Maybe there's no relationship between the events."

"And maybe the Pope is not a Catholic," Dugger said.

"Well, now that he's not an Italian—"

"Have you contacted my other former agents?"

"Not yet. We're arranging to have them watched."

"That's not good enough," Dugger replied. "If Heidigger and Schraeder were killed, you owe it to the others to warn them they might be next in line."

"Except," McCoy pointed out calmly, "that one of them is our leak. When we warn them, we notify them how much we know at this point—and never learn anything further."

"So you're just going to sit back and see if anyone else dies?"

"We're watching them. I told you that."

"What if I notified them?"

"Don't."

"I don't like the idea of them walking around like ducks in a gallery."

"Stay out of it, Joe."

Dugger came back to his chair. He did not sit down, but stood with his large hands jammed into the pockets of his Levi's. His expression showed how little he liked it. McCoy was not worried. Dugger had been a professional for almost two decades before he left the Agency. He would obey orders even now, when he was a relative outsider.

"We'll keep you informed," McCoy told him. "And if you have any further thoughts, I'm in the office there at

Kelly, outside Stuttgart. Give me a call."

"Are you telling Obutu?"

"No. Not at this time."

Dugger did not like it. He told himself not to worry about it. He reminded himself that he was fifty years old, not only past his prime physically but emotionally, too. Let younger men handle it, ones whose blood pressure wouldn't shoot up, whose hands wouldn't shake. He couldn't help anyhow. He didn't even know the new procedures. All he would do was screw things up.

In the days following McCoy's visit, Dugger worked hard at convincing himself of this.

June passed and July came, still cool, rainy. On the Fourth of July Dugger pan-fried a steak in his tiny backyard between showers and thought about firecrackers and band day picnics. His wife had been dead four years now. The pain would never go away.

On an evening more than a week later, a little before dark, someone knocked on his door. The man was young, Scandinavian in appearance, wearing American double-knits. He had a briefcase.

"Mr. Dugger?"

"Yes?"

The man extended his hand. "I'm Bob Nathan." The hand held an identity card from the Agency.

"Come in." Dugger took him into the living room.

"It's very kind of you to see me," Nathan told him. "I realize that you've retired now, but frankly, we have a situation on our hands. It dates back to the Regensburg thing, actually."

Dugger had no idea what "The Regensburg thing" was. "Go ahead," he said carefully.

"We need to confirm the identity of a couple of the people who once worked for you," Nathan said easily, "because we may have a special need for one or the other of them and we don't have time to go all the way back through the old files."

"I'll help if I can," Dugger said.

Nathan looked around the crowded room. "I'm sure there's no need for extra security, but I've been in the car all day and could stretch my legs anyway. What would you think of taking a stroll down around the castle? It looks like a real doozy."

Dugger filed the archaic slang, "I'll get my jacket."

They left the house and walked downhill, heading for the river and the castle area. A light mist was falling, and darkness was coming fast. No one else was on the street. The castle, the longest in Germany, jutted out on the promontory ahead, gray walls eerie in the half-light. Nathan showed no inclination to return to the topic at hand, but chatted instead about this region of Germany and the history of the castle. He was surprisingly knowledgeable.

Their walk took them through side streets of the town and across an open grassy field, where a gravel walk began. It could be seen vaguely in the mist ahead, winding uphill past ancient wall ruins to higher ground where later castle walls stood black against the obscurity of the night. Their footsteps scraped the wet gravel and they moved up the steady incline, past the first wall remnants, to an area where a high grassy knoll rose to the right and the ground to the left dropped off sharply to treetops.

"I can't imagine attacking this place with a battle-ax," Nathan said.

"They did it," Dugger said, his hands in his jacket pockets.

"It's almost spooky. I don't see anyone else around."

"I walk this way often. I seldom see a soul."

They reached higher ground. Near an ancient round turret was a newer construction, a low rock wall with a metal gate. Behind the gate were neat rows of brambles . . . vegetation covering mass graves. Here lay more than three hundred Jews killed by the Nazis and buried by the 4th Armored and the people of Burghausen in 1945.

Dugger turned toward the small metal gate, giving Nathan his back.

Nathan's feet stirred the gravel.

Dugger swung back around swiftly, seeing the small, pipelike instrument in Nathan's right hand. The man's eyes widened as he realized his mistake, but it was his last reaction. The .38 hidden in Dugger's right-hand pocket made a frightful noise when he fired it. Nathan was staggered backward a step, and then he fell.

Dugger listened to the echoes of the gunshot ringing over the hills, to the lake and the ancient walls beyond. His coat pocket smoked through the ragged hole torn by his bullet. Kneeling, he examined Nathan briefly. Of course there was no identification other than the card, which Dugger pocketed. He also took the aerosol gun.

It took him less than ten minutes, walking fast, to get back to his house. He threw clothes into a bag and did not bother to lock the door when he left. They would break it down anyway if they came again to find him.

He backed the Volkswagen out of the driveway and started to drive away. Only then did he realize that he had also left a light burning inside the house. That did not matter either. He drove on.

It took about an hour for reaction to set in. Dugger had to pull off the winding mountain road in the darkness beside a black granite cliff. The shaking was very bad for a while. He smoked a cigarette, watching the highway behind his car. A Mercedes truck passed after a few minutes, and then a Cortina and a microbus close together. Dugger did not think there had been two of them, but there was always that chance. He was surprised by the clarity with which a part of him was thinking. Old self-protective reflexes were coming back to life quickly despite the sickness at having just killed a man.

When he felt steadier, Dugger resumed driving in a now steady rain.

His impulse from the time of McCoy's visit had been to ignore suggestions and find ways to warn the others. But he had told himself it was better to follow orders even though they didn't really have the right to issue orders anymore. He hadn't wanted to get back into the slime.

But he was in it now. There was no more room for doubt. Something had happened at Regensburg; the man calling himself Nathan had slipped when he said that. Dugger had no idea what it had been, but it related somehow to the leaks about Joseph Obutu and the deaths of both Heidigger and Schraeder.

Dugger realized that he would be dead now too if he had not had the luxury of almost accidental warning. He doubted that he would have picked up the would-be killer's verbal mistake, that old-fashioned bit of slang, if he hadn't already been warned by the ID card. Case officers did not use CIA identification cards, not outside the U.S.

He had been lucky.

He intended to give the others who remained alive the same chance.

2

Zurich, Switzerland

Dugger drove through the Tyrol to Zurich, with brief stops near Innsbruck and Bludenz. A light, steady rain pelted the two-lane asphalt highway all the way, and there was snow in the passes. This part of the Alps was changing very rapidly; majestic mountains towered into the low-hanging clouds as they always had and perhaps always would, and beside the twisting road were the fields of hay and villages dominated by sharply pitched church steeples in dark red or green. The country was breathtakingly lovely. But along the rushing streams, floury with rock powder from melt high above, more and more silver-blue high-tension lines ran, and more and more huge cranes scooped out rocky earth for industrial development. Startlingly vivid flowers still grew in profusion from window boxes everywhere on tall houses with exterior timbers, and Dugger, driving with the collar of his windbreaker turned up against the chill air, told himself there was always hope as long as the people cultivated the flowers.

It was late when he reached Zurich and found a hotel room in a small establishment in the section of the city he liked best, not far from the two thirteenth-century churches on the River Limmat. He then drove to a parking garage a number of blocks distant and bought a week's time for the Volkswagen, using a false name and address on the registration ticket. Walking back to the hotel, he found himself using old techniques to be sure he was not being watched. There were no signs of danger. The drive had left him very tired, but sleep did not come easily.

Walking along the river on the next morning, he watched the boats and street traffic with a soft sense of shock. The air was very cold, the sky with an opalescent quality that promised more rain and perhaps wind. He shivered in his windbreaker and battered Irish hat. The old feeling of total isolation had continued to seep back into his bloodstream, and he wondered how he had ever forgotten the precise, existential feel of being so alone.

He found the jewelry shop without difficulty, and his friend was still there. His friend asked no questions and promised to deliver the required items by late afternoon. He used a Polaroid camera to take the pictures in the back room. Dugger paid him $223 in Swiss francs in advance, a like amount due on delivery. It was a lot of money. Dugger felt he had no choice.

Using a telephone directory, Dugger next secured some of the information about his old friend Frank Bauer that was necessary. The taxi driver was sullen at first, but cheered up when he learned that Dugger required several stops, a handsome tab.

Bauer's house was in the northeastern part of Zurich, a small two-story home with a detached garage in the back. Trim on the house needed paint, and the pavement of the driveway was crumbling. The yard was neat. There were apartments at the bottom of the hill, mansions at the top. Bauer's house was halfway up.

The local grocer talked freely about the Bauers. He liked them. Their daughter was certainly a lovely young woman, and so intelligent. Frank Bauer's bakery goods were the best, and the grocer sometimes himself stocked some Bauer pastries, although the bakery was not large enough to provide stock on a consistent basis. Of course the gentleman knew that the Bauer bakery was located downtown? Dugger casually got the address.

The people at the city building were more difficult. Dugger managed to learn that yes, the home at the address given was occupied by the Bauer family, and no, there certainly was no local litigation involving the property, and yes, as far as the tax office knew, there was indeed a mortgage on the property.

The bakery shop near the Zurichhorn was small and neat, and seemed to have a steady flow of clientele. It appeared to be a neighborhood bakery, many of the customers elderly men or women who carried out bags containing fresh-baked bread or small pastries. Frank Bauer seemed to have a delivery boy who moved to and from his small, decrepit truck in slow motion.

Sitting in the cab, observing the bakery, Dugger also picked up one of the Agency people McCoy had promised would watch Bauer. He was youngish, blond, so obviously an American tourist that he could not be one. He was sitting on a bus stop bench, but when the bus went by, he remained seated, reading an English-language newspaper. Dugger saw him watching customers of the bakery over the top of the paper.

A second man, elderly, sat on a bench nearer Dugger's taxi. He was feeding the pigeons from a bag of peanuts. Everything about him was just right except the way he fed the pigeons. He tossed the peanuts out a few at a time, well away from the bench. When pigeons pranced closer to him, he moved his feet nervously, making them scatter. The old man did not like pigeons.

Dugger had the taxi driver give him an hour's tour of the city, then take him back by the bakery. The Agency man was now in a parked car. The elderly man was gone, and Dugger could not spot his replacement.

Back at the jewelry shop, Dugger's friend had the items. Dugger paid him and walked through several department stores, then took another taxi back to the bakery, getting out a block away. He walked down the alley and rapped on the bakery's delivery door in back.

A fat man in a white apron and cap opened the door. "This door is not for customers."

"I am sorry," Dugger said with an apologetic smile. "May I please go through to the front? You see, it has started raining again."

With a sigh, the fat baker led him through, past great

ovens and butcher block counters laden with breads and cakes and delicacies that turned the air sweet and warm. The two young women icing cakes and spreading powdered sugar on cookies did not give him a glance.

The front was small and immaculate, with steamy windows looking out onto the streets, glassy under the rain. A robust middle-aged woman was just making change for a customer who departed clucking about the weather. The woman clerk walked to Dugger's place at the counter.

"Yes, sir?"

"Mr. Bauer is not here?" They were speaking German.

"No, sir. He has been away on business today, but should be back soon."

"I am an old friend. I wish to leave him an important message."

"Of course, sir." She handed him an order form and a pencil.

Phrasing the note, he paused only briefly before suggesting a meeting place. He signed with his old code name, feeling a bit old-fashioned and foolish. Folding the paper carefully, he gave it to the woman. "You will see that Bauer gets this most important message today?"

"Yes, sir. I promise you that."

"I stupidly parked my car in the back. May I exit that way?"

Once in the alley, he walked two blocks before cutting back to the street to hail another taxi. This time he gave the name of a small hotel near the Odéon, Zurich's famous old literary cafe. Entering the hotel, he used the rest room, then sat in the lobby for a while. A radio on the clerk's desk was playing a local station. The music was out of the past: Glenn Miller, Benny Goodman, Artie Shaw. It was still the popular music in many parts of Europe.

A few minutes before six, Dugger walked to the cafe. He found a booth near the front windows. The cafe seemed shabby and down-at-heel, but he realized that the management kept it this way to better provide the ambience it must have had in the days when men like Lenin,

Mann, and Joyce met friends here and argued endless arguments. Rainy light filtered through the high windows, glinting on dusty chandeliers and beaded glass. Working-men and college students mixed at the tables. Dugger had cappuccino.

A little after six, a heavy-set, gray-haired man wearing a rain-soaked overcoat pushed through the doorway. His slightly bulging eyes swept the room. Dugger saw the anticipation and possible nervousness in his eyes. When he spied Dugger, he smiled and came over like a man on uncertain ice.

Dugger stood to greet him. "Hello, Frank."

"It really is you, Colonel. After so long—"

"You look fine, Frank. Sit down."

Bauer made a thing of his umbrella and coat, then sat facing Dugger. Sweat streamed down his florid face, effect of coming in from the cold. He watched Dugger closely, but kept looking away as if nervous. He did not know what to make of the rendezvous after so long.

"I was passing through," Dugger told him after the waiter had brought a beer, "and I couldn't resist seeing you. I hope this is not too inconvenient."

"It is my pleasure, Colonel, I assure you! But tell me: you . . . ah . . . are no longer . . . ah . . ."

"I am no longer in the service," Dugger told him.

Bauer's shoulders slumped a bit with relief. "It is very kind of you to remember me after so long."

"Your bakery is handsome, Frank. I'm glad you're doing well."

Bauer patted his ample belly. "I eat my profits."

"Is Katrina well?" The name and details came easily. Once they had held Bauer and others like him in a brotherhood with Dugger, serving him. "And your daughter, Ilka?"

"Katrina is fat, like me." Bauer grinned amiably. "And Ilka is attending the university."

"The university! She is that old?"

"She is very beautiful and very bright. She is going to be a doctor."

"Frank, that's wonderful. I'm happy for you."

"Everything has changed since the old days, Colonel."

"Yes, it has. For all of us."

"You are in Zurich on business?"

"Just passing through."

"I see. And you have . . . have you remarried, Colonel?"

"No."

Bauer showed alarm, reaching across the table to put his hand on Dugger's arm. "Please do not take offense, Colonel. It is just that I remember your wife, so young, so beautiful. I have always thought how sad for you, to lose such a one—"

Shockingly, Dugger felt his eyes get wet. He coughed and looked toward the traffic in the street beyond the window, using the excuse to wipe his eyes. "It's past, Frank."

"I am very, very sorry to mention it when it obviously still upsets you, Colonel. I am a fool."

"No, Frank, you're no fool. And that's part of the reason I'm here."

Bauer's bulging eyes became wary. "Oh?"

"There's danger. I don't understand the source, or the motivation. I feel I owe it to you to tell you about it."

Bauer nodded, leaning back in his chair and fiddling with a cigar. Dugger told him in general about the deaths of Heidigger and Schraeder, and about the attempt on him. He told very little about McCoy's visit.

Bauer took it well, although perhaps his face was paler when Dugger concluded. He leaned forward again, his voice lower. "They are after me, too, you think, Colonel?"

"Frank, I know for a fact that the Company is watching you. I have every reason to believe you're safe. I wanted you to know the score."

"I know nothing anyone could want to kill me for!"

"I don't see that I do either."

"But who is doing this? Why?"

"Frank, I don't know."

"But this is terrible," Bauer said, his eyes far away. "If the Agency is watching me, it could come out somehow that I once worked for you and against the Soviet Union. My business could be ruined. I could become a target for radicals. My life could be in worse danger than whatever is now threatened!"

"Is it such a disgrace to have old CIA ties?" Dugger asked, knowing the answer, prompted by his bitterness to have a confirmation.

"My friend," Bauer said not unkindly, "you must know that everything is different today. Now we have detente. We have friendly relations with the Soviets. If there is a monster in Europe today, it is West Germany, with its new industries and its great army. The violence today is against the Bonn government, its jingoistic maneuvers."

"Which is damned nonsense," Dugger said.

Bauer held up a thumb and index finger. "Twice in this century. Twice, Germany has overrun the continent and brought death and starvation to everyone. It is not Russia that has done these things. Today the fear is of Germany becoming so strong it can try it again. I myself have heard young Germans say that the third time will be different— the third time Germany will have the United States on its side against Russia! They talk of World War Three in terms of *hope!*"

"Not many of them," Dugger said.

"The Nazi party is alive again," Bauer said somberly. "The German national character has not changed. I tell you, the majority of people in Europe see *Germany* as the menace, not the Soviet Union. For me to have my past revealed—for people to know I worked inside Germany against the Russians—could be very bad for my business."

"Maybe it won't come to that," Dugger told him. "Maybe people will never have to know you did nasty things to wonderful men like Taltkin and Crognoi."

"You are bitter. But it is a different world today."

"I've told you what I had to tell you, Frank. I guess there's nothing more."

Bauer held up a finger to halt him. "You are seeing all of us who remain?"

"Yes."

"Please do not mention me to any of the others. Especially to Pierre."

"LaFontaine? Why?"

"I have heard he is very wealthy now . . . money earned partly through German investments."

"That's so bad?"

"I just do not want to be identified with anyone who is making money out of the new German war machine."

"If you're in danger, Frank, it isn't from *Germany*."

"The fight is no longer with the Soviets. Those days are gone. It is as logical to assume that the Bonn government is behind these things as it is to blame the Soviets."

The statement was too absurd to give a comment. Dugger walked out.

On the way back to the hotel, he was depressed. Frank Bauer had been one of the last men he would have expected to voice such nonsense. Dugger knew the Agency had been far from blameless in the sixties and early seventies. But he had not anticipated that the smear jobs perpetrated by spoiled idealists could have affected people like Bauer, along with the truly innocent. And the fact that Bauer had followed the trend toward mistrust of the Bonn government was even more upsetting.

Dugger knew that Bauer had echoed ideas widespread in Europe today. Dugger himself would never forget the evils of the Nazi regime or the way the Bonn government had tacitly approved wholesale shipment of stolen art treasures entirely out of Europe as recently as the mid-1970s. But the idea that the enemy today should be Germany, rather than the Soviet Union, struck him as absurd. The fear simply did not square with the facts. It had not been Germany that slaughtered the Czech freedom fighters, maintained bellicose puppet states in Poland and a dozen other once free nations, encouraged chaos in Africa. It was not Germany with the big bombs and the big rockets to deliver them. It had not been

German operatives he had struggled against so many years down here in the slime.

But he would never convince men like Frank Bauer, and he mourned the fact. Perhaps they had to go with the popular fallacy, nurtured in so many popular novels and films, that Germany was a monster waiting only the slightest chance to rise and destroy its neighbors again. It was not popular today to be a realist; the fantasy fear of a possible Germany was more pleasant than the fear of an existing Russia. Businessmen like Frank Bauer could not swim against such a popular tide and still maintain a faceless free enterprise.

Nearing his hotel, Dugger again used an alley. Entering the back door of the building, he ascended to his floor via the darkened rear stairway. Feeling foolish, he walked softly on the thin carpeting to his door, leaned close, and examined the frame. The small piece of masking tape was broken.

Moving on quickly, he summoned the elevator and rode down to the lobby. There were a number of men and women there. Dugger caught the attention of a bellhop, a wizened old man in shapeless gray uniform, and pressed fifty francs into his palm.

"I am going into the coffee shop," he explained to the old man. "If you will please take a bottle of rum to my room and adjust the windows for ventilation, there will be a handsome tip for you."

The old porter nodded eagerly. "You will be in the coffee room, sir?"

"Yes. Will you deliver the bottle, adjust the windows, and report to me there just as soon as you have done it, so I can pay you?"

"Of course, sir." The porter scurried off, Dugger's key in hand.

Dugger went into the steamy coffee shop. His stomach ached. He ordered a glass of milk. He thought about what he would do next. Bauer's comment about Pete LaFontaine had been disconcerting. Dugger thought Paris might logically be his next stop.

The milk was only half gone when the old porter came back into the coffee shop. He placed Dugger's key and change on the table. "There you are, sir. All done. Oh, and the gentlemen waiting in your room had to leave."

"I see," Dugger said. He gave the old man five francs, got up, and walked quickly into the lobby. There were too many people, no way to pick anyone out. His man was probably among them. Dugger had to act swiftly now.

Cold rain dashed steadily against his face as he left the hotel and walked rapidly eastward, staying in the strong light of storefronts. Night was coming on and some of the cars had their headlights burning. He judged the traffic carefully and stepped from the curb without warning, zig-zagging at a dead run across four lanes of traffic. A horn sounded angrily. He reached the far curb and ducked into the revolving doors of a fashionable department store.

Inside, the store was stuffy and crowded. Voices murmured, a clerk's call chime sounded insistently over the discreet racket. Lights gleamed on glass counter tops of gloves and jewelry. Dugger managed to squeeze in as the last person entering an elevator whose doors had already started to close, earning him hostile stares from the other shoppers.

He was still breathing hard when the doors swung open onto the second floor. He got out first and walked fast past chalky, staring mannequins dressed in boldly colored summer styles for women, through a department filled with coats, and to the down escalator. Stepping on, he rode to the basement.

It was louder and hotter in the basement, or perhaps only the low ceiling made it seem that way. Acres of tools and hardware stretched out ahead of him. He moved fast between rows of lawnmowers, camping equipment, and automotive accessories, reaching the concrete stairs going up a half flight to doors leading outside.

The rain was letting up. He walked swiftly to the next corner and cut down the side street, a narrow, cobbled thoroughfare with rows of tiny shops, residences above, where most of the lights for business had already been turned off. The street sloped sharply downward, seeking the level of the river a few blocks away, and he realized his mistake if indeed he was still being followed. But it was too late.

He reached the next corner. Another street, even narrower, intersected. There was a Mercedes sedan parked nearby, but it was deserted. Only a block off the thriving main street he was completely alone.

There was a little whining noise, and something spatted hard into the rock wall near his head, throwing biting rock fragments into his face. He dived for safety behind the wall, getting the briefest glimpse of the two men in rain slickers halfway up the block behind him. Then he had no more time for observing anything because he was running just as hard as he could.

It was steep uphill in this direction, the cobbles slippery underfoot. He reached the next corner and turned blindly left. There was a little retaining wall which he climbed upon. The drop over the far side was about five feet. He took it, hitting heavily in soft earth.

He had dropped into some sort of small municipal park, about an acre on high ground that looked down toward the river, with rooftops intervening. Aged oaks were spaced across the gravel floor of the little park with almost machine-like regularity. At the far end was an iron railing and a gate that led down to somewhere else. He ran again.

At the gate, he hurled himself around the corner and kept on going. He was quite near one of the ancient churches, saw its ivory-colored steeple over rooftops ahead as he ran. It occurred to him to head that way. But old churches were a *cul-de-sac*, almost always. He kept running, turning left again.

At the next corner, he was back out onto a busier street. There was a newsstand, and a taxi driver had left his cab long enough to buy a newspaper. Dugger rushed to the taxi and got inside.

The driver came back nonchalantly, perhaps irritated at finding a fare when he wanted to park and read. He took an eternity getting behind the wheel.

"The airport, if you please," Dugger said. "Please hurry."

The driver sighed as if to say that everyone was in a hurry, and he disapproved. But he started the car at once and pulled away smartly. Dugger leaned back in the shadows of the back seat and did not see any sign of his two pursuers.

Where had they picked him up? he wondered. At the bakery? The cafe? Only at the hotel itself? And who were they? There were no answers.

At the airport, he paid his driver and promptly hailed another to ride back into the city. He bought a raincoat and hat and a few other things at a cheap tourist shop, then walked to the park. He spent most of the night there, just about as cold and uncomfortable as he had ever been in his life.

At dawn he made himself somewhat presentable in the rest room of a dingy hotel, went to a Eurocar agency, and rented a Cortina sedan. He signed the papers to match the passport and other false identification he had procured earlier from his friend at the jewelry store, so that for all anyone could know, it was not Joseph Dugger, American, but John Baxter, West German, who drove north out of Zurich about 8 A.M., headed for Stuttgart.

3

New York City

A steady drizzle had turned Fifty-first Street into a gleaming black mirror beneath the ornate streetlamps. It was very late. Even a block west, up on First Avenue, traffic was only sporadic. Slumped behind the wheel of the parked Chevrolet sedan, Bill Corbin lighted another cigarette.

He instantly regretted it. The Kent tasted foul and stung his tongue. The inside of the Chevy, already steamy and rancid from the humidity and all the other cigarettes burned through more than four hours of vigil, felt like a prison again. Corbin was hungry and he had a headache. He allowed himself a glance at the digital watch. Two more hours before his relief man showed.

Corbin tried to scrunch his butt around on the seat to relieve some of the stiffness. It didn't work. He rolled his window down another inch or two, letting more of the smoke from the cigarette escape. Rain pelted in, cool on his shoulder and arm.

The Chevrolet was parked on the left, or north, side of Fifty-first just west of Beekman Place. Corbin had both mirrors adjusted so that he could look back at an angle to watch the apartment door partway up the block on Beekman. Light shone behind the heavy draperies at the front window. Nothing at all had changed since his man had entered hours ago.

The neighborhood, perhaps New York's most expensive and fashionable, and in the shadows of the United Nations

43

complex just to the south, was hardly the customary type for such a watch. But Corbin had been here five different nights now and was becoming accustomed to it. At least there was very little traffic or commotion. Just a short half block behind him, east of Beekman, Fifty-first dead-ended to all traffic. There was a barricade, a railing, stairs on the left side which twisted downward to a little courtyard and a sidewalk which led on down to the FDR Drive and the river just beyond.

Corbin tossed his cigarette out and scrunched around in his seat again.

If he was tired and frustrated, his awareness of these feelings was distant and controlled. He was a veteran of more than ten years, and had spent many other nights in other cars on other possibly foolish errands. Even bitterness played no part here, although it had certainly occurred to him that the people he was watching probably derived much of their diplomatic income from taxpayers of the United States, just as he did, although theirs came through the considerably more circuitous route of foreign aid and a foreign payroll. Corbin managed not to be bitter even with the added knowledge that the people he was watching made many, many times the money he was paid, and yet evidently were dedicated to working against the country whose largesse they enjoyed. Corbin did not indulge such thoughts because he was a veteran.

After tonight he would have four days off. He was looking forward to this. He and Jill would leave in the morning and be in the shack in Connecticut for a late lunch. People said the fish were biting like crazy. It would also be warm enough to swim, if you kept moving around.

Corbin sighed, reached for another cigarette, put it back. He would be glad when the operation was over, if it ever was. The long hours of surveillance and crazy travel had played hell with both his nerves and his home life.

The trouble was that he had no idea how close they might be. He did what he was told, went where he was sent. It was for others to put it together. About all he knew was that it was Big. Capital B. There were too many working on it for it to be routine, too much pressure from high up for results. And God knew some of the people being watched were themselves considered very, very important . . . in their own nations.

It did not occur to Corbin to feel impatience at how long the probe had already gone on, or about his ignorance of what it really involved. His job was often like this.

About the time he was again seriously considering a cigarette, there was a slight change in the illumination around the sunken bricked entry to the apartment under scrutiny. Corbin perked up and watched his mirror. The door of the apartment had been opened. He saw his man come out, briefcase under his arm, umbrella unfurled.

The man said a final word to his host, out of sight in the doorway, and turned to walk in Corbin's direction. He would now, Corbin thought, walk to his Buick, parked on the other side of the street not far behind Corbin's Chevy, and either drive west on this street or turn south on Beekman. Corbin was to tail him if he went west toward First. If he turned left onto Beekman instead, Corbin would use his Handie-Talkie to alert the boys on Mitchell Place.

His man walked slowly to the corner, not thirty feet from Corbin's car. He then turned to his right, walking toward the car he had left hours earlier. Light from the streetlamp made diamonds on his black silk umbrella.

He walked past his car and headed for the barricade at the end of Fifty-first, lengthening his strides.

Corbin grabbed his Motorola off the seat. "Four," he said into the microphone-speaker.

There was the briefest pause before the little transceiver popped as the voice came back, the volume very low: *"Four, go ahead."*

"Subject eastbound on Fifty-first on foot."

"Is he going down the steps to the lower level?"

"It looks like it."

"Keep him in sight. Six, get onto FDR below Fifty-first."

It was unexpected. Corbin stepped quickly from the car, the rain pelting him. Hooking the Motorola onto his belt, he slammed the Chevy door and headed up the sidewalk. His man had just turned left at the end of the street and disappeared down the steps leading to the lower level. *Mustn't lose him*. Corbin walked faster, stretching his legs, not bothering to get out of the deserted street.

He was within two car lengths of the dark-colored van on his left when he heard the engine idling. He turned toward it but he was too late. The van's engine roared and he heard a slamming sound as a brake was released. The van leaped away from the curb, coming right at him.

Corbin tried to leap out of the way to the right. His foot slipped. *Fucking leather soles*.

The bumper of the van caught him at the knees, breaking both legs. In virtually the same instant the entire broad front of the vehicle slammed into his body, bowling him over backward. His skull hit the pavement with killing force and two wheels ran over him. The Motorola went skittering across the wet pavement as the van rushed on west to First and made a skidding, high-speed right turn.

Fully three minutes passed.

A car squealed around the corner of Beekman, rocking to a halt in the intersection. Its headlights picked out Corbin's broken body, lying face down. Both car doors popped open, and two men, wearing rumpled business suits, leaped out and ran to kneel by the body.

They examined briefly and stood.

"Shit," the taller man said. He walked over and picked up Corbin's radio and thumbed it. "Six?"

"This is Six."

"Have you got him?"

"Negative."

The man put down the Handie-Talkie for a moment. "Shit," he said again. He raised the radio once more. "Eight?"

"Eight."

"Get over here. They got Corbin."

There was a pause, then: *"How bad?"*

"He's dead."

"Eight rolling."

The taller man belted the Handie-Talkie alongside his own. His face, lantern-jawed and heavily lined in the harsh glare from the headlights, was tight and angry. "The God-damned bastards," he said.

The other man, who had not yet spoken, only stared at him. The shorter man was crying without a sound.

"They've blown our whole fucking operation," the taller man said.

"Screw the operation!" the shorter man said. "Corbin is *dead*. He was a friend of mine! Wasn't he a friend of yours? And you can only think about the *operation?*"

The taller man started to reply, then seemed to think better of it. He stood watching his younger companion weep, and then the other car came and they all stood there in the rain.

Quantico, Virginia

For Eileen Arrington, there was no warning.

One moment he was moving cautiously toward her, open hands outstretched. Then he put his right hand behind his back, and when it reappeared he had the knife.

Of course he had had it hidden in the back of his belt. Eileen knew she should have expected such a trick, but for an instant the surprise was total. The knife was about seven inches long, dull silver in appearance, with a thick black handle. It looked capable of opening her body from sternum to pelvis.

He glided toward her, moving on the balls of his feet, the knife describing a small circular motion of intense readiness. Eileen was not a small woman at five feet, six, and one hundred and twenty pounds, but she suddenly became intensely aware that he stood eight inches taller and weighed over two hundred.

He was within five paces.

He lunged toward her.

Eileen moved in automatic response.

Sliding to her right, she resisted the impulse to move back from the blade. Instead she moved *in* on him, making his slashing attack miss over her shoulder. He was off balance in this moment, and she brought her right elbow around sharply into his throat. He staggered. She caught his knife arm over her hip in such a way that his weight worked to her benefit. Twisting, she flipped him. He went over in a somersault, hitting the floor with a resounding thud. The knife spun free. She kicked it off the mat, spun, and leaped as if to bring her full weight down on heels into his chest. At the last possible distant she diverted the strike, her feet landing inches from his side.

"*Damn* it!" he panted.

There was a mixture of ironic applause and playful booing from the Academy students ringing the practice mat.

Giving them a mocking bow, Eileen walked over and picked up the knife. She touched her index finger to the tip of the blade and pressed down on it, hard.

The blade, made of pliable plastic, bent double.

"At least," she told the group, "you have some sense."

One of her gym-suited students, a young woman named Jefferson, made a wry face. "You said you wanted the drills realistic, Eileen."

Eileen smiled at the row of husky men and women in their gray tee shirts and shorts. "It never fails. We get you along into the twelfth or thirteenth week, and you think you have to start testing the instructors. All right, wise-acres. We'll just practice with the knife awhile. Jim, get out here with Barb." She handed the muscular trainee the knife. "You get an A for the session if you can bend the blade on her belly."

"No fair!" the girl named Barb protested. "What do I get if I stop him? Nothing?"

"You get to have the knife next . . . to attack the class-mate of your choice," Eileen said sweetly.

"Super!" Barb walked lightly onto the mat. "Come on, Jim." She pranced around in a comical burlesque of the self-defense posture. "Try it!"

As Eileen stepped back into the line of her students to

observe, she noticed that the class was no longer itself unobserved in the echoing gymnasium. Near a doorway at the far end of the echoing room was a short man with the thick arms and legs of a professional wrestler. She recognized the way he overfilled his military-cut summer suit.

John Micheals, deputy director for training at the FBI Academy here in Quantico, gestured that he wanted to speak with her. She walked over to him after designating a student as referee for the contest about to get under way.

"It looks like a good group, Eileen," Micheals said as she reached him. Up close it was easy to see his smashed cauliflower ears and the tiny old scars around his eyes. Yet, at sixty, he glowed with good health.

"It's not a bad group at all," Eileen told him as she toweled face and hands. "I enjoy working with this bunch."

"Do you suppose it would break your heart if you had to turn them over to another instructor for the last three weeks?"

Eileen stared at him, trying to read his dark green eyes, the granitic expression. "Meaning what?"

"Meaning we have a request for you to go operational."

"When?"

"Now."

"Today?"

Across the gym, behind her, there was some hooting and jeering. She did not turn to see the outcome. She was still trying to read Micheals' expression. It was impossible, even with her question hanging in the air.

He told her, "I'll be waiting in Conference B. We'll talk."

She nodded, turned, and walked back to her class. Barb was holding the plastic knife aloft like a trophy, and Jim was still sitting on the mat. He seemed to have a bloody nose.

"People," Eileen told them, "this is your lucky day. I have a meeting to attend. Take a shower."

Surprised and delighted, the trainees broke up. Hurrying to the instructors' locker room, Eileen was conscious of hurrying. She had thought this day would never come.

Washington, D.C.

Quite late the same evening, John Micheals was escorted into a meeting of his own. The director's office was quite large and impressive. Micheals had a bad case of sweaty palms. He had been here only twice before, and both of those occasions had been ceremonial picture-taking only.

The director stood behind his massive desk and reached across it to shake hands. "Thank you for getting here so quickly, John. I'm sure you know Francis Cooper."

Micheals turned from the towering figure of the director to shake hands in turn with the lank, completely bald Cooper, whose function was assistant director for intelligence. The three men exchanged brief pleasantries about the flight and the weather. Then the director sat behind his desk and motioned for Micheals and Cooper to take the two leather chairs facing him.

"She accepted," the director began. "Good. And I believe you told us on the telephone that she can be in New York tomorrow?"

Micheals took a sheet of paper from his attaché case and put it on the edge of the desk. "This is a copy of her itinerary."

The director's eyes swiveled momentarily to Cooper. "She will be met and assisted, then briefed on details tomorrow afternoon."

"Yes, sir," Cooper said, making a note.

The eyes swiveled back to Micheals. "You have a copy of the updated basic file?"

"Yes, sir."

"Review the highlights for us, please."

Micheals took the folder from his case and summarized it: "Eileen Arrington. Age twenty-eight. Marital status: divorced. Born in Downey, California. Public schools. BA in modern languages, UCLA. MA in the same field, USC. French with a minor in German. She is also proficient in Italian and Dutch, and studied three years at the Center for African Studies, learning to speak and write Swahili and three other African dialects. I think you remember her athletic achievements in college: Pac-Eight champion in the women's 880 and mile runs, anchor on the UCLA distance medley relay team that still holds the world's record, and third in the women's mile at the last Olympics."

"About her African ties," the director prompted.

Micheals thought they all knew the information, but it had to be talked out—reviewed for something possibly overlooked. After tomorrow there would be no pulling back; she would be committed.

He said, "She married a government official in Marandaya while studying there four years ago. She tried to live in the capital, Atavi, but her husband was in the process of going back to traditional native ways of life—the family living with him and Eileen, complete freedom for him to indulge in affairs, and so on. She left after eight months and divorced him. He later died in a small plane crash, so that while I said she is technically divorced, the fact is that she is also now a widow even under Marandayan law.

"Of course we all know that she'd black, frighteningly bright, and one of the best physical and language instructors we ever had on the women's side down there at Quantico."

The director allowed him a wintry smile. "You hate to lose her."

"She wants the assignment," Michaels countered.

Cooper spoke up. "There's no one else we can try."

The director nodded. "She has that great advantage. In addition to being black, of course, and familiar with African affairs, *and* conversant in the language, she met socially with the chief Marandayan delegate to the UN, Clarence Endidi, during her months in Atravi."

Cooper nodded agreement. "Once she's on the job with the Secretariat, there's every reason to hope that she can get close to Endidi and the others on the Marandayan delegation faster than anyone else we have possibly could hope to do. Assuming, of course, that Endidi remembers her and accepts her at face value."

"He'll remember her," Michaels said.

"You're sure?" the director asked.

"Sir, a man does not meet Eileen Arrington and forget."

The director studied him. Michaels had the eerie sensation that behind those eyes were memory discs and voice tapes, turning and correlating things. Then the director nodded. *Analysis complete. Move to Program II.*

"She won't have an easy job," the director said. "It is mandatory that she take some risks. I want her to understand the urgency factor. We know that the cobalt program, once stolen, went through that delegation on its way out of the country. We know that the man we picked up in Utah had a third-party connection with Endidi himself. Our African people believe there's a concerted effort under way to pilfer copies of the Rhodesian contingency plan, and our friends over at the Agency are all upset about a leak that reveals President Obutu once had some connection with them operationally. She has got to get inside that delegation and find out who is the focus of this espionage activity. And we can't wait two years, either."

"I think," Michaels said carefully, "Eileen can do it if anyone can."

The director's heavy hands rested on the top of the desk. His fingers began to drum. "We don't have forever," he said.

"How long do we have?" Michaels asked, knowing he might be going too far.

The tapes turned behind the eyes for a few seconds and a decision was made. The hands folded. "The rebel activity int he provinces seems to be intensifying, and the Agency thinks there are Cuban troops involved for support. Obutu may be on thin ice. He's also negotiating with the French for a new mutual defense pact . . . could be going to Paris to state a public signing within weeks or even days. As shaky as he may be, it's imperative that we discover who is behind what in his delegation at the UN. The answer could determine what our response could be if it looks like he might be toppled."

Cooper added quietly, "Even if none of that were involved, we still would have to crack this ring that's operating in and around Endidi and his people."

"You think Obutu countenances it?" Michaels pressed.

The director shrugged.

Michaels pointed out, "He's erratic. Not as bad as Amin was, of course, but a real son of a bitch, isn't he?"

"He may be a son of a bitch," the director said. "But what we have to determine is whether he's our kind of a son of a bitch."

"I think Eileen will do a hell of a job, sir."

The director stood, signaling that the meeting was over. "We all hope that, Micheals."

Michaels shook hands with the director, with Cooper. Squeezing the deputy's hand, he risked one last question. "Will she be told about the agent who got killed the other night?"

Cooper looked genuinely surprised. "Of course not."

That was probably unfair, Micheals thought. But he could see that it also was probably necessary.

He hoped she would make it. He genuinely liked her.

4

Stuttgart, Germany

Dugger drove north out of Switzerland on an indirect route, and soon he was in the rolling forest of southern Germany. The two-lane highway was crowded for a while, truckers pushing their Mercedes rigs through curves and corners in villages as only European drivers could. Then Dugger struck off on a lesser-used route, Hutingen and Beuron, on the Danube, and heading north toward Tübingen, skirting the Black Forest. There was no sign of pursuit.

His nerves felt surprisingly good. He was running on adrenalin. There was nothing like two attempts on your life to key you up.

He did not understand what was going on. There had to be answers, and now the finding of those answers might be the difference between life or death for him. But he did not have enough information yet and he could only induce unnecessary mental fatigue by cycling and recycling the same questions. Using an old mental trick, he tried insofar as possible to think of other things.

Southern Germany could not compare with Austria and Switzerland for sheer grandeur, but Dugger was conscious now of a feeling like he was back home again. The quiet vastness of the fir woods, heavily timbered yet always fresh and clean, as if no man had ever entered them, touched something deep inside him. He drove through one village, then others, with perfectly clean streets, shining windows, brilliantly well-tended flowers at every point where flowers might be displayed. Later he drove past undulating fields of hay, studded with small barns, and saw elderly men and women working with hand tools as other generations had worked before them. Along distant slopes, sunlight glinted on phalanxes of high-voltage power lines carrying modern life into Germany from the tireless streams in higher elevations. It was cool, clouds were gathering, and it began to rain.

About noon, Dugger stopped in a village and bought some pale cheese, a loaf of fresh bread, some *Wurst*, and two bottles of dark beer. Back on the road, he ate and drank as he drove. The road climbed, and he had to turn on the defroster fan to blow fog from the windshield.

Except for an occasional car met coming from the other direction, Dugger might have been alone on the planet. Few German families lived on their farms, preferring to live in the towns. The result was uncluttered countryside even where intensive farming was taking place. But most of all the drive was through forest, the somber conifers now close along the highway, throwing it in shade, now moving back a few hundred feet to loom overhead from hillsides. The terrain seemed grand, rugged, unassailable.

No wonder, Dugger thought, it had been German peoples who contributed so much in earlier ages to tales of heroism on an epic scale. Their country had these qualities. And in their love for their country, the Germans had maintained its vistas. The French might clutter and chop and wear out their land. The British might create picturesque agricultural gardens. In America, the huge machinery might mow down every tree from coast to coast, filling in the space with endless houses and gigantic farm-factories crawling with machines that looked like something designed for the moon. But in Germany the land was a part of the national heart and mind—in this area, at least, inviolate.

Dugger did not look forward to Stuttgart. The western industrialized cities were a part of the nation he did not fully understand. With their rows of gleaming, Dallas-style buildings, they symbolized for him all the worst things that had been done . . . were being done . . . to what he considered his Germany.

He knew he was dangerously sentimental in all this. Anything done to the German people or land, they had brought it down upon themselves. They had done terrible things in two major wars, unforgivable things in World War II. And now, it seemed, they would never be allowed to forget it. They would pay *forever*.

Poor Germany, Dugger thought, driving. Cut into pieces, each fragment still filled with troops decades after the end of hostilities, a generation on one side brought up to believe the Soviets, a generation on the other brought up to believe the West—both sides told endlessly of the evil things their country had done, how lucky they were to have such charitable conquerers . . . and protectors against the other side.

The mistake, in Dugger's view, had been in stopping Patton. Once the Russians were all over East Germany, it was too late. Now Germany as a true nation no longer existed.

It was a very unfashionable view. Dugger had explained it to his editor in New York a year before, and that bright young woman had at first laughed, thinking he was joking. "No *one* thinks that way anymore!" she had told him. "I'm a dinosaur," he had replied, a bit angrily. "That's why I write adventure, where it's still allowable to have people who are good and other people who are bad."

The young woman had been terribly amused.

Well, Dugger thought, the hell with all the sophisticated idiots of the world. They had not been shot at.

After a long time the steady slapping of the windshield wipers dulled his senses. He had had very little sleep. Finding a small, perfectly clean little *Parkplatz*, he pulled to its edge overlooking an airy drop from the side of his mountain. He did not have to worry much about roving thugs on motorcycles or staunch middle-class citizens ready to hop out of a $30,000 camper in order to break a window and steal a fifty-cent ballpoint. He locked the car doors and slept.

When he awoke, it was still raining but the sky appeared brighter. He had slept an hour, and felt better. Getting out into the cold, pelting rain, he doused his head under a rusty pipe pouring spring water endlessly from the rock wall of the mountain. Climbing back into the car shivering but wide awake, he lighted a cigarette and drove on.

Late afternoon found him approaching Stuttgart on one of the *Autobahnen*, crazy German drivers passing on the left, bumper to bumper, at over a hundred miles per hour. The rain had stopped and the terrain was now rolling, like that of south-central Ohio or Indiana.

Originally built in a great natural depression in the earth's surface, the city was virtually surrounded by rings of higher ground, some natural and some the result of enormous, grassed-over landfills. Dugger left the *Autobahn* and drove downhill toward the distant center of the city, aware that the air became denser and smokier as he progressed. At first the route twisted between endless rows of three- and four-story houses, jammed wall to wall in the old European fashion. As he neared the city center, however, he came upon gaping parking lots and walls of glass. Advertising signs flashed and reflected, traffic roared. At its heart, Stuttgart had been gutted by Allied bombers. Madison Avenue had had a lot of influence on the rebuilding. The streets teemed with ambitious Germans chasing money.

Dugger registered at a small hotel under still another name, then took a walk looking for a telephone booth. He had to call Information to get the listing for Kelly Barracks, then deal with a recalcitrant operator at the installation.

"Three-four-five-four," a woman's voice answered the telephone.

"Mr. McCoy, please," Dugger said, watching traffic and pedestrians stream past the glass walls of the booth.

"Who is calling, please?"

"Joe Dugger."

There was a pause. The woman came back on the line.

"Mr. McCoy is not in the office, sir. Mr. Garfield would like to speak with you."

"All right."

Garfield came on the line. "Mr. Dugger?"

"Yes."

"Where are you, sir?"

"I'm in Stuttgart."

"God! We didn't know what happened to you!" Garfield sounded young. "What are you doing here?"

"Mainly trying not to get killed."

"I beg your pardon?"

"Look, where's McCoy?"

"He's in Norway today. What is it you want?"

"I want to talk to somebody. Things have happened."

There was a pause, and Dugger thought Garfield might be whispering to someone else. Then the youthful voice came back on the line. "Maybe we could meet somewhere."

"Maybe I can just come out there."

"No, we don't think that would be wise. Look. We could meet tonight."

"Where?"

"Well, if you're downtown, how about the Königshof? It's sort of a beer hall—"

"I know the place."

"Good." Garfield sounded relieved. "Okay, tell me what time you'll be there and what you'll be wearing. I'll—"

"No," Dugger cut in. "You tell me what *you* look like and what *you'll* be wearing. And you will be reading a newspaper if anything is wrong."

Garfield was silent again, probably another conference. He probably didn't like it. Dugger didn't care. He was not about to sit around the Königshof and wait to see if Garfield or anyone else thought the coast was clear. He intended to be the one who looked things over and made the decision as to whether the contact would be made.

Garfield came back. "I'll meet you there about nine

o'clock, sir.''

"Describe yourself."

"I'm thirty, six feet tall, a hundred and seventy. I have very blond hair, cut short, and a mustache. I'll be wearing . . . uh . . . wait a minute . . . I'll be wearing a light tan sportcoat, dark brown slacks, a white shirt, and check tie.''

"The upper level?"

"That will be okay."

"You'll be alone."

"Yes, sir."

"And a newspaper to read if you have any doubts."

Garfield's patience seemed to break. "Look, Mr. Dugger, I know you've probably had a bad time. But I know my business.''

"So do they," Dugger said, and hung up.

The hotel supper was heavy but good: sauerkraut, weiners, green beans, potato pancakes, dark bread, steaming strong coffee. When Dugger left to walk toward the Königstrasse a little after eight-thirty, the rain had stopped and the night air was brisk and cool.

The Königstrasse was a primary thoroughfare that had been closed to vehicle traffic and turned into a mall. It was wide and clean and pleasant, with trees planted in garden plots, and fountains. Windows of fashionable stores and shops drew continuous streams of pedestrians. Dugger was walking a few steps behind a British couple when the man tossed a cigarette butt to the pavement. An elderly German man in a dark suit saw the action and hurried over at an angle. He picked up the offending bit of litter, then hurried after the couple. They stood in astonishment as he lectured them, waggling a finger in their faces, before stalking to a nearby container and depositing the trash where it belonged.

Smiling, Dugger walked on toward the distant yellow sign that marked the Königshof. He knew there were people who could have found something sinister in the old man's actions. The German national mentality was such that it might, in mass-meeting circumstances, propose penalties out of all proportion for such crimes as littering. Could and had. There was something in the German people that led to excess in zealous causes.

Dugger recognized this, but was not terrified by it as many people—perhaps people like Frank Bauer—seemed to be. It was not a strictly German tendency to overreact. In America there were still those who would have supported the death penalty for homosexuals. Given a choice, Dugger preferred the German zeal for order.

He arrived at the Königshof at ten minutes before the hour. Theater-type display cases out front showed pictures of the band and vocalist playing an engagement. Dugger went in, walking to the upper level.

The place was very large, with a long bar to the back and right, and a sort of balcony area to the left overhanging part of the first floor and looking down on a brilliantly illuminated bandstand. The orchestra was doing a Glenn Miller arrangement of "String of Pearls." About half the tables were occupied, mostly by young German couples, and everyone seemed happy.

Dugger stood at the bar and ordered a beer. The bartender brought a large stein of the only beer sold, Dinkel Acker. Dugger sipped it and listened to the band, which he could not see this far back on the upper level. He wished they had another kind of beer.

At two minutes before nine, his man came in.

Garfield appeared younger than thirty, but otherwise he matched his description. He appeared a bit nervous as the waiter showed him to a table set against the railing on the front edge of the balcony. Garfield glanced around, missing Dugger, and then concentrated on *not* looking around. He had a newspaper in his coat pocket. He made no move to take it out.

Dugger nursed his beer and waited. The band played a traditional polka, and the crowd clapped in unison and cheered. Then there was more applause and the vocalist did a number. She had a nice voice. Dugger wished he could see her.

At ten minutes after the hour, a middle-aged German

man wearing gold spectacles came in. He asked for and was given a table partway across the room from where Garfield was seated. Dugger saw the man watching Garfield.

There was also another man. He was dark, with shelves of dark eyebrows and clothing that seemed too heavy for the weather. He was eating *Schnitzel* and drinking beer, and Dugger had no idea why the man looked wrong to him.

It was too much, a pair of them not looking right. Dugger wondered if he was getting paranoid as he paid his bar tab and walked out.

The next morning, Friday, Dugger drove out of Stuttgart to the suburbs to the south. The sky was blue porcelain, relief after all the foul weather. A brisk breeze flew. Following small road signs with an American flag and the words KELLY BARRACKS on them, he turned off a routine German street and found himself approaching a gate to the military installation like any of a thousand others around the world. There was a high chain-link fence, a black-on-white sign, broad paving, and a guardhouse manned by smartly uniformed MPs.

A battered Volkswagen microbus and a gleaming white Mercedes diesel, both bearing the distinctive dark green United States personnel tag, were in line ahead of Dugger at the gate. The MP glanced at tags and decals and waved both vehicles through. When he saw Dugger's Swiss plates, he strode over. He was a sergeant and wore a white armband and a .45 under a leather-flap holster.

"Good morning, sir. Can I help you?"

"I'm here to see Charles McCoy or a Mr. Garfield in his office." Dugger handed over his genuine passport and driver's license.

The guard scowled at them. "Do you have Department of the Army ID, sir?"

"No."

"What area do Mr. McCoy and Mr. Garfield work in? Headquarters?"

"Sergeant, I'm sure they're listed in your directory."

Two other cars had pulled in line behind Dugger. The guard seemed perplexed and cautious. "Sir, if you will pull your car over there to the right, I'll check this out."

Dugger cranked the wheel hard and pulled to the wide space in the pavement, letting the other vehicles pass. He shut off his engine and waited. Through the fence he could see mature trees, winding cobbled roads, towering brick buildings in the sterile architectural style of the Nazis who had built them in 1936 and 1937. Soldiers and a number of civilians walked the sidewalks. Dugger spotted British, German, and French uniforms as well as U.S. ones.

Inside the guard building, the sergeant hung up the telephone. He came out, still frowning, and walked to Dugger's car. "There will be a slight delay, sir. Will you wait in the guard shack, please?"

"The car is fine."

"No, sir." The guard rested his hand lightly on the top of his holster. "Just step out of the car, sir, and accompany me to the building."

Dugger obeyed with a sense of irritation. The guard held the screen door for him out of courtesy or caution. Inside, the shack was standard GI, roughly hewn counters, OD desks, a rack of temporary visitor cards to hang from car radio antennas, a half dozen gray steel straight chairs with gray plastic seat cushions.

"If you'll just have a seat, sir, I'm sure it won't be long."

It was forty minutes.

The sergeant remained at one of the desks, ostensibly studying reports. In point of fact, he was keeping an eye on Dugger. The building was too warm with the thin sunlight beating on its roof. Dugger's slight headache began to grow.

The screen door banged open. The sergeant stood as Garfield, wearing pale slacks and a shirt open at the collar, walked in. An ID card flapped in a plastic holder attached to his shirt pocket. He did not look happy.

"Mr. Dugger?" He did not offer his hand. "I'm Bryan Garfield."

"Sorry about last night."

"So am I. We didn't want you coming out here."

Dugger was aware that the sergeant was listening, but to hell with it. "You had a friend tailing you last night, maybe two."

Garfield's jaw set in a stubborn line. "I don't think so, sir."

"You're wrong. Now do we go inside somewhere and talk or do I just go my merry way, getting shot at and leaving bodies?"

Garfield's fair cheeks spotted with angry color. He turned stiffly to the guard. "Thank you, Sergeant. I'll vouch for the visitor."

The sergeant handed over Dugger's license and passport. Dugger pocketed them. "You didn't look at these, Bryan."

"We got photos of you . . . this morning."

They left the guard shack together and walked to Dugger's car. Dugger got behind the wheel. Garfield got in the other side.

"Rent car, Mr. Dugger?"

"Do you want to see my green card?"

Garfield puffed his cheeks. "All right. What do you say we just start over? You're pissed. I was pissed last night. Let's just forget all that and start over."

"Where do I drive?"

"Straight ahead, and then to the left."

Dugger drove slowly past a big stone building on the right. Over the doorway was a large pastel mural showing German soldiers, in coal scuttle helmets, with rifles stacked nearby. All around the Reich warriors were farmers, artisans, workers, and housewives, their labors clearly, in the crude symbolism, going directly to the war effort.

Garfield noticed Dugger's glance. "Nazi, of course. It was painted over when we took the place in 1945. Not long ago, building cleaners found it again and we've had it restored for its historical significance.''

''Painted over in forty-five, restored in the early eighties,'' Dugger said. ''The way things are going, I suppose you'll have to paint it over again one of these days.''

''I beg your pardon?''

''Nothing.''

''Turn left here, sir.''

Dugger obeyed, going down a narrow street lined by old brick buildings. His hands felt puffy on the steering wheel. Tension caused fluid retention. He lighted a cigarette.

Garfield said, ''You've given us something of a start, coming here like this.''

''I've had something of a start myself.''

''You really think I was followed last night?''

''I'm sure of it.''

Garfield looked glum.

''We all make mistakes,'' Dugger offered.

''Yes,'' Garfield said, brightening. ''Like your man in Burghausen.''

''*He* made the mistake there. Not me.''

''Who was he?''

''I have no idea. I'm glad to know you picked up on it, anyway.''

''Oh yes. That, and your house there being empty, and your car gone. Then last night we learned about your car in Zurich. Of course we already had heard from you here, so we knew you weren't in it.''

Dugger tightened up. ''In it?''

''When it blew up. Oh. You didn't know about that. Of course.''

''Suppose you tell me.''

''Pull right in there behind the Citroën, sir. Well, the attendant in the garage where you left it had to move it for some reason. He used the ignition key you left at the office. When he turned the ignition lock—boom.''

Dugger looked at the younger man, losing patience. ''Boom?''

''Boom,'' Garfield repeated. ''Poor guy was killed

instantly."

"Jesus Christ."

"The police were interested, of course. We picked up your identification papers quite routinely. Gave us something of a turn until we could establish you weren't in it. May I ask why you left the car there?"

Dugger parked and turned off the Cortina. "I left the car there, Bryan, because somebody took a couple of shots at me earlier. They chased my aching ass all over the back streets of Zurich, and I considered it wiser to change IDs and high-tail it."

"I see." Garfield smiled boyishly. "Good show. Well, shall we go in?"

They entered the building, which was stark and cold in a way only military buildings could be: gleaming dark green tile floors, buff walls with water stains from exposed pipes and wiring in the ceilings, a steel staircase going up. Beside the staircase was a sergeant at a desk with a gun. Garfield signed the register for Dugger and they went up, Dugger clipping his visitor's pass to his shirt pocket.

"Is this where the office was when you were with us, Mr. Dugger?"

"Yes. It used to be quite an operation."

They reached a high floor and turned down a narrower, similarly barren corridor with closed doors studding its walls. "We've been cut down rather severely today, I'm afraid," Garfield told him.

They walked through an unmarked door with frosted glass in the top. Dugger knew it well; once it had been the busy outer office, with a dozen clerks and secretaries in a constant clamor of activity. Now the tall barred windows on the far side of the large room shone bleakly onto a single desk, a small row of metal filing cabinets. It looked unused, abandoned.

A young woman walked out of the next office, which looked through the door to be just as bare. "Hello, Bryan."

"Millie, is he in?"

"Yes. He's expecting you. Go right in."

Garfield led the way into the next office, a large, square room with barred windows on two walls. Standing behind a large desk flanked by American and West German flags was a short, sandy-haired man with age-faded freckles. He wore rumpled blue slacks, a tan tie that was too wide, and a pale gray corduroy sportcoat open over an expanding midsection. His eyes were bright green.

"Hello, Bryan," he said. "And this is our Mr. Dugger."

Dugger shook hands with him. "I thought I knew everyone in Europe who was on the payroll."

The man smiled faintly. "My name's Cunningham. Spent most of my days in Southeast Asia. You don't know me, but I know a lot about you. Sit down. Let's talk."

Dugger started toward one of the chairs facing the desk. Bryan Garfield slumped into the other one. Dugger stopped where he was. "I want this to be between you and me, Cunningham."

Cunningham raised sandy eyebrows. "Yes. Well, leave us, then, Bryan. All right?"

Garfield frowned, stood, and walked out of the room. Cunningham followed him to the doorway. He called, "No telephone calls unless it's the A line, Millie. All right?" He closed the door and came back to his desk.

"Nothing against Garfield," Dugger began. "But—"

"I understand perfectly," Cunningham said, smiling. "He is something of an asshole, isn't he?" The man sat down and folded his hands. "All right, then, Mr. Dugger. Let's talk turkey."

5

Moscow

Thin crowds of tourists moved across the vastness of Red Square beneath a thin, unwarming sun. In a stark little office in an upper floor of one of the ugly buildings nearby, Victor Surin faced his superior, General G. J. Svintitsky. The rotund general was eating Swiss chocolates, but his mood was anything but sweet.

"Victor," the general said, licking chocolate from his thumb, "the assignment was not complex."

"We had no way of knowing that the man had already been contacted by a genuine CIA officer, General," Surin said nervously.

"Bordoff was hardly the experienced man who should have been sent in any case," General Svintitsky said, picking up a dark creme and experimentally poking a fingernail through the chocolate crust to sample the color of the filling. "Bordoff lacked experience, finesse."

"General, forgive me, but Bordoff had many years' experience, an impeccable record—"

"Insufficient to send after a man like Joseph Dugger!" General Svintitsky popped the creme into his mouth and chewed angrily, a dribble leaking from a corner of his lips. "Do you know this man Dugger's *background*?"

"He was retired, my general, with an undistinguished record—"

The general's fist crashed onto the desk top. "Where did you get *that* information?"

"Out of the files! I studied them closely!"

The general sighed and rummaged in the chocolate box again. "I suppose it is possible, although I intend to check that file for myself, Victor. You may be sure of that. My God, this bureaucracy will be the death of me! I suppose some piddling idiot put the best face possible on everything. Do we even have to lie in our own secret files to preserve our image?" The general tried to crack the crust of another chocolate, which burst and sent rivulets of red juice down all his fingers. He tossed the candy back into the box and resumed, angrily licking. "What did the file say about Dugger's work at Geneva, eh? I suppose it said *that* was routine? And what did it report about Essen? Or Rome in 1978? Eh?"

Victor Surin hesitated, terrified to reply. He *knew* the file had painted Joseph Dugger as a routine operative with no special talents. But he feared insisting on the fact. Clearly the file was wrong. The files seemed so often to be wrong. And Victor Surin had compounded whatever initial error he had made several times since then. His promotion folder, he remembered with acute anxiety, was on the general's desk somewhere. At this rate it would stay there, buried under chocolates and cookies, forever.

"Oh, never mind," General Svintitsky growled. "The fact of the matter is that he escaped us in Burghausen and he escaped a grossly amateurish effort against him in Zurich. The fact also remains that we now have lost track of him altogether."

The general waited, glaring, so the unhappy Surin murmured, "Yes, sir."

"He has been warned and he has gone to ground," the general added.

Victor Surin said nothing.

"IS THAT CORRECT?" the general bellowed, his face going crimson.

"YES, SIR!"

The general resumed poking around among the chocolates, his voice instantly becoming mild, thoughtful. "And how do you propose finding him again, if I may be so bold as to inquire?"

"General, he cannot return to Burghausen—"

"Do not say he cannot, not with this man, Victor!"

"I do not believe he will return to Burghausen, my general, although we do have three men in that city on watch against the unlikely possibility—"

"Good. Go on."

"We have analyzed his situation and we believe he has only two or three options—"

"Which is it, two or three? God of our fathers, man!"

"Three," Victor Surin said, sweating. "Whichever of these he exercises, we have men waiting to identify him and resume our operation against him."

"There will be no slipups," General Svintitsky said.

"Absolutely none, my general."

"This man Dugger is not a major part of the operation in progress. You know that and I know that. It is very complex. But Dugger could ruin everything. It was decided to eliminate the slight chance that he might do so. He must be located and taken care of. You do understand that."

"Oh yes, my general."

"We have little time left," General Svintitsky said, glancing nervously at the calendar on the otherwise bare concrete wall.

"I am fully confident he will come to us, my general."

"He *must*. There must be no more stupidity. I am feeling grave pressures from higher authority, Victor." The general stopped, a chocolate poised to pop into his mouth. "That surprises you, that I, too, feel pressures from above?"

"It is only, my general, that your position—"

"My position, Victor, is that of a worker like any other worker. I have superiors. They reward me if I do well. They punish me if I fail. There is great interest in this operation at the highest levels . . . at the very highest levels." The general put the chocolate into his mouth and chewed thoughtfully, glaring.

Victor Surin watched, unable to speak. In point of fact, General G. J. Svintitsky had but four possible superiors in the entire structure of the government. He was a most powerful man. Yet he was clearly worried . . . was being pressed just as he was pressing Surin.

It gave Victor Surin his first realization of just how important the operation, in all its unknown facets, must really be.

"You will report again this evening," the general told him. "There will be nothing that is not reported at once. You will gloss over no new failure or uncertainty. I *must* be fully informed. You understand?"

"I understand, my general," Victor Surin said reverently.

The general thrust the box of candy toward him. "Have one! Enjoy it!"

Victor Surin looked into the box. Many of the cremes had been crushed by the general's testing fingernail, and others were half melted. All had escaped their dark brown wrappers and were riding in a thin coating of yellow-pink goo that covered the entire bottom of the box. But the general had made a friendly overture, and the general did not issue conditional offers.

Victor Surin selected one of the candies that looked least crushed and put it in his mouth. He chewed rapidly, smiling around the sweetness, while his stomach lurched.

Stuttgart

Cunningham had stuffed a pipe with foul-smelling shag, and his office was now layered with gray smoke. The cup of coffee he had produced was somewhat akin to battery acid, most of it now scalding the lining of Dugger's stomach.

"We agree on a couple of things, then," Cunningham said in his deceptively calm voice. "There's a leak somewhere, it's going to hurt Joseph Obutu, and somebody clearly wants you dead."

"Point number three tends to take priority in my thinking," Dugger said.

Cunningham chuckled. "I understand."

"Do you have anything on the man who tried to hit me in Burghausen?"

"We managed to run a complete check on him. There's absolutely nothing to indicate any possibility of a Soviet connection."

"What connection did you come up with?"

"None."

"That's very helpful."

"Some of our people have a line of speculation."

"That being?"

Cunningham put down the pipe. "We obviously have a move to discredit Joseph Obutu. We don't know the source or the reason as yet. Perhaps someone wants all of Obutu's old contacts dead to eliminate the possibility of their vouching for him against new phases of the smear campaign."

"It isn't very convincing," Dugger said.

"I admit that. Of course if we can locate the leak that provided some of the information McCoy showed you, then perhaps . . ." Cunningham puffed the pipe again.

"Any leads on that?" Dugger asked, knowing the answer.

Cunningham surprised him. "We lean to the theory that it's Frank Bauer."

"*Why?*"

"The most obvious reason: He's still alive."

"I can't accept that," Dugger said. "I talked to him. He isn't a traitor. And there's a compelling reason for him to want *all* information about Obutu, me, himself, and all the others kept quiet. Publicity that mentions his connection with the Agency will hurt his business, be considered a black mark by people his daughter evidently associates with."

"Yes," Cunningham said thoughtfully. "We're looking into the people his daughter associates with."

"It isn't Bauer. I feel sure of that. Why pick on him? What about Rudi Wetzel, if you're looking for—" Dugger stopped, because he had caught Cunningham's change of expression.

"I was going to get to that, actually," Cunningham told him.

Dugger waited and said nothing.

"He was in Oslo, you know. That's why McCoy is up there today. It seems there was quite a bad accident yesterday."

"For Rudi?" Of course Dugger knew.

"It seems he tripped climbing some stairs at his rooming house. Fell several flights. Broke his neck." Cunningham puffed the pipe furiously for a moment, then made a face and put it back down on the desk as if giving it up permanently. "Strange thing to happen to a man with a background in Alpine climbing, wouldn't you say?"

Although he had begun to guess moments earlier, Dugger still felt severe shock. He did not reply at once.

"So," Cunningham said through the dense smoke, "only you and Frank Bauer and Pierre LaFontaine remain alive. Assuming that the information about Joseph Obutu was leaked by one of your group, our list of suspects is radically narrowed. The attempts on your life have been legitimate—"

"You've satisfied yourself about that, have you?" Dugger asked sarcastically.

"Yes." Cunningham gave him a cool smile. "And it's absurd to think LaFontaine would be the leak."

"Why?"

"In the first place, he has no need of money. He's a wealthy man. In the second place, he has considerable interest in maintaining the status quo in Marandaya."

"What the hell does Pete have to do with Marandaya today?"

Cunningham stood, went to the windows, and drew the draperies. Going to a side table under a wall of maps, he turned on a small reading lamp beside a motion picture projector; Dugger now noticed that the machine was loaded with film, ready to operate.

Cunningham walked once more across the room, turned off the overhead fluorescents, and returned to the table where the small lamp now splashed a single bright yellow cone of light up the wall over the maps. The illumination turned his face into a gargoyle as he leaned across it to start the projector. On the far wall, the whirring machine cast a pale rectangle of uncertain color.

"These were taken last month," Cunningham said over the machine noise. "They're grainy, but under the circumstances, remarkable."

A series of red numbers flashed by on the wall. Then a picture took form: a yellow undulating field of brush and weeds, with a mountain range indistinct in the far background. The camera seemed to be hidden behind netting of some kind because there was a silk screen effect to the picture. Dugger made out a vehicle distantly moving away from the center of the picture out in the field.

There was a sudden out-flushing of smoke and dust from the far portion of the field, and then a flaring red light. A slender silver pencil—a rocket—soared up out of the obscurity, trailing a hot line of fire. It made a brief arc across the brilliant blue sky, and was gone with only a distant squiggly vapor trail to prove it had ever been.

Before Dugger could react, the picture changed. It looked like the same kind of vegetation, the same background. But the lens was considerably longer. Through shimmering heat waves he could clearly make out a long burnished aluminum rocket standing on a launching pad of some sort. There was a two-prong support tower beside the pad, its jaws retracted from the rocket. Again there was a flare as the rocket engines fired. The rocket lifted off and was gone.

The film changed again. This time the picture was from an aircraft looking down at a dizzying angle through broken cloud toward the green earth perhaps fifty thousand feet below. A rocket flew into the field from the right, indistinct because of camera movement, yet unmistakable in contour. The engine was still firing; Dugger could make out the angry fire of the booster. As he watched, the camera tracking at a fantastic rate of speed which blurred the cloud cover below, the rocket engine shut down. The rear section of the rocket—then another section—tumbled free, jettisoned. As the rocket vanished into a layer of cloud, a bright glow announced the firing of another stage. The rocket clearly was tilting over to return to earth with its final engine still thrusting.

The picture on the wall showed flashing numbers on their sides, some sprocket holes, and whiteness.

Cunningham shut off the projector, went to the wall switch, and reestablished normal illumination in the room. Dugger blinked in the resumed brightness.

"Those were shot in Africa," Cunningham said as he opened the drapes. "To be specific, in central Maran-daya."

"OTRAG?" Dugger said, surprised and puzzled.

"Oh, you know about Orbital Transport-und Raketen-Aktiengesellschaft," Cunningham said, returning to his desk with a nod of approval. "You've been keeping up."

"I know a little," Dugger replied. "They're a West German firm that's headquartered right around here, as a matter of fact. They're building rockets and hardware on the free enterpise system, nominally under the flag of Zaire. Some people seem to think they're an Agency front."

"A logical assumption," Cunningham said surprisingly. "Treaty forbids the Bonn government from certain kinds of rocket research, and the UN space treaty forbids free-lance exploration in space. So we're to assume the Agency is using this kind of phony private business front to let the West Germans experiment with anything they want."

"And?" Dugger said.

"It's all bullshit," Cunningham said amiably. "The bastards really are going off on the ultimate exercise in entrepreneurship—their own rockets and launchers, designed to be offered in direct competition to NASA, and at a drastically reduced cost to users. The European Space Agency paid NASA forty-seven million last year for a launch. It failed, but the money wasn't refundable. There are a lot of people interested now in seeing if

OTRAG can really make it work with their windshield-wiper motor-fuel pumps and all this other incredible crap they seem to be using.''

"So those pictures were taken in Zaire? That's where OTRAG tests, isn't it?"

"Yes," Cunningham said. "But that rocket wasn't OTRAG. There was a competing company out of Cologne. And its testing is being done in Marandaya."

Dugger rubbed his aching forehead. "I begin to see glimmers. Why haven't I ever heard of this outfit? What's it called?"

"It's got a name as long as your arm. We call it Volks-rocket." Cunningham allowed himself a slight smile. "And if you haven't heard of it yet, you're reading the wrong newspapers. *Afrique-Asie* called it 'the German knife in the heart of Africa.' The Russians are fit to be tied. Their puppets in Angola have let it be known that they're supporting the rebels in Marandaya specifically be-cause Joseph Obutu has leased eighty thousand kilometers to Volksrocket for their testing range. *Pravda* is foaming at the mouth."

"Which explains their motives for wanting to discredit Obutu and bring about his downfall politically if they pos-sibly can," Dugger said. He slammed his palm on the edge of the desk. "Which explains *why* the leaks. But it doesn't say a thing about why Pete LaFontaine is *ipso facto* innocent."

"LaFontaine," Cunningham told him, fiddling with the pipe again, "has something like nine million dollars in Volksrocket."

"Good God. Frank Bauer *said* Pete had big investments in Germany."

"LaFontaine wants Obutu ousted—obviously—about like he wants lung cancer."

Dugger leaned back in the chair. His headache was con-siderably worse. It made sense in the foggiest way; he now had at least a theoretical reason for the evident plot to dis-credit and topple Joseph Obutu in Marandaya. But that in no way explained who had leaked the information, or why someone wanted a number of people—including Dugger —dead.

"What are you doing about Pete?" he asked.

"About LaFontaine? He's being watched, of course."

"Has he been warned that some of us have been killed?"

"Oh no. We couldn't make him aware of our interest. You see, there's considerable evidence that the Volks-rocket is going to have possible military applications. If they go off the deep end and start selling military launchers all over Africa, we have to have the advantage of being well out of sight for our operations."

"In the meantime, what if somebody just blows Pete's head off?"

Cunningham squinted through smoke. "Oh, he's wealthy enough to have his own security. I wouldn't worry."

"I'm sure Rudi and the others weren't worried either."

"Calm down, Mr. Dugger. I've told you all this only to assure you that we're on top of the situation . . . and to explain why we feel pretty sure our leak is your man Bauer down there in Zurich. We'll get this ironed out, believe me."

"And what am I supposed to do?"

"Well, that is a little sticky, isn't it? We've only had preliminary discussions of that, but it looks like you could either stay here on base a few days or weeks, until we get this thing unraveled, or we could arrange transport to the U.K., where you could have a vacation under an assumed name."

Dugger thought about it, conscious of a simmering anger. He could not believe Frank Bauer was the traitor be-cause there was no motive. Now that left only Pierre LaFontaine, who seemed even more unlikely. But LaFon-taine was either the traitor or the next candidate for assassi-nation. In either case, his office in Paris was the next likely place for Dugger to go.

But he was moving across Europe like the plague, drag-ging death behind him. He had no solid information. It was clear that Cunningham was not about to volunteer any information about the unspoken compartment of the puzzle—Regensburg. Perhaps it was all too much. Perhaps, Dugger told himself, he was too old, too rusty.

Perhaps he should accept the enforced vacation and wait for the other side to forget him . . . wait for his own suspicions and worries to subside. *It will take time for me to become useless again.*

Dugger stood, jamming his hands in his pockets. "I need some time to digest all this."

"Sure," Cunningham said. "All the time you want."

"I'll go back to my hotel, collect my stuff. It's obvious I don't want to stay there anymore."

"We can have somebody pick them up for you, Joe." Cunningham's washboard forehead was sincerely concerned.

"I'm confident no one picked me up there. I'll be all right." Dugger walked partway to the office door. "If I drive off, can I get back on this afternoon without quite so much hassle?"

"I'll arrange it." Cunningham shook his hand and walked out to the car with him.

Dugger drove back into Stuttgart.

They tailed him, of course. It took a while to lose them. Then he checked the rent car in at the downtown agency and carried his bag to the *Hauptbahnhof*, where he consulted the schedule boards for trains west. This left him just enough time to buy a ticket, a poor boy sandwich, and a small pastry, which he carried on board the 1 P.M. *rapide* for Paris.

6

New York City

When Eileen Arrington returned to her small furnished apartment, she found Rick Kelley waiting for her.

"It's all right," Kelley said, his long, skinny legs stretched out from the plastic couch to the small coffee table. "I won't just barge in again, but the big guns are very anxious to know you're all right after your first contact over at the UN."

Eileen put her purse and briefcase on the dining table by a dusty window in the kitchen alcove. The view was of a brick wall across an alley. She was keyed up but well in control. "It went fine. I'll be translating documents on an informal basis. I don't know how you got me in there. No one seems aware that I'm any different from any other clerk in the Secretariat, but the job will get me to the African delegation areas constantly."

Rick Kelley smiled lazily. He was tall, sandy-haired, with wide-set eyes. He looked too young for his post of responsibility, an effect that was heightened by the casual knit slacks and open-throated sport shirt he had worn for this contact today. "*I* didn't get you in there, lady. That took some doing by someone a lot higher up."

"Well, I'm in, anyway."

"Good. And all is well?"

"I'll have some materials to deliver to the Marandayan and Liberian delegations on the floor of the General Assembly. I'm to find a spokesman for those delegations this afternoon to arrange delivery."

Kelley's eyes snapped. "Great. Then you may very well make contact with Clarence Endidi right away."

"I'm going to give it my best shot," Eileen said with more confidence than she really felt.

Kelley got up and walked restlessly to the window, then turned and strode back to a frayed chair standing forlornly under a crooked reading lamp. His movements revealed that he, too, was feeling the pressure. Jamming his hands in his back pockets, he glared at her. "Just remember: you're here to finger the spy in the Marandayan delegation, but you're not supposed to take risks that might get you dropped in the East River."

"I'll be careful."

"I mean, I know you've been stuck in the training area and I know you want to give a good showing on this. We're pressed for time. But . . . uh—" He stopped, seemed to think of saying something more, and then clamped his jaws tightly. "Enough said."

Eileen was moved. She knew he was trying, in his clumsy way, to show his personal concern for her. Their backgrounds were drastically different—he from an Ivy League college, with money, and she from a poverty line family in Los Angeles' black ghetto. But last evening and early today they had immediately felt a friendship growing. He was a very decent man, and she sensed that she needed him in more ways than one.

"I'll be careful," she repeated. "I'll be fine."

"Just remember your cover. You went back to graduate school and then you worked for that textbook firm in Atlanta. You got fed up with that and came up here hoping to latch onto an editorial job in the foreign books division of some publishing house. The UN job is a stop-gap, and you're doing some free-lance copy editing—"

"I know," Eileen cut in. "I remember. I'll be *fine*, Rick!"

Kelley looked around the room. "You're all moved in and it still looks bare. Maybe I ought to go out and get some more books and magazines and stuff to scatter around."

"It ought to look bare," Eileen told him. "I did just move in, remember? My cover story takes care of that. If we moved things in, it would all look like . . . things moved in. If anyone smart enough to check up on me came by, they would spot planted clutter faster than anything else."

Kelley went back to the couch, dropping onto it like a collection of loose bones. "You're right. I just worry. Clarence Endidi is a son of a bitch. I want you to watch it."

"You forget that I know Clarence Endidi from earlier days," Eileen said.

"Then you know he's a son of a bitch."

"He's a very strong man, a self-made man who obviously has a lot farther to go . . . much more to accomplish. He's tough and very, very smart. But I think under all the guise of cynicism and hate there's a good and even gentle man who truly cares about his country and the world."

"You've read the file," Kelley replied. "He's one hundred-percent black nationalism, Africa-for-Africans, anti-American, Marxist, and all the rest of it. He's dangerous."

"I managed to like him once, for all of that," Eileen said. "I think I can handle him."

Kelley stood again, pacing, his jaw working. He was under a pressure that Eileen did not understand. "Things are heating up in Marandaya. Gero Paasaad and his guerrillas are tearing hell out of Joseph Obutu's army in the western highlands. There's unrest all over the place. Endidi might be more suspicious of you than he would be even normally."

"Rick," Eileen said, putting her hands on her hips and facing him squarely so that he had to stop his restless pacing, "what is it you *really* want to say?"

Kelley's eyes widened. "I don't know what you mean."

"You've got something else on your mind. What is it you're not telling me?"

Kelley looked at her, clearly troubled. "Hell," he said explosively. "They didn't directly *order* me not to tell you.''

"Tell me what?''

"There was someone else on this case. A lot of people, as a matter of fact. But there was an agent named Corbin. He had Clarence Endidi's apartment staked out a few nights ago. Watching a man who had been followed to the Endidi address.''

"And?'' Eileen's pulse began to murmur at a faster rate.

"He was killed. Hit-and-run, while trying to follow the guy when he left Endidi's place.''

The information hit her hard. She was conscious of her altered breathing and heart rate. "I see.''

"*That's* why you've got to be extra-careful,'' he told her.

"I will,'' she promised.

"You must *not* press too hard. If you can't find a lead naturally, then the operation has to be terminated and they can try something else. Agreed?''

"Agreed,'' Eileen said, managing a smile.

He stepped closer and took her lightly by the shoulders. "Because I don't want to lose a partner, and you're my partner. Right?''

"Right.''

He released her and stepped back. "Okay. I'll get out of here. What time do you have to be back over there?''

"Right away. I pleaded meeting a mover.''

"Okay.'' Kelley went to the door, opened it, looked back. "Remember how to get in touch.''

"I will, Rick. And thanks. Really.''

He grinned, winked, and was gone.

Eileen hurried to the kitchen, where she made a cold meat sandwich. Standing at the window without a view, she chewed thoughtfully. She still felt sure she could handle it. But she wondered if this new emotion inside was fear.

Atravi, Marandaya

In the walled compound just beyond the main courtyard

of the palace, the guards had trouble tying the prisoner to the post for execution. He kept collapsing and falling to the sun-scorched dust. Finally the guards managed it and put on the blindfold. The prisoner was a boy of perhaps fifteen, naked except for raggedly cut-off jeans, his black skin like velvet powdered with the yellow dust where he had repeatedly fallen.

President Joseph Obutu stood in the hot shade near the gate and watched as the guards marched away. The military drummer played a drum roll, to preserve the niceties. Obutu, sweltering in the brocaded uniform, encrusted with gold leaf and medals, wished they would hurry it up. But the captain in command insisted on marching the firing squad in with full ceremony and then ritualistically inspecting their rifles.

Finally everything was ready. The firing squad loaded and stood at attention. The prisoner was collapsed against the ropes that bound him, weeping hysterically.

Obutu waited, also at attention. Sweat trickled down his cheeks, wilting his collar.

"Ready!" the captain cried sharply. *"Aim! Fire!"*

The rifles barked. The boy was smashed back against the post as all the bullets hit, and then he hung there in the ropes with a different kind of slackness. The captain marched up with a small pistol and shot him in the head to make sure.

The drummer did another roll.

Joseph Obutu did an about-face and marched back through the stone gate into the courtyard of the palace. All the water sprinklers had been turned off for his walk to the execution, and the flagstone walks were rapidly drying. The roses, begonias, vinca, and hothouse chrysanthemums made the inner courtyard a blaze of vivid color. Against the backdrop of the huge, castle-like stone palace building, the blue Marandayan flag cracked in the hot wind buffeting a fifty-foot flagpole.

Obutu walked partway to the palace doors, trailed by four of his uniformed aides.

He stopped then, turning to a major, and pointed at a

bed of mums. "These are wilted. Have them replaced immediately."

The major saluted. "At once, Mr. President!"

Obutu marched on into the shade of the palace. The front doors stood open, a smartly uniformed and armed guard at each side. Obutu went in, through the vast, echoing marble foyer, and to the special elevator. Another guard swung the door open for him as he approached, and he stepped directly inside. The officers started to follow.

"Not now!" Obutu barked, and they froze, expressionless, as the door slid closed in their faces.

Riding to the second floor, Obutu maintained his glacial control. He walked past other guards in the gleaming second-floor corridor, each of whom snapped to frightened attention as he passed. Through the outer office to his own sanctum he walked, head up, shoulders back. The male clerks and officers at the desks watched in covert fear.

General Marcos Arman, chief of Obutu's staff, tried to intercept him at the general's desk near Obutu's office door. "Mr. President—"

"Not now," Obutu snapped, and went on inside alone.

He slammed the door behind him, removed the gold-crusted military jacket and cap, pulled the tie loose, opened the collar.

And wept.

He was a very large man, bearish shoulders and thick chest and arms of great power, with legs that were too short for his torso. His large head rode on a thick neck. A broad nose and heavy shelf of eyebrow, under close-cropped kinky black hair, gave him a perpetually angry look except on those rare occasions when he allowed someone to see his smile. He did not look like a man who could be shaken by tears.

Standing alone in his big office, however, Joseph Obutu trembled from head to toe. He held a hammy black hand to his mouth, biting hard on his coiled index finger in his attempt to maintain silence. No one could know. If they knew the waves of revulsion that swept through him after these executions, they would see him as weak . . . incompetent. That must never be allowed to happen. They would be on him like a jackal pack, tearing his flesh from his bones.

After a few minutes, Obutu regained control. He walked to his big mahogany desk, set against huge windows thrown open to the humid Marandayan wind, and stood looking down at the military analysis maps spread on the surface. Small crosses marked the latest places struck by Gero Paasaad's rebel forces.

I will strike with full force and destroy him, Obutu thought. *What does it matter if these few villages are also destroyed? I must be strong, avenger for my people.*

No. I must be calm, a statesman. I must exercise restraint.

Do other leaders feel so torn?"

Is it true what some of them say? Am I mad?

Obutu told himself to be calm. He bent over the maps with a small magnifying glass. A large drop of his sweat dripped onto the glass, making it blur.

He walked to the office door and swung it open. General Marcos Arman stood quickly, questions in his eyes.

"What progress, General, on repair of the air-conditioning plant?"

"I have spoken to the chief of the plant, Mr. President. He promises restoration by tomorrow afternoon."

"Please inform the chief of the plant, General, that he will be shot if it is not repaired by nightfall today."

Arman stiffened. "Parts must be flown in from Rome—"

"Let him improvise!" Obutu shouted, making every head in the room jerk. "Are the Americans the only ones in the world with ingenuity? Are we ignorant savages ready to rush back into the jungle?"

"No, Mr. President," General Arman said softly.

Obutu glanced at the solid-gold quartz watch on his wrist. "He has seven hours! Inform him of this fact immediately!" He turned, slamming the door again, and strode back to his desk.

The air conditioning in the palace had been down for two days. Now the blazing African sun had thoroughly heated the four-foot walls of the building, and every room hovered over the 100 mark, Fahrenheit. Obutu's large office, with windows on only one wall, was among the worst in that it lacked any cross-ventilation. The heat here was insufferable.

Obutu walked again to the windows, remaining somewhat back out of the direct sunlight in an automatic gesture of caution. There had been two attempts on his life in the past ten months.

Below in the courtyard, the sprinklers were all going again, filling the air with little rainbows. In the compound beyond, the firing stake was empty, the prisoner taken away. Beyond that wall, a handful of people stood in the dusty street, watched by the armed soldiers in the jeep and the personnel carrier. A soldier had his head stuck out of the top hatch of the personnel carrier. He had his helmet on. *His brains must be frying*, Obutu thought.

South of the courtyard, the compound, and the dusty road where the soldiers were, an area of several hundred yards had been cleared and transformed into bare lawn which the sun had now turned uniform brown. Beyond this safety perimeter, the outskirts of Atravi began. The city's rising modern skyline loomed vaguely in the distance over mile after mile of squalid clutter and slum. French colonial rule had considered the slums good enough. Joseph Obutu was rebuilding it block by block. The entire job, he estimated, would take another hundred years.

He did not have a hundred years.

An army chopper puttered over a far part of the city on its endless routine sweep for signs of threatening activity. Obutu followed the craft for a moment, his sense of frustrated depression growing. If Gero Paasaad tried to spread his insurrection to Atravi, he would not succeed. Obutu's army had the firepower here. But how many innocents would die because Marandaya's army had to kill them to reach the rebels?

Obutu thought briefly about sending another message to Castro. In the last one, he had bluntly promised to mount an expedition and invade Cuba itself if Castro did not immediately withdraw his "advisers" from Paasaad's forces. The newsreels had shown Castro reading the message to a huge throng in Havana, and laughing until the tears streamed from his eyes.

Patience.

In his few years in office, Joseph Obutu had tried to attack all his country's myriad problems at once. Tax benefits had been offered for foreign investment. Rental for the miles of land used for the West German rocket testing had provided valuable added income, as well as contractual guarantees of first bid on military rockets when research and development climaxed in an operational vehicle. After Regensburg, the deal with the United States had helped enormously. There were other aid packages from both the U.S. and France. A totally new educational program was getting under way, teachers being trained here and abroad by the tens of thousands. He had rooted out much of the corruption in the army, and the new military force was smaller, better equipped, skillful. The U.S. had been only too happy to sell arms, including Phantom jets. If the Russians had not insisted on three submarine bases as part of their offer to build new hospitals, that deal might have gone through as well. The Russians were a problem. Obutu hated the Russians.

He could survive without them. In another decade, the political parties would have been purified, the electorate educated, and a genuine election could be held. In his lifetime, Obutu would drag Marandaya into the twentieth century as an independent power. Then, one day—God! —he could step down.

The telephone on Obutu's desk flashed. He picked it up. "Yes?"

"Mr. President, the gentleman from the United States embassy is here."

"In a minute, General." Obutu hung up and looked back down at the maps.

The crosses marking the latest strikes showed that Gero Paasaad had, as usual, planned well and daringly. Each attack had been in the highlands, along passes looking down upon narrow roads. The worst had been along the Andalui River; some sixty rebels with automatic weapons and anti-tank rockets had struck there. More than one hundred of Obutu's soldiers still lay dead in the smoking wreckage of their vehicles. Obutu had seen enough combat to imagine the scene . . . the heat, the smoke, the congealed blood and staring eyes and flies and carrion hovering nearby, eager to begin their work. . . .

The rebels said they wanted democracy now. Obutu was struck by a strong irony. The rebels had grown up out of the very groups in the highlands which had first been given the benefit of education and medical assistance. It was as if, in giving them hope for the first time, he had created a monster.

He ought to go in with the gas and the flamethrowers and all the rest of it, incinerate and kill everyone—

He caught himself.

Patience.

He picked up the telephone.

"Yes, Mr. President?"

"Marcos, you and Mr. Lawrence come in now, please."

"At once, sir."

Obutu took a cheroot from the ivory box on a corner of the desk and fired it up. He had taken only two puffs when the office door opened at the far end of the room and General Arman, wearing his heavily medaled jacket now, came in. He was followed by a thickset, balding man with silver-rimmed glasses. This man, Jeb Lawrence, the American, wore a pale linen suit and fresh white shirt and dark tie. He looked like a middle-echelon diplomat. It was an open secret that he represented the Central Intelligence Agency at the U.S. embassy.

"Gentlemen," Obutu said, "sit down." He indicated the red leather chairs facing his desk.

Lawrence and General Arman complied. They exchanged pleasantries about the hot weather.

Then Obutu asked, "There is later news?"

Lawrence leaned forward to point at the map near the crosses. "We believe they moved out through this pass, Mr. President, and are moving to a bivouac . . . here." He pointed with a blunt index finger.

"In what strength?" Obutu asked, holding his temper. That he had to ask the CIA to get accurate intelligence in his own country!

"The strike force," Lawrence told him, "was between fifty and seventy men."

"They had trucks?"

"No. No trucks."

"My colonels tell me they had to have trucks."

"I can assure you, Mr. President, there were no trucks."

Obutu jumped to his feet. "How do you know there were no trucks? How do you *know?* God damn you, is your country flying over the sovereign soil of Marandaya?"

"No, sir," Lawrence said quickly.

"If you are flying over Marandaya," Obutu shouted, "my air force will seek your planes out! We will intercept them and shoot them down with our heat-seeking rockets, and we will send our soldiers into the fields and find the pilots and bring them to Atravi and hold them up for the whole world to see how America cheats its own allies and friends!"

"We are not operating aircraft, Mr. President."

"Lies! All lies! Do you think we are ignorant savages? Your satellites are not that good that you can see a truck in the jungle!"

"They are that good, Mr. President," Lawrence said calmly.

Obutu fumed. He relighted his cigar. The smoke calmed him. He realized that he had been very loud. He laughed. "Your information is that good, then?" He scowled. 'It is unfortunate that your excellent intelligence-gathering did not extend to warning us before the attack took place!"

Lawrence's rather large ears turned pink. "We warned you of the attack in the coastal areas last week. We don't claim infallibility. Guerrilla warfare is not that easy to combat.''

Obutu showed his teeth. "Tell me about that, Mr. Lawrence. I would like to have all the correct words of wisdom at my disposal for explaining it all to the widows of the dead soldiers."

Lawrence's color darkened across his cheeks. He kept a finger stubbornly on the map. "You could strike here, sir, and intercept them."

"We have insufficient forces in the area for an attack. You know that."

"An air strike, then?"

"Our fighters must remain close to Atravi."

Lawrence frowned at the map. "Three Phantoms would do a hell of a number on them."

"I do not have three fighters to spare. I do not have *one* fighter to spare! Nor the pilots to risk if I had the machines."

"When are your next pilots due back from training in the States?"

"I think you know that as well as we do, Mr. Lawrence. They will graduate in two weeks. Thirty of our finest young men. And when they come back here, not all of them will have machines to fly."

"I am sure, Mr. President, that my government's offer on new F-4s still stands."

"No more fighters from the United States."

"I'm sure the credit is available."

"No more credit. I cannot bankrupt my nation. I cannot risk further antagonizing the Russians."

Lawrence looked up too casually. "You still plan to accept the offer of aid from the French?"

"If the treaty can be worked out, yes."

"When do you plan to go to Paris for final negotiation and signing?"

"Mr. Lawrence, you are too transparent. You know my plans remain a secret. Would we advertise my absence to help Gero Paasaad plan some indecency while I was gone?

Would we provide advance information for international terrorists in Europe who support scum like Paasaad?''

"You needn't give up mining claims to the bauxite and diamonds," Lawrence said quietly. "You can get help elsewhere. You don't have to have those Mirage jets."

"I consider the negotiations with the French vital to Marandaya's future," Obutu replied. "I intend to move increasingly away from the United States—with its companion irritation to the Russians—and to European allies. All that has been made clear to your government."

"You're putting a lot of eggs in one basket."

"My friend," Obutu said softly, "it is the only basket I have."

Lawrence seemed to accept it. He remained another few minutes, then left. General Arman stayed back with Joseph Obutu.

"I do not trust that man," Arman said grimly.

"Nor should you," Obutu agreed. "But I think we can trust him far more than some of our own officers."

Arman bristled. "The army is completely loyal."

"I hear the rumors, Marcos. I know there are many who, like you, would go to any lengths to crush Paasaad immediately."

"This is not disloyalty, Mr. President!"

"Not unless it reaches the point of plotting against me to accomplish your aims, Marcos."

"That will never happen!"

Obutu put his arms around Arman in a brotherly hug. "You disagree with me on policy; this I know; yet you stand firm, supporting me in everything. You are my rock, Marcos!"

General Arman's eyes were bright with tears. "For you, Mr. President—anything!"

"If it were not for you, I could not even go to Paris."

"I can only hope, Mr. President, that the negotiations in Paris go as well as you anticipate."

"They will, Marcos. They must."

The conversation was interrupted by the opening of the

door at the far end of the room. A small brown face peered through the crack below the level of the ornate doorknob. "Father?"

"My son! Come to me!" Obutu spread his arms wide.

The door swung open. A little boy, wearing only native shorts, scampered barefooted across the tile. Behind him came a slender black woman wearing a wraparound gown of the finest silk. She was young and beautiful, with multiple golden earrings and bracelets which tinkled gently as she moved with a dancer's grace.

"Shana," Obutu said gladly, "please come in."

"We are not interrupting?" she asked softly.

"Of course not!" Obutu caught his little boy's rush against his legs and, laughing, swung him into his arms. "My fine son!"

General Arman moved tactfully out of the room. Shana Obutu, the president's wife, walked to the desk and smiled as Obutu tickled their boy, reducing him to squirms and giggles. After a few moments he put the child down, and the lad promptly scurried to the other side of the room, where a large world globe rested on its pedestal. He pushed the globe and it spun, the colorful continents blurring.

"The boy insisted on seeing his father," Shana Obutu said. "We will be brief."

"You are always welcome, my dear. You know that!"

She touched a linen to her forehead. "Is there word on repair of the air-conditioning equipment?"

"It will be operating again by nightfall."

She smiled. "You are sure?"

"Quite sure."

She moved to him and touched cool fingertips to his forehead. "You're overheated—tired."

"It's been a hard morning. Paasaad has been busy again. I will be glad when the Paris trip is behind me and we have our new agreements and French arms. I hope we may have the Foreign Legion assisting us within thirty days. We will see how Paasaad likes that!"

Shana Obutu sighed. "I wish I could go to Paris with you."

"But you can! I want you to go. You know that."

"We agreed. The family should stay here. That way there can be no chance for false rumors that you are staging an escape, an abdication."

"I know . . . I know. Of course it will not be all that pleasant in Paris. I am sure there will be demonstrations against me there. My enemies have ways."

"But if your arrival is a secret . . .?"

"I can only keep my arrival and specific plans quiet, my dear. I will be seen. There will be a speech, eventually, of announcement. My enemies will know then."

"Can we dine together tonight?"

"I don't know." Obutu looked at the desk. "There is so much to do."

"I thought we might dine privately."

"You, me, and the boy?"

"Just you and me." She gave him a small, sly smile. "I have a new dress."

"Oh?" He was not sure he understood the smile.

"Yes," she told him. "It is suitable only for a very private dinner, though. The material is so very transparent, you see."

"I think we should have our private dinner then, by all means."

She laughed. "Suddenly you have less work?"

For answer he pulled her close. "Ah, God, Shana, how I love you!"

"And I love you, Joseph."

In the corner there was a yelp from the boy, then a loud crash. Obutu and his wife spun. The boy was all right, but his violent turning of the globe had caused it to tip and crash to the floor.

"I am sorry, Father! I did not mean to!"

"It is all right, my son. Don't be frightened. There you are! What a good boy!" Obutu scooped him up and kissed him before the tears could start. "Go with your mother now, and your father will make things right again.''

Mother and son left together. Obutu righted the large globe on its stand. As he did so, he noticed that the thin metal sphere had been badly dented in the fall. It had struck the hard floor on the continent of Africa, and the paint cratered off—as if from some terrible upheaval—directly over the gray-green area that marked the nation of Marandaya.

Paris, France

Carrying a West German passport identifying him as Franz Bertell, the killer arrived in Paris on a Lufthansa flight from Hamburg. His single carry-on bag went through customs without a ripple, and he caught a taxi for downtown. It was a warm, hazy day. Seeing the Eiffel Tower and the dome at Les Invalides appear through the murk, Bertell smiled. No one could return to Paris without some feeling of having come home. Its dingy grandeur was one of the few sights left in the world that could stir Bertell after so many years . . . so many missions like the present one.

The hotel three blocks off the Rue Royale was modest but entirely adequate. The room was stuffy. Bertell opened the windows and leaned on the dirty metal railing for a few minutes, watching the insane Paris traffic below. Then he unpacked his handful of clothes and made his telephone call.

Two hours later, driving a rented Citroën, he pulled through the gates of the estate west of Paris near the Seine. The sky here too was smoky from new industries farther west on the river, but the grounds and trees had a manicured freshness. He parked in front of the house and walked to the front door, where he rang.

A man answered the door. ''M. Bertell, is it?'' He used German.

''We will speak in French,'' Bertell told him.

''*Oui*. Of course. Tell me: the weather is sunny in Hamburg?''

"The weather is sometimes cloudy, sometimes with bright sun."

Bertell's host relaxed, coming outside and closing the door behind him. "All is well. I am the only one here today."

"Then we will conduct the business at once. Where may I park the car?"

"Please to park it at the side, out of sight. I will go get the golf cart and meet you there."

Bertell obeyed, pulling the Citroën out of sight. His host drove around the asphalt driveway from the rear in a white electric golf cart. He had a rather bulky long carton, well tied with heavy twine, on the seat beside him. Bertell climbed in and they drove back around the house, through formal gardens, and down a long, curving pathway that went downhill under fruit trees and into a kind of meadow. There were hills in the distance, and somewhat nearer at hand, a creek. Bertell's host carefully pointed out certain landmarks as they drove.

After a few minutes, they reached the far end of the cart path, a skeet and target range in the low terrain where the creek drained. The range was deserted, the shooting pads empty, scrubby grass whipping in the breeze.

Bertell helped his host untie the box. Inside, each wrapped in heavy oilskin-type paper, were three identical rifles. Springfield Armory Match Grade M1As, they appeared brand new. Each had a telescopic sight and a numerical identity number tied to the trigger guard with light twine.

Bertell picked up the first rifle and brought it to his shoulder with a smooth, practiced motion. The faded sunlight glowed on its blued metal surfaces and custom walnut stock. "They have been test-fired?"

"As you specified, sir."

"Who did your firing?" Bertell was examining the second rifle.

"I have a very fine man. One of the best in the French army, and a leader in international competitions."

Bertell clearly was not impressed as he picked up the third rifle and repeated his examination. "Did he state a preference?"

"The rifle marked number two gave him better results."

"What types of ammunition did he fire?"

"He fired 165-grain Sierras, spitzers, boat tails; also 165-grain hollow-point—"

"The powder, the powder," Bertell cut in.

"With the Sierra spitzers, 39.1 grains."

"Three-oh-three-one?"

"Yes."

"He tried the lighter Speer?"

"Yes. The results—"

"I will fire this number two rifle with my loads."

His host was startled. "Now?"

Bertell's eyes were slate. "Why not?"

"No targets are up—"

"You have the bullets I ordered?"

"Yes."

"It should not require any great feat of cunning to attach one target on the range board and hand me ten of those bullets."

The other man hurried to obey. Within ten minutes, the target had been rigged against the primary backing board on the side of the embankment, and Bertell stood on the paved shooting pad slightly uphill a full 350 yards away. He tested the weight and balance of the M1A, then carefully inspected and loaded each of his ten shells into the clip. Slipping his left arm through the shooting sling, he knelt, and then lay fully prone on the warm, dusty concrete, leveling the barrel on the distant target. He paused, attended to the range-finding scope, and then worked the bolt to feed in the first cartridge. His host stood to one side, watching nervously.

Bertell began to fire. The rifle spat with a clean, hard, chest-quaking ferocity. Bertell did not wait long between shots, but squeezed them off at regular brief intervals as if his kind of shooting did not allow the luxury of taking one's time. When he had finished, he climbed to his feet and unslung the rifle.

"Now we see," he said.

They drove the golf cart to the target stand. At the center of the paper target, perhaps two inches from the center and slightly low, the target had been repeatedly punctured by the shots. Bertell examined the holes with some care, probing the edges with a small metric rule.

"Seven-point-four centimeters," he announced.

"My God! The best my man could do—and he is internationally renowned—was over ten centimeters!"

Bertell examined him with those dead gray eyes. He showed no pleasure or, for that matter, any kind of feeling. "The grouping can be improved. I will have to load my own shells. I will give you a list of the items I will require."

"Yes, sir."

"Take this rifle to the house and arrange for its delivery to my hotel with all precautions. I must find a gunsmith to make a minor modification."

"I know a man."

"Good."

They started back to the golf cart. Bertell crumpled the torn target and tossed it into a trash container.

"What about the other two rifles?" the host asked.

"Keep them hidden here in case of difficulty. I will also require a handgun."

"A .38 S&W, perhaps? I have a fine—"

"No, no. A terrorist weapon, preferably with a full-automatic option. And a silencer. It must have an excellent silencer."

"I'm not sure I understand the need for such a gun."

"As a backup, if the first plan fails."

"Ah, I see. Then I believe I know where to find what you would require. I can get a Skorpion."

Bertell nodded.

"It shoots a .32 Colt ACP," his host told him. "It's a Czech weapon, very popular with terrorists. Twenty rounds in a magazine forward of the trigger housing, low velocity, but reasonably accurate in close, and the slow bullet eliminates sonic boom. The silencer is excellent—''

"I know the weapon," Bertell said impatiently. "It will do nicely."

"Will you wish to test-fire the model I can procure for you?"

Bertell gave him a venomous look. "Not unless you have an unlimited supply of silencers. The rubber seal shoots out after ten or fifteen rounds."

"Yes," his host said, cowed. "Of course. I am sorry."

They rode back toward the house. A gust of wind picked the discarded target out of the trash container and tossed it into the creek.

7

Nancy, France

Dugger had had the six-chair compartment to himself from Stuttgart through Strasbourg and into the rolling tank country of eastern France. In Nancy there was a brief delay, and he looked out through the large picture window at other red electric trains on many adjacent tracks, the skyline of the city beyond. Just as the train again jolted silently into motion, a young man came up the outside aisle and opened the door to the compartment.

"It is permissible to join you?" the man asked with a slight Dutch or German accent. He was tall, fair, wearing tweeds too heavy for the weather, carrying a single small shoulder bag.

"Come in," Dugger said.

The man settled himself into the far facing seat, nearest the door, and lighted a cigarette. The train moved swiftly out of the city and into the open countryside. There were distant hills, but everything near at hand was open country, pastureland with a few hedges and lines of scattered trees, yellowish green under the pale sun. It was much like pastureland in parts of Nebraska, Kansas, and Oklahoma. No wonder Patton had run wild.

When the Russians went on the attack—Dugger, like many military men said *when*, not *if*—they would have to be stopped back in the more rugged terrain of Germany if they were to be stopped at all. Once they crossed the Rhine and got into this kind of country, even the tactical nukes might not stop them for long.

Thinking about this, Dugger wondered, as he often did, whether there would be much of a chance to stop them anywhere. He had some idea just how strong they were, and how weak the NATO forces were in critical locations. It might be easy to sit back in Washington or New York and say such an attack was unthinkable, as his editor had done, but Dugger knew better. He had stood at many points along that thousand-mile wall that slashed Europe north to south—had studied the barbed wire, the stainless steel fencing that amputated fingers, the concrete, broken glass, tubing, ditches, horizontally aimed trip-wire shot-guns, guard dogs as big as wolves, electronic sensors, barricades, and guard towers and he had *known*, in the gut, that a power so cruel and bellicose as to build this obscenity was capable of anything.

"We're going to stop them," a Luftwaffe colonel had told him one time in a matter-of-fact tone. And Dugger had wanted badly to believe him. But of course the West Germans had to have that faith or they might go mad.

Dugger was not so sure. One day, he believed, the test would come. And every day between now and then would involve smaller battles, part of the same immense struggle.

Somehow, he thought, he was now again involved in that struggle. He did not understand everything that had happened. But he was committed now and he would not try to back out. The shortest way through this swamp was out to the far side.

He became aware of the young German watching him through the cigarette smoke. He returned the stare.

The young man smiled. "You are Mr. Dugger."

"I beg your pardon?"

"I said, you are Mr. Dugger." The man took a small photo out of his inside coat pocket and briefly studied it. "Yes. There can be no doubt. Mr. Dugger, I work out of the office in Nancy. I have been asked on very short notice to ride a few kilometers with you."

Dugger watched him and said nothing.

The man told him with a slight smile, "Mr. Cunningham is very upset."

"Really?"

"I do not know the details. But I have been asked to give you certain information, Mr. Dugger. I have been asked to make it clear that Mr. Cunningham's superiors wished you to be deactivated in Stuttgart. Mr. Cunningham believes he made this desire clear to you. You were then reported boarding this train. Mr. Cunningham urgently wishes to know your plans."

"I'm going to Paris," Dugger said, "to visit the Louvre."

The younger man sighed. "Mr. Dugger, my orders are to tell you that authorities are exploring every possibility. You orders are to return to Stuttgart without delay. I have a telephone number for you here on this card, which you are please to call when you are back in Stuttgart. Mr. Cunningham has instructed me to tell you that there is nothing more that you can do, and your continued activity can only complicate matters."

"Once I was helping," Dugger said. "Now I'm only a complication."

"Sir, forgive me, but it will do no good for you to play games with me. I know no details. I am only relaying information as ordered."

"Is there any more?"

"Yes, sir. I have been instructed to tell you that if you persist, you will not receive any assistance whatsoever from anyone in Paris or elsewhere. If you place yourself in further danger, no one will aid you. I have been asked to state that you cannot help, but may damage operations in this case, whatever it may be. I have been told to make it clear to you that, far from helping, you may actually put not only yourself but others in great jeopardy. I have been told to tell you that persistent action by you in this matter on an unauthorized basis may result not only in suspension of your retirement benefits, but in direct action designed to prevent your further interference. I have been asked to make it clear, sir, that Mr. Cunningham and his superiors will take whatever action may be necessary to cause you to cease and desist in your interference against orders."

If Dugger had harbored any lingering doubts about the German's authenticity, the rolling-thunder parade of threats had eliminated them. A committee obviously had had an emergency meeting and had drawn up a list of threats. Then they had disagreed on which threat to make. A compromise vote had been to deliver all of them.

He said, "Please thank Mr. Cunningham for his concern and advice."

The train was slowing. A few tile roofs slid by the window, then older walls of buildings that had been there for centuries.

The young man said, "Here is the station. If you wish to get off with me, I will assist you in making bookings for return to Stuttgart."

"No, thank you."

"May I ask your plans?" The train was shuddering to a halt in the little station.

"I'm going on. Tell Cunningham that."

"There is nothing more you can accomplish."

"Son, I don't think you can understand this, but some of my people are dead. Others of them are probably on the same hit list. I've been chased, shot at, and rolled in the garbage. Tell Cunningham this: tell him that if he didn't want me involved, he should never have pulled my chain."

"Pulled your—"

"Tell him. He'll understand."

"Mr. Dugger—"

"*Tell him.*"

The German sighed, pulled the door of the compartment open, and went down the corridor. Dugger saw him leave the train and walk across the platform to a point where two other men stood waiting. The train jolted into movement again. Dugger leaned back and closed his eyes.

New York City

It was very late in the afternoon by the time the papers were ready for Eileen Arrington to deliver them to the two delegations in the UN General Assembly. She crossed from the Secretariat Building to the General Assembly Building by way of one of the interior courtyards, noting that the tall structures had already created a false evening in their shadows. When she reached the great Hall, she saw at once that the session had already adjourned; only a few delegates remained in or near their seats, and some areas of the floor were entirely vacant.

Dismayed, Eileen hurried down the right-hand aisle between rows of green leather-covered desks and blue upholstered chairs. Rotation had placed the Marandayan delegation quite near the front of the Assembly, near the podium. The slanting gold-slatted walls and great seal of the organization seemed to bear down on her as she hurried. She was disappointed to see that the Marandayan half of the desk had been cleared.

A young black woman, tall and striking in a broadly striped blue-and-black gown with matching head wrap, had been standing nearby. She noticed Eileen and walked over. "Could I be of assistance?" she asked in impeccable British tones.

"I have documents for the Marandayan delegation," Eileen told her.

The woman glanced at Eileen's ID tag, recognized her as a mere employee, and immediately became frostier, more condescending. "You might find some of them in the delegates' lounge next door. Do you happen to know where that is, dear?"

"I think I might just be able to find it," Eileen told her, and walked back up the aisle.

The adjacent lounge, one of several in the building, was more crowded than the General Assembly Hall. Under the bluish illumination from an entire wall of glass, couches and chairs seemed scattered rather haphazardly among potted ferns and palms. The effect was open and contemporary, yet it created many small conversational islands. The view was to the north, with a view of gardens and the river, but none of the hundreds of delegates here seemed to be noticing that view. Everywhere men and women were talking in small groups.

Eileen worked her way through the crowd, moving between men and women in standard Western dress, the crumpled uniforms of Maoist countries, colorful robes and gowns from African nations. Mixed polyglot sounds touched her ears, including Arabic, French, Swahili, Italian, Spanish, English, Russian, Chinese. Finally she spotted Clarence Endidi standing with two other men near the wall of windows.

Pressing through the crowd toward him, she was aware of a tightening in her nervous system. She would have remembered him anywhere, and could only hope his memory was as good. Otherwise she might have to jog it.

Endidi looked very young in the evening light, a long cigarette smoking between his tapered fingers. He was not very tall, very thin and black, with keenly edged features. His hair was cropped quite short. He wore an ivory-colored linen business suit, white shirt, and lemon-colored tie. The hand not holding the cigarette carried a thin attaché case. His companions were older men, one dark brown and one chocolate, both with gray in their hair. The darker man wore very thick glasses.

Endidi was talking heatedly: "If they follow through with their threats, all they can accomplish is polarization—" He saw Eileen as she moved between him and the older man with glasses. He stopped talking and frowned, clearly trying to recognize her.

"Excuse me," she said. "I have some documents for the chief of the Marandayan delegation?"

The man with glasses extended a thick hand. "I am Guy Arata," he said, giving the first name the French pronunciation, "chief of the delegation."

Eileen handed over the thick envelope. "Here you are, Mr. Arata. My name is Eileen Arrington, and if you could just sign this receipt—"

"Of course!" Clarence Endidi burst out, startling both older men. "Eileen! But this is impossible! How very pleasant!"

"Hello, Mr. Endidi," she smiled.

"You remember me?" His eyes traveled up and down

her body with pleasure. "After such a long time?"

"Of course," she said, explaining to the others, "Mr. Endidi and I met in Atravi."

"You know our country, then?" Guy Arata asked with keen interest.

"Yes," Eileen began. "I—"

"She was married to a countryman," Endidi broke in, his face suffused with pleasure. "I may say, Eileen, that I have often mourned the end of your marriage. Our country needs women of your beauty and intelligence as a contribution to its gene pool."

Eileen hesitated. It was obviously meant as a compliment, but it was a remark either amusingly naïve or frighteningly cold. In this instant she was reminded how unpredictable and puzzling the man had always been. "You're too kind, Mr. Endidi. . . . You remember that my husband died a few months later."

"Yes." A scowl creased Endidi's forehead. Then he brightened again. "But you once were not so formal, Eileen. You used to call me 'Clary,' as my friends do."

"I work in the Secretariat now. I'm quite new. I must mind my manners."

Guy Arata finished signing the receipt and handed the small blue card back to her. "You are American, Miss Arrington?"

"Yes."

"It is a pleasure. May I present the delegate from the Republic of Cabinder, Mr. Grover Matsoon?"

Eileen shook hands with the other delegate. Matsoon's smile was gracious, and she saw that, despite his graying hair, he was not as old as Arata by a number of years. There was an urbane, possibly even dangerous quality in Matsoon's manner as he held her hand a bit too long. She put him down as a womanizer, but a very clever one.

"We were speaking of an early supper and return to work," Matsoon told her. "If you are not otherwise engaged, perhaps . . . ?"

She must not appear too eager, but it was a chance she could not allow to slip away. "That's very kind of you, Mr.

Matsoon, but perhaps these other gentlemen prefer pri-
vacy to continue their talks?"

"You must go with us," Clarence Endidi said in his
impulsive way. "I may even persuade you to call me by my
first name again, Eileen."

"If," Matsoon said good-naturedly, with a glint in his
eyes, "the young lady remembers you at all after she and I
have had a chance to become better acquainted."

Endid's fine white teeth showed in a tight grin. "You
must watch out for Grover, Eileen. He is what was once
quaintly called a cad."

Matsoon placed a diamond-encrusted hand over his
heart. "You injure me, sir!"

Guy Arata joined in the amusement, but then grew
sober. "I can see, Miss Arrington, that you bring out the
competitive instincts in my colleagues. I regret that circumstance will not permit me to join you to watch more
of their obvious performance." He turned back to Endidi.
"We will conclude our planning when you return this
evening."

Endidi also turned serious. "I think we have covered
nearly everything."

"Yes, and the plane leaves very early in the morning. I
hope to get a good night's sleep." Arata turned back to
Eileen. "It has been a pleasure, Miss Arrington. Good day
to you."

Eileen watched the distinguished man move away from
them in the crowd. "Is he being called home for consultation, Clary?" she asked.

"Actually, no," Endidi said. "I envy him. Paris is beautiful at this time of year." He looked over heads in the
crowd, standing on his toes to do so. "As soon as Tella arrives, we can be off."

"There she comes now," Grover Matsoon said.

"Yes." Endidi waved. "She sees us. Good."

Eileen saw with some surprise that the person coming
toward them was the same beautiful and rather formidable
young woman who had spoken to her in the General

Assembly Hall. She moved with a sinuous grace, although the colorful gown did not fully conceal a dazzling figure.

"There you are," Endidi said to her as she joined them. "Tella, may I present an old friend, Eileen Arrington? Eileen, this is Tella Rhonta, a member of the delegation from Nown."

Tella Rhonta extended a slender hand. Her grasp was cool and hard. "Hello, Miss Arrington. I see you found them."

"You found . . . ?" Endidi asked.

"Miss Rhonta was kind enough to give me directions," Eileen explained.

"Excellent! Tella, Eileen is joining us for supper."

A quickly suppressed glint of irritation showed on Tella Rhonta's classically beautiful face. "How delightful. Shall we go?"

Together they left the delegates' lounge and used the wide staircase to descend to the visitors' entrance, with its impressive façade of windows looking out toward the plaza. Once outside, they turned north, moving onto the sidewalk of First Avenue. Heavy traffic honked and scratched its way by them, and the sidewalks were crowded.

"I know a place quite nearby," Endidi told Eileen. "We go there seldom, but this is a special occasion."

"I hope," Tella Rhonta said surlily, "you don't mean that bogus French restaurant."

"Bogus?" Endidi said, eyes widening. "I consider the cuisine superb!"

"You have been in this wretched country too long," she responded. "You have begun to acquire a taste for their plastic culture."

"Will you now lecture me about my taste in food, too, Tella?" There was a bit of anger in Endidi's voice, and in the instant he looked into Tella Rhonta's angry eyes, Eileen knew they were lovers.

"Children, children," Grover Matsoon said with ironic smoothness.

"It's quite possible," Tella Rhonta said spitefully, "to be seduced by the decadent luxuries of the imperialist society."

Endidi's color changed. He set his jaw as if afraid of what his temper might reveal if he spoke.

Matsoon took Eileen's arm. "Where are you from, Eileen?"

"California, originally."

"And you lived in Marandaya for a while? How extraordinary!"

"Since my divorce . . . and my ex-husband's death . . . I've done graduate work in languages, and then editorial and sales work for book companies. In New York, I hope to expand a part-time job as editorial consultant—"

Tella Rhonta cut in, using fluent Swahili, "So the job with the United Nations is only a stopgap?"

Eileen replied in the same language, using the formal inflection, "Indeed not, Tella. I believe I revere the goals of the UN more than many of its own member delegations."

Clarence Endidi laughed aloud. "Ah, Eileen, I remember anew how much I yearned after you in Atravi. You have become even more beautiful and witty."

Tella Rhonta said nothing, but Eileen saw the killing look in her beautiful eyes. *I have just made an enemy.*

"You're living here in midtown?" Grover Matsoon asked.

"In the East Sixties," Eileen told him vaguely.

"A very expensive neighborhood," Matsoon said approvingly. "Have you a rich lover, then?"

Eileen laughed at him. "I wish I did!"

"Perhaps you can find one yet, dear," Tella Rhonta told her. "Or failing that, a number of less well-to-do ones."

Endidi turned up the side street. "Here we are. I hope we will like it, Eileen, regardless of Tella's feelings in the matter."

They entered. The main dining room was not large, and appeared crowded even at so early an hour. Gold carpet and white walls reflected multifaceted chandeliers over small tables outfitted to perfection with white linen and gleaming silver and crystal. The maître d' who greeted them was tall, balding, impressive in a dark tuxedo and mint-colored ruffled shirt.

"Good evening. Party of four?"

Endidi gave his name, his face glacial when dealing with a social inferior.

The maître d' consulted his book. "I am sorry, sir. The reservation list shows no such name."

"Obviously you have made a mistake," Endidi snapped.

"Yes, sir." The maître d' was composed, but clearly uncertain about whom he was dealing with. "If you will wait a moment, sir."

Endidi took a wad of bills from his coat pocket and peeled off a ten. He handed it over. "Be quick."

The man went away somewhere. Waiters were moving between tables, and the murmur of conversation was everywhere. Eileen was a bit puzzled. "Did we have a reservation, Clary?"

"Of course not," Endidi said. "But they're all barbarians. The tip will buy anything in this country."

"They're all such fools," Tella Rhonta chimed in. "After we are seated, they will probably offer us a menu that includes ersatz *coq au vin* and strawberry pizza!"

"The last days of Rome," Endidi said thoughtfully.

"One can *hope*," Tella added.

The maître d' returned, his face showing nothing. "Mr. Endidi, I regret there will be a delay in seating you this evening. If—"

"Delay?" Endidi's voice went up. "How long?"

"It should not be more than ten minutes, sir—"

"Ten minutes?" His voice went up in volume several more decibels, causing heads to turn in the dining room. "These reservations were called in yesterday! Now your stupidity forces further delay?"

"I am very sorry, sir," the maître d' said, his own voice even lower, his ears getting red. "If you would care to wait in the bar—"

"No, sir!" Endidi began shouting shrilly. "Who is the owner here?"

"The owner is out, sir. If—"

"Jesus Christ, man! Do you think we are some of your Georgia niggers, to be shoved outside? We represent three nations here! I demand to be seated at once, or you may be sure there will be serious repercussions!"

The last was practically screamed. Everyone was looking, some startled, some curious, not a few resentful and angry. The maître d' was quite pink. "If you would be willing, sir, we might seat you at once in the private dining room."

Endidi glared. "We will look at it."

"Yes, sir. This way, sir, please."

The maître d' took them through the main room to a small, lavishly furnished private room beyond. The long table was empty, but the handsome wallpaper, carpet, and ceiling fixtures showed clearly that this was a private room reserved for the most distinguished customers.

Endidi looked around peevishly. "We are a party of *four*, man! Not *forty!*"

"We can set a small table aside, sir."

"All right, then. Be quick about it. Jesus Christ!"

Once they had been seated, with a pair of waiters hovering near each chair to anticipate every possible whim, Eileen saw Clarence Endidi transform himself again from the arrogant boor to the charming gentleman. He chuckled something aside to Tella Rhonta, who was vastly amused by his entire performance. Then, while the meal was being prepared, he turned his full attention to Eileen. She practically felt the high wattage of his deliberate charm.

"You come to the United Nations at a most interesting time, Eileen," he told her. "These are days when Marandaya is in the forefront of many thoughts."

"Do you really expect the General Assembly to debate the case of the revolutionary movement next week, as one of the newspapers said?"

Endidi set his jaw grimly. "Yes."

"It seems a strange time," Eileen added, probing, "for the chief of your delegation to be going to Paris."

"Not at all. It is well known that President Obutu will be in Paris soon for possible conclusion of new aid pacts with the government of France."

"I see. Does this mean that President Obutu is going to try to beat the General Assembly to the punch by going to Paris right away?"

"Eileen, the president's plans are a secret."

"I'm not sure I understand why secrecy is so necessary."

"Gullible people have been taken in by Gero Paasaad's so-called revolutionary activity in my country. If they knew President Obutu was going to be in Paris at a specific time, they would surely stage all kinds of disruptive and dangerous demonstrations."

Grover Matsoon nodded agreement. "Not to mention the fact that Paasaad would undoubtedly take advantage of Obutu's absence by making a maximum effort to attack the capital while he was out of the country."

"You think Paasaad is strong enough to mount such an attack?" This was interesting and might be valuable. "I had heard—"

"He is not so strong," Endidi said bitterly. "If President Obutu would strike forthrightly, Paasaad would be ground under and this entire insane debate would be headed off."

"President Obutu," Tella Rhonta said, "is a bit like the American military presence, a paper tiger."

"No," Endidi said quickly. "He has the force. It is only that he has not chosen to use it."

"Why?" Eileen asked bluntly.

"If I knew that, Eileen, I would be a genius."

She did not reply. To hear Clarence Endidi speak in this bitter, almost defeated tone about his own president was a real surprise. She did not know how to proceed, although the information about Guy Arata going to Paris was clearly an item that Rick Kelly would be questioned about most closely by his superiors.

It was Tella Rhonta who spoke loftily: "Whatever

Marandaya does, the momentum of Gero Paasaad's crusade on behalf of freedom will not be blunted." She smiled at Endidi with a curious gentleness. "All freedom-loving peoples clearly see the nature of his drive, Clary, which is why I am sure we will benefit from next week's debate."

Eileen waited for Clarence Endidi to counterattack. Amazingly, he did not. The muscles of his jaw worked and his eyes were bleak. But he said nothing. *What was going on?*

"With each passing day," Tella Rhonta added, "Gero Paasaad strikes new blows for ultimate victory."

Eileen needed clarification of the undercurrents here. She risked attack. "What sort of blow was it when his men attacked that school bus last week, killing forty small children?"

Tella Rhonta's eyes widened with shock. "A blow for peace—"

"And when they shelled that hospital the day before yesterday? It seems to me, Miss Rhonta, that your hero has very bloody hands."

"I could expect stupidity like that from an American imperialist."

Eileen smiled back into her venomous glare. "You support Paasaad, then?"

"Of course! I agree with the view of my government! All freedom-loving peoples must support the just cause of suffering minorities."

"It strikes me, Miss Rhonta, that the minority doing the most suffering consists of the children and aged hospital patients who are being slaughtered by Paasaad's mercenaries and Cubans."

Tella Rhonta tossed down her napkin. The table was jostled badly, water spilling from glasses, as she got to her feet. "I'll listen to no more insults from the cow granddaughter of a field slave." She turned and started away, then spun back. "Clary?"

"Tella, wait!" Endidi pleaded.

"Are you coming with me?"

Endidi hesitated, then glared. He turned back to his plate, saying nothing.

Tella Rhonta stormed out of sight.

"My, my," Grover Matsoon said mildly.

"I'm sorry, Clary," Eileen said. "I baited her."

"No. She was the one who started it, Eileen." Endidi allowed himself a slight smile. "You said things I should have been saying." He paused and swallowed. "Thank you."

Eileen was again surprised. Didn't he support his own government? She said nothing.

Grover Matsoon chuckled. "Most third world countries tend to share Tella Rhonta's view, Eileen. There is great admiration for Paasaad—"

"For a terrorist?" Eileen asked. "Is that how one gains acceptance in the world community today? By becoming a terrorist?"

Matsoon showed gold teeth and spread his hands wide. "I'll not argue with you. You're clearly a woman of fire and principle. I hope that you'll restrain yourself tomorrow night, however, at the party in our mission."

"Am I invited?"

"You just were, my dear."

Clarence Endidi spoke up: "Please accept, Eileen, and come as my partner."

"I thought you and Tella—"

Some humor had come back to Endidi's eyes. "Tella will get over her anger, I'm sure. But by tomorrow night? I doubt it. You *must* come with me, then; after all, you have just robbed me of my usual companion."

Eileen turned to Matsoon questioningly.

Again the elder diplomat spread his hands. "I seem to have been outmaneuvered."

"Then I accept, Clary, and thank you," Eileen told him.

Late in the evening she walked to a convenience store near her apartment and used the telephone booth.

"Yes?" the male voice answered.

"Is this Allied Special Products?" Eileen asked.

"Yes, it is," Rick Kelley told her. "Are you all right?"

"Rick, I am perfectly fine."

His tone relaxed. "What happened?"

She told him briefly about the things she had learned, and about the date with Clarence Endidi tomorrow night.

"It sounds great," Kelley said.

"That's what worries me," she admitted. "Maybe it's too easy."

8

Paris

Hazy warmth cloaked Paris when Dugger left the train at the depot and took a taxi to a small hotel not far from the Place Vendôme. The innkeeper had a small room at the rear, overlooking a murky alley. Dugger paid for a week in advance.

Leaving the hotel on foot, he walked about a block to the square, heading for the shops along the Rue de Rivoli, beyond. The square had been overlooked by most tourists, as it often was, and was virtually deserted. Dugger's footsteps echoed off the cobbles to the arcades, with their steeply pitched roofs, which uniformly surrounded the central paved area. The sun was going down, painting the ornate buildings on the east side a golden tan and bringing out dull green-and-gold highlights on the Austerlitz column in the center. In another city, this monument, made by entwining the core with the melted-down bronze from twelve hundred cannon captured by Napoleon at Austerlitz in 1805, would have been a wonder. Here it was almost ignored, a bit off the beaten paths, the eternal yellow dust of Paris thick on its ornate convolutions.

In another few moments, Dugger had reached the Rivoli. Here the sidewalks were crowded. Across the street was a corner of one wing of the Louvre, and beyond, to Dugger's right, an edge of the Guileries Gardens. A small flock of the Tuileries' big wood doves banked over the busy street and swung back for the relative quiet of the woods in the gardens.

Dugger used a pay telephone and called the home listing he found for Pierre LaFontaine. A servant answered. No, Mr. LaFontaine was not at home, and no, M. LaFontaine could not be contacted at this time. Was there a message?

Dugger hung up, found the number for the corporate offices of LaFontaine's conglomerate, MTR Enterprises, and dialed it. A switchboard operator put him through to LaFontaine's office. A secretary answered in French, and Dugger responded in kind.

"Is M. Fontaine in at this time, please?"

"May I ask who is calling, please?" the woman asked.

Dugger detected the accent and switched to English. "I'm an old friend, in Paris for a visit."

She sounded relaxed as she also changed to English. "You're an American."

"Yes. The name is Joe Dugger."

"I'm sorry, Mr. Dugger, but Mr. LaFontaine is away from the city today."

"When do you expect him back?"

"Not until Sunday, I'm afraid. May I take a message?"

"I'll write something out for him and bring it by your office in the morning. Will someone be there?"

"I expect to be here from about nine to noon."

"Fine. I'll bring you the note, then. You're his secretary?"

"One of three, yes. My name is Anita Courtright."

"And you're an American, too."

Her voice was warm and friendly. "Milwaukee, Wisconsin."

"I'll see you in the morning, Miss Courtright."

It was a letdown. He had hoped to find LaFontaine at once. There was nothing to do but wait. He walked to a nearby cafeteria where he had eaten many meals during long and lonely operations in Paris in earlier years. The food was plain and heavy. He carried his tray to a corner table and took his time eating. Two-story ceilings in the place created walls where someone once had painted agrarian murals, but not very well. The years had faded all the bright pastels to shades of tan and brown against a yellowed backdrop of ordinary wall paint. At a nearby table, five Parisian laborers were having a loud political argument. Dugger felt his mood begin to change, his usual refusal to think of the past faltering, and he tried to prevent it.

When he left the cafeteria, the street was in full shadow but the illumination of the dingy evening sky showed that sunset had not quite come. Crossing the street against traffic, he climbed a few worn stone steps and walked up into the Tuileries. He had come out on a raised platform of earth, with scattered trees, which looked down on the octagonal pool. Sunlight slanted across the gardens from his right, glinting on the large pool. People were everywhere around it, strolling, sitting, talking. A few children perched on the ledge of the large pool had little sailboats adrift on its surface. The big classical statues on high pedestals surrounding the area looked down with an ageless silence. Birds flew.

Dugger sat on an empty bench close to the pipe railing at the edge of the overlook. Hiking one foot to the lower pipe, he lighted a cigarette and leaned back to think.

What came, however, was not rational thought but emotion: totally unexpected, so that it struck him all the harder—a stark, devastating sense of loneliness.

He had been very stupid to come to this spot, and at this time of day. The last time he had been here had been more than four years ago, with Susan.

They said time healed. All time actually did was allow the survivor to experience the pain of loss at greater intervals.

Now, Dugger looked at the empty seat on the bench beside him. For a few seconds he remembered the last time so vividly that it was like present reality: he dressed much as he had today, smoking a cigarette, complaining about shin splints and flat feet after their three hours' walking in the Louvre; she smiling, radiant, teasing him—dark hair framing that astonishingly beautiful face, those eyes. She had been wearing jeans and a short-sleeved blouse in a tiny check pattern, open at the throat, and she was looking through the Michelin guide.

"*We missed the 'Mona Lisa'!*"

"*Congratulations to us, then. We may be the only people who ever visited the Louvre and missed the 'Mona Lisa.'*"

"*Joe, we're just going to have to go back tomorrow.*"

"*Next trip.*"

"*No! I want to see her smile for myself.*"

"*It's just sort of a crooked smile, baby. Da Vinci couldn't paint mouths.*"

She made a face and nudged his leg with her foot. "*I heard it was the smile of a woman who just had intercourse.*"

"*Hum.*"

"*Do you think I have an enigmatic smile after we have intercourse?*"

"*I never noticed. Come on. Let's go back to the room and find out.*"

Dugger had been well into his forties when he found her and they were married. He had imagined there never would be anyone—that he was far too old to succumb to any romantic bullshit, that he was too set in his ways to take a woman into his life-style, that no women would want to share his kind of life. Then along had come Susan, an employee at the embassy here in Paris, and it had been bells, beautiful music, skyrockets, incredible highs and equally unbelievable depressions, telephone calls, dinners, talks by the hour, soul-searching, pleas, jokes and arguments, and a stern French magistrate who lectured them about the folly of short engagements just before he married them to climax a six-week courtship.

She was a war orphan, thanks to a German buzz bomb that hit Coventry late in 1944, killing both of her visiting parents. She had been married before, briefly, to a son of a bitch. She brought to Dugger more beauty, wit, understanding, excitement, and sheer joy than he had ever expected so late in what he considered a misbegotten existence.

During the Essen operation, years ago, Dugger had been following a Volkswagen that he believed was driven by a Soviet assassin named Alexi Crognoi. Crognoi was one of their very best; no known photograph of him was known to exist, and the only likeness in the Agency's files was an artist's drawing done from descriptions by Dugger and some of his agents who had tentatively identified him during the operation. Dugger was following the Volkswagen that day because he believed Crognoi was at the wheel, headed for a vital appointment.

As the Volkswagen left the city and moved into the hillsides that day, however, it had shown signs that the driver knew of Dugger's pursuit. It sped up, beginning to take high turns at reckless speeds. Dugger followed, driving at the outer limits of his skill. He was one long inside curve behind when he saw the Volkswagen skid, swerve, and plunge off the road over a three-hundred-foot embankment.

The body authorities took from the burned wreckage was that of a young woman, unidentified, a clever decoy.

Crognoi vanished.

Seven months later, while Dugger was on a simple operation in Stockholm, Susan left their apartment in Geneva and drove into the countryside, evidently to look around small village markets. On a narrow blacktop road on the side of a thousand-foot-hill, the Mercedes went through the guard rail and took her to her death. Authorities could not explain the cause. They ruled accidental death.

Dugger had no evidence except his senses, and his knowledge of how the Russians—and men like Alexi Crognoi—operated. But he was quite sure that Susan had been taken from him not by accident. *An eye for an eye.* No one was better at living by the old cruel scriptural injunctions than a Russian. The girl in the Volkswagen had been avenged.

One of the children's sailboats had tipped on the Tuileries pond. Dugger watched a young mother and father help the boy retrieve it. He noticed all the people here seemed to be in couples. It was the time of day for couples, with the last crimson rays of the sun gleaming through the trees to the west, where the guillotine had hammered out its bloody work.

God, I miss you, Dugger thought.

This was no good. Tossing his cigarette to the grainy earth, he stood and walked out of the gardens and back to the street.

In the morning, he wrote a note to Pierre LaFontaine, put it in his jacket pocket, and walked to the nearest Métro station. A cool front had come in the night, and the big blowers in the tube had made the underground ramps and tunnels uncomfortable. Saturday traffic was lighter than usual when he emerged from the tunnel in the newer business section of Paris. It was not hard to find LaFontaine's offices in four middle floors of a twenty-story glass building. A receptionist directed him to another set of offices, where he found another reception desk, unoccupied.

He waited in the large paneled room. In a few minutes he heard the sound of heels on the tile floor of the corridor beyond, and then a rather tall woman, perhaps thirty, walked in. She was blonde and striking, with unusual brown eyes, high cheekbones, and a pretty mouth. She was wearing a summer dress, belted at her small waist, with an open collar and a small slit in the skirt which revealed flashes of handsome tanned leg as she moved. She wore medium heels, dark tan, almost the color of the dress.

"May I help you?" she asked in French.

"My name is Dugger," he told her in English, "and I think you must be the one I spoke with on the telephone late yesterday."

She smiled and extended a hand devoid of jewelry. "Hi. I'm Anita Courtright."

"I have the note for Pete."

"Pete?" For an instant she drew a blank. "Oh. Mr. LaFontaine."

"Pardon me. We are old friends, as I told you."

Still smiling, she took the folded paper. "I'll be sure he

gets it at once, Mr. Dugger. Could I offer you a cup of coffee?''

"That sounds good.''

She led him down the hallway to an office in the corner of the building. Floor-to-ceiling draperies were open on two walls of glass that gave a stunning view over other rooftops toward the Seine, the distant Eiffel Tower, and other Paris landmarks. Office furniture included a large walnut desk, devoid of paperwork, a file cabinet, and several comfortable chairs.

"You have an outstanding office.''

"Mine is the cubbyhole out there,'' she told him. "This belongs to Mr. LaFontaine. Sit down. I'll be right back with the coffee. How do you like it?''

Waiting for her, Dugger examined the photographs on the walls. They were of uniform size, about 28 by 20 inches, and uniformly framed in smoothed oak. There were no captions or titles, but they evidently showed pieces of the LaFontaine empire. There were offshore oil drilling platforms, what looked like a gasoline cracking plant, a textile mill, what might have been a motion picture studio, an automobile factory with acres of small sedans parked in lots beyond.

He was studying the picture of the automobile factory when Anita Courtright came back, carrying two white plastic cups of steaming coffee.

"You like the art work?'' she asked, placing his cup on a corner of the desk next to a chair.

"Very impressive. But where are the pictures of the rockets?''

Anita Courtright sat down and crossed her legs. Her expression showed nothing. "Rockets?''

"I'm an old friend, Miss Courtright. I told you that. Pete may not advertise his interest in West German rocketry, but it's hardly a state secret.''

She smiled ruefully. "It's not something we put pictures up on the wall to illustrate, either.''

"Is that where he is? In Cologne or someplace?''

"Actually, no.'' She sipped her coffee. "You ask a lot

of questions, Mr. Dugger.''

"It's all right. I'm harmless.''

"I find that very hard to believe.''

"Do I look like a dangerous man?''

"Actually, no. But Mr. LaFontaine called late last night to order some papers prepared, and I told him you had called. He was quite pleased. He said he might find his way clear to get back earlier tomorrow than he had planned. He wants to be sure you leave your Paris address and telephone number. He also told me a bit about how the two of you worked together in the past.''

"The number and address are in that note on his desk. As to the past, whatever Pete may have said was probably an exaggeration and a lie.''

"You're no longer active with the CIA?''

"I never was.''

"I understand.''

She interested Dugger. In addition to being lovely, she had a quick, bright edge of intelligence. He hoped he would be able to use her for some of the information it would be nice to have.

"You've been with the company a long time?'' he asked.

"Two years.''

"You've moved up fast.''

"The job is mainly secretarial. Occasionally I handle minor negotiations with my counterparts in other organizations. But I think that's why Mr. LaFontaine stole me from another company; he needed someone like me.''

"And what is a person like you, Miss Courtright?''

She betrayed what might have been irritation by swinging a golden leg ever so slightly. "Efficient. Completely loyal. Capable of speaking six languages, with a background in engineering.''

"Did you come before or after Pete's interest in rocket development and manufacture?''

"Actually, with.''

"Do you think, Miss Courtright, that the Germans will

ever get one of those Rube Goldberg things off the ground?''

She smiled. ''We certainly hope so.''

''I can imagine little play rockets, but big boosters are pretty damned complicated and expensive, aren't they?''

''There are a lot of shortcuts, Mr. Dugger. The Russians and our own country tend to overengineer. Did you know, for example, that NASA spent a half million dollars to develop a ballpoint that would write in the light gravity of the moon? A half million dollars. They could have used a pencil.''

''But you can't build a booster out of pencils.''

''No. But the West Germans are intent on manufacture from commerically available parts, and you might be surprised. The fuel tanks, for example: ordinary stainless steel pipe, given an extra hardening process.''

''What kind of fuel?''

''Ordinary diesel fuel with nitric acid for an oxidizer.''

''That's not very efficient. And you can't have a very big booster from a piece of pipe.''

Anita Courtright smiled again. ''But you can strap six pipes together with six small engines for a small rocket, and just keep adding pipes and engines for bigger ones.''

''It'll never fly.''

''We already have three launches sold for later this year, and options on three more early next.''

''Satellite launches?''

''Of course.''

''How does your rate compare with NASA's?''

''About a third.''

''Have you flown a rocket yet big enough to achieve orbit with a meaningful payload?''

''We will.''

The conversation continued. Dugger learned that MTR had no visible stock holdings in the West German rocket firm, all exchanges of money and technical assistance being by way of confidential memorandum of agreement.

Anita Courtright spoke frankly about hostility in some quarters from people who feared and/or distrusted any new German excursion into rocket technology. Dugger reminded her of the peace accords which explicitly forbade such research by West Germany.

"That treaty was almost forty years ago," she told him.

"Which makes it void?"

"They had long since finished their coffee, and now Anita Courtright stood and collected the cups. "Oh, my. We are into deep water when we talk about international agreements. I'll give your note to Mr. LaFontaine, Mr. Dugger. But I really do have some work to get done now."

Dugger stood with her, suddenly more aware of how attractive she was and how he had been enjoying this beyond the value of information gathered. He heard himself ask, "What are you doing for lunch?"

"Why, nothing," she said, and the smile came back.

"I know a terrible place near the Bourdelle museum that has the worst food and nastiest wine in Paris, but also the best old-time atmosphere. If it's still there."

"It sounds lovely. Do you want to wander around the neighborhood for about an hour until I get my work done?"

"I'll be back in an hour."

"It sounds nice, Joe."

It was nice. He found her waiting when he returned an hour later, and she was the one who insisted on the cheap mode of transportation via the tube. The cafe was still there, even rattier and nastier than before, with the same old war veterans and youthful whores sitting at the sidewalk tables. Dugger and Anita sat just inside the door, examining the hundreds of autographed pictures on the grimy walls along with the few aging oil paintings. At one point, Anita got up to walk to one of the paintings and examine it closely.

"My God, Joe!" she said softly when she returned. "I think it's authentic!"

"Nothing would surprise me here," Dugger told her.

They got along very, very well. She told him about her

earlier jobs and how she was lured to MTR. They compared notes on their feelings about Paris. For a little while, although he gave her absolutely no useful information, Dugger almost forgot someone was trying to kill him.

It was past three when he returned to his hotel room. It was as he had left it. He lay down on the bed and caught an hour's restless sleep, then carried the heavy shaving kit into the bathroom and ran a bath.

Soaking, he thought about how high Pierre LaFontaine had risen since the dangerous days in Geneva. He looked forward to seeing LaFontaine again, and had every reason to believe LaFontaine would welcome him with equal pleasure.

LaFontaine had been a very, very good agent. But after both of them were out of the muck, one of LaFontaine's earlier operations had come back to haunt and threaten ruin for him. It had been then that Dugger had repaid old debts—and sealed the friendship—by getting the Frenchman out of a bind that was very tight indeed.

LaFontaine had been on the brink of both civil and criminal actions against him. LaFontaine was accused of selling French industrial research materials to a Soviet agent.

Dugger could not explain that the materials had been evaluated by his own people as useless, and that the sale had allowed LaFontaine to win the confidence of an agent who later led them to several others of much greater danger to the Western world. What Dugger could do, however, was arrange a meeting at LaFontaine's castle-like estate for the principal complainants.

When Dugger walked into the meeting, he found LaFontaine's major business partner at that time, an Italian copper merchant named Izzezzio; a Swedish financier named Bergen, and the spokesman for the majority party in the French government. Izzezzio and Bergen claimed irreparable damages from LaFontaine's actions in earlier years, and the government official was preparing to file charges.

Also at the meeting with Dugger and LaFontaine were a

well-known writer for *Le Monde* and a much more famous American attorney flown in by the Agency, at Dugger's request, specifically for the session.

The injured parties were not in a mood for bargaining. LaFontaine had gone too far, they said, had tarnished the reputation of French business and government, they said. Unless stern action was taken against him, there would be serious political repercussions outside as well as inside France. Pierre LaFontaine had compromised the nation's security, they said—and probably for personal gain. He would be made an example.

At this point, Dugger explained to them that LaFontaine had been working for him at the request of the United States government. He told them no real secrets had been divulged. He suggested that some of LaFontain's business enemies might be spearheading this "moral" war against him.

The gentlemen were adamant. LeFontaine's actions could not be condoned under any circumstances. As a leader in the business community and adviser to the government, he had to be completely pure. He had sullied his reputation, and there could be no compromise.

Dugger turned the floor over to the famous American lawyer, who had flown in at the controls of his own Learjet. The attorney stood, brushed a hand through unruly hair, and began reciting some facts. He listed CIA payments made to Izzezzio through intermediaries prior to the last two Italian elections. These payments had been earmarked for a certain party, he said, but there were affidavits on file suggesting that Izzezzio had pocketed some 70 percent of the money. The attorney then discussed certain instrument sales made by Bergen to both Britain and West Germany, and outlined legal actions that might be taken due to a 50-percent defective rate in said instruments. He then turned to the French leader and asked him how his secret holdings in Rhodesia were doing.

The gentlemen were bitter, pointing to the newspaper reporter who had avidly been taking notes. Dugger explained that the reporter was an old friend, sworn to secrecy under an agreement that would turn him loose to print everything only if the gentlemen failed to be reasonable in the matter of Pierre LaFontaine.

Toweling himself after the tub, Dugger opened the door from bathroom to bedroom and started through. He knew, remembering that night long ago, that LaFontaine would always be a friend. If—

He stopped, all thought collapsing in surprise.

Two men stood in the middle of his bedroom. They wore wrinkled business suits, and were quite young, in their twenties. Americans.

"Mr. Dugger?" the heavier one said diffidently.

"What is this?" Dugger demanded, making a show of being more startled than he actually was. "Who are you guys?"

The heavier man took a billfold from his hip pocket and extended it toward Dugger in the palm of his hand. "I think you recognize the credential, sir."

"I don't understand! FBI agents *here?* How did you guys get in here, and what do you want?"

"We're sorry, sir, but we have to ask you to get dressed and come with us."

What Dagger really wanted to know was how they had picked up his trail so swiftly. He felt sure he had not been followed from the train station. Had they checked every hotel in the city with an ID picture? Physically impossible in such a short time. *How, then?*

But he couldn't speculate now. Standing here naked, dripping on the bare floor, he sized up the two men. The heavier one was a year or two older, clearly in charge and more experienced. He had bushy blond eyebrows, a scar that turned the corner of his mouth down. The younger man, with a little monk's fringe of beard around his thin chin, was clearly watching and keeping his mouth shut. Dugger made out the bulge of shoulder holsters under both coats although the rigs fit well.

"This is outrageous!" he protested shrilly. "My name is Dean—Helmut Dean—and I have the papers to prove it! I intend to report this indignity—"

"Mr. Dugger," the older one said, "just get dressed."

"Why? On what charges? I don't understand!"

"We'll dress you if we have to. In your raincoat."

Muttering complaints, Dugger got underwear from his suitcase and put it on. He made it a point to hop around comically on one foot, then the other, as he put on his socks. The younger man stifled a smile. Good.

"I don't have a clean shirt," he moaned, rummaging in the suitcase. The older man tossed one to him roughly. "But that one is all sweaty!"

The younger man's smile came through this time.

Putting on the shirt, Dugger reached for his trousers and got into them. "This is terrible," he said fretfully, buckling the belt. "I tell you, this is all some kind of ghastly mistake."

"Hurry it up."

Dugger sat on the edge of the bed to lace his shoes. "All right, all right! I admit it! I'm not a German. My real name is Smith—Jack Smith. But I'm here strictly on business. That girl I had up here last night didn't mean a thing to me. I never even saw her before. If she's in some kind of trouble, it doesn't involve me!"

"It looks like it might rain," the older man said. "Do you have an umbrella?"

"Look, you can call my home office. Smith Implement Company, Cedar Rapids!"

The younger man grinned, amused and off his guard. The older man, however, showed no expression. "Let's go."

"Look, am I going to be back in an hour? I have an important appointment in an hour."

"Close his suitcase, Bill, and take it."

"This is awful!" Dugger said. "This is the worst thing I ever heard of! Here I am, with only a couple of days to see Gay Paree, and then you guys barge in here with a wrong ID—"

"Mr. Dugger," the older man said more sharply, in warning.

Dugger watched the younger one close the suitcase. "All right," he sighed. "Only wait. My shaving kit is in the bathroom." He turned at once and stepped through the door into that room.

It probably dawned on them within five seconds that his sudden and unexpected move had put him entirely out of their sight, and the more experienced man muttered an oath and did—to his credit—move very quickly. But Dugger had had those five seconds with the false bottom of the shaving kit, and that was long enough.

The agent's eyes went wide as he reached the bathroom door and looked into the muzzle of Dugger's .38.

Dugger shoved the revolver into his midsection and muscled him out into the bedroom, shoving him roughly back beside the younger man, who stood with mouth agape.

"Against the wall," Dugger told them. "Brace. You know the routine."

"This is a mistake, Dugger."

"Move or I'll blow your ass off."

Both men hesitated. Dugger knew what they were thinking.

"No, I wouldn't want to kill you," he told them quietly. "But I'm out of practice. I might shoot for your thigh and tear your pelvis to shreds. Or I might try to hit you in the shoulder and hit you in the face. Don't make me risk it. *Move.*"

They turned and faced the wall. Spreading their legs, they leaned outstretched hands against the wallpaper.

Dugger grabbed the shaving kit, false bottom flapping, and tossed it into the suitcase. He put it by the outside door, then reached into each man's holster and removed identical revolvers. He tossed them onto the bed and flipped the cover over them. "All right, gentlemen. Into the bathroom."

"This is really stupid," the older man said. "The pick-up is for your own protection."

Dugger stood well back, carefully tracking them with the gun as they entered the bathroom. "All the way to the back, away from the door. That's it.'' He reached in and slammed the stout old door, then turned the rusty skeleton key in the lock.

"I'm sure someone will come along after while to let you out,'' he called through the door. "Oh, and just in case, I think I left a used razor blade there on the dresser if you want to slash your wrists or anything.''

Pocketing the revolver, he picked up the suitcase and hurried down to the street. There was a taxi stand at the corner, with three taxis in line. To be safe, he tipped the front taxi and took the second one in the line.

9

New York City

Tella Rhonta sat up angrily in bed, the afternoon sunlight from the apartment window bright on the chocolate curves of her nude body. "If that little whore will be at the party, then I'm not going!"

Clarence Endidi remained supine on the bed beside her. He had feared an outburst when he broke the news. "I tell you, my dear, she might be useful to us."

"You and Grover have the same use in mind, too. You want to use her cunt!"

"Gutter language doesn't become you, Tella."

"She's an enemy of the people, I tell you! I think she must be some kind of spy!"

"She's an innocent, Tella. It's sheer chance that we met again."

"Don't you find that kind of chance unusual? Doesn't that speak for itself? She could be a plant! She could—"

Endidi put his hand on her bare thigh. "Tella, Tella! Do you think I'm that much of a fool? I'll watch her, of course. But it would be much more suspicious if Grover and I *didn't* show an interest in her."

"Are you having her story checked out?"

"Of course we're having her story checked out. But I know her, if you'll remember. I feel confident she's okay. And there may come a time when we need someone in the Secretariat."

"You'll never convince me she can be trusted."

"I plan to question her closely . . . watch her." Endidi moved his hand across Tella Rhonta's belly to her breasts. He began stroking her left breast in the way he knew she liked best. "Now come on, Tella. Relax."

She made a sullen face. "I intend to do some checking on her myself."

"Fine. Excellent."

She plopped down beside him, rolling to a face-to-face position. "I wish this next week were over."

"Everything is going according to plan," Endidi assured her. "We have nothing to worry about."

Which was, of course, a very great lie. Their lives and the fate of a nation rode on the events of the next few days. And any broken thread in the complicated fabric of their plans could ruin everything. But Endidi had a sense of destiny in his gut. He believed the worst parts were behind them, that they had done their planning well. So in this small sense it was not a lie at all.

After their lovemaking he tried again to convince Tella Rhonta to attend the party that night at the Cabinderian mission. She again refused. So he was alone a bit after eight o'clock when he called for Eileen Arrington at her apartment.

Eileen was nervous, but tried to hide the fact. Endidi complimented her on her new gold-colored cocktail dress, which pleased her. Seeing his calmness as they drove away from the apartment, she knew he had not heard the recent news. She debated, then decided that the subject should be broached in order to let her watch his reaction.

"Have you heard any news in the last hour?" she asked.

"No," he said, smiling. "What new calamity has warmed the hearts of our American newspaper people?"

"There's a story out of Paris. A quote, responsible source, unquote, says President Obutu will definitely fly to Paris early next week for final negotiation and signing of an aid treaty."

Endidi's jaw set, and she thought she saw his hand tighten on the wheel. He said nothing.

"Did you know?" she probed.

"I knew, of counsel, that a trip was probable. But this sounds like it has become a certainty. I suppose I should have assumed that when Guy Arata flew over there."

"Are you pleased?"

His eyes flared with sudden anger. "Should it please me that President Obutu seems hell-bent on concluding a pact with France that will either make Marandaya a lackey for a capitalist slave state or bring full-scale revolution to the streets of Atravi?"

"I thought you supported President Obutu. I had no idea."

"Of course I support him in public. He is the leader of my country. And I support him—as my president—at all times. But my God, Eileen, surely you can see how foolhardy his present course of action is! It can only bring new discord, rejection by other African nations—ruin!"

Surprised, Eileen cast about for a way to keep him talking. "But your country needs aid. I assume you support Obutu's refusal to take more direct aid from the United States?"

"Of course I support that. Marandaya cannot become another puppet government in the struggle between East and West."

"Then the French bargaining—"

"Only substitutes dependence on one capitalist state for another. France has a history of oppressing black people that goes back even longer than America's. I will admit to you, Eileen, I have argued *bitterly* against a new treaty with France."

"The treaty, as I understand it, would strengthen Marandaya."

"Eileen," Endidi said wearily, "you have been away from my country too long. You don't know the tensions there now. It is a tinderbox. Why else do you imagine President Obutu has kept his forthcoming visit a secret for so long? Even with this premature announcement in Paris, I will wager that all details will remain a secret until the very end. But even this semi-official leak will fan the flames. Gero Paasaad will strike with renewed intensity.

He will discover new allies over the world among the poor and the helpless. There will be demonstrations everywhere. And any hope we might have had to keep Paasaad out of the General Assembly is now gone.''

''Paasaad? In the—''

''A dozen countries,'' Endidi told her bitterly, ''have been working behind the scenes to arrange a formal invitation to Paasaad, for him to address the General Assembly. Now—''

''*Address the General Assembly!*'' But the man is a terrorist! A murderer!''

''Do you think other murderers have not addressed us?''

It shocked her. She said little more as they drove to the Cabinderian mission.

Like many UN missions, the one run under the supervision of Grover Matsoon was an old brownstone that had been turned into a showplace within. Eileen was still trying to cope with Endidi's reaction to her news when they arrived, but she forced herself to think only of the moment once they were inside.

The main portion of the party was held in two very large rooms connected by a double doorway. Crystal chandeliers shone down on dozens of guests, most black but a surprising number of whites and Orientals. Waiters moved through the throng with trays of champagne, and a three-piece combo was playing in a far corner of the second room although no one seemed to be paying any attention whatsoever. Clarence Endidi put on his best face as they entered, and for several minutes she was given a constant stream of introductions: the gentleman from Chad, the lady from Niger, the gentlemen from Cameroun and Sierra Leone, the American novelist Jeremy Whittier, businessmen from three continents. Then Endidi excused himself to speak to someone privately for a moment, and Eileen found herself standing beside a delegate from Chad and a striking white woman who might have said she was from Great Britain.

"Clarence Endidi looks tired," the white woman observed.

"We have had very long sessions this week," the gentleman from Chad told her, showing his teeth.

The woman turned to Eileen. "Do you think he'll be the president of Marandaya someday, as people speculate?"

"The idea had never occurred to me," Eileen blurted with total honesty.

The gentleman from Chad chuckled. "He has the fire" —he pointed to a small but ample midsection—"here. In his belly."

"Yes," the other woman said. "He's a man to be watched."

Before Eileen could respond, a burly man in a white tuxedo, the left breast buried in brightly ribboned medals, approached them. He had rough, Slavic features, and his gray hair had been cut within a quarter inch of his gleaming pink scalp. In his fifties, he gave off an aura of great strength.

Bowing to Eileen's companions, he showed that he already knew them. With a little bow, he extended a ham hand to Eileen. "Allow me to present myself. I am Mikhail Parkov."

Eileen allowed her hand to be engulfed. She realized that it was a measure of her nervousness that she had not instantly recognized the chief delegate of the Soviet Union.

"I saw my friend Clarence bring you here," Parkov said, showing a gold tooth. "And then he has abandoned you, eh?" He offered his arm. "Come. I will introduce you to people you have not met."

Eileen allowed him to take her away from the others. He moved her from group to group, making a bewildering round of new introductions. Wherever he paused, the conversations stopped politely and opened up to him. He was clearly the star of the party.

After a little while they chanced to stop beside a bar set

up in the front room. Other conversations buzzed nearby, but they were effectively isolated for a few moments. Parkov handed her a fresh glass of champagne and beamed down at her. She was very aware of his strong animal magnetism.

"You wonder why I take you under my wing, eh?" he asked.

"It crossed my mind, yes."

Parkov comically held an index finger to the side of his rather large nose. "Perhaps I am, ah—how is it said in English?—perhaps I am after your body, is it not so?"

She laughed. "That wasn't my impression."

"No. I will tell you." He leaned closer. "I consider Clarence Endidi a very good friend. I would like to have you as a very good friend, too. Can this be so?"

"I'm very flattered, Mr. Parkov. It would be a pleasure to count you as a friend."

"Good! It is done, then!" Parkov turned and nodded toward a man edging through the crowd toward them. "And here is definitely someone else you should meet, eh?" He held out a big hand to the man who had joined them. The newcomer was tall, gray, with a hawkish quality about him. "Miss Arrington, please allow me to introduce Mr. Leonard Jenkins. He is a fellow countryman of yours."

Shaking hands, Eileen had the uneasy feeling that she knew Jenkins. She had an extraordinary memory—an attribute red-flagged in her personnel file at the Bureau—and the name meant nothing. But in the instant before either of them spoke, his face engraved itself on her consciousness: thin hair that might once have been red, a long, narrow noise, rather close-set green eyes, a mouth that even in a smile, as now, was thin and cruel. He was in his froties, and carried the ravages of smallpox on his cheeks and chin. She noted, too, that his expensive suit was cut in a style a bit too youthful for him, and she marked him down as a vain man.

"A great pleasure, Miss Arrington," Jenkins told her, squeezing her hand a bit too long.

"I have the feeling we've met," Eileen said frankly.

"I very much doubt it. I think I would remember."

"You're with one of the delegations?"

"No. I have a small company in Upstate New York. A number of the people here are my customers."

Parkov patted Jenkins on the shoulder. "And if your government ever relaxes, my country, too, will probably buy your teaching machines, eh?"

"I sincerely hope so," Jenkins said, smiling.

"And here," Parkov chuckled, "comes Miss Arrington's escort. I didn't think he would feel comfortable, seeing her with two such handsome men."

Clarence Endidi joined them. He shook hands with both men. "I see you're making friends, Eileen."

"It's a lovely party."

Parkov patted her hand. "I must mingle. I hope we can talk again later." He turned and moved across the room, where he joined another grouping.

"And how are you, Leonard?" Endidi asked. "Is all well?"

"Everything is as it should be, my friend. I hope to have a word with Grover before the evening is over."

"I believe you might find him in one of the back rooms, or in the garden."

Jenkins adjusted the lapels of his slim-cut jacket. The tip of a brown manila envelope showed on his chest for a second, then vanished as his coat was rearranged. "I may go look for him shortly."

Endidi took Eileen's arm. "Would you like to meet some of the members of the British group? They're in the next room."

The party wore on. Eileen met a confusing number of people. Much of the conversation was "shop talk" about a resolution on South Africa, the famine in India, and Marandaya's unrest. After a while, Eileen found herself again separated from Endidi, who seemed intent on conversing with everyone in the building. She drifted toward the back of the place, looking for the garden he had mentioned in connection with Grover Matsoon. •

As she entered a back area that once had been a solarium, she found about a dozen persons in three different conversational groups. Near sliding doors to a garden, she saw Matsoon and Leonard Jenkins, evidently in earnest conversation. Before she could react, the two men turned and strolled out into what was evidently the garden beyond.

Eileen studied what she could see from her position. The garden was surrounded by wings of the house. Through dense greenery she could see the lights from windows beyond its rear border. Making a quick decision, she walked across the room to a door that was ajar.

Pushing through it, she found herself in a hallway leading deeper into the building. Here were the rest rooms, but the corridor went deeper, turning to the right. Her heart beat faster as she passed the rest rooms and moved on around the corner.

She came to another room that was lighted, a kind of sitting area. Its windows were the ones she had seen from the far side. The light was too bright against the glass to allow her to see anything in the garden beyond, but there was one more door at the end of the hall. She moved on to this one and tested the handle. It turned.

She stepped into darkness and a musty odor, and her foot struck something. Bending in the dark, she felt the edge of a cardboard box . . . then a crate of some kind. So she was in a storare area.

Feeling her way between items, she moved across the room partway toward the single window. Finally a big crate blocked her way. Kicking off her shoes, she hiked her gown and climbed up onto the rough planks of the crate.

It was a precarious perch, but it allowed her a view across the rest of the room and into the garden. There was a small fountain, flagstones, and shrubbery everywhere. Standing quite near her window were Grover Matsoon and Leonard Jenkins, the latter with his back partly turned to her.

Straining, she tried to make out their voices. But the dusty window was closed and she could hear only the distant rumble of conversation from the party at her back. Jenkins seemed to be doing most of the talking, and Matsoon occasionally nodded agreement. There were no smiles.

Her knees were beginning to kill her, rough splinters biting into them. She knew she couldn't stay in such a cramped position more than another minute or two, but she hung on, hoping she wouldn't get so weak that she tore something climbing down.

After a moment, Leonard Jenkins reached inside his coat and withdrew a long manila envelope, the one she had seen an edge of. He handed it to Matsoon, who glanced around furtively, took it, and quickly put it in his own inside coat pocket. Jenkins started saying something else, but Eileen's knees wouldn't take any more punishment. With a little sob of relief, she let herself back down to the floor.

Fumbling around, she found her shoes and made her way back out of the room, closing the door just as it had been. She could only hope no one would notice footprints on a dusty floor. It was too late to worry about that.

She made her way back down the hall and to the ladies' room. She dabbed cool water on her face, touched up her makeup and washed her hands, then flushed the toilet and went back outside again.

By midnight some of the guests were departing. She had been with Endidi for a while again, and then had been separated once more. A gentleman from Burma had made a clumsy pass. Now, going toward the front room, she encountered Endidi and Matsoon standing alone near the bar. She saw that Endidi appeared angry, and was talking swiftly, in a low tone. She moved toward his back as swiftly as she dared.

'' . . . stupid and reckless!'' Endidi was saying angrily. ''It's practically a public place, and he ought to know better . . .''

Matsoon saw Eileen coming and gave Endidi some sign which shut him up. He spun, saw her, and gave a transformation to his features by sheer will. The anger vanished in a twinkling and he was relaxed, smiling. ''There you are! I was just telling Grover that I can't get you to myself for five minutes!''

"I noticed some of the guests are leaving," she told them, "and I wondered if it was time for us to go as well."

Endidi shrugged. "We've done our duty. And we certainly want to thank you, Grover, for your part in making it a fine evening."

Matsoon's smile was wan. "I wish I could also escape. My face aches from so much polite smiling."

"Why don't you, then?" Eileen asked, getting an inspiration.

Matsoon's eyes widened. "*Leave*, you mean?"

"Of course!"

"But, my dear, that just isn't done."

"Everyone will only assume you're off on some matter of state. And the party does seem to be running itself. Come on. The three of us can go to my apartment. I'll play a record for you and cook breakfast."

"An American breakfast? Eggs and fat bacon?"

"I was thinking of pancakes."

"My God, I adore pancakes, my dear!"

She gave both men her most dazzling smile. "Come on, then!"

Matsoon looked at Endidi. Endidi slowly smiled. "Why not, indeed?"

With conspiratorial winks, the three of them moved through the front room. Matsoon fetched their umbrellas and hats, and within moments they were out on the nearly deserted streets. Endidi had trouble getting his car out from between two others that had parked too close, and his hearty cursing reduced Eileen and Matsoon to giggles. The trip partway across the island was at breakneck speed, a reminder that diplomatic immunity extended to traffic laws.

Eileen led them up the stairs to her apartment. Her heart was thumping and she had a coppery taste in her mouth. She did not think Matsoon had had opportunity to get rid of the envelope handed him by Leonard Jenkins. She believed it was still in the inside pocket of his coat. She had to get a look at it.

Opening the apartment door, she ushered them in. The inadequate floor lamps cast yellow shadows up the dingy walls, and she realized that it looked extra-shabby after the grandness of the Cabinderian mission.

"Eileen," Endidi said, looking around, "we need to find you a decorator!"

"On my salary, Clary, this is it." She stepped out of her heels and pointed toward the tiny kitchen. "Will you fix drinks? I'll put a record on the machine. . . . Oh, Grover, you look like you're burning up in that heavy suit coat! Let me start the air-conditioner. And just give me that coat, and I'll hang it in the bedroom."

Matsoon peeled off the coat and handed it to her, heavy with his sweat. "I'll start the air-conditioner, my dear."

"All right," she said, hurrying toward the bedroom with the damp coat hugged against her. "It's the big knob on the right."

"My dear," Matsoon's voice trailed her jovially, "I once studied to be an enginner. I believe I can manage it."

She reached the bedroom and swung the door lightly closed. Putting the coat on a hanger, she placed it in the closet among her things. Then, with a deep breath, she plunged her hand into the inside pocket.

The envelope was there, soggy with sweat. There was no writing on the outside. She tested the flap. It was glued, but the moisture had made the glue sticky. The flap opened under her thumbnail.

More frightened now, she pulled the contents out of the envelope. It consisted of three or four pages stapled at the top left corner and folded in three. Her hands shook as she opened the pages and glanced at the top sheet.

> TOP SECRET   TOP SECRET
> File: *730447*
> Copies: *1 only*
> This material is classified TOP SECRET.
> SUBJ: *Obutu, Joseph A.*
> TYPE: *Activity report*
> *Central Intelligence Agency Cross-indes 428-CD*

"Eileen?" Clarence Endidi's voice called, shockingly close.

Nerves jangling, she refolded the papers without a chance to look further. Stuffing them back into the envelope, she mashed the gooey flap between her fingers and put the whole thing back into the dank interior of Matsoon's coat.

"I'm coming, Clary," she called innocently.

"Where are you?" Endidi sounded concerned, and she heard his footsteps just outside the bedroom.

She opened the door and went out to him. "I was just hanging up Grover's coat and freshening myself up a little. Have you made the drinks?"

"Your ice trays are empty," he told her gloomily.

"Oh, Clary, I'm such a *dunce*! What are we *ever* going to *do*?"

10

Paris

The stone gate off the side road leading to Pierre LaFontaine's estate was obviously ancient. The high mesh fencing extending in both directions from it into the woods—and the electrically operated steel gate and brick guard building—looked painfully new in the bright Sunday sunlight. The elderly man who came out to check Dugger's credentials, then make a telephone call somewhere else, might have been a retired French policeman. He looked like nobody's fool, and Dugger noted that he was armed with a quite professional-looking Colt .45 automatic.

"Please to follow ze road, M. Duggair, and M. LaFontaine will meet you at ze house."

Dugger obeyed, keeping the rented Renault in low gear up the twisting gravel roadway. For about two hundred yards the grade was steep, through dense woods. Then the road leveled somewhat and moved out of the trees and across a sweeping acreage of manicured lawn. Atop the hill was LaFontaine's rambling stone mansion. Three stories tall, with steeply pitched clay roof studded with dormer windows, it was flanked by two lower, newer structures of equally massive appearance. Great old trees crept close to the east and west wings, softening somewhat the sheer monolithic effect of the architecture. LaFontaine had had the stone sandblasted since Dugger's last visit years ago, but the granite blocks were already staining again.

As Dugger negotiated a large circular driveway around a

fountain and formal garden in front of the house, the front doors opened and Pierre LaFontaine strode down the many white steps toward the parking. He looked older: wearing gray slacks and white shirt open at the collar with a tan safari jacket, he was thicker in the midsection and had now gone entirely gray. Reading glasses perched on the tip of his slender nose, he had a long cigarette holder clamped in his massive jaw, and a broad grin that showed his big teeth. Someone had told LaFontaine once that he looked just a bit like Franklin D. Roosevelt. He had liked that; the use of the cigarette holder could be dated to the compliment.

Dugger stopped the Renault, got out, and walked around to greet his old friend.

"Joseph!" LaFontaine pumped his hand. "Wonderful to see you again, old man!"

"You're looking fit, Pete."

LaFontaine patted his gut. "I tell Maria there's more of me to appreciate all the time. Come in! Come in!"

"I have a bag."

"One of the servants will park your car and bring the bag inside." Arm over Dugger's shoulders, LaFontaine, a massive man at least six feet, four inches tall, led him up the stairs toward the house entry. "I hope this can be a fine, extended visit, as I told you on the telephone."

"I wanted to see you, Pete. But you said you have some other guests coming later today—"

"That's no problem, no problem at all! Just some friends and business associates in later for the evening, and two other house guests. The house is as big as a bloody hotel, and if you don't like them, you'll never even have to see them much. You're always welcome here. You know that."

They entered the house. A massive curved staircase dominated the foyer, gilt banisters gleaming under the illumination of a hundred bulbs in a gigantic chandelier. Their voices echoed as LaFontaine led Dugger through a book-lined library room to the right and into a living area at the rear. High beamed ceilings created an extraordinary effect of great space. Contemporary furniture was scattered on bright shag rugs. The rear wall, virtually all glass, looked out onto a garden and, behind a discreet low hedge, a swimming pool. There was a gardener working in the roses.

"Too early in the day for a small bracer?" LaFontaine asked, walking to a large, curved bar with its own suspended walnut lattice roof.

"I might consider a beer."

"Sit down! Sit down! I'm sure Maria will be with us in a minute!"

Dugger took a white leather chair near the rocked-in fireplace. LaFontaine brought two bottles and sat facing him across a massive oak coffee table. "I think this is your favorite, Joseph—or was at one time."

Dugger looked at the label. "My God, Harp lager. I haven't had any Irish beer in two years."

LaFontaine chuckled with pleasure. They tasted. After so much dark German beer, Dugger had almost forgotten the bright, clean taste of Harp. He lighted a cigarette and LaFontaine joined him, putting an acrid French smoke into the long holder.

"You look fine, Joe! Fine!"

"It's obvious you're doing well, Pete."

"You know the story of Midas? In the past few years, I believe the myth. Everything I touch—gold! Magic!"

Dugger smiled, knowing better. The LaFontaine family had been all but wiped out in the Second World War. Pierre LaFontaine had still been scrambling, fighting to retain control of this ancestral home, in the days when he had worked as an agent for Dugger out of Geneva. If he was now wealthy and powerful once more, it was due not to fairy tale magic, but to the alchemy of intelligence, courage, and an incredible capacity for work.

Dugger said, "The fencing and the guard make it look like Fort Knox."

"They're new. How was the guard? How did he strike you? He's quite new. You're one of his first customers."

"The guard was professional. You say it's all new? Has

something happened to demand greater security?"

"Several things." LaFontaine scowled, swirling the beer in the bottle. "Italian-type terrorism is becoming fashionable in my country, Joe, God help us. Of course you know that. One of my affiliated companies is dabbling in nuclear energy as well as offshore oil, so I have the environmental crazies after me. A man could be attacked . . . kidnapped for ransom." He gave Dugger a hard, direct stare. "And then there is the matter of our old friends being assassinated."

"You know about that."

"I still have friends . . . contacts. Is that why you're here? To warn me?"

It was simpler to lie. "Yes."

"You are a good friend. But I have already been warned, and as you can see, I have taken precautions."

"Do you have any idea why we seem to be under attack?"

"I thought, my friend, you might be able to tell me."

Dugger watched LaFontaine very carefully. "It might have something to do with Regensburg."

If the word meant anything, LaFontaine was a consummate actor. "Did you say Regensburg?"

Dugger remembered that LaFontaine *was* a consummate actor. "It's been mentioned. It means nothing to you?"

"Nothing at all!"

Better to switch tactics. "In your case, of course, it could also have something to do with the West German rocket research."

LaFontaine grinned broadly. "You have heard about that, eh? I tell you, Joseph, the German people have lost none of their genius in engineering. I fondly hope they are going to make me truly wealthy."

"There are people who take a dim view of the whole operation, I understand."

"Did that ever stop the Germans? They are like your bulldog; they sink their teeth in, and nothing can dislodge them."

Dugger smiled. "It's the Brits who have the bulldog."

"Regardless." LaFontaine waved the cigarette holder. "The German genius will overcome all difficulties. They are an amazing race, Joseph! Once they nearly destroyed my family's fortune, but now they are going to help me rebuild it beyond anything my father, and his father, ever dreamed."

There was a slight sound at the far end of the great room, near the interior doors, and Dugger turned. Maria LaFontaine had entered. A tall and elegant woman, she had kept herself reed-slender, handsome. Her hair, too, had gone to gray, but was cut in a fashionable tight coiffure. She wore heels and a starkly simple black afternoon dress with a single strand of pearls.

"Joe," she said, coming to give him her hands, "it has been such a very long time." She offered her cheek, which was cool, antiseptic. "We were so very sorry about your wife."

"Thank you. I appreciated your letter at that time."

"You're . . . alone?"

"I haven't remarried."

"One day you will, I am sure." She came around the coffee table and took a chair in the grouping with them. LaFontaine started toward the bar, but she shook her head.

He sat down again and reached for his beer. "Joseph and I were just discussing the German national character."

Lines of distaste appeared on Maria LaFontaine's forehead. "Surely there are more pleasant topics."

LaFontaine sighed and got to his feet. "Excuse me a moment. I have to consult with the kitchen staff about the wines for dinner." He strode stiffly out of the room.

Maria LaFontaine sighed heavily.

"I take it the German character is a touchy topic," Dugger said.

"I hate the Germans."

Was her vehemence directly related to her husband's business connections with the rocket-makers? Dugger tested. "I've been living in Germany, you know."

"I know, and I will never understand it!"

"But you were born in Austria!"

"Austria is quite different. There is a flaw in the German national character. It goes back centuries. It will *never* be erased."

Dugger hesitated, then decided to ask, "You prefer the Russian national character?"

Maria laughed. "My poor friend! Still the Cold War warrior."

Dugger's cheeks warmed. "That doesn't answer my question."

"The Russians are still peasants, animals in people's clothing. They are barbarians, and they will always be barbarians. But the Germans have more in common with the Russians and the Poles than they have with France or Great Britain or America. In the West we have centuries of individualism in our heritage. We are the children of ancient Greece. They are the children of the barbarian hordes. We are like great oaks and pines, able to stand alone in the darkness. The Russians and the Germans are like the fir trees in those German forests you so admire; they cannot stand alone; they are stable only when crowded together, their branches locked into those of their brothers. *That* is their darkness, Joe. That is why I will always fear and hate them."

Dugger looked into Maria's intense, beautiful eyes and did not reply. He thought of La Fontaine's fine new mesh fence and guardhouse. They had not walled out conflict. LaFontaine's ties to the German manufacturers must be extraordinarily precious to be justified in the face of opposition from a woman like this.

By midafternoon Dugger was no closer to understanding LaFontaine's precise relationship with either the West German manufacturers or the rocket testing in Marandaya. LaFontaine, driving a white golf cart, took him on a brief tour of some of the grounds, showing the ultrasonic detectors and trip wires that complimented the new mesh fench. LaFontaine was cheerfully confident in the system at the same time he questioned Dugger closely about the deaths of their former comrades. When Dugger tried to talk to him about the arrangements that existed with Joseph Obutu, and whether there could be some tie-in between the leak of information concerning him and the deaths, or between the rocket research and political unrest in Obutu's country, the Frenchman was charmingly but stubbornly evasive.

Shown to his room upstairs by a servant at three, Dugger showered and changed clothes, and tried to review his information to make sense of some of it. *Someone clearly wanted him and at least some of his former agents dead. Someone clearly was plotting to smear Joseph Obutu, and perhaps bring him down. LaFontaine's business associates were testing West German rocket hardware in Marandaya. Something—sometime—had happened in or near Regensburg.*

And something in Dugger's gut told him that LaFontaine knew exactly what had happened in Regensburg.

There were too many missing pieces to the puzzle. He felt farther from an answer than he had in Zurich. But he felt the answer was here somewhere, around Pierre LaFontaine. He had to find it and he did not have forever. He could not expect his whereabouts to remain unknown long when both his highly irritated friends at the Agency and the people who wanted him dead were looking for him.

When he went back downstairs a little before four, the first guest had arrived. The rotund distinguished black man was in the large living room, having a cocktail with the LaFontaines.

"Joseph," LaFontaine smiled, "allow me to introduce another old friend, Mr. Guy Arata. Mr. Arata, may I present Joseph Dugger?"

Arata's handshake was robust, and his face glistened with his smile. "A pleasure, sir! I trust that you, like me, look forward to a pleasant vacation here, away from our usual duties!"

Dugger knew both the name and the face. He could not make a link in his memory. "Will you be in France long, Mr. Arata?"

"A few days"—Arata beamed—"A few days only, I fear. Then it will be back to my usual business in London."

"Mr. Arata is a very fine bridge player, Joseph," LaFontaine told him with relish. "And I recall that you once considered yourself good at the game. If we can convince Maria, we can anticipate some fine, cutthroat competition in the next day or two!"

"I'm pretty rusty," Dugger said, still shuffling memory cards.

"As I am," Arata chuckled, rocking back and forth in his chair. "But we can try, is it not so?"

He spoke with a definite British accent, but his phrasing was not British. Dugger could not quite place him. Recognition was on the edge of consciousness.

Then, as Maria LaFontaine said something mocking about her husband's manic delight in playing no-trump, the recognition came. Dugger had some difficulty in maintaining an even expression, and now he had another question to add to his list: *What was the chief of Maranday's UN delegation doing in Pierre LaFontaine's house?*

There were seven other guests for the dinner. Georges Trouveau, the second man in the French ministry for defense, was a handsome, classically Gallic man of indeterminate middle age. Both he and his wife, a rather dour and portly woman, chain-smoked harsh French cigarettes. Wilhelm Dortmund, a German business associate whose precise business was not stated, was accompanied by his wife, Marlene, a brittle blonde whose icy Germanic good looks were shown to maximum advantage in her silver sheath gown. The third couple was black, Francis Corbinere, the Marandayan ambassador to France, and his wife, a very young and very frightened woman who spoke hardly a word and watched everyone with the eyes of a startled fawn.

The seventh guest was Anita Courtright.

"I hope you're not angry," she told Dugger the moment they had a few seconds away from the general conversation.

"Why should I be?" he asked, surprised.

"I feel sort of silly—the unattached female for the un-attached male."

"Pete is old-fashioned. I'll overlook his social match-making if you will."

She laughed, and it was all right.

It was a congenial group, and good conversation started at once with Maria LaFontaine prompting. After a few minutes, Dugger noticed LaFontaine slip out of the group, to be followed by the two black men, Corbinere and Guy Arata. They were gone for nearly fifteen minutes. No one else seemed to notice.

When they returned there were more drinks, and soon the head butler, a man named Crouex, announced dinner. Dugger gave Anita Courtright his arm and they went into the large dining room, ablaze with candlelight, to a long, perfectly prepared table whose silver and crystal seemed to glow under the candles.

Again, the conversation was light and amusing. It was not until nearly time for dessert that Corbinere mentioned the future-indefinite visit to France by President Obutu and the German, Dortmund, picked it up.

"We are all most interested in your president's visit," he said.

Corbinere showed fine white teeth in an apologetic grin. "It can only be regretted that security prevents discussion of my president's plans."

Georges Trouveau sighed. "The need for maintaining secrecy about President Obutu's plans is indeed regret-table. But it is also obviously necessary."

"Obviously?" Dugger echoed.

Trouveau spread his hands. "My friend, even the know-ledge that President Obutu is to visit our country some-time in the near future has brought all sorts of extremists out of the walls. Already there have been ugly demonstra-tions . . . even violence."

"I've seen nothing about that in the news."

"The media are cooperating fully with the government in order to prevent provocations of an even worse kind.

And yet—this is in confidence—only today there were demonstrations at the palace and at the Marandayan embassy. Notes have been delivered threatening that President Obutu, if he visits our country, will never leave it alive.''

Corbinere nodded. "It is also true that events in my own country would be . . . unpredictable . . . if dangerous elements could plan with certainty for a time period when our president was absent.''

There was a sober silence around the large table. Crouex, the chief of the domestic staff, moved inconspicuously around the table, refilling wineglasses. Dugger absorbed the new information: the game was more deadly, on a grander scale, than he had imagined. And yet none of it really made sense.

The conversation shifted quickly to other topics. Soon the party moved back into the living room, where a fire had been started in the fireplace against the creeping evening chill. Breaking with tradition, LaFontaine preceded the demitasse with a splendid Sauterne. The old wine's golden sweetness had a mellowing effect on everyone.

It was Marlene Dortmund who returned briefly to the subject of terrorism: "The terrorists should be executed.'' She snapped her fingers. "Like that.''

LaFontaine smiled at her fondly. "So there might be utter tranquility, Marlene—as there is in Germany today?''

Marlene Dortmund crossed her legs, and the slit skirt of her silver gown opened above the knee. "You know, Pierre, that we have dealt with the Stuttgart terrorists, and those in Cologne. We would never allow rabble to drive a state visit practially underground.''

Maria LaFontaine murmured, "Ah, yes. The efficiency of the German people.''

Marlene did not look at her. "You'll not make me lose my temper this evening, Maria.''

LaFontaine chuckled. "Then we will all miss a great show.''

Marlene turned to Dugger. "You have heard the term 'love-hate relationship'? Pierre and I have been friends for

many years. I love him, but he and Maria can infuriate me
like few people in the world!"

"It gives us such pleasure, Marlene," LaFontaine said,
"to witness your capacity for passion."

It was said lightly, as a joke, and there were smiles. But
Dugger saw the brief look that passed between them as
well as the stiffening in the faces of both Maria LaFontaine
and Wilhelm Dortmund. He wondered if LaFontaine and
Marlene were lovers.

Marlene told LaFontaine ironically, "You are a scoun-
drel, sir."

Maria LaFontaine said in French, "Perhaps you only
bring out the wrost in him, my dear. He does tend to show
off in your presence, like a naughty puppy dog."

The phraseology in French formed a cutting *double
entendre*. But there were again smiles, as if no one else had
noticed.

"I have a treat for everyone," La Fontaine announced
abruptly. "In a few minutes, after coffee, we can go to the
film room, where I have a film classic prepared for showing."

"Oh, Pierre," Marlene Dortmund moued, "not the
Marx Brothers again?"

"Perhaps," Wilhelm Dortmund said with a stiff attempt at good humor, "he has a true classic for us this
time."

"But Pierre has such dreadful taste in old films!"

"My dear," Dortmund said, quite still this time, "we
are guests here."

"Don't be such a stick, Willy. Pierre knows I was teasing."

"This film," LaFontaine announced, "is Laurel and
Hardy."

Maria LaFontaine made an almost inaudible clucking
sound.

"The one," LaFontaine added, "in which they have a
moving company!"

Corbinere was smiling with blank politeness. His wife
leaned toward him to whisper a question. He silenced her

with a wiggle of his fingers.

LaFontaine caught it. "You do not know Laurel and Hardy? My friends, you are in for a great treat!"

The film room, where they were led a few minutes later, had once been the great ballroom of the mansion. A large permanent screen had been lowered from the ceiling at one end, and Dugger saw a projector window in the opposite wall. Easy chairs had been arranged in a loose pair of semicircular rows in front of the screen. As the last person was seated, the room was plunged into darkness. The screen flickered and came alive, and the Laurel and Hardy theme music boomed scratchily from speakers beyond the screen somewhere.

For about ten minutes, Dugger watched the comedy drowsily. He was missing far too much sleep. The flophouse he had spent the night in last night, after escaping the boys from the FBI, had not been conducive to decent rest. He was about half asleep when a movement to his right alerted him and he saw Pierre LaFontaine slipping out of his easy chair and moving unobtrusively to the back of the room.

On the screen, Stan and Ollie were trying to get a grand piano up an Everest of San Francisco steps. The Corbineres were chuckling, and so was Marlene. Dugger watched more alertly.

Behind him there was another very slight sound. He turned and saw the back of Wilhelm Dortmund. He also moved soundlessly to the back of the room, where an open door led to a darkened hallway.

Dugger thought about it, then started to ease out of his own chair.

Beside him, Anita Courtright caught his hand and whispered, "*Where are you going?*"

Dugger leaned close to her, breathing her perfume. "*Outside.*"

She stood and moved with him through the blackness of the doorway. Mildly irritated that she was coming along, he went down the corridor to the lighted foyer. Glancing in the library, he saw no one. The fire still burned in the empty living room. He crossed the room, opened a sliding glass door, and went out onto the patio. She followed.

There was no one in view. Lighting a cigarette, Dugger walked off the patio and into the garden, staying on the walk. Earlier clouds had drifted away and the sky was filled with stars. A cool breeze moved the trees. With another glance around, he turned to look back at the house. On the second floor, two windows side by side glowed with interior light. The draperies were open, and he could see the high ceiling of the room.

"I wish I hadn't stopped smoking," Anita told him companionably.

He looked down at her. She was beautiful in the starlight. "Start again if you feel that way."

"It isn't that simple." She smiled.

"Of course it is. You want to smoke? Smoke."

"Why are you angry?"

"I'm not."

She sighed and followed his gaze to the second floor, the row of windows over a narrow stone balustrade encircling the building. "That's his home office."

"Pete's?"

"Of course. I imagine he and Wilhelm slipped off for a few minutes of shop talk."

"What's Dortmund's business connection?"

"Oh, they have several interests."

The answer was evasive enough to tell him that she was not going to give him anything. He smoked his cigarette in silence, watching the lighted windows. He had not known LaFontaine had an office at home. It was a room he very much wanted to see.

"Do you plan to stay long, Mr. Dugger?" she asked.

"Before, it was 'Joe.' Now we're more formal again?"

She smiled. "You're very distant tonight."

"Sorry. In answer to your question, I expect to be here a few days."

"Are you doing research for a book?"

"You know about that?"

"Yes. And you used to be a spy."

"Pete has a very big mouth."

"He's very impressed with you. I think he's proud to have such a distinguished friend from the world of letters."

"I'm afraid I don't measure up. My books are entertainment, and my idea of a great time is a walk in the woods or a drive to a *Parkplatz* to cook sausage on the grill."

"I knew you were like that. I'm glad."

He was surprised, and paid attention to her. "You don't strike me as an outdoors person."

"I might surprise you. We have more in common than we discovered at lunch. That's why Pierre invited me here tonight to be your companion."

"I'm sorry he made you extend your working hours so late."

Her smile faded but did not entirely vanish. "You seem to want very much to fight with me. I didn't come tonight on orders. I wanted to come. I enjoyed lunch with you. I like you."

He was conscious of the growing attraction. She was much too young for him and the situation was impossible. But there was something about her which spoke to him at a level beyond rationality.

He flipped his cigarette into the flower bed.

"Ready to go back?" she asked, starting to turn.

Without thought, he reached for her. He heard her breath catch as she yielded, coming into his arms. She was electric there, fully against him, her mouth raising. It had been a long time since he had touched a woman, and as her mouth opened to him, his need hit the back of his skull with hammer force. Their kiss extended, moving from the tender and exploratory to bruising heat. She did not try to break from him. She returned his intensity with naked desire of her own. She was strong.

Shaken, he released her. She remained loosely in his arms, staring up at him with eyes that were darkly filled with mystery and excitement.

"I didn't plan that," he told her.

"I know."

"We'd . . . better get back inside with the others."

"If you're in the city you can call me," she told him. "And I'll be back out here Tuesday or Wednesday. I expect to be here at the house through the weekend."

Upstairs, the lights went out in LaFontaine's office.

"We'd better hurry back," Dugger told her.

11

Paris

On Monday it rained. Pierre LaFontaine did not go to the office in the city, but a steady stream of business visitors occupied him through much of the late morning and early afternoon. Dugger swam in the indoor pool and browsed the downstairs library. LaFontaine's interests ran to history, politics, engineering subjects, and modern methods of warfare. There were many documents from the United Nations, including its recently updated reports on *Basic Problems of Disarmament*. The volume had been thoroughly read and annotated, but the pages that showed the most wear were those on Chemical-Biological Warfare. Dugger noticed a seeming contradiction: these worn and finger-marked pages were the only ones in the volume which did not have marginal notes in LaFontaine's hand.

During the afternoon, he wandered upstairs. Locating the door to LaFontaine's office, he tested it. The knob turned and the door swung open into a large, deeply carpeted room with a high ceiling. There were more bookshelves on one wall, stuffed with journals and reports. The desk was massive, ornate, with a spotless top. Two filing cabinets stood against the other wall.

Dugger walked into the room and went to the nearest casement-type window. The latch was bronze, an ornate handle that thrust a rod into a slot. Dugger looked for security alarm devices such as studded all downstairs windows and doors, but found no wiring. He lifted the window lock and left it unobtrusively open. He then left the office quickly.

Downtown, at about the same time, the killer's rifle had been delivered. Unwrapping the package, which had been padded to considerable bulk to mask the real dimensions of the contents, the man identified as Bertell gave the weapon a minute inspection. The modifications had been done expertly to his precise specifications.

Sitting on the bed of his hotel room, the man traveling as Bertell rewrapped the rifle in oil-impregnated paper, taping it carefully. He then examined the custom-loaded cartridges, using a small magnifying glass. The loader had done a fine job as far as could be told.

Putting the wrapped rifle and box of shells on the bed, he tossed a coverlet over both. Turning to the telephone, he asked the desk to ring Room 20, the one directly below his. He listened to the telephone ring a dozen times before he hung up. Then, walking rapidly, he left his room and used the stairway to go down to the floor below. The hall was empty. He walked to the door of Room 20 and rapped loudly on it. Again there was no response.

Satisfied, Bertell went back up to his room and again locked himself in. Taking his suitcase out of the closet, he opened it and peeled back the lining of the lid. Beneath the lining was a thin saw blade approximately seven inches long, with one end sharply tapered.

The killer pushed his bed to one side a few feet and knelt on the bare plank floor. He inserted the thin saw blade between two of the floorboards and began sawing with vigorous care.

Within a very few minutes, the tapered end of the saw had started cutting through one of the boards, and Bertell was able to saw with full-length strokes. This speeded the work. Soon he was through the first board.

Less than twenty minutes later he had two of the floor planks sawed at both ends. Levering the boards out of the floor, he created a hole three feet long and six inches wide. In the cavity beneath the boards were joists, brightly fresh sawdust, and ancient dust and lint. Bertell carefully placed the wrapped rifle and box of bullets in this cavity.

Replacing the sawed boards, he took from his coat pocket a small can of precolored putty. Working carefully with a wide blade of his Swiss army knife, he filled the cracks in the boards he had removed. This done, he carefully picked up sawdust on the floor with pieces of wet toilet tissue, then used dry tissue to stir around some of the dust and lint balls that had been discovered when he moved the bed. Standing, he examined his work.

The boards would be removable in minutes. But no careless housekeeper would ever notice that they had been disturbed.

After moving the bed back to its proper place, Bertell replaced the saw blade in the suitcase lid. He then took the Skorpion from the bottom of his big camera case and examined it carefully before replacing it. He could not afford to hide this weapon. Use of the rifle would be carefully done, with time. If it came to using the automatic, he would need maximum speed because he would be in an emergency situation.

Bertell washed his hands and smoked a cigarette, standing at the window and looking down at the rainy street below. He felt an instant of stark isolation. These moments sometimes came when the preliminary work had all been done and it was a matter of waiting for the time of the killing.

It came to him that he might hire a whore. Although the whores of Paris were vastly overrated, as well as grossly overpriced, a few hours with one might calm him. He thought of his wife in Riga and decided that he owed it to her to relax himself just as much as possible. She did not want to become a widow, and in the hours ahead his life might depend on his state of rest and relaxed efficiency. A whore, then, for the therapy. Yes.

With nightfall the rain slacked off. Pierre LaFontaine wanted to play bridge after supper, but his wife begged off with a headache, retiring early to her room. The youthful wife of the Marandayan ambassador also went upstairs early, leaving Dugger with LaFontaine and Francis Corbinere.

"A chance to demolish you at bridge, and it's ruined!" LaFontaine said, throwing up his hands.

Corbinere said apologetically, "My bridge is really not so very good. It is Mr. Arata who is expert. Perhaps we could not have defeated them after all."

"I know your bridge." LaFontaine winked. "I was intending to saddle Joseph with you as a partner."

Dugger put down his brandy glass. "Maybe you gentlemen would rather talk business, anyway."

"Business?" LaFontaine looked blank.

"When does he arrive?" Dugger asked, electing the frontal approach.

"Arrive?" LaFontaine repeated.

"Pete, cut it out. Mr. Corbinere is here because Joe Obutu's arrival in Paris is imminent, and because it's obvious you plan to meet with him during his official visit. Tell me: does he get here tomorrow?"

LaFontaine studied him with sagging eyes. "You don't miss much."

"Is it tomorrow?"

LaFontaine glanced at Corbinere.

The diminutive African smiled nervously. "If we knew, Mr. Dugger, we could not reveal it to you."

"But it's soon, isn't it?"

"Oh yes," LaFontaine said. "It *could* be tomorrow."

"Will he be out here?"

"You mean at this house? Lord, no!"

"But you are going to meet with him."

"I may, yes, Joseph."

"I'm trying to put things together," Dugger told both men. "Portions of that manuscript I mentioned to you, Pete, could be leaked to the press at any time. Given the international mood today, it's sure to fan worse reaction against Obutu both here and at Atravi. All right; evidently someone is waiting for the perfect timing, to do him the maximum possible damage. *Why?*"

Neither man spoke. Both watched him somberly, expectant.

"It ties to your rocket investments," Dugger said. "A great many people don't want West German rocket research going on, especially in an African state. The Soviets don't like it. The other satellite nations don't like it, and neither do the Chinese. I'm not convinced the United States cares a whole hell of a lot for it, the way it's heightening tensions all over the place. And certainly all the loosely allied anti-German elements here in Europe don't like it—and neither do any of Marandaya's neighbors, I imagine, like Zambia and Cabinder and Nown.

"Presumably," Dugger went on, "Joseph Obutu is the man who has approved the testing. Presumably there are elements in every country and faction I just mentioned who feel strongly enough against the testing—for fear of Germany or fear of a rocket-armed Marandaya—to want Obutu overthrown or assassinated if they thought that would put an end to it. So my problem in identifying who leaked the information on old Joe is complicated by a plethora of suspects. *Everybody* wants him out, or dead. And a lot of them want you dead, too, I imagine, Pete."

LaFontaine puffed out his cheeks, then fitted a cigarette in his long holder and clamped it between his teeth to light it. "But I'm alive, Joseph, and well."

"Which puzzles the hell out of me, frankly. If *you* had been the one killed, instead of, say, Heidigger or one of the others, it might make sense. I might even be able to theorize that some of the rest of us were killed to screen the real motive for killing you. But here you sit."

"Proving?" LaFontaine puffed smoke and struck one of his FDR poses.

"I don't know what it proves. I think Joe Obutu is going to be in damned dangerous water when he arrives here in Paris. I think *you're* in danger, too. I can understand that. But somebody has tried to blow *me* away. I can't understand where I fit."

"It sounds," LaFontaine said with a faint smile, "like the puzzle is nowhere near a solution."

"I think you could move me a lot closer if you would, Pete."

"Me?" Again LaFontaine feigned astonishment.

"Are you planning broader tests in Marandaya? Bigger boosters? Sale of some of the rockets to Obutu as weaponry? What?"

"What makes you think *any* of these things are likely?"

"Because you're meeting with him when he gets to France. Because one of your West German business associates had to come out here last night for a quick consultation. Because"—he pointed at the African—"Corbinere is here, evidently to help arrange some kind of secret meeting. What are you up to? What are you planning with Joseph Obutu that has one or more terrorist groups printing a book and killing my old agents and God knows what else?"

LaFontaine glanced at Corbinere, then back at Dugger. His face was totally unreadable. "I don't know what you're talking about, Joseph."

"Regensburg," Dugger shot at him. "What happened at Regensburg? How does that tie in? God damn it, Pete, my life is among those on the line here, and you're holding out on me!"

"Joseph," LaFontaine said wearily, "I wish I could help you. It's all just as much a mystery to me as it is to you. I mean that sincerely."

Dugger reached in disgust for his brandy. He was thoroughly angry, but not so angry that he had missed the flickering change in Francis Corbinere's expression when he had mentioned Regensburg. *Corbinere knew about Regensburg, too.*

It was a key that both of them were holding out on him.

At midnight Dugger said good night and went to his second-floor bedroom. He turned out the lights, but removed only his shoes, lying on the bed fully awake. A little before one he heard LaFontaine's and Corbinere's voices distant in the long hallway. He consulted the luminous digits of his watch and waited.

By one-thirty the mansion seemed totally quiet.

Dugger waited another hour.

When he silently opened the tall windows of the bedroom at two thirty-five, he felt a freshening moist wind that riffled the curtains around his body. His room faced west, and on the distant horizon he could make out the sullen flickering of thunderclouds. Overhead, an occasional star could be seen through swollen black clouds.

Dugger stepped out through the window and onto the narrow concrete rail atop the balustrade surrounding the house at the second-floor level. The rail was about ten inches wide. It was a sheer drop of about thirty feet to the dark shrubs along the west side of the house.

Flattened hands against the cool stone facing of the building, Dugger edged to his right, leaving his room behind. He came to another set of windows, dark. He moved past this pair, and another, and came to the corner of the structure. The railing did not go around the corner smoothly, but broke on each side with a gap at the angle. Dugger paused, sweating. The window to the office was halfway around the south side and there was no way to get there but around this corner. But he did not want this risk.

There was no choice and no way to go at it cautiously. Leaning out from the protective wall as far as he dared, he swung his right leg out around the corner—trusted to luck that he was reaching far enough—and thrust his weight around the corner to the far side as he reached a clawing hand around at the same time.

His foot came down on the ledge but perilously near the edge. His heel started to go down into nothing. He strained his weight forward on the ball of the foot, clutching for any handhold as he felt his body swinging out to fall. His fingernails tore against the stone and then caught a little chink, digging in. He hopped on around the corner, slamming flat against the wall with eyes closed.

He had made it. He stood still, catching his breath.

The wet wind picked up, and lightning flickered nearer.

All he needed was a thunderstorm. He not only had to get to LaFontaine's office this way, he had to get back the way he had come. The office might have been left momentarily unlocked during daytime hours, but Dugger had no doubt that it was locked at night, and secured by an alarm device that prevented his opening it from *either* side.

He moved down the south face of the building. A distant security light seemed to put him in shocking glare, but he knew that his eyes had merely adjusted. Anyone below would have to stare directly at him to make him out in the darkness. He could not even see the pavement below this position, and although he could hear the whisper of water in the outside pool down the slope, he could not see it.

Reaching the window of the office that he had earlier left unlatched, he tested the metal frame with his fingertips. For a second or two it refused to move, and he thought someone had discovered it and relocked it. Then the metal casement moved outward sharply, very nearly propelling him backward off the ledge. He caught the other part of the window frame and swung himself onto the sill, then stepped down onto the carpet inside.

Fighting the impulse to gasp his breaths, he stood very still in the darkness. The edges of the room were indistinct, black. He could make out the corner of LaFontaine's desk and the fronts of the filing cabinets.

Moving silently, he went to the desk. He took a small penlight from his pants pocket and flicked it on, the tiny cone of light so bright to his dark-adjusted eyes that he winced. He tested the drawers. They were all locked.

Breaking them was out of the question, and Dugger had no lock-picking tools. Not that he would have known how to use them if he had had them. He shone the narrow beam of light across the top of the desk, empty except for a lamp, a letter tray with nothing in it, and the leather-framed green blotter. There were several scrawled notations on it, and he looked briefly at each of them.

One said 88.40 in large black-ink letters. A doodle box had been drawn around the numbers.

Letters must be signed, another read, underscored.

A third, written at an angle, said, *Corbinere*.

The fourth, nearer the bottom of the blotter, had three circles drawn around it: *Winged V.—4.*

There were several crudely drawn stars in the upper right-hand corner, and below them, partway down, a final scrawl: *Late winegrape harvest.*

The credenza behind the desk held only a small lacquered vase and the telephone, and Dugger realized that LaFontaine's scrawls had probably been done while he faced the desk, talking on that telephone. The mention of the French ambassador's name was intriguing, but could have meant anything—or nothing. He would remember the various words and symbols, but doubted that they were in any way helpful.

Kneeling, he gently opened the doors of the ornate credenza. The shelves contained stationery supplies, nothing else. He reclosed the doors and moved down the bookshelves, touching spines of journals and report folders with his fingertips as he scanned them. They all seemed to be technical stuff on a variety of subjects.

The top drawer of the left-hand two-drawer file cabinet was empty. The bottom drawer contained folders with such markings as *Routine repair, Household maintenance costs, Wine inventory*, and *Automotive*. Dugger pulled a few of the folders to be sure. Pierre LaFontaine was nothing if not a stickler for precise detail. Each folder was as labeled, and many contained tediously compiled lists of routine expenditures, guarantee cards, or canceled checks. It was beginning to look like Dugger had wasted his time.

Closing the drawer of the left-hand cabinet, he slid back the top drawer of the other one. The front of the drawer was filled with closely packed folders, some crammed with papers. In the back of the drawer were piled about a dozen reports of some kind.

Tabs on the folders were blank. Dugger pulled out one of medium thickness and opened it.

The top document consisted of about thirty stiff Xeroxed pages stapled together at the top left. Dugger had only to glance at the cover to get a shock. A depiction of the American eagle was emblazoned on the sheet with a circle around it formed by the words *Department of Defense* and *United States of America*. Dugger scanned the rest of the cover:

Report Bibliography

DEFENSE DOCUMENTATION CENTER
Defense Logistics Center
Cameron Center   Alexandria, Virginia 22314

TOP SECRET

Dugger hurriedly flipped the page. The next one was blank, and the one after that contained the Top Secret notation again and a warning about distribution or disclosure. The one after that contained a search control number and some verbiage that might have been significant to a scientist about the ''search strategy'' used by the computer in compiling the bibliography. He hurried past this to the next page:

UNCLASSIFIED

DDC REPORT BIBLIOGRAPHY   SEARCH CONTROL NO.
996557

AD-896   351L   15/2
DUGWAY PROVING GROUND UTAH

Behavior of BW Aerosols in Sub-Freezing Temperature, ''Operation Icicle,'' BW 330-B, Trials 3, 4, and 5.

DESCRIPTIVE NOTE: Interim Report
          Mar 57   8P
REPORT NO. DPG-IR-1007

UNCLASSIFIED REPORT

Distribution limited to U.S. Gov't agencies only; Test and Evaluation 19 Sept 72. Other request for this document must be referred to Commanding General, Desert Test Center, Attn: STEPD-TT-JP-I (S). Fort Douglas, Utah 84113.

DESCRIPTORS: (*BIOLOGICAL WARFARE AGENTS, COLD WEATHER TESTS). (*BACTERIAL AEROSOLS), (*BACILLUS SUBTILIS), FREEZING, ATMOSPHERIC TEMPERATURE, BIOLOGICAL BOMBS, BOMBLETS, GUINEA PIGS, SAMPLING, RECOVERY.

IDENTIFIERS: DECAY RATE, 3-61R4 BOMBS, E-61 BOMBS, FIELD ACTIVITIES, ICICLE OPERATION, PT-12 AEROSOL GENERATORS, RESPIRATORY INFECTIVITY, SLURRY AGENTS, *UL AGENTS, U/A REPORTS, VERTICAL GRIDS.

This report presents the results of three separate tests in which three PT-12 text fixtures, filled BG, and two E-61R4 bomblets, filled FP, were functioned simultaneously under sub-freezing temperatures. The total decay rates for the BG and UL aerosols were measured and compared for a distance of three-quarters of a mile from the source. The infective capacity of the UL aerosol was also ascertained.

Dugger turned the page to find a similar summary. He began to get a crawling sensation. He had never been called a bleeding heart, but chemical-biological warfare had always filled him with a sense of loathing and disgust. He had heard the callous arguments that death was death and CBW was just another weapon, and he knew the great effort expended by the army during the 1950s and '60s to try to convince the public in America on the same point. He had never been convinced. There was something obscene about CBW.

And this bibliography, page after page after page, summarized reports done over the years during the intense period of experimentation and development in CBW in the United States.

Most of the pages were stamped as unclassified. Dugger kept turning them, knowing that some pages had to have the top secret classifications to entitle the entire document to that classification.

Four pages from the back he found it:

TOP SECRET   TOP SECRET

DDC REPORT BIBLIOGRAPHY   SEARCH CONTROL
                                                          NO. 996557

AD-989   070L   15/9
BRADLEY PROVING GROUND S. PACIFIC

Test Report DPG-BW79-79
                    TOP SECRET REPORT
DESCRIPTORS: BIOLOGICAL WARFARE AGENTS, TESTS, GUINEA PIGS, MONKEYS, DOGS, INFECTIVE AGENTS, RESPIRATION, WATER, BIOASSAY, NERVE GAS COMPOUNDS, DECAY RATES, CONTAINER INTEGRITY, SOILS, PLANTS, CONTAMINATION, CULTURE MEDIA, UNKNOWN SUBSTANCES.

IDENTIFIERS: AGAR, FIELD ACTIVITIES, PETRI DISHES, PERSISTENCE, SLURRY AGENTS, LEAKAGE, ENVIRONMENT.

This report contains a summary of information and recommendations developed as a result of intensive testing of unknown CBW agents found in deteriorating containers near Regensburg, Germany. The first part of the report summarizes lethal agents and mutations isolated and identified during tests. The second part of the report discusses mass population dangers and problems of removal or disposal.

TOP SECRET REPORT

Dugger read the page twice with growing shock and incredulity. Kneeling, he glanced at the final pages, but hardly saw them. There was no possibility of coincidence. This explained too much—raised too many new possibilities. He had sought the meaning of "Regensburg."

Now he knew a part of it: the United States, only recently, had found a cache of CBW weapons near Regensburg. Whatever might have happened since that time, the discovery somehow had triggered many of the events in which he was now swept up.

His hand shook slightly as he replaced the file folder and started to withdraw another. Then he thought he heard a slight sound somewhere—outside, in the hallway or nearby in the house.

Distantly he heard a toilet flush, and rushing water. It sounded like the far end of the building. But it meant someone else was awake . . . might be prowling around.

He had to hurry. Pulling another folder, he opened it to find another Department of Defense document, also on CBW. He replaced it and pulled a third. This, classified secret, contained drawings of CBW bomblets. *Christ, the entire drawer was filled with stolen secret documents!*

There was no time to read everything. Pushing in past the folders, he lifted out several of the thick reports at the back. Most were tied together with ribbon. The top one was separate.

He opened it, skipped past the classification pages, found the title:

CBW AGENTS FOUND AT REGENSBURG, GERMANY
Report of Field Testing
TOP SECRET REPORT

Dugger was stunned. LaFontaine not only had bibliographies and directories, he also had many of the secret reports themselves. For whatever reasons, and however accomplished, he had compiled a fantastic cache of CBW secrets . . . probably over a period of at least three or four years.

How? Why? Dugger was still too close to shock to begin looking for these answers. And there was not time now. He had already been in the locked room far too long for safety.

But he could not leave quite yet. Not before reading the Regensburg report.

Kneeling, he began to read.

12

New York City

Tuesday morning.

Eileen Arrington had been standing at her apartment door for more than five minutes when she saw the taxi with the designated number glide by. Gathering up her purse and portfolio, she hurried down the steps, waving frantically. The cab squeaked to a halt several car lengths past her address. She hurried to catch it, climbed in, and slammed the door.

The driver was hunched low behind the wheel and wore a battered baseball cap. He did not turn. "Where to, lady?"

"The UN Building, please."

Flipping the meter flag down, he pulled away, making the clutch chatter. At the corner, he turned left into dense traffic with the right-fender aggression of a born cabbie.

Only then did Rick Kelley turn and give her a quick smile. "You okay?"

"Yes, but your call didn't reassure me any."

"The signal only said I needed to contact you this way, babe."

"Yes, but this is for emergencies. What's gone wrong?"

Kelley turned right, nosing off a Lincoln. "I'm going to drive downtown a few blocks and then double back. Give us time to talk."

"All right. What is it?"

"I'm not sure it's right or wrong, but the big boys wanted me to update you pronto. We watched for Leonard

Jenkins, the man you fingered after the reception the other night, and sure enough we found him having lunch with Grover Matsoon. Got a picture and a positive make on him.''

"We identified him from files?'' Eileen said tensely.

"The son of a bitch's real name is Haas. Fritz Haas. The Bonn government wants him for espionage. That dates back to 1978. A couple of years later he came back home to Brooklyn and was linked to that guy who sold copies of the Early Bird satellite manual to the Russians. Since then he's been on *our* wanted list.''

Eileen leaned back against the slick, dirty seat of the taxi. She pressed her hands to her cheeks. Her fingers felt cold. "Have you picked him up?''

"Nope, that's part of what I needed to talk to you about. We might have enough to make something stick on him and we might not. In either case, picking him up now would scare everybody else off. The decision is to leave him alone awhile longer and see how much more you can pick up.''

"How much more *I* can pick up? It looks like you could follow Jenkins or Haas, or whatever his real name is, and get it all that way.''

"They've been wary as hell lately. We think they've picked up on our surveillance teams, and are being super cautious. Thanks to your efforts, the big boys are convinced we're close to busting this thing. So what they're going to do is let Haas-Jenkins swim right along, and in addition they're pulling the surveillance off Endidi, Matsoon, and everybody else.''

"Pull the surveillance *off?*''

"Yep. The theory being that Jenkins-Haas *et al* will figure we gave it up, or are looking at our hole card or something, and they'll promptly get active again. Which is where the big shots figure you come in.''

"I'm not sure,'' Eileen said dazedly, "I see how.''

"They figure you're trusted inside the group now. They figure you've already accomplished more than all the rest of the boys had in a period of months. So they're pulling everybody else off and leaving it to you to make the big break single-handed." Kelley made another turn, prompting angry horn-honking from the right. "You're the fair-haired girl, for sure."

Despite her tension, Eileen smiled. "Hey. Is that a racist remark?"

Kelley glanced back at her. "Oh, shit. I forgot. I'm sorry."

"Don't be sorry," Eileen told him with real fondness. "People *have* been known to forget."

"Shit, you're the *last* person I would—"

"Rick, I understand that. It's okay. Forget it."

"Anyway," he sighed, waiting in line to turn onto First Avenue, "they wanted you brought up-to-date. They think there will be a flurry of all kinds of activity—including the clandestine kind—in the next forty-eight hours. It looks like the General Assembly will invite Gero Paasaad to address them real quick-like, and that's bound to lead to things. The big boys hope it will also motivate your friends to do some plain-and-fancy secret-passing, and you can tip us off when to pounce on 'em."

"The debate on an invitation to Paasaad is this morning."

"I know."

"The Bureau thinks the vote will be positive?"

"The boys seem pretty sure."

"The people I've talked to at the UN aren't that sure."

"Bet on it," Kelley said, turning left onto First.

"All right," Eileen said dubiously. "But are they *sure* they want to trust to me to get this done?"

"You're the star, kiddo. Surveillance hasn't worked anyhow. So this is a wing-and-a-prayer deal now, and you're the angel. Hey, get a couple bucks out to pay me when we pull up over yonder."

Eileen dug in her purse. She felt shaky. "I hope I'm up to this, Rick."

"Hey," he growled. "Of course you are. But just remember one thing, okay? With the surveillance off, you really *are* going to be on your own now. So for Christ sake don't try anything dumb and heroic. I mean it!''

"Why, Mr. Kelley," she said softly, half teasing him, "if you weren't a good southern boy, I might think you cared."

He pulled the cab to the curb and slipped the transmission into neutral. As he turned to take her fare, there was no smile in his eyes. "You just be careful, like I said. When this operation is over, I intend to have a talk with you about . . . caring."

Their fingers brushed as the money was transferred. She felt electricity.

Saying nothing, head down, she got out of the cab and walked briskly toward the Secretariat Building.

At 11:15 A.M., the General Assembly voted to issue a formal invitation to Gero Paasaad as spokesman for the Marandayan rebels. The invitation, worded by Tella Rhonta as a spokesman for Nown and introducer of the resolution, asked Paasaad to address the Assembly "at your convenience."

Paasaad, according to the representative from Zaire, was already at a secret retreat in Canada, and would fly to New York to address the Assembly Wednesday morning.

The vote and subsequent announcement of availability were met by prolonged and enthusiastic applause from a majority in the Assembly Hall. Only members of the Marandayan delegation and most of the white delegates were notably silent and unmoved by enthusiasm. Exceptions were the members of the Soviet delegation who left with broad smiles.

Eileen Arrington was in the public gallery for the vote, and made it a point to intercept a glowering Clarence Endidi when he left the Hall.

"It was inevitable," he told her, a steely self-control masking his expression. "Paasaad has a great following, and Marandaya's unrest was one of the three reasons the special session was called this summer."

Eileen kept up with his long strides in the corridor. They passed a heroic oil painting done by a Scandinavian artist.

"But it makes him out a hero when he's a mass murderer."

Endidi mustered a thin smile. "He is seen as a freedom fighter."

"Killing children and old people from ambush? Mailing letter bombs?"

"My dear Eileen, there is certainly precedent for inviting terrorists to speak to us."

"You're taking it more calmly than I expected. There's nothing you plan to do to try to head it off?"

"There is *no way* to head it off. He will speak tomorrow."

"And what will that do to your country? It *has* to make things worse!"

"From the standpoint of President Obutu's government, yes."

"You represent President Obutu's government."

"I know that very well," Endidi snapped.

"Did you see the Russians?" Eileen fumed. "They were chortling."

"Of course. The Soviets officially support Paasaad. Just as your inept government, in its interfering way, tries to support President Obutu."

"When *we* take sides, it's 'interference.' But I don't hear you condemning the Soviets."

"Eileen, you understand nothing. The Russian government has always supported freedom movements. The United States has always worked against them to maintain a corrupt status quo. This is simple history."

"So you don't blame the Russians?" Eileen asked, astonished.

"They appear wrong in this case. But their motives are pure."

"My God," Eileen said. "I suppose you don't blame Tella Rhonta for her part in issuing this invitation for the same reason. Her 'motives' are pure!"

"I support the Obutu government," Endidi told her stiffly. "But I do not see communist conspiracy behind every bush. Tella is acting on instructions of her government; she, too, has been misled.''

They stopped in a corridor intersection. People flowed past them on all sides. Eileen studied his angry, troubled face. ''What would *you* do, Clary, if you could have it any way you wanted?''

''I would strike Paasaad with full fury,'' he announced with suppressed ferocity. ''His head would hang in the square in Atravi. But my president plans social outings with effete whites in Paris, instead.''

Eileen could not reply. *This* was an honest response. It showed her not only the depths of Endidi's suffering and concern for his country, but the extent of his disillusionment with the government he served.

Clarence Endidi, she thought suddenly, was a man in a trap. Trapped into speaking for a government whose policies he did not wholly support . . . trapped in an idealism that was amazing in its naïveté. For the first time, she saw how he might also be a dupe. He might not really understand the motives of some of the people around him, or the things they were doing against Marandaya . . . against the national interests of the United States.

One hundred feet away, Tella Rhonta walked into the broad hallway and looked ahead to see Eileen standing in the intersection with Endidi. Tella snapped her fingers impatiently.

''Jealousy,'' her companion smiled amiably.

''No,'' Tella snapped at him. ''Why would she be here *now?* She has been all over this place! She's a spy, I tell you!''

''But your inquiries have—''

''Damn the inquiries, then! There's another way to prove what she really is.''

''How?''

''I know how to bait a trap for her.''

''Tella, you could be taking a big chance. If you are wrong—''

''I am not wrong! And I will prove to you I am not wrong. Tomorrow.''

Atravi

A blinding sun baked the concrete apron of the Atravi airport. Dust devils whirled across the patchy grass beyond the long runway. The military bandsmen, sweltering in their heavily brocaded red uniforms, bravely played the Marandayan national anthem, the hot wind tearing their harmony to tatters. In the distance, military helicopters shuttled back and forth on top-priority security patrol. In the shadow of the presidential jetliner, the crack palace brigade stood at rigid attention as Joseph Obutu walked past them.

Obutu reached the stairs of the jet and stood on the red carpet, his new shoes hurting his feet. His wife and small son stood nearby, along with General Marcos Arman and three other high military officers. Obutu had already bid farewell to the mayor of Atravi and four tribal leaders.

General Arman saluted sharply. "Your staff is aboard, Mr. President. The crew reports it is standing by for immediate departure."

A quartet of F-104 military fighters screamed overhead in tight formation. Obutu glanced up in appreciation. "And our escort is ready."

"Yes, Mr. President."

"You have your instructions for the time I will be in Paris, Marcos."

Arman was in full-dress uniform, and sweat streamed down his face. But he stood at full attention and clicked his heels sharply. "I will follow them precisely, Mr. President."

Obutu turned to the other officers and shook hands with them. He turned back to Arman.

"God give you the wisdom to conclude a fine treaty in Paris, Mr. President."

"And may our gods make your work here in Atravi wise and fruitful," Obutu said, using the formal, almost ritualistic language.

Arman's face worked with obvious emotion. Touched, Obutu stepped forward impulsively and grabbed him in a bear hug. "Take care, my friend!"

"We count the hours until your return, Mr. President."

Tears in his eyes, Obutu knelt to hug his little boy, then rose to embrace his wife. Her lips brushed his cheek before he stepped back, still holding her arms.

"It will be only a few days," he told her.

She smiled. "We will be here, waiting, my husband."

He pulled her close again for an instant, then turned and strode briskly up the stairs to the plane. The moment he was inside, the ground crew closed the hatch and the starboard engines whined into activity. The stairs were rolled back, General Arman solicitously escorted the wife and child to an air-conditioned Lincoln waiting nearby, and the port engines got rolling. The band played a tattered anthem again as turbine wash buffeted them in the wake of the taxiing plane.

Each principal was filled with emotion.

For Joseph Obutu, it was regret at having to leave his family at such a time. But they had to remain behind to void any rumors that the trip was an abdication. And it would not be long, he told himself. There were only a few wrinkles yet to be ironed out of the mutual aid pact in Paris, and when he returned, he would be in triumph.

For Shana, the president's wife, the feeling was a loneliness that had begun the moment she turned from the plane. She was also afraid. He was risking his political future—perhaps his very life—on this mission to France. He could not return to Atravi too soon for her.

For General Marcos Arman, however, the feelings were more complex. Watching the aircraft turn onto the distant runway and nose into the gritty wind, he felt a burst of elation that was mixed with mind-numbing awareness of the dangers and complexities that lay immediately ahead. For in seventy-two hours, Joseph Obutu would be dead. And he, Marcos Arman, would be the new, self-proclaimed president of Marandaya.

13

Paris

Pierre LaFontaine had gone to the city very early Tuesday morning, which gave Dugger some time for hard thinking. When LaFontaine returned a little after noon, a young aide helping carry in armloads of contract folders and other work, it was obviously an appropriate time.

"Into the city?" LaFontaine repeated, frowning. "My driver could take you, Joe."

"I have some shopping," Dugger said. "So I think it would be better if I drove myself."

"All right, my friend." LaFontaine cocked an ironic eye at the work folders piled on a table in the living room. "I have something to keep me occupied."

There was a chance that friends from the Agency might intercept him the moment the rental car poked its snoot out of the estate, and he was prepared for this eventuality. It did not happen. He drove quickly into Paris without incident.

The usual roaring traffic around the monuments of the Place de la Concorde was complicated on his arrival by city trucks and crews which seemed to be everywhere. French flags were being strung from every standard, and bleachers being thrown up along the east end of the Champs Élysées, where it fed into the Concorde, and in front of the Obelisk. The commotion made no sense until Dugger remembered the date: Thursday would be Bastille Day, and the great holiday would be marked with parades and other events likely to draw hundreds of thousands of French villagers to this spot.

He wondered if Joseph Obutu would choose the great French holiday for his arrival.

Finding a place to park with great difficulty, he walked to the corner of the Concorde and through the gate in the barred fence to the American embassy. He was stopped at the door by a marine guard acting on information relayed from the gate. After a little while, he was passed on to someone else, and it took almost an hour to make his point clear:

"I want your man representing the Central Intelligence Agency. I have some vital security information. That's all I'm saying until I see some credentials."

Finally he was escorted into a small office that was dusty from nonuse. The dingy windows, without curtains, looked out into trees of the side yard. He paced up and down, smoking cigarettes and wondering if he had made a serious mistake.

After a while, the office door opened. He turned. "For God's sake," he said, feeling a little better.

Charles McCoy closed the door behind him and walked across the room to shake hands. "Hello again, Joe. It's been a while since my visit to Burghausen."

"And considerable water has gone over the dam."

McCoy sat down behind the dusty desk. "I won't go into explaining why I'm in Paris except to say I'm probably here for the same reasons you are. You gave my associate in Stuttgart a start on a new ulcer, Joe."

"He thought I ought to hide out."

"I know that."

"Then I got to Paris and he sent a couple of assholes to take me into custody."

"I know about that, too."

"And you know where I've been recently?"

McCoy gave him a thin smile. "Pierre LaFontaine's."

"Maybe you also know," Dugger said, "that Pete has a filing cabinet full of stolen secret documents out there. American documents."

McCoy's smile went away. "How do you know that?"

"I crawled around the ledge of the house in the middle

of the night and burgled his office.''

McCoy studied him for a moment as if to decide if he was telling the truth, then evidently decided. ''Sounds like fun.''

''Oh, it was a barrel of laughs.''

''What kind of documents?''

''I didn't have time to look at all of them. All I saw were CBW.''

McCoy made a tent with his fingers and sighed.

''And I know all about Regensburg,'' Dugger told him.

''Do you, now?''

''Maybe not all. Enough to make some guesses. I know the army found eighty tons of the stuff in an underground laboratory-factory that had been buried under the old *Panzer Kaserne* at Regensburg ever since 1945. Some of it was in explosive shells for artillery use and some in experimental warheads for a rocket that was supposed to follow the V-2. A lot more—the report wasn't too specific on this point—was raw, in containers approximating fifty-gallon drums.''

''Your information is pretty good,'' McCoy said, watching him.

''Some of the stuff was pretty straightforward,'' Dugger told him. ''Zyklon-B and the newer stuff the Germans developed late in 1944 and considered using on the eastern front.''

''That was one possibility they considered,'' McCoy told him. ''They also talked about using it on the Brits after we destroyed Cologne in that big fire-bombing.''

''Why didn't they?''

''Fear of retaliation. They knew we had mountains of similar stuff. Roosevelt had already warned them that we would use it if they gave us any provocation. There are some who think we *wanted* to try it out. Everyone knows the Brits would have used gas if the Germans had invaded across the channel. General Marshall and the Joint Chiefs wanted to use it on every landing in the Pacific after the pasting we took at Iwo Jima. There was a detailed plan for using it in invading Kyushu, and we already had modifications to allow the B-29s to drop all kinds of CBW material the minute someone gave the green light.''

"So the Germans just left it lying there," Dugger said. "Yes."

"And then it got buried in the hasty retreat, and no one ever told."

"Your information is still accurate."

"I know a lot more."

"Do you know what was found at Regensburg, specifically?"

"Oh, hell yes," Dugger said sarcastically. "Zyklon-B. Phosgene. Plague. Cholera. Tabun. Sarin. Typhus. Yellow Fever. Mustard Gas. Arsinol. Adamsite. All that good stuff.''

"All of that," McCoy said. "And then some."

"The report got very technical, and I'm not too bright. But as nearly as I could make it out, some of the compounds had deteriorated and some of the germs had sort of died of old age. But some were just as virulent as when they had been packaged, and some had recombined— either through a process we don't understand very well or through sheer bad luck—into some nice new things that scared hell out of our technicians when they started trying to test them."

McCoy nodded again, his face somber. "It isn't in the report you're evidently quoting from, but seven technicians died during the testing."

"Jesus Christ. From what?"

"They called it Strain C. It wasn't definitively identified. As soon as they realized how virulent it was, they destroyed the remaining specimens in the lab by fire. That was when they decided they couldn't risk simply detoxifying everything still underground at Regensburg. It was *all* deadly stuff, Joe. But there was enough of some of it, especially Strain C, to start an epidemic that would kill half the people on the globe."

"So what did they do?" Dugger asked, thinking he knew.

"It couldn't be buried where it was. No one had any

estimate of how long those microbes and viruses might go on living, even in an airless environment, and there could always be an accident. And destroying it all on the spot was out of the question; it would have taken a thousand men a hundred years, working with Bunsen burners and test tube quantities, and bulk destruction just ran too much risk of some crazy spore escaping into the atmosphere and starting a plague like none we've ever known.''

"So it was moved," Dugger prodded.

"Yes."

"Where?"

McCoy's eyes showed a trace of irritation. "Don't you know? Aren't you playing games with me?"

"I can guess: Marandaya."

"You've got it. Give that man his cigar."

"*Why?*" Dugger demanded. "Of all the places in the world: the oceans, the Antarctic, little atolls in the Pacific . . . !"

"The ocean was considered," McCoy told him. "It's always been a good garbage dump. The Brits dumped 175,000 tons of CBW weaponry into the North Sea between 1945 and 1948—"

"Don't lecture me, God damn it. Answer me."

"Danger of leakage and contamination. Strain C and at least one other mutated strain do not dilute and die in either fresh or salt water. Still, it was considered. Crews went in and sealed all the stuff at Regensburg in large blocks of solid poured concrete. One of these was flown to the Pacific for testing. A ship took it out about halfway between Pitcairn Island and the coast of South America. It was dropped over the side and suspended on an anchor cable, and a couple of depth charges detonated close to it to destroy the integrity of the concrete housing.

"The idea," McCoy continued, "was to allow a medical team on board to see if any disease organisms might do damage to the environment if a container ever broke open by accident on the ocean floor."

"There was a fish kill?"

"Tides carried the stuff east. Three months later there

was a massive fish kill reported off the coast of Chile, south of Santiago. You might have read about it at the time. It was a worldwide mystery: ocean perch, crab, and even sharks and whales were reported in countless numbers all up and down the beaches and at sea. Scientists reported an estimated hundred million birds dead along the coastline. It's a very isolated region of the world, but the World Health Organization estimates that as many as six hundred people died also.''

Dugger felt a distinct chill. ''From one container a thousand miles away?''

''More than two thousand miles away. And the container was approximately fifty imperial gallons.''

''All right,'' Dugger said after lighting another cigarette. ''The stuff is deadly—one more wonderful thing from the guys who brought you World War Two. It had to be buried. It's buried in *Marandaya?*''

''In their southern highlands.'' McCoy nodded. ''If you're familiar with the plate theory of geology, you know that these massive plates are sort of floating around on the earth's core. Where plates collide, there are geologic anomalies.''

''The earthquakes on the west coast of America.''

''Yes. The San Andreas fault is one sign of plate movement. So are volcanoes in Central and South America. So, for that matter, are the Alps. In Marandaya there's a plate convergence. There—and also in Zaire, which is obviously out of the question—the pressures have produced enormously deep caverns, breaks in the earth that go down, in the case of Marandaya, to a depth of as much as six miles.''

''The world's greatest natural dump?''

McCoy did not smile. ''We thought so at the time, apparently. The stuff was flown out of Germany in C-130s direct to Marandaya and buried there. The shafts were sealed with concrete plugs, and Joseph Obutu leased us fifty thousand acres around it for construction of high-power radar and radio monitoring apparatus beamed at Russia. That gear is all there, incidentally, but it was put there to give us an excuse for a continuing presence. In case you're wondering, the terms of the secret lease paid Marandaya a hundred million outright, and twenty million a year in perpetuity.''

Dugger smoked furiously, assimilating it. ''I begin to see why we have such an interest in keeping old Joe in power.''

''Yes. It would look very nice if the Russians could expose the site and talk about how we were willing to risk the lives of millions of Africans just to save ourselves a little bother.''

''That's why they want him discredited,'' Dugger added, seeing it. ''Either they get a pro-Soviet leader into power, and get the chance to expose the site, or—''

''Or they force us to step in directly to prop him up, which makes us look like mud anyway,'' McCoy concluded.

''How does the West German rocket testing tie in?''

''It doesn't. They're drawing attention and unfavorable criticism to Marandaya when that's the last thing we want. We want their asses *out* of Marandaya.''

''But here's Pete LaFontaine with a drawer full of secret papers about CBW. I'd bet he knows as much as you've just told me. Why? What does *he* want out of this?''

McCoy looked at him.

''Oh, shit no,'' Dugger said.

''It makes sense, doesn't it? He's into building rockets. The ultimate weapon—''

''You mean that stuff could be recovered?''

''With modern drilling techniques, yes. It would be dangerous, but with modern techniques it definitely could be brought back up again.''

''I'm convinced LaFontaine plans to meet with Obutu when he comes to Paris,'' Dugger said. ''Is *that* what he's trying to get Obutu to agree to?''

''We don't know,'' McCoy said.

''Who is going to so much trouble to bring more trouble down on Obutu? The Russians? For reasons already stated?''

"We don't know," McCoy repeated.

"Is Paasaad, the rebel leader, one of their boys?"

"We can't be sure."

"How do *I* tie in? Why did someone take a crack at me? Why are my former agents dead—all of them but Frank Bauer and LaFontaine? I can see why someone would want Obutu out of power, or dead. I can see how LaFontaine has put himself in the middle of a target for all sorts of groups, and that's a risk he's running with his eyes wide open. But what about me? What's my connection? What made me a target?"

"We don't know," McCoy said for the third time.

"I'll stay with LaFontaine," Dugger said, "unless some of your boys want to practice arresting me again. He's a key. And I think you know you've got your work cut out for you when Obutu arrives. They'll leak information from that book about the time he gets here. There will be demonstrations. I wouldn't be surprised if someone made an attempt on his life."

"You didn't see the morning papers," McCoy said.

"Meaning?"

"The story has already leaked. The demonstrations have already started here and in New York and in Atravi. And Obutu's jet touched down at Orly about forty minutes ago."

At the same time Dugger sat in the embassy office with Charles McCoy, Joseph Obutu was being ushered into the hotel suite which would be his headquarters in Paris. His three aides and the two gentlemen representing the French government joined him in a champagne toast to success of the mission.

"You will meet this evening with our president and minister for defense?" the French spokesman asked.

"I look forward to it," Obutu told him. "My position papers are ready, and I hope to begin seeking final answers to our treaty language problems at once."

"I believe I speak for our government, Mr. President,

when I state that no problem remaining is insurmountable.''

Obutu strode to the windows and looked out on the maniac Paris traffic. ''It will give me great pleasure, sir, if we can announce details of our accord the day after tomorrow, during your Bastille Day ceremonies.''

''We will all work toward that end, Mr. President.''

Obutu turned back to smile at the men in the room. But even as he did so, he felt a distinct chill deep in his body. The sensation startled him, and he remembered that the British or Americans had an explanation for such a sensation. *Someone*, he thought, *is walking on my grave*.

He brusquely dismissed the thought. He was here. The historic meetings were about to begin. He had General Arman back in Atravi to watch after things while he was gone, and he knew Arman was the one man in his country whom he could trust implicitly.

The feeling was only a touch of homesickness, he told himself. It felt distinctly strange to be back in Europe after so many years. It had changed. He had changed. The world was different.

The chill struck again, and to combat it he walked directly to the chilled bottles of champagne at the sideboard. Raising a bottle high, he grinned and walked around, refilling glasses.

''Another toast, gentlemen! To friendship, and our future!''

A quarter of the way around the world, in Atravi, General Marcos Arman handed a list to three of his trusted lieutenants. It contained seven names.

''At once,'' he told them. ''In absolute secrecy.''

His men saluted and marched out of the office without a word.

Arman then went to his desk and took a .45-caliber revolver from the locked bottom drawer. His heels clicked loudly in the corridors as he made his way from the main palace building to the even older building next door which housed the offices of the Assembly. It was dusty here, and silent, but he knew that his man would be here even though the Assembly was not in session.

On the second floor, which seemed deserted, he opened the office door.

Tavecki Vi, the presiding officer of the Marandayan Assembly, was alone in the suite. Bent over a thick law-book, the skinny, bald old man was trying to read the small print with the aid of a large magnifying glass. It was not an unusual occupation for a man whom some called the first father of Marandayan independence, a fierce spokesman for individual liberties whose dedication to freedom and law was surpassed only by his near-legendary friendship with Joseph Obutu, the man he himself had called his spiritual son.

Tavecki Vi's colorful floor-length robe swirled sharply as he turned, realizing someone was in the room behind him. He was eighty now, but looked far older. His rheumy eyes widened at sight of Arman's gun.

"Come on, old man," Arman said sharply.

"What is it?" Tavecki Vi asked in a reedy voice of alarm. "What has happened?"

"What has happened, old fool, is that you are under arrest. It is a pleasure I have reserved for myself. Come. You are a student of history. You know the palace compound. I will let you lead me to your new quarters in the royal dungeons."

With a sharp cry, Tavecki Vi launched himself at Arman. Arman stepped away from his rush and slammed the barrel of the revolver onto the bald crown of his head. Blood spurted, and the old man went down with a sound of bones hitting the concrete floor. He did not move.

Muttering, General Arman went looking for a guard to drag him.

By the time Dugger returned to the mansion in the country, it was very late in the afternoon. Maria LaFontaine was on the rear patio, sipping a drink alone. From far back on the grounds came the sound of distant gunfire.

"Pierre is amusing himself on the range," she told him, shading her eyes to look up at him. "He invited you to join him when you returned. Or if you prefer, you can have a drink here with me."

"The drink with you sounds better," Dugger told her, "but I might just go let him know I'm back."

She was wearing a white pleated skirt with a pale lavender blouse and leg-flattering high heels. Reclining partially on the chaise, she moved her left leg slightly so that her skirt slid partway up her thigh. "Does he really have to know at once?"

Dugger hesitated, trying to read her eyes. The invitation was there, and he saw that she was not just practicing. He was surprised, but then he remembered Marlene Dortmund and the surprise went away.

He said, "Actually, I do have something important to tell him at once."

Her slight smile held, disappointment entering her eyes. "Of course," she said indifferently.

Dugger turned and started toward the back of the gardens.

"Do remind him that our guests will arrive soon," she called after him.

He grinned and waved. Her expression was thoughtful; both of them knew that the possibility had been raised and a final answer withheld.

Dugger hiked through the gardens and past a small metal gate in the wall. Beyond the wall, the grounds were carefully mowed, punctuated at formal intervals by clumps of shrubs and trees. A gravel path wide enough for a cart wound downhill and to the west. Shoes crunching, he followed the path and in moments had walked around a small grove of fruit trees on the knob of earth that blocked vision from the house. Down the hill several hundred yards, at a point where a small stream traversed the meadow, Pierre LaFontaine stood alone on one of the shooting pads of a skeet range. A white golf cart was parked on the path nearby. As Dugger watched, LaFontaine foot-tripped an automatic device, and a clay target sailed from the squat shed nearby. LaFontaine's shotgun belched gray smoke, and he was moved slightly by the recoil. The target disintegrated. Only then did the sound of the report reach Dugger's ears.

As he walked on down toward the range, Dugger considered his options. Neither McCoy nor the FBI legate who had later been called into the meeting at the embassy had any clear idea of what was going on. They believed Joseph Obutu's life was in danger in Paris, as did the French police. Elaborate security precautions were being taken. They were not sure how LaFontaine tied in, unless he was another logical target.

"LaFontaine is going to try to have a meeting with Obutu," Dugger had told them.

"Of course," McCoy had replied. "The question is, when? And where?"

It was an oversimplification. There were many more questions than that.

Reaching the range, Dugger watched his old friend shoot a few more targets. LaFontaine was monotonously good. Dugger noticed that there was a rifle range set up downhill from the skeet range, with the target area against a man-made hillock near the creek.

LaFontaine broke the shotgun to insert two fresh shells and turned toward him, eyes obscured by the yellow shooting goggles. "About six more, Joe."

Dugger waved assent.

"Want to have a try?"

"No, thanks."

LaFontaine went over to the throwing shed and made some sort of adjustment to the machine inside.

Dugger strolled on down the path toward the rifle range. The shooting line was thirty feet long, and its place in the tufted grass was marked by the litter of small-arms cartridges. He walked on down to the target area and examined the concrete trench positions behind the target area. LaFontaine had not spared expense in installing target-raising devices. Several could be operated by a single attendant. A trash container nearby was stuffed full of the paper targets, and others had blown out of the container into the creek bottom. Dugger went down the little embankment to the narrow, swift-moving stream and knelt to test it with his hands. It was cold and clear. Careful not to stir the gravel bottom, he scooped a handful and tasted it, then drank.

One of the wind-blown targets was quite close to his position. Tangled in grass, it had not been carried downstream. He pulled the soggy sheet loose and looked at it, then smiled. LaFontaine had not done this shooting. The tiny punch holes of small-arms bullets were scattered all over the target.

Another target was also near, and he picked it up also, still smiling. This one was older, the paper almost disintegrated by rain. But the shot pattern was still clear. Just to the left of the bull's-eye, and a half inch low, the target was simply torn to pieces.

His smile dying, Dugger examined it more carefully. The pattern was incredibly tight. By examining the edges of the pattern, he could see that it had been repeatedly punctured by slugs of heavier caliber than the usual sporting load.

Behind him, LaFontaine's shooting had stopped. Dugger crumpled the target and put it in his coat pocket. As he climbed back out of the creek bottom, LaFontaine whirred up in the golf cart.

"Sure you won't have a go, Joseph?"

"Thanks, Pete, but Maria sent me down to remind you that your company will be here soon."

LaFontaine winced. "More business companions. It's a cruel life."

Dugger got into the cart and they started back up the path. "I imagine your business started turning especially hectic today."

LaFontaine glanced at him. "Why would you guess that?"

"Obutu landed a few hours ago."

"Did he *really?*"

"Come on, Pete," Dugger said wearily.

"Well, all right. Of course I knew."

"You're going to see him when?"

"Oh, I doubt that I'll see him, Joseph. It would be very pleasant, and useful in terms of assuring that we're all on the same wavelength about future testing for our boosters. But I rather imagine he's going to be much too busy with weightier matters."

"Too bad."

"Yes, it is."

"You have a very nice rifle range. Judging by the shell casings on the ground, it's well used."

LaFontaine steered the cart with his knee while fitting a cigarette into the holder. "We allow the local police to practice there sometimes, and there is one rod and gun club."

"Big-bore stuff?"

"Oh no. The police sometimes fire their service pistols, but they're dreadful shots, totally unlike American police, and they don't really seem to enjoy it. Everything else is target caliber."

Dugger did not reply. For the first time, deep suspicion of Pierre LaFontaine took root in him. He had assumed that LaFontaine's interest lay in keeping Joseph Obutu alive as well as friendly. The fact that someone—someone very, very good—had used the range now changed that. Perhaps LaFontaine had already tried to get to the Regensburg cache through Obutu and Obutu had steadfastly refused. Perhaps now LaFontaine's interests could be achieved only with Obutu out of the way.

It was a bad thought. It changed everything.

Within an hour, the guests had arrived. The French official Georges Trouveau had returned, again with his dour, chain-smoking wife. After spending most of the day somewhere in Paris, the Marandayan spokesman Francis Corbinere was also again on the scene, saying that his wife was slightly ill in a hotel in Paris. To Dugger's mild surprise, Anita Courtright also returned, bringing with her a tall, cadaverous man who was introduced as Dr. Jacques Clabon.

While drinks were being served in the warm evening air on the patio, Pierre LaFontaine promptly vanished with Corbinere. Maria LaFontaine, now wearing a strapless black cocktail dress that seemed uncharacteristic of her, although it did wonders for her figure, presided over the conversation. Dugger caught her eyes on him at several points and sensed that the dress was for him. He felt slightly uncomfortable. Although her almost severe business suit paled in comparison, Anita Courtright was the one who engaged his interest.

"Do you plan to come into the city for any of the great events?" she asked Dugger during a lull.

"Bastile Day, or President Obutu's visit?" Dugger countered.

Maria commented, "They do seem to be getting mixed."

Trouveau said, "The Marandayan president's activities will surely be private, especially after the events of this afternoon."

"Events?" Anita echoed.

Trouveau scowled at his drink. "Two small bombs were detonated in the city today. A continuing demonstration goes on at the hotel of President Obutu. Rumors are everywhere. Our police are very busy, I can assure you."

Maria LaFontaine stirred. "Let's do talk about something more pleasant."

Dugger turned to Dr. Clabon, who had sat silent, drinking steadily, through earlier conversation. His bony frame looked collapsed inside an ill-fitting dark suit, and a slender cigar was clamped in his bearded jaw. "You're a medical doctor, sir?"

"I do not treat patients," Clabon said, his bass voice touched by only the slightest accent. "My specialty lies in research."

"Dr. Clabon," Anita Courtright said, "is a consultant for our medical publishing firm in Brussels."

"What brings you to Paris, Doctor?" Dugger probed gently.

"A client-author is here," Clabon replied, puffing a dense cloud of smoke and reaching again for his drink. "Certain questions have arisen concerning his manu-script."

"It's quite fascinating," Anita told the group. "The man here is writing a complete history of chemical-biolog-ical warfare."

"How dreadful!" Marie LaFontaine murmured.

"At least," Dugger said with a smile, "such a book would be short."

Clabon cocked his head. "How would that be so?"

"CBW is a very recent invention. A history would have little—"

"Quite to the contrary," Clabon snapped, flicking ashes from the cigar in the general direction of an ash stand. "Biological warfare goes back for centuries."

"Is that so? I had no idea." Dugger wanted to keep him talking.

Maria LaFontaine, however, was clearly uneasy. "Is this a subject for cocktail conversation? I really find it less than pleasant."

"It's fascinating," Anita Courtright said. "Do tell them a few of the highlights that have been uncovered, Jacques."

A trace of color appeared in Dr. Clabon's cheeks, proving he was not impervious to the attention of a beautiful young woman. "Biological warfare is an an-tiquity," he said. "There is a book I have seen, Varillas' *Histoire de l'hérésie de Viclef, Jean Hus et de Jérôme de Prague*. It was published at Lyon in 1682, and tells how attackers of the city of Carolstein threw the corpses of soldiers, and thousands of carloads of excrement, over the walls in 1422."

Maria made a tiny clucking sound and showed her dis-approval. Clabon glanced at her with surprise, but con-tinued:

"It has been suggested that such tactics date back even

earlier. Some believe that besiegers of Kaffa, a Genoese trading post in the Crimea, hurled plague victims over the wall in about 1346. There are those who believe that survivors of the attack carried the plague back to Europe subsequently, leading to the first outbreak of the Black Death on our own continent.''

Maria LaFontaine was growing more restive, but Dugger found this interesting for several reasons. He tossed the doctor a new stimulus: ''If I remember my early American history correctly, Doctor, the American Indians were exposed to smallpox in a similar way.''

Clabon rolled bulging eyes. ''Indeed, sir, that is so. A British officer gave chieftains gifts of blankets and handkerchiefs which had been heavily infected. This led to a great epidemic in the Ohio country.''

''But what *we* know as CBW is modern,'' Anita Courtright observed.

''Indeed, yes,'' Clabon said, warming to his topic. ''Most advancement has come since the turn of this century. In the early days of World War One, the German army tried to spread anthrax and glanders by injecting horses and cattle. Chemical attacks—chlorine gas—began at Ypres in 1915. By 1918, the Germans alone had produced almost five hundred tons of chemical weapons.''

''Of course it was very crude in those days,'' Dugger prodded.

''By today's standards, perhaps, sir. But the early weapons were not ineffective. Tear gas was improved continually. Chlorine was soon supplanted by phosgene, a much better killer—six times more deadly, actually, and with a desirable delayed effect. Then, once all combatants had finally laid aside all vestige of concern for the old Hague agreements, there were further refinements. The French people developed hydrogen cyanide, the British hydrogen sulphide. The Germans then found ways to use 2-chloroethyl sulphide in their yellow cross shell, and development became very rapid: Betholite, Clairsite, Collongite, Zusatz, CG, Forestite, Cyclon, Surpalite, Klop, diphosgene, CB, PS, Perstoff, Acquinite, Vitrite,

CBR, green star, and so on.''

For a moment no one spoke. Dugger stepped in. ''I'm amazed, Doctor, at the amount of knowledge you carry in your head from a single manuscript.''

Dr. Clabon looked at him sharply. ''I do not understand.''

''You speak like a man with a consuming interest, and not merely a copy doctor.''

Clabon's smile was forced. ''It is much on my mind at the moment, since I soon meet the author to discuss problems.''

''Does the book also cover more recent developments?''

''*Must* we continue this?'' Maria LaFontaine asked crossly.

''But it's so fascinating!'' Anita said.

''I find it distressing in the extreme.''

''Just one more question,'' Dugger said. ''Does the book tell also about German development of the nerve gases?''

''Indeed it does,'' Clabon said, appearing uneasy.

''Wasn't the first real nerve gas Tabun?''

''Yes.'' Clabon wanted it ended now. Dugger first wondered why, then realized that someone had come into the room behind him and now stood in the patio doors. Clabon had already seen who it was. Dugger could guess.

He said, ''I recall that it was I. G. Farben who developed Tabun as part of research into so-called insecticides. Wasn't that in 1936?''

''Indeed,'' Clabon agreed. ''And of course there was intense experimentation into germ warfare—plague, cholera —many things—at the special SS post in Posen in later years.''

Pierre LaFontaine walked out of the doorway and into the group. His smile was tense. ''What are we discussing?''

''Germ warfare, my darling,'' Maria said with distaste.

LaFontaine went gray. His eyes spat sparks at Clabon, but then he caught himself. ''Well, enough of that, eh? Let us have one more drink, and then soon we can have dinner. . . . Georges, I understand the government has a new program planned to bolster Peugeot. Tell us about that, eh?''

After dinner, Dugger was again on the patio, now in almost total darkness. Most of the others were in the living area. Anita Courtright came outside and walked over to join him.

"A solitary smoker," she smiled. "Very dangerous."

"Thinking."

"Pierre was very angry with Dr. Clabon."

"Yes," Dugger agreed. "That was what I was thinking about."

"I can't imagine why he was so angry."

"Can't you?"

"No."

"Clabon is no book research expert," Dugger told her, "and I think we both know that."

"I'm not sure I understand you."

"Anita, your job for Pete may require a pose, but we're alone. I know pretty well what you know and I also know exactly who you really are."

She looked at him, the lovely lines of her face grim as she studied his expression. Finally she said, "You know that, do you?"

"Yes."

"When did you guess?"

"Today sometime. I don't know exactly when."

"I thought," she said ruefully, "I was better than that."

"Oh, you're very good. I'm sure Pete and the others accept you absolutely at face value. Which is good. But it's getting late in the day for you to bullshit me anymore."

She sighed and reached into his shirt pocket for a cigarette, which he lighted for her. She exhaled smoke. "It was fun, getting to know you . . . wondering which direction we were going to go."

"Part of the assignment?"

"Don't be a bastard, okay?"

"Okay. I'm sorry. Tell me: are you Bureau or Agency?"

"The Agency—the same as you are."

"Were."

"Were, then."

"Who is Clabon?"

"He's legitimate, a scientist-editor."

"There really is a publishing firm?"

Anita smiled thinly. "Oh yes."

"Is he here for the reasons he said?"

"As far as I know, yes. But Pierre went white when he found him drinking, and talking so freely. You noticed that, I'm sure."

"I noticed," Dugger admitted. "Which makes me think Clabon is more than he appears—more than an editor. But I also suspect that Pete wouldn't have had him here if he had known his weakness for booze and tendency to blow off his face."

"He gave you a lot of information, but I'm not sure I know what to make of it."

"I'm not sure either. But Pete considered his talkativeness very bad news. I intend to file that. Clabon probably drank too much too fast because he's feeling a lot of pressure. I intend to file that, too."

She nodded. "Yes. Clabon was a mistake. Maybe we can capitalize on it."

"We?" He looked at her.

"We're allies now."

"Are we?"

"I know a little about your meeting with Charlie McCoy today."

"Jesus. Everyone knows more than I do. All right. Let me tell you one you don't know. Somebody has been target-shooting—recently—with a high-powered rifle down on Pete's range. The man is a crack shot, one of the best I've ever seen, judging from the pattern. And Pete pretends, at least, not to know anything about it."

"Have you told anyone?"

"You. That's part of your job, isn't it? To report back on me?"

"It might have been, as an extra duty. It isn't now.

You're back in the fold and you know it. You're just wanting to be a bastard again.''

"Be that as it may, you might want to pass the word along about the shooting.''

"What do you think it means?''

"I don't know,'' he said wearily. ''We'd better get back inside.''

She touched cool fingers to his arm. "Joe?''

"Yeah.''

"The part about . . . liking you. That wasn't operational.''

"I'm glad of that,'' he said.

He would have liked to say more. The feeling was there. He could not allow it. Not now. The pressure was too great from every other direction, and he needed all the control he could muster. There were too many decisions to make.

He walked back into the house, allowing her to follow on her own.

14

Paris

In the morning, it was almost like a holiday. Francis
Corbinere had stayed over, as had Anita Courtright. Guy
Arata, chief of the Marandayan delegation to the UN, was
in a private meeting with Pierre LaFontaine when Dugger
got downstairs. Before Dugger had finished his coffee and
rolls, Dr. Clabon appeared, having also stayed the night.
Then Georges Trouveau drove in, using a government limousine.

LaFontaine shuttled from private meeting to private
meeting in the house.

Dugger managed a few words with the dour Clabon over
coffee.

"It's a difficult day to meet your author, Doctor, with
so many other meetings in the wind."

"Yes," Clabon said, munching a hard roll. He was
sober and pale. "But I will manage."

"Your talk about CBW last night interested me. I
wonder if I might pose a hypothetic question."

Clabon looked at him and said nothing.

"Suppose," Dugger said, "some very old CBW
weapons were found. Would they, you think, pose a
present danger?"

Clabon's forehead furrowed. "I have no comment."

"Old weapons. Say, CBW materials produced by the
Germans in World War Two. Would such materials be of
any value today?"

"I doubt it," Clabon said. "I do not wish to discuss it."

"There are no known methods of maintaining potency?" Certain germs, for example, couldn't still be in lethal powder form?"

"This is not my interest," Clabon said stiffly, uncomfortable.

"I see," Dugger said. "I was thinking that possibly certain nerve gases might remain potent, and that some kinds of disease organisms could still be deadly in one form or another."

Clabon sipped his coffee and abruptly got to his feet. "If you will excuse me."

The fishing expedition seemed to have been fruitless. Clabon had been told about his loose talk last night, Dugger thought; there would be no more such mistakes from him.

A few minutes later it was Guy Arata who entered the glassed-in sun porch. "M. Dugger. Good morning." Arata looked pin-neat in a gray summer suit and narrow dark tie. A diamond ring glittered on his left pinkie. He seemed tightly strung, overalert. "These are exciting days."

"Are the negoiations going well?" Dugger asked.

"My information is that they are proceeding well indeed, sir. There is to be a reception late today at the palace, and it is my high hope that the new accords may be announced at that time."

"That's good news," Dugger said. "But I was talking about your negotiations with Mr. LaFontaine."

"I know of no such negotiations, sir."

"When does Mr. LaFontaine meet with President Obutu?"

"Why should such a meeting be contemplated, sir? You talk in riddles!"

Dugger changed tack. "Will you be seeing your president at the reception?"

"No, sir. I will not attend the reception. You had something in mind?"

"I have met President Obutu," Dugger told him. "I

hoped you might pass along my regards, and a small personal message.''

"I regret then, M. Dugger, that I will not see our president at all today. If you will excuse me now?''

As he walked out, he was met in the doorway by the chief of LaFontaine's household staff, the dour man called Crouex. Crouex was bringing a fresh pot of coffee for the warmer on the tile-topped sideboard. He gave Dugger a curt nod, replaced the coffee, and turned to leave.

"Do you have a moment, Crouex?'' Dugger asked.

The small, angular servant turned, his face a polite mask. "Yes, sir?''

"When Mr. LaFontaine is away, and also Mrs. LaFontaine, who runs the house?''

"If both are away, sir, then I make whatever minor decisions may need to be made.''

"You would also make decisions about such things as, say, who got past the gate?''

"The gate system is very new, sir, and no formal protocol has been established.''

"But you would make such a decision.''

"Yes, sir.'' Crouex's close-set eyes betrayed curiosity. "If I may ask, sir, is there relevance to your question?''

"I'm curious about who might have been using the rifle range in the last few weeks.''

"The rifle range, sir? No one.''

"You're quite sure of that?''

"Yes, sir. Quite.''

"When would you say the last time was that the range was used?''

Crouex frowned in thought. "March, sir.''

"Oh no,'' Dugger told him. "Much too early. It's been used since then, Crouex.''

"No, sir. I believe not.''

"The range was used within the last three weeks,'' Dugger told him. "Someone fired with a high-power rifle. I found the target. The man was an expert.''

Crouex's face showed no expression. "There were two

days when I was on holiday, sir. It is possible some member of the police used the range in my absence. If it's important, I could query other members of the staff—''

''Don't bother,'' Dugger said indifferently. ''Thank you.''

Crouex left the porch.

Dugger found Anita Courtright in an upstairs room, typing pages from stenographic notes. She stopped when he walked in.

''They put me to work,'' she said ruefully.

''Important?''

''I think it's busywork to smoke-screen things: routine letters.''

''Who is he with now?''

''Corbinere.''

''What are they talking about?''

''I don't know.''

''I'm going into town,'' Dugger told her. ''I think McCoy needs to know who's out here and our best estimate of what's going on. He ought to be told about finding the target on the range, too. I just questioned Crouex about that, incidentally.''

''My God, was that wise?''

''Possibly not. I don't know if he has a role here or not. I want him to sweat if he is involved.''

''Adding pressure?''

''Yes.''

''That can be dangerous.''

''Also productive.''

She thought about it and sighed worriedly. ''You're going now?''

''I'll be back by lunchtime.''

''I could ride along with you.''

''Will the boss allow that?''

''I think so.'' Standing, she smiled as she covered the typewriter. ''I need the air.''

Crouex himself brought the rented car around to the front. It seemed to be running rough, but smoothed out once they had gone through the guarded front gate and onto the highway. To reach the village, it was necessary to leave the main road and take a narrow one, the paving none too good, through a series of valleys and along several hillsides. It was dairy cattle country primarily, pastoral today under a brightly hazy sky. The temperature was about 20° Centigrade.

Halfway to the village, on the right-hand side, they passed a crumbling chalk cliff. Perched on top was the ruin of a very old castle. Slowing the car to negotiate the hairpin turn below its position, Dugger asked about it. Anita Courtright knew only that there had been some talk of restoration, talk which so far had obviously accomplished nothing. The ruin was isolated, stark-looking against the high clouds.

"This is still Pierre's property," Anita told him. "So if you really want to know, you could ask him."

"Why the hell," Dugger asked, "would a man like Pete need to get involved in trying to buy—or steal—old CBW weapons when he already has so much?"

"Profit?"

"I suppose so. But doesn't he have enough?"

She smiled ruefully. "Does anyone ever have enough? Having more just creates bigger wants, doesn't it?"

Dugger did not answer. It made as much sense as any other theory he had come up with.

In the village, there was a pay phone at a service station. Dugger got into the embassy in Paris, and McCoy was available. Dugger told him about the shell casings on LaFontaine's range and the people at the mansion. McCoy said security had already been tightened around Joseph Obutu as a result of a demonstration at his hotel which had almost overwhelmed the police on duty. He had no— or would not admit any—information on the talks in progress with the French government.

"Someone is going to try to kill him, Charlie."

"I know. What are your plans?"

"Until I know exactly where LaFontaine fits in, I'm going to do my best to keep my eye on him."

The clouds had thickened slightly after Dugger gassed

the car and started back toward the house, taking the same winding road. A blue BMW tagged after them as they headed again into the remote countryside.

"I can't believe Pierre knows about anyone practicing for an assassination attempt on his range," Anita said.

"It could be practice for an attempt on him," Dugger said.

"Doesn't he *know* that half the governments in the world will take action to prevent removal of those weapons from Marandaya?"

Dugger delayed his reply as he glanced in the small rear-view mirror. The blue BMW had speeded up considerably, was coming down the hillside behind them at a high rate of speed. There was deep ditch, and trees, on both sides of the narrow roadway. He relaxed pressure on the accelerator pedal to give the car room to pass.

"He's crazy," Anita Courtright said, glancing back.

Dugger did not reply, inching his wheels closer to the crumbling edge of the blacktop and slowing further.

The BMW flashed out beside them on the left. Tires squealed. The BMW veered to the right, into Dugger's fender. The steering wheel was almost torn from his hands, and he felt his right-side tires wobbling on the edge of the drop. He hit the brakes and cut the wheel sharply left. Metal grated. The BMW veered left again and swung back behind them.

"He's trying to run us off the road!" Anita said.

Dugger had no time for talk. The bumper of the BMW crashed into the rear of his Renault, snapping his neck. He jammed the accelerator to the floor, downshifting to second. The combination of impact and acceleration moved him perhaps five feet in front of the BMW, which veered left again, trying to get alongside.

"Who's driving it?" he yelled.

"I can't see—the sun on the windshield—"

Dugger sawed hard on the wheel as the Renault drifted around the tight turn at the bottom of the hill, tires screaming. He shifted up, gaining speed, but the BMW was on his bumper. Again he was jolted hard as the two cars touched. He was again on the brink of losing control and on the wrong side of the road, and the BMW tried to move alongside on the *right*. He jerked the wheel back hard, regaining a measure of equilibrium. In the rearview mirror he saw the grille of the BMW, blinding in the sun, move rapidly from right to left again.

The road ahead vaulted up a brief, left-turning hill and then around a sharp curve to the right for a downhill slope on the far side. Dugger tried to remember the road beyond, but was too busy maintaining control. The speedometer crept up past 65 kph. Inexplicably, the BMW dropped back a few car lengths, then started closing again as the driver evidently shifted. Dugger clawed for his shoulder harness and managed to buckle it, and saw Anita doing the same.

They reached the crest of the sidehill with the BMW inches behind. Dugger fed power mercilessly to the little engine as he started the sharp curve. He felt the wheels chittering on the brink of loss of control, but they held. The BMW dropped back a few feet again as they skidded around the turn and started down the far side.

"Have you seen who it is yet?"

"No! I can't!"

The road clung to the side of the hill with trees tightly packed along the sharp embankment on the right. On the left, the drop was sheer for seventy or eighty feet, with a creek meandering below. Up ahead, the road reached the valley level and turned right again, sharply. There was heavy brush on both sides, and some trees. Dugger was vaguely aware of the castle ruins off to the left and beyond. He poured on the power. They were going far faster than he would have ever dared under any normal circumstances.

"We're not going to make that turn!" Anita cried.

"No choice," Dugger grated. A glance in the mirror showed the BMW on the left side of the road again, and he felt the jarring impact as the other car's right front sawed into his left rear. The wheel tried to saw out of his control again as he spun it left, forcing the BMW back to avoid itself going off the road.

Rear end swishing from side to side, the Renault pounded down toward the curve at the bottom. The BMW was close. Sweat stung Dugger's eyes as he eased up marginally on the accelerator. There was an immediate heavy impact, and something came off the car with a loud clatter of metal against roadway. He saw bright metal flying over the precipice and then was too busy again, keeping a semblance of control.

The impact had driven them faster and the curve was just ahead a few car lengths. It was perhaps already too late, but Dugger saw that they could not possibly make the curve. Behind him there was screaming of tires, and he had an instant to observe the BMW swerving wildly, smoke billowing from all four tires, their brakes locked. Dugger stood on his own brake pedal, but now it was too late. The little car simply slid straight ahead, the rear end fishtailing very slightly right.

The curve—a guard rail—filled the windshield. There was no chance of making it. He heard rather than felt the impact as the car went through the flimsy rail and flew entirely over the shallow ditch. It hit in deep brush and small trees with shocking impact, and the windshield went. Fragments stung his face and hands, and Anita Courtright cried out. Somehow the car hit on all wheels. It seemed buried in a torrent of green and black—deep shrubbery and tree leaves. The ground underneath was muddy, and he could feel the wheels striking rocks or stumps in the mud as it continued its mad slide.

Then, suddenly, the car stopped.

Dugger sat stunned, his rib cage afire from being thrown against the belt. He knew he was bleeding from the face, but he could see. Where the windshield had been there was now a ragged opaque opening. Steam billowed from the shattered hood. The car was in a shallow ditch of some kind, almost entirely buried in tree limbs and brush.

Beside him, Anita groaned. He turned and saw her unbuckling her belt. She appeared dazed but unhurt.

"We have to get out," he told her. "Fire."

She nodded. Pushing violently against her door, she

didn't budge it. Dugger tried his side. The door opened a few feet, scraping loudly, and then refused to go farther. He rolled out into wet brush and leaned back across to help her scramble out through his side.

"I've hurt my shoulder," she said matter-of-factly, clutching it.

Dugger helped her stand. Trees formed a broken canopy over them. Looking back, he could see with amazement the distance they had come through guard rail, leaping the ditch, practically tunneling through the underbrush. They had left a ragged swath more than a hundred feet in length.

It was then that he heard the sound of the car engine. He stepped past the end of the wrecked car to get a view up the road beyond the site of their crash.

The blue BMW was partway up the far hill above them. It was backing back down toward them.

Dugger grabbed Anita's hand. "Come on!"

"Where?"

"Away from this car, *anywhere*."

They thrashed through the tangling underbrush and encountered the steep embankment of a small stream, perhaps the one they had seen from the road. Dugger tumbled down into it and helped Anita down behind him. It was shady and dank, with water running an inch deep over pebbles.

"Which way?"

Dugger pointed. "Up."

It occurred to him that the sound of their splashing might be heard all over the field, but they had no choice. They could make faster time by staying in the creek bottom than by fighting the dense vegetation. Their pursuer had not been satisfied to run them off the road; he had been coming back to make sure the job was done. If Dugger could not escape, at least he could find some ground where the odds were slightly closer to even.

He knew he had been stupid, leaving his gun in the suitcase in his room. But it was supposed to be a routine trip to the village.

The creek bottom became steeper as it went uphill, and within minutes they had to abandon it as it became a trickling waterfall. Great boulders were tumbled over the hillside, and Dugger saw that they had come out not far below the crest of the hill that held the castle ruins. Directly overhead, an ancient stone wall stood blackish against the brightly cloudy sky, vines and creepers everywhere.

Below their position, the blue BMW was pulled off the edge of the road. The driver's side door stood open. There was no sign of the driver.

"We can hide somewhere in there," Dugger said. He had to grasp Anita's hand to help her upward. Her shoulder was hurt worse than she had said, and she was deathly pale. But she made no sound as they clambered upward.

They started across a gravel slope. The end of one of the castle walls was just ahead a few paces, towering overhead. As Dugger stepped forward, something hummed off the ground nearby with an ugly, spiteful sound.

"Run for it!" he said. "He's shooting!"

There was no sound of gunfire, so he had a silencer. Something cracked into a rock nearby, and then a piece of the wall flew off in tiny fragments as they ran behind it. They leaned against the wall, momentarily out of the line of fire, catching their breath. Anita bent over, her hair hanging down around her face, and a thin brown stream of vomit extended silently to the ground. She shuddered, wiped her mouth with her sleeve, and faced him again.

"I'm all right now."

"He's not giving up. We have to keep moving."

The wall that hid them extended downhill from another, older one which intersected at right angles. The main walls of the great structure lay beyond the second wall. Holding her hand, Dugger led the way up to the second wall. There had been a gate, but stones had fallen out of the arch, partially barring the way. They climbed around the fallen rocks and found themselves in a small grassy enclosure where a few small oaks had begun to sprout. To the right, the declivity which had once been a moat was now choked with creepers and ivy. The narrow wood drawbridge had fallen.

Dugger led the way to the fallen drawbridge. Rocks had fallen from th massive interior wall, forming a natural stairway. He climbed up first, perching on top to reach back and give her a hand. Together they went through a tightly enclosed stone fighting station and then through another narrow hole in an ancient wall.

They had emerged into what had once been the central courtyard of the castle. The sun moved in and out of clouds, casting harsh, moving shadows. The effect was almost like standing on the floor of a stadium; wings of the castle surrounded the yard, throwing most of it in deep shadow. Stairs led upward at several points, and a second-level rock platform ran almost all the way around the buildings at a height of about fifty feet. There were turrets at the corners, sheer rock walls everywhere with gaping slot-windows.

Dugger pointed. "Up there."

They hurried up the centuries-worn stairs to the upper level. Doorways without doors opened everywhere into black interior caverns. There had been tourists or pick-nickers; sandwich wrappers and other bits of trash littered the dusty stone walkway.

Narrower stairs went still higher, evidently toward the roof, with its jagged sawtooth top where perhaps archers had once been stationed. Dugger hesitated, trying to pick the best hiding place. Something slammed spitefully into the rock wall above his head, showering both him and Anita with fragments.

Back in the courtyard, the figure of a lone man darted back into the shadow of a broken wall.

Dugger pushed Anita ahead of him into the nearest doorway. Inside it was warm and stale-smelling. He moved forward, intent on going deep into the structure—and bumped solidly into a wall not ten feet from the door.

"I can't find the way out!" Anita whispered.

Dugger made his way around the solid stone walls as his

eyes adjusted. There *was* no way out. They had blundered into a *cul-de-sac*, some sort of ancient storage room that had only the single door.

He moved back to the door, flattened against the wall, and signaled Anita for silence. Beyond the door was the slight sigh of the wind through rotting timbers some where, over the old stones. But then he caught another sound, regular, almost inaudible, a slight scraping.

The man coming up the stone steps below them.

Dugger risked a glance out through the door. He could not see the top of the stairs, but knew it was only a few steps to the left. The man would come off the steps and walk almost directly to this door. The stone railing of this upper walkway was partly eroded or fallen away, so that there was nothing at this point on the edge—it simply stopped, with a sheer drop all the way to the courtyard floor. It provided absolutely nothing for Dugger and Anita to hide behind if they tried to make a run for it.

Dugger looked at the floor of the room, wishing for a rock or some length of wood that might make a club. There were cigarette butts and candy wrappers, nothing more. Anita stood against the far wall, hands pressed back ward against the rock, watching him with keenly fright ened eyes which understood their predicament.

Outside and out of view, a foot scraped stone. The gunman had reached the top of the steps. Dugger wiped sweat from his own eyes and then froze, breathing shallowly because he could hear the other man's labored breathing.

Anita Courtright had not moved. To Dugger's light adjusted eyes, she seemed perfectly exposed in any view from outside the doorway. The man would look in and see her instantly.

The scraping sound outside resumed. Dugger gauged the sound and realized it was getting fainter. The man was moving in the other direction, away from them. He almost began to hope for a few seconds, but then there was a louder scrape and the footsteps sounded louder again. He was coming back.

Dugger slipped a bit closer to the door, standing now just behind its edge. He could hear the other man breathing again, harsh breathing, as if the man had a touch of asthma. Dugger could imagine him, gun in hand, moving with great caution now until he could again spot their location. It was not fun for the other man, either. He must know by now that they were not armed, but he had lost all sight of them and could not predict their actions. He must feel reasonably secure, the other man, but hardly sanguine. His instincts undoubtedly were telling him not to risk this lone pursuit. But his orders clearly were to see that they were dead, and no slipups.

The man was closer to the doorway. Dugger's nerves strung tight, and it was all he could do to keep from moving because the man was *very close*, perhaps just on the opposite side of the stone wall.

In another moment he would look into the doorway.

Dugger waited, and watched Anita Courtright.

She stood flat against the wall, the reflected light seeming bright on her body and upturned face. Her eyes were riveted on the doorway, expectant.

There was the slightest scraping sound outside.

Anita stiffened, her eyes widening.

Which meant he was looking in, blinded by the relative brightness outside.

Dugger moved into the opening. The figure was there, black against the bright sunlight. The figure grunted surprise, but by that time Dugger had slammed both hands into his chest, clawing for the rough material of a suit coat, and driving him backward with all the strength in his legs.

The gun went off deafeningly beside Dugger's ear and he was blind for an instant. He kept driving, with churning legs. The man staggered and then suddenly pitched backward, out of control, and Dugger let go. The figure went off the edge of the walkway and plunged out of sight.

Through his deafness Dugger heard tatters of the scream. And the thud.

He had fallen much too far to survive it. When Dugger

and Anita rushed down the steps and found him sprawled on the bloody pavement stones, he was not at all pretty. But he was identifiable.

He was Pierre LaFontaine's household chief, Crouex.

15

General Marcos Arman looked up from his handwritten list to the ramrod-straight young major standing in front of the presidential desk. "You have a trusted and capable man in the headquarters of Colonel Irgundi?"

"Sir, Captain Iru is with the colonel."

"Excellent. You stressed that he is to take no action until the order comes from me personally?"

"Yes, sir. Each man understands this most important provision."

"Everything will remain normal for the remainder of today. We are only a handful at this time, Major. Not until we have succeeded, and shown dramatically our dedication to the new Marandaya, can all the slaves and lackeys become aware of our actions."

"I understand, sir. Each of us understands."

Arman consulted his list. "The guards for the radio stations?"

"On alert, sir, but out of public view."

"The newspaper?"

"Sir, the editorial staff will be placed under arrest at 1800 hours, and the facilities padlocked. The telephones to and from the building will go out of order ten minutes prior to that time."

"The president's family is locked in quarters?"

"Yes, sir."

"They are comfortable? You understand they are to be

treated well. We will not outrage world opinion by mistreating them in any way.''

"Yes, sir.''

"The foreign diplomatic corps and newsmen?''

"Sir, within the hour I shall personally appear in the press ministry offices to give the first information on the serious battle beginning in the Anwami Province. At 1630 hours, the unmarked aircraft will strafe the airport for three minutes and fly away. I will announce details of this unprovoked attack immediately. The release stating details of the attack on the hospital and orphanage in Anwami will be given at the same press conference. I shall state, as planned, that a pitched battle is under way near the Catholic mission of St. Barbara.''

"Excellent,'' Arman said, smiling as he considered the effects of the carefully wrought fabrications. "I will be here in the office with Captain Zarbo. He and I will handle personally all calls from members of the Assembly.'' He glanced at his list. "The telephone cables, wireless facilities, and satellite access terminal?''

"All will be placed under military control and censorship promptly at 1630, sir, and disabled at 2330.''

"And the airports will be closed.''

"Yes, sir. As the schedule indicates.''

Arman clapped a hand on the major's shoulder. "By tomorrow this time, Major, our victory over Gero Paasaad will be complete!''

The major was youthful for his rank, and fanatically dedicated. He actually got tears in his eyes. "We have waited long for this day, sir!''

Arman dismissed him and remained in the office for some time, studying his list and searching for flaws in the long-planned sequence of events. He was so excited that he felt slightly ill. The false reports of heavy fighting in the Anwami Province, followed by the attack on the airport, would create a sensation around the world. The members of the world press here in Atravi, he thought, would flock to the scene just as planned. With them out of the way, and the communications blackout total, the rest of the plan could be carried out. It would be important to complete the arrests and assassinations within a very few hours, followed by the announcement. . . .

Leaving the office, he secretly marveled that the office staff was at work quite normally. Lieutenant Sissiwim was even flirting with the young encoding clerk again, and she seemed to be enjoying it. And the old crone, Mrs. Julo, was covertly watching them, and pursing her mouth in bitter disapproval, just as she so often did. This normalcy was just as it should be, but Arman was still amazed that it could all be going so splendidly, with no one suspecting.

Entering the elevator, he rode to the lowest level. The corridor into which he stepped at the bottom was brightly tiled, immaculate. But the odor of dank rot permeated the modern fixtures and partitions.

He walked briskly through the power monitoring station, nodding to the corporal on guard, then entered a concrete tunnel. Occasional bare light bulbs in the curved ceiling showed seepage running down the walls, forming puddles here and there on the floor. He walked carefully to avoid marring the finish of his gleaming leather boots.

At the far end of the tunnel was a steel door. It led to another tunnel, one much older, with rough rock walls and heavier seepage. He walked through this to an intersection tunnel, and then went deeper into the earth again, taking two more side turns. At last he came to a widening, with heavily barred doors. The light was quite bright here, and it was cold. Two soldiers snapped to attention, the butts of their rifles hammering the stone floor.

General Arman saluted casually and waited while they unlocked the doors. The same doors thudded closed behind him, and even knowing that he could walk out at any time, he still felt a quick chill at the sound.

The light was faint, from a single bulb in a high rock ceiling. Grayish slime grew on the walls. Arman squinted in the dimness until he made out a very slight movement on the far side, then walked to it.

Tavecki Vi, the old man whose legend and intelligence ruled the Marandayan Assembly despite his great age, was hunkered on a half-rotted army blanket in the middle of his cell. The blanket was sodden from water on the floor, and so were the old man's robes. A pan of maggoty broth lay untouched near the barred door, and as Arman approached, a mouse or small rat scurried away from it. Tavecki Vi was shaking steadily, as if from a chill. Dried blood caked his face.

"Eat, old man," Arman told him, his voice echoing and re-echoing. "You will need your strength."

"Why am I arrested?" Tavecki Vi asked in a strong but quavering voice. "On what charge? When is my hearing?"

"You are under arrest on my authority. There will be no hearing. Surely you have worked that out in your mind."

"The Constitution guarantees—"

"You can forget your milksop Constitution, old man! This is now a military government! Our dedication is to one thing and one thing only: the destruction of Gero Paasaad and his rabble, which will deliver us from the tyranny of fear and uncertainty!"

"The people will never allow you to take over, Arman. When President Obutu hears of this, he will return immediately to rally his—"

"Are the maggots already in your brain, you old fool? Obutu is in Paris, and in a very few hours he will be dead. I am in charge now. The months and even years of weakling government are at an end. Paasaad and all his ilk are about to feel the full force of our power!"

"You will never succeed," Tavecki Vi said, but his voice trembled.

"Tomorrow," Arman told him, "after the tragedy of Obutu's death in Paris, the formation of the provisional government will be announced. There will be nothing you or anyone can do about it by then. You will be released at that time. You will call the Assembly into emergency session, on my command, and formally authorize all emergency powers and actions I stipulate to you."

Tavecki Vi's skinny shoulders squared. The look that

flared from his runny old eyes was shockingly youthful and full of vigor. "Never!"

"The new government," Arman told him, "will not pursue the milksop policies of the old. Paasaad will be executed, his troops shot. There can be nothing to prevent this."

"The rights of every citizen—"

"Old man! There *are* no rights as of this minute! *This* government will be *strong!*"

"I will never cooperate."

"Then you will be shot . . . or allowed to sit here until you rot. I advise you to think about it most carefully."

With that, General Marcos Arman turned and walked out of the dungeon.

New York City

Eileen Arrington had never seen Clarence Endidi like this.

Hurrying up the staircase toward the General Assembly Hall, he moved with strides that were long and urgent, as if they were late, although they were in the mainstream of the multinational throng flocking to the Hall to hear the speech by terrorist leader Gero Paasaad. Endidi's face was so tight with tension that his teeth were actually bared. His eyes were dark and wet, fiercely angry.

"Will he speak at once?" Eileen asked, hurrying to keep up.

"Yes," Endidi said. "Finally."

It was 2 P.M. There had been a delay, and for a while wild rumors had circulated that Paasaad would not speak at all, was even at this moment heading back for some hideaway in Canada.

About 1 P.M., Paasaad, wearing native dress, had swooped down upon the First Avenue entrance in a huge Lincoln limousine, surrounded by a fleet of New York's finest. A huge crowd, containing demonstrators both for and against Paasaad's appearance, was held well back behind barricades manned by seemingly countless policemen. As usual, a visit by an international figure was costing city taxpayers a million dollars.

As Paasaad stepped from the limousine, the warm breeze swirling his robes, a half dozen of his strong-arm aides boiled from the other doors of the limousine, brandishing automatic weapons.

A stunned police colonel in charge, along with the chief of UN security, hurried forward to protest the weaponry. Paasaad, surrounded by his armed men, began to shriek protests and insults, saying he would leave immediately if his men were not allowed to protect him every step of the way. The police were adamant. Paasaad stormed back to his limousine and sulked while a frantic call went out to higher authorities.

Within minutes, the Undersecretary-General for General Assembly Affairs, the chief for UN security, and representatives of five nations cosponsoring the invitation were on the sidewalk at the side of the car.

The diplomats pleaded, and finally a deal was struck: Paasaad and his men would show no weapons, and they would not be searched. Since the flowing African robes could conceal an arsenal, a few Western diplomats were heard to complain bitterly that the compromise was one of form only. These decadent Western remarks were ignored, and Paasaad was now in the building with his men, presumably waiting to speak.

The hallway outside the Hall was a madhouse. Eileen went with Endidi through one of the delegates' doorways and into the great Hall. It was abuzz. Most of the blue tables were already filled, and other delegates hurried up aisles to take the remaining places. Behind the glass partitions high on the side walls, the translators and observers were at their stations. The press gallery was packed, and Eileen could see only a few scattered seats left in the public gallery area.

"Will you speak immediately after he does?" Eileen asked Endidi.

His eyes swept the throng with angry intensity. He did not look at her. "After perhaps a brief recess."

"Clary—good luck."

Endidi turned his back on her and started down the aisle toward the site for the Marandayan delegation.

Moving into the visitors' section, she squeezed into a chair and waited. The golden glow of the walls and the sheer vastness of the Hall lent it an austere dignity. Voices murmured in the vastness like those awaiting the opening overture at a great play. The architects of this room, she thought, had had a sense of greatness and historic destiny. It was a place like no other in the world. Had any of those designers ever dreamed that this great forum would one day lend its majesty to men like Gero Paasaad?

At the green Italian marble podium in the very front of the Hall, the President of the Assembly took his chair, flanked by the Secretary-General and the Undersecretary-General for General Assembly Affairs. A hush fell. There were brief formalities. A great hush was over the crowd.

One of the men at the podium spoke. His voice, amplified many times, filled the Hall: "The distinguished representative from Nown, for the purpose of an introduction."

Tella Rhonta, in a flowing crimson gown and headpiece, moved to the podium below the officers. Its light shone up into her face, showing a gleam of perspiration. She looked electric, alive, and beautiful. Her voice, when she spoke, was husky but strong. She spoke in an Indiric derivative that Eileen did not know well; Eileen quickly plugged in an earpiece for translation.

"It is my honor and pleasure," the machine-like voice of the simultaneous translator said in her ear, "to introduce to this assembly . . . a man . . . a man who today carries the burden for all freedom-loving people in the world.

"My country . . . like all free African nations . . . honors this man whose courageous struggle for decency and honor . . . has inspired the world. In keeping with . . . the vote of this assembly on date last . . . I have the high honor to introduce to you one of the great men of this century. I present to you at this time the Honorable Gero

Paasaad, director of the People's Liberation Army of Marandaya.''

There was a stir in the curtains to the right as the applause started to build. Gero Paasaad, his scuffed brown boots swirling the hem of his robes, strode forcefully toward the podium. His bodyguards stepped out behind him, the bulges in their robes obvious. Most of them were unshaven. Paasaad himself had a two- or three-day growth of beard, and his headpiece hung in back with an oily limpness.

As Paasaad reached the podium, the applause became an avalanche, rolling over him. Many delegates were on their feet. Eileen saw to her amazement that most of the visitors' gallery, predominantly American, were also standing.

Paasaad did not look up. The podium light shone up into his face, highlighting the folds of fat under his jaw. He was not as young as Eileen had somehow expected, or as tall and vigorous. He arranged his sheets of paper before him, scratched his bearded chin, and looked up for an instant, giving the throng a smile that more resembled a nervous grimace. The applause redoubled as if he had given them a blessing.

Paasaad then raised his hand, signaling for silence. Slowly the applause died down and people began resuming their seats. Paasaad waited, looking out stonily. A deathly silence fell.

''Thank you,'' he began, ''for this opportunity to speak out on behalf of the suffering majority in Marandaya.'' He was speaking fluent French, and his voice was surprisingly reedy. ''I believe this invitation is long overdue.'' He looked around and his eyes flashed with a dangerous light, the passion of a true believer.

''I had wondered,'' he added, ''when this august body''—he paused with heavy sarcasm—''when this *most* august body would begin to recognize the facts of life in our part of Africa.''

There was scattered applause, quickly hushed.

''This august''—again the sarcasm—''body has, I am

sure, many vital matters to consider. But allow me to remind you"—a finger stabbed the air—"that you came here to defend the rights of the oppressed peoples against fascist capitalism and imperialist tyranny. But the tardiness of this invitation proves how many of you have forgotten your sacred duty."

The silence was complete, unbelievable.

"I have been told," Paasaad went on, singsonging with mocking irony, "that, after all, 'These delegates want to do the right things; these delegates have very many grave and vital matters of concern; these delegates are very . . . important . . . personages.'

"I have been patient. I have waited. After all, mine is a small country. It is a weak country, and it has the support in its tyranny of many imperialist powers. What—I have asked myself—if a few thousand additional political prisoners are tortured or executed? What if a few thousand more innocents are chained, beaten, starved, torn limb from limb on the fascist Obutu's machines of torture?"

He paused and swept the Assembly with his eyes. When he spoke again, the savage sarcasm dripped from every word: "After all, *one* day they will find time for Marandaya."

Paasaad paused again dramatically. Suddenly, with an explosive sound that boomed through all the loudspeakers, he turned and spat on the floor. "I spit on your complacency!"

After an instant of shocked silence, the applause began. Delegates from African nations were the first to leap to their feet. Others joined. The applause became tumultuous. Again Eileen was stunned. They were cheering insults to their own integrity and decency. But then she immediately understood. Crudity meant sincerity; insults meant moral outrage; vulgarity meant strength. In this topsyturvy forum, traditional manners signified decadence.

Paasaad spoke cleverly through the applause as if he did not care about it, so that it hushed with miraculous speed.

"Here are facts of my country today:

"Under house arrest or constant surveillance by the

dread secret police—fifty thousand.

"In prisons without trial—three hundred thousand.

"Already dead in combat against Obutu's terror squads —twelve thousand.

"Executed for political protest—seventeen thousand.

"Starving and diseased—three million.

"Oppressed and held in check by force and terror— eleven million—every living citizen of my country.

"Fighting to overthrow the yoke of tyranny for our people—sixteen thousand—the men and women in my army of revolution!"

The applause boomed again. Paasaad dropped his scowl after a few seconds and looked up to give the Assembly a quick, brilliant smile. The uproar became incredible.

As it rolled through the Hall, Eileen looked down at the table where Clarence Endidi sat with others on his delegation. Hunched over like a hermit crab, he and a handful around him stared straight ahead with eyes that were bleak. Her heart went out to him. He not only had to take all this now. In a little while he had to try to answer it before these same delegates. And the delegates were already proving beyond doubt that Paasaad, in his bloodstained robes, with his hired guns on all sides of him, was a Messiah whose every word they would swallow without question.

"Lies!" Endidi repeated with dazed anger. "Almost everything he said had no foundation in fact whatsoever! The man did not even require some thin basis of fact for his fabrications. And they believed him!"

"Many of them see the tide of history as with him, my friend," Grover Matsoon said somberly.

Endidi looked miserably at Eileen, then at the surprisingly subdued Tella Rhonta across the table. The four of them were in the Four Seasons, having walked there after the close of the tumultuous session. Gero Paasaad had talked for two hours and fifteen minutes, and Endidi's response on behalf of the formed government of Marandaya had been postponed until a special evening session.

Endidi said, "It will be a very difficult speech to answer."

"Perhaps this will awaken your President Obutu, or others within your government," Tella Rhonta said.

"How," Eileen asked heatedly, "can you show concern for Marandaya after introducing Paasaad?"

Tella Rhonta turned astonishingly solemn eyes to her. "I take no pleasure in what I have done today. But perhaps only in this way can Marandaya be fully awakened to the danger it faces before men like Paasaad eat up all of our part of Africa."

"If that happens and my country awakens," Endidi said, "then some good may yet come from this evil day."

Eileen tried to hide her amazement. "You mean, Tella, that you don't actually support Paasaad?"

"Of course not," Tella Rhonta said calmly. "This is all political, as Clary and Grover very well understand."

"But everything rides now on quick action," Endidi said darkly.

"We'll have an early dinner at my apartment," Tella Rhonta said. "I have invited a handful of other influential guests at six. I need to go back to the office for a while, but perhaps some of you would like to go to my apartment now, and be there to greet any early arrivals."

"Out of the question," Endidi snapped. "I will have contacts from my government at my office."

"I really have to stop by my mission," Matsoon said.

Tella Rhonta turned to Eileen. "You are off this afternoon, no?"

"Yes," Eileen said. "But—"

"Help me in this way," Tella Rhonta said. "Please. I will write my address and give you the key to the door. It is very warm and the air-conditioning is not turned on. You could start that and still have time to relax awhile before any, early guests arrive. I will try to get there by five-thirty."

Eileen hesitated. She was surprised that Tella would trust her in this way, but it had not been a normal day and she saw that perhaps she had misunderstood some aspects

of Tella's behavior. It also occurred to her that it would be
a golden opportunity to look through the apartment.

She said, "All right, Tella, if you wish."

"Excellent." Tella Rhonta took out a small notebook
and pencil. "Here is the address."

Riding to the apartment off Central Park, Eileen considered calling Rick Kelley but decided there would be
time enough before the evening session. She needed some
time to sort out what had happened.

Tella Rhonta, she saw, had pushed Gero Paasaad's
visit to the UN as a pressure tactic. Far from being at odds
with Clarence Endidi, apparently, she shared his angry
belief that Joseph Obutu had to take stronger action
immediately against the rebel chieftain. And Grover Matsoon evidently was an accomplice.

The surprising turn of events tended to make certain
things that had happened earlier easier to understand.
Whatever details Tella Rhonta and Clarence Endidi might
disagree about, they apparently were united in stark fear of
Gero Paasaad and a determination to make the Marandayan government take sterner action against him. Surface
disagreements of a minor nature might pall into insignifi-
cance beside this central agreement. So there was no great
chasm between them. This explained how they could seem
so at odds, yet be lovers.

Seeing this, Eileen felt a bit let down. Not that she felt
anything serious for Clarence Endidi, but she still could
not like Tella Rhonta, and knew Tella was a spy. Was
Endidi also an active spy, or in this was he being deluded?

Having the key to Tella's apartment might give her an
answer.

The taxi deposited her in front of the twenty-story apartment building, and she showed the doorman the note
from Tella to gain entry. The elevator carried her up to the
ninth floor, and she found the apartment without difficulty.

The apartment was large and expensively decorated,
with African masks and other art objects displayed on the
walls. There was a television set with a six-foot screen, an

elaborate stereo system, and handsome furniture. It was stuffy from having the air-conditioning shut down, as Tella had indicated. Eileen found the controls and reset them and was promptly rewarded with a quiet rush of cooled air.

Eileen's watch showed past 5 P.M. She had time to look over the apartment, although she did not really hope to find anything very incriminating. On the other hand, Tella Rhonta might assume that no one would look even in the obvious places.

There was a tall, narrow bookcase in a corner of the living room. Eileen systematically removed books, looking inside and behind them. She found nothing. Moving across the room to a small desk, she tested the drawers, found them unlocked, and looked inside with equally unhelpful results.

The bathroom, redecorated in gold and platinum to suit the most sybaritic taste, contained nothing of genuine interest to her. This left the bedroom.

It was large, dominated by a circular bed covered with crimson covers. White furniture completed the arrangement. There was a dresser, and a night stand matched it. The vanity and bench were covered with Tella Rhonta's cosmetics, brushes, and perfumes.

Eileen started through the dresser drawers. In the bottom drawer, partially covered by filmy underthings, she found a thick manila folder. Her heart beating slightly faster, she took the folder from the drawer and tested the flap. It was sealed only by a string wrap. She untied the folder and slipped the contents out onto her thighs as she knelt on the carpet.

The thick pages were copies of engineering documents. They showed wing and empennage structural details of what appeared to be a very advanced jet fighter.

Eileen consulted her watch again. She still had perhaps ten minutes. Hurrying, she carried the documents to the bedside table and turned the lamp on to the full brightness position. Taking the little Minox out of the bottom of her purse, she focused and started shooting.

She had nearly finished when the slight sound behind her sent her entire nervous system into spasms of warning. Flipping the folder closed, she spun toward the far door into the living room.

Tella Rhonta stood in the doorway. Her eyes were bright with angry triumph. "So, Eileen, at last."

Eileen looked into the muzzle of the tiny nickle-plated automatic. There was nothing to say. It looked like Tella was alone. It was the only hope she had.

"Come here," Tella ordered. "Place the camera, your purse, and the papers on the edge of the bed."

Eileen obeyed. The action halved the distance to Tella. They remained ten feet apart. Tella increased the distance now by backing through the doorway. "Out here. Move very slowly."

Eileen again did as she was told. Going through the doorway, she passed a large, heavy-looking piece of African statuary—a standing giraffe—on a white pedestal. Just as she passed it, the telephone rang and Tella's eyes moved toward it for a part of a second.

Eileen hurled the bronze piece. It hit Tella's arm. The gun spun through the air. Eileen closed the distance between them in one long, athletic stride and chopped her stiffened hand onto the side of Tella's throat. The woman collapsed like a feed sack.

Eileen ran back into the bedroom and grabbed up her purse, tossing the Minox into it. Jerking the front door of the apartment open, she ran down the hall. The elevator doors were just sliding open. Clarence Endidi and Grover Matsoon looked out at her, surprise in their expressions. They stepped out of the elevator.

"Tella sent me out for some mix," she ad-libbed hastily, starting to brush by them to catch the elevator doors. "I'll be right back."

Matsoon reached out and caught her arm in a strong grip. "That has to be a lie," he said.

Eileen turned desperately to Endidi. He was now her only hope. He might not know—might be a dupe. "Clary! They're spies! She has an entire folder of secret aircraft drawings in there, and I've seen Grover exchange stolen documents with that man Leonard Jenkins. For God's sake, help me!''

Endidi reached out a hand as if to assist her. But his hand grabbed her left wrist and he pivoted so that he jerked the arm sharply behind her, between her shoulder blades. It was a swift move, an expert one. She was now held by both of them, and truly helpless.

''My dear Eileen,'' Endidi said with a grim sadness, ''I am so sorry.''

16

Paris

"My God!" Maria LaFontaine exclaimed, meeting them at the door of the mansion. "I thought you were never going to get back!"

Pierre LaFontaine briefly embraced her, then put an arm around both Dugger and Anita Courtright, drawing them toward the living room. "I think we can all use a drink."

"Do you know it's almost midnight?" Maria demanded.

"I told you we would be very much delayed when I called you, my dear."

"But that was hours ago!"

LaFontaine went behind the bar and began mixing drinks. "We had the local police to contend with, Maria. Then the Paris authorities, and finally the national inspectors."

"The national inspectors? Why them?"

Dugger told her, "I asked for them."

"Why?"

"It crossed my mind that Crouex has been a member of your staff for more than a year, and Pete has some interest in the visit by President Obutu. I thought there might be a tie-in."

Maria's forehead wrinkled. "I'm not sure I understand."

"None of us understands a lot of things right now," Anita said.

"Crouex!" LaFontaine said, shaking his head as he brought martinis. "I still can't believe it!"

"And there is no idea why he tried to kill the two of you?" Maria asked Dugger.

"Not really."

Maria seemed to notice Anita's sling for the first time. "How badly hurt is your arm, my dear?"

"It's my shoulder, and it's not serious. I can remove the sling tomorrow." Anita glanced at Dugger. "We're both lucky. Me a sprain, Joe a few minor facial cuts."

"But *why?*" LaFontaine asked for what must have been the hundredth time.

"Our other guests have all gone back to the city," Maria said after a lengthy silence. "Francis Corbinere and Guy Arata were going to the reception, although it started quite late."

"Why late?" Dugger asked.

"You haven't heard? There's been bad news on the radio. Fighting in one of the Marandayan provinces, apparently quite a large battle, and an aircraft strafed the airport at— What's the name of the capital?"

"Atravi."

"Yes. At Atravi. Now evidently there's practically a complete communications blackout. Guy Arata was very excited. The reception was being delayed while President Obutu and his staff tried to get information."

"*More* trouble," LaFontaine said, his teeth clicking together angrily. "If those damned rebels are making a serious attempt to topple the government while Obutu is in France—"

"You told me the rebels were weak," Maria cut in.

"I probably told you our household security was absolute, too," LaFontaine countered bitterly. "Now my friends have nearly been killed. And I do not even know the motive for such an act. I can no longer take anything for granted."

"Who was directing Crouex?"

"We have no idea."

"There were no papers, codes . . . ?"

"My dear, clues such as that turn up only in popular novels. He had nothing on him, and the people who came here and searched his quarters found absolutely nothing of interest."

Maria turned to Dugger. "Do *you* have a theory?"

"It's not the first time someone has made an attempt on my life," Dugger told her, rubbing one of the little bandages on his face.

"*Why?*"

"If I knew the answer to that, a lot of things might be clearer. It's possible Crouex acted because I had just questioned him about a certain target I had found on your husband's range. Possibly Crouex had let an unauthorized person onto the range and feared I might be getting too close to identifying that person."

"Why would someone be using our range?"

"He might be an assassin."

"An assassin! Against whom?"

"Your husband. Or Joseph Obutu. Or both."

"But—again—why? They have no real connection!"

"I think we can all drop that pretense," Dugger told her.

LaFontaine said, "I beg your pardon?"

"Your rocket firm tests in Marandaya," Dugger said, editing his remarks most carefully. "I think you must have other interests there also. Reliable people have estimated that as many as three million persons in this part of Europe are actively involved—*actively* involved—in doing everything they can to prevent Germany from ever becoming an independent military power again. The West German army already is probably the fifth most powerful in the world, thanks to us. And German industrialism is healthy —wealthy, too, obviously. Those millions who fear another round of German militarism are already alarmed. Your rocket interests are a red flag to them. If you *are* planning other activities connected with your company in Africa, that just exacerbates the situation. You have plenty of connections with Joseph Obutu, Pete—and there are plenty of reasons why people would go to great lengths to sever those connections.''

"Next," LaFontaine scoffed, "you will be saying I have connections with ODESSA."

"No," Dugger said very seriously. "I don't think so. But to some people you probably look just as dangerous."

"As if there were a new Reich organization, an ODESSA, or any of the rest of it."

"There is," Dugger told him. "No, don't look that way, Pete. There is a Nazi presence in Germany yet today. People like Mengele and their supporters exist. Some people could equate you with Naziism, Pete, and God help you if they do."

"Surely you don't think Crouex was a member of an anti-German group."

"I don't know what to believe."

"Speaking of Germans," Maria said, a tinge of hate in the way she said the word, "your associate M. Dortmund called."

"Wilhelm? When?"

"About an hour ago."

"You told him what had happened?"

"Yes, a little. He asked that you call him back."

"Where is he?"

"His telephone number is written beside the instrument in the hall."

Frowning, LaFontaine got to his feet. "It could be urgent. Please excuse me." He walked out of the room.

Maria looked after him a moment, then also rose. "I will be back," she said, and went out.

Dugger looked at Anita, who gave him a pale smile. "You're all right?" he asked.

"It hurts, to tell you the truth. How's your face?"

"Itchy and sore. You'd better finish your drink and get to bed."

"I'd better not finish it if I want to take the pain-killer they gave me."

"Cigarette?"

She accepted one. "This is our first chance to talk alone. Do you have any better ideas than what you admitted to the police or Pierre?''

"Not really. Only the vaguest theory.''

She leaned closer. "Do you think there is any chance Pierre sent Crouex after us?''

"No. I really don't.''

"Then he truly is as upset as he acts.''

"Yes, I think so,'' Dugger told her. "He sees that Crouex could have succeeded as easily as not—or Crouex could have hit him instead of us.''

"You really have no idea why he came after us? After you?''

"The question I asked about the range. I really think that. But it's no solution.''

"If it was your question about the range, then someone else may still be out there someplace.''

"I don't have any doubt about that,'' Dugger said.

"Is the target Pierre?''

"He may be. But I think Joseph Obutu is the primary target. The news from Marandaya reinforces that. They're going to go all out to oust him. Or kill him.''

"And there's nothing we can do?''

Before he could reply, Maria LaFontaine walked back into the room. She noted the way they were leaning close to talk, and Dugger saw the flash of jealousy in her eyes.

"Well,'' she said, sitting down with a careless flip of her skirt, "I hope I didn't interrupt anything intimate.''

"Nothing that can't be continued later,'' Anita told her with a sweet smile.

"The call is business,'' Maria told Dugger as if Anita did not exist. "He seems to be concluding.''

"I'm going to turn in soon,'' Dugger said. "My nerves seem to be going to jelly.''

"Everyone is overwrought. When the news was coming in about the fighting in Marandaya, I never saw anyone as upset and tense as Guy Arata was this evening. I feel sure he believes someone is going to attempt to kill President Obutu.''

"He said that, did he?''

"No, but when a man like M. Arata—a diplomat of his

age—carries a weapon, it shows how frightened and worried they all are.''

Dugger and Anita exchanged looks as LaFontaine came back into the room.

"Please excuse me," LaFontaine said, reaching for his drink. "A little problem—"

"Wait a minute," Dugger said, holding up his hand and riveting his attention on Maria. "Guy Arata had a gun?"

"Yes. He arranged some papers in his briefcase and I saw it, a little revolver in the bottom under some folders—"

Dugger remembered something else that he had stupidly ignored earlier. "And Arata said he was going to the reception?"

"Why, yes—"

"He told me earlier he *wasn't* going," Dugger said. Then it clicked for him. He turned to LaFontaine. "Where is that reception being held? Get on the phone! Christ! Unless it's already too late!"

The reception was drawing to a close. More than half the guests had already departed. Standing near the center of the flag-draped room in the embassy, Joseph Obutu was anxious for it to be over.

Receptions had never been his favorite activity. He had been standing for hours, a constant smile pasted on his lips, answering some of the same polite questions over and over. Yes, he believed the final questions over wording in the treaty could be hammered out in the morning session. And indeed yes, it would be grand if the announcement of the accords could be made a part of the historic Bastille Day celebrations tomorrow. And no, there was, unfortunately, no late word from Atravi. But he was confident all was well. Yes.

Obutu was soaked with sweat, the shirt of his tuxedo wilted and pasted to his chest under the too heavy jacket. His legs throbbed with the pain from an old injury after standing so long.

A gentleman from Holland, along with his youthful wife, came over. Obutu could not remember their names, so he clasped a hand of each and gave them a brilliant smile. "My good friends! I hope you have enjoyed the evening!"

"Thank you, Mr. President," the man said. "We are going now, and wanted to wish you a final word of good luck."

"Thank you, my friends! Thank you!"

A couple from Luxembourg, or possibly Sweden, followed with their parting words. Obutu again clasped their hands, showing a smile of serene confidence. When they had passed, the thinning crowd swirled around him for a moment and he was able to turn to two of his aides standing nearby.

"Is there any further word?"

"I am sorry, Mr. President. No. Every effort is being made—"

"Yes, yes." Obutu turned back to wish someone else good night.

He was more worried than he could let anyone know. The reports of a pitched battle in the Anwami Province had been confused, and were a brutal shock. He had known of no rebel activity in the Anwami. Had Paasaad moved his troops so far, so fast? Yet how was that possible, with the damned Paasaad basking in infamous glory at the United Nations, half a world away?

Nothing seemed to be going right.

The first reports of Clarence Endidi's response to Paasaad's speech, completed only recently in an extraordinary evening session at the UN, were also disturbing in the extreme. The news reports said Endidi had spoken less than twenty minutes. The reports had used words like "quiet," "withdrawn," and even "ineffective" to describe Endidi's rebuttal. Yet clear instructions had been drafted over Obutu's signature, telling Endidi to mount an all-out verbal attack on Paasaad, documenting his many atrocities and pinpointing the obvious lies in Paasaad's speech as reported by the news agencies. Obutu did not understand why Endidi had apparently failed him. Endidi was not a weak or stupid man, an opinion shared by Obutu and Guy Arata. Obutu would never have asked Arata to come here and assist him with the myriad diplomatic protocol problems associated with the visit if there had been any doubt whatsoever about Endidi's abilities.

So why, then, had Endidi been so ineffective? What would explain the fighting in the Anwami and the subsequent blackout from Atravi? It was not even clear what sort of airplane, under what colors, had done the strafing at the airport. It was all mixed up . . . insane.

Obutu had ordered Guy Arata to proceed with most urgent telephone calls, both to Endidi and to Atravi. He knew Arata disagreed with many of his policies, and was a leader in the opposition party. But Arata had mellowed in the year since Obutu had sent him to New York, the honor deactivating most of his opposition, and no one could say he had not been helpful in the past two days. Obutu looked for Arata, did not see him.

"Thank you very much, madam. Yes, I am sure all will be well!

"So kind of you to join us, Mr. Ambassador! Please to convey my warmest regards to the king!

"Yes, yes, I am sure we can conclude in the morning!"

Minutes passed. More guests departed. Obutu saw Guy Arata come out of the private wing of the house and make his way through the crowd toward him. Arata was sickly-looking with sweat, his eyes at pinpoints of tension.

"Is there word?" Obutu asked him quietly.

"From New York, no, sir. From Atravi there is a communiqué."

"What is it?"

Arata gave off a strong odor of sweat and nervous tension. His eyes darted around. "We must be alone for a few moments, Mr. President."

Obutu took a deep breath of irritation. No one seemed to be waiting for him to offer final words. "A minute only, Guy," he said.

"This way," Arata said, leading him past two neatly

tuxedoed, beefy-faced security men into the hallway.

Beyond there were several rooms. One was an office with walls of books and a large wooden desk. It was into this room that Arata led him.

They entered and Arata closed the door.

"Now, then," Obutu said impatiently.

Arata walked to the chair beside the desk. There was an attaché case on the chair. He opened it. "Mr. President, the crisis in Marandaya is more serious than you have imagined. You have never truly understood the nature of the threat posed by Gero Paasaad. That is your tragedy. We can only hope that Marandaya itself can still be saved."

"What are you talking about?" Obutu demanded. "Do you think I came in here for some political lecture from—" He stopped.

Arata pointed the small revolver at him. The distance between them was more than ten feet, but the muzzle looked as big as the mouth of a tunnel. "For Marandaya!" Arata cried in a high-pitched voice.

The door crashed open. Obutu dived for the floor. Arata fired.

"Why don't they *call?*" Anita Courtright asked, pacing the floor of the living room.

"If it was a false alarm, Joseph," LaFontaine said, "the diplomatic repercussions will be severe."

"Damn that," Dugger said, lighting another cigarette. "It's no false alarm. It all fits. Trouble in Marandaya. Lying to me about going to the reception. Arata taking a gun. He would be one of the few guests not even subjected to routine scrutiny during that reception."

"But Guy Arata?" LaFontaine said. "Why should he do such a thing?"

"That's obvious, isn't it? Because he didn't agree with the way old Joe was running the country."

"But Arata has been loyal for a long time!"

"Times change. Paasaad just made a successful speech at the UN. The reports of new fighting—if truthful—may mean a major coup attempt under way."

"By Paasaad? When he is out of the country?"

"That may all be part of an elaborate plan to strike when least expected."

"It still makes no sense," LaFontaine said. "All the renewed fury in Marandaya just now—why?"

"Oh hell," Dugger said, despite himself. "You know that, Pete."

LaFontaine froze. "I beg your pardon?"

"Joe . . . ." Anita Courtright said in a low warning.

"No," Dugger told her, angry. "Joe Obutu may be lying dead down there and a country may be going up in flames. And I'm a little sick of pretending we don't all know one of the underlying causes of all the unrest."

No one spoke. LaFontaine, his wife, and Anita all stared at Dugger.

"It's your rocketry testing," he told LaFontaine. "That and whatever deal you're trying to pull off regarding the CBW weapons buried in those deep shafts."

LaFontaine's face underwent a transformation. Layers of polite veneer fell away, and his expression was harder and grimmer than Dugger had ever seen it. "You know about that, do you?"

"I know enough, Pete. It wasn't enough for you to be testing West German boosters in Africa and getting everyone from the anti-German crowd to Zaire and the Soviet Union all bent out of shape. Now you're trying to work out some crazy scheme for the CBW—"

"Crazy?" LaFontaine cut in. "How many African nations do you think would fall all over one another to bid for rockets with CBW warheads? We're talking billions here."

"You're talking madness."

"That remains to be seen."

"I can see why you must think you can bring it off," Dugger said. "My God, you've stolen secrets from several countries without trouble—" He saw that in his anger he had given away too much. He stopped.

Too late. LaFontaine's eyes flared. "On what basis

would you make such an allegation, Joseph?''

Dugger took a deep breath. There was no turning back, and he wondered how much damage he had just done himself. ''Your files, Pete.''

LaFontaine was the color of chalk. ''You come to my home and act as a burglar in my office here?''

''It's a measure of your arrogance,'' Dugger counter-attacked, ''that you would keep things like that here at your home, unlocked—''

''Far safer from industrial espionage than any office in the city. That room upstairs is kept locked, too, except when I am nearby. I did not anticipate that an old friend would betray me.''

''If there has been betrayal, Pete, it started with you.''

The telephone in the hall rang. For a moment Dugger and LaFontaine stood watching each other, gazes locked, the woman on either side of them silently engrossed in their conflict.

The telephone rang again. LaFontaine turned abruptly and went to it.

Dugger walked into the hall after him and listened.

''Yes, this is he,'' LaFontaine said. ''Yes.'' Glaring, he handed the telephone to Dugger.

''Dugger here.''

''Mr. Dugger? Bert Lasmeck here. Associate of Charlie McCoy. I'm at the site of the Obutu reception.''

''Yes,'' Dugger said, frozen.

''Your call was none too soon, sir. Arata had a .32-caliber revolver in a briefcase. He got President Obutu aside, started spouting slogans, and blasted away with the thing.''

''Obutu?''

''He's fine. The first shot went a bit high, the second hit the wall after he ducked, and the security boys grabbed Arata without further damage.''

Relief flooded through Dugger. ''Arata wasn't hurt either?''

''Nope, he's in custody. So far he isn't saying anything helpful, but there's always hope of getting it out of him.''

"I'll be in touch," Dugger said, and hung up.

Turning, he found not only LaFontaine but Maria and Anita standing in the hallway behind him.

"It's okay," he told them. "Obutu is safe and they have Arata in custody."

LaFontaine accepted the news stiffly. "You understand, Joseph, that I must ask you to leave my house at once."

"I understand," Dugger said. "I'll get my bag."

Going upstairs, he was conscious of a mixture of relief about Obutu and regret over the rest of it. Probably he had been very stupid to face LaFontaine about the stolen documents. *Never let the other man know how much you have*. A cardinal rule violated. Now he would have no direct way of knowing whether LaFontaine would still persist in his scheme. Now he might be farther than ever from the questions remaining . . . crucial ones.

Because he still did not know why he had been a target, and he was sure that Guy Arata had not been the man with a high-powered rifle. And that meant this was far from over.

17

New York City

"More coffee, Eileen?" Clarence Endidi asked politely.

"No," Eileen Arrington said.

Endidi sighed, took the cup from her, and carried it to the table, placing it with the other dirty dishes. He then walked back to a battered old wicker chair and sat down again amid the wreckage of the morning paper. He stared moodily into space. Tella Rhonta, her face puffy from sleep, sat curled in the corner of a mildew-speckled old sofa nearby, and Leonard Jenkins stood near the wooden stairs, chain-smoking cigarettes.

They were in the basement of an old frame house off Bay Street in Stapleton, Staten Island. It had been Jenkins who appeared not long after Eileen's capture the previous night to drive her here, hands and ankles tied, under cover of darkness. Endidi, Tella Rhonta, and Grover Matsoon had appeared about midnight, and all but Matsoon had spent the night.

The basement room had once been a recreation room. Some of the acoustical tiles had fallen from the ceiling, revealing bracing for the floor above. Only one of the three fluorescent lighting fixtures worked, and it flickered eerily, making shadows dance on the dingy paneled walls. The old furniture was haphazardly arranged on a moldy linoleum floor.

Eileen had slept little, and had a raging headache. She was no longer bound, but both Jenkins and Tella Rhonta had revolvers and were constantly between her and the wooden staircase leading up. Once she had heard creaking in the floor above, and thought another person might be on the ground level. The shock of her capture had passed, and she felt clearheaded despite the pain in her forehead.

Tella Rhonta stood and began pacing nervously. "Grover should be back by now."

"He may have been delayed in making the contact," Leonard Jenkins said. He was pale, his face drawn into lines that had not been there before. "This was hardly in the plan, you know."

"I told all of you from the start that she was a spy!"

Endidi looked up at her, his eyes drooping with fatigue. "Enough of blame, Tella."

"How much has she jeopardized that we don't know of?"

"Nothing," Endidi said.

"We should give her the drug and make sure."

"It could kill her, too. None of us is a physician."

"Does that make a difference if she first talks? She will have to be eliminated in any case."

"Crazy talk," Leonard Jenkins said. "Our friends will tell us what to do. Now that Arata has failed, everything else may be changed. We'll do nothing on our own."

Tella Rhonta was about to reply, but boards creaked overhead. The door at the head of the steps, out of Eileen's line of sight, opened audibly. Jenkins looked up sharply. There must have been a signal. He gestured to Tella Rhonta and both of them went up the stairs, leaving Endidi alone with Eileen. The door above closed behind them.

"It will not be much longer," Endidi told her. "Whatever happens, it can't be much longer."

"I don't know what's happening, Clary!"

"You know very well!" he flared. "You betrayed our friendship and the bonds of race, and you have been caught. Now what happens to you will depend on decisions made by the people who are our true friends."

"Who are they? Why have all of you been spying on the United States for them?"

"God, woman! You know the history of the race struggle! This vile country has always stood behind dictators and other imperialist oppressors. Only the Soviet Union has been steadfast in supporting the struggle of downtrodden peoples."

"And do they also pay well, Clary?" Eileen asked softly, with regret. "Is that how Tella can have a luxury apartment?"

"We act out of principle!"

"Was it *principle* when Guy Arata tried to kill your own president last night in Paris? Clary, my God! It's insane!"

"You should not know of that."

"You talked about it in front of me late last night when you got here from making your speech at the UN. You wanted Arata to *succeed*. Your own president, Clary!"

Endidi's dark face twisted with angry pain. "Obutu has failed to stop the terrorists. A stronger man must take command."

"And you think you're helping your country by plotting to kill Obutu? Oh, Clary!"

"There is no other way. We will still succeed. The coup is already under way in Atravi. Even if we have failed in Paris, General Arman is in control of Marandaya and there is nothing Obutu can do about it."

"And 'the friends' Leonard Jenkins mentioned, they're Russians? They're helping you in this? *Why?*"

"Obutu has been a tool of the CIA. General Arman will be a neutral leader, and has the strength to beat down Paasaad and his murderers."

"Do you really believe the Soviets would prefer Arman to Paasaad?"

Endidi looked surprised. "Of course. The Soviet Union wants only peace and justice in my country. They recognize Paasaad for what he is."

"You're wrong—tragically wrong—Clary. What kind of regime can be set up when it begins with murder?"

"It is not so unique, Eileen. Your own country did the same in South Vietnam, as I seem to recall."

"And did it lead us to *victory?*"

Endidi slashed the air with his hand. "Enough talk. Arata has failed, but I know him well. He will never reveal a thing. Even if Obutu lives, we have won. We have you, and my weakling speech in the General Assembly last night sealed world opinion against the Obutu government."

"Your . . . weakling speech?"

"Of course." Endidi gave her a bitter smile. "I presented the picture of a delegate without adequate instruction—without sound answers to Paasaad's allegations against my government. Now General Arman will announce new policies, and the world will see that they are needed. When he strikes a deathblow to the Paasaad forces, the world will support him because he is clearly the leader Marandaya desperately needs."

"Did it ever occur to you," Eileen asked, aghast, "that your purposely weak speech also supported *Paasaad?*"

"Of course. But General Arman's rise to power removes the supports for the rebels. Their cause will disintegrate without popular support. And General Arman has the will to destroy any diehards who remain."

Eileen looked at Endidi with growing dismay and astonishment. He believed every word he was saying. She saw that he had been driven from the outset by a love of his country that was not only misguided, but blind.

"They're using you," she told him.

"*I* am not the one who sold himself to the secret police of an imperialist state! Now be quiet!"

Minutes passed. Eileen sat silent, trying to imagine some way to escape. She knew it was up to her. Surveillance had been removed to give her a clear field. No one had followed . . . or knew where she was. If she did not escape, she was going to die.

It was hard to imagine that she would actually die. She thought of her excitement when they had come for her in the training room. *My first real assignment.* She was filled with bitter regret.

Endidi nervously walked around the room, going not for

the first time to an old radio, a floor-model Zenith, shoved against a wall. He had plugged it in earlier and twirled the dials, getting only whistles and static. He turned it on again now. The loudspeaker popped and crackled as he turned the large dial.

"If only there was news!" he exclaimed angrily.

The door at the head of the stairs opened and Leonard Jenkins came back down, followed by Tella Rhonta and a man Eileen had not seen before. He was tall and heavy, with the shoulders and arms of a dock worker. He wore Levi's, work boots, a blue denim shirt, and a battered baseball cap. He looked fifty, a gnarled workingman with shaggy eyebrows and a big nose.

In his hands he had a small black leather case.

"We will wait for news," Leonard Jenkins said, his face a mask. "In the meantime, it has been decided to inject her for information."

The dock worker went to the littered wood table and opened the black case. He removed a bright syringe and length of rubber tubing.

Clarence Endidi stood by the radio, his eyes wide with shock. "Are you a doctor?" he demanded hoarsely.

The dock worker ignored him.

"I said . . . !" Endidi began, starting toward him.

Jenkins caught him by the arm, spinning him. "He knows his business! We have our instructions!"

"The danger is too great!" Endidi said. "I—I forbid it!"

"You are not in position to forbid anything," Jenkins told him.

It was not much of a chance, but it was the best she had. Eileen saw they were preoccupied. She jumped from the couch and darted toward the stairs, brushing past Endidi.

Tella Rhonta cried out shrilly and moved to intercept. Eileen backhanded her out of the way and vaulted up the first few steps. Behind her, someone shouted. The door above opened and Grover Matsoon—and another man—appeared. Eileen tried to bolt past them, but her lower position made it impossible. They grabbed her. She struggled and lost her balance and tumbled heavily back down the stairs, cracking her head hard on the floor.

Tella Rhonta and the dock worker stood over her. Dazed, she had difficulty getting them into focus.

"Whore!" Tella Rhonta said furiously.

The dock worker knelt and snaked the rubber tubing expertly around Eileen's upper arm. She tried to struggle. His fist exploded on her mouth. She went limp, stunned.

The last thing she was aware of was Clarence Endidi standing over her, somewhere beyond Tella Rhonta in her blurred field of vision. His eyes were wide with impotent shock.

Then the needle bit into her vein and she tumbled into blackness.

The white Ford van parked on the side street near Eileen Arrington's apartment was identified by its lettering as a plumbing shop. Inside, it was packed with electronic gear. Rick Kelley sat at the microphone on a side bench, and he was fit to be tied.

"Shit, I'm going to call them again," he muttered.

"Take it easy," his companion, a man named Berg, advised.

Kelley ignored him and thumbed the mike. "Seven to four."

A small loudspeaker on the wall panel crackled to life: *"Four."*

"Anything?"

"Negative."

Kelley bit a fingernail and spat it against the panel of equipment. *Four* was one of the mobile units watching Clarence Endidi's apartment. No one had entered or left it since 4 A.M., the hour they had set up the watch. Another unit was parked outside the Marandayan mission, and another across the street from the Cabinderian mission. No one had seen Eileen Arrington, or any of the people she had had under suspicion, for that matter.

It had been Kelley, after a sleepless night, who convinced the special agent in charge to set up full-bore operations again after Eileen had failed to make contact or appear.

"Shit, they've got her," Kelley said now. "I just know it."

"Take it easy," the phlegmatic Berg repeated.

"That's easy for you to say," Kelley snapped. "She isn't your partner."

"She might have just gone out of town with some of her pals. You don't know she's been had, man."

"She would have called."

"Maybe there wasn't time."

"No, God damn it, she would have *called*."

Berg wisely did not reply. Time oozed away. Kelley turned the inside of the van dense gray with his cigarette smoke. Berg cracked a vent in the roof. The radios were silent.

Kelley punched an encoder and accessed a telephone line. He jabbed in Eileen Arrington's apartment telephone number, then craned his neck to look up the side of the building at the shaded window of her apartment as the telephone rang and rang.

He broke the connection. "Well, I'm going up there."

"The orders are to sit tight."

"I'm going up there."

"She's not there. She would answer the phone."

"It's just possible she could have left a note or something."

"You know the drill. If you go up there openly, you blow the last vestige of her cover. Someone could see you enter. McTeeg said to hang tight and wait."

"Well, I can't just sit here anymore. I'm going up."

"You're going to get your ass in a sling," Berg warned as Kelley moved to the back door of the van and stepped out into the street.

Morning traffic was heavy along the street. Kelley waited before jogging across in a break in the traffic. In the lobby of the building, the doorman walked over to intercept him. The doorman was an old man with a perpetually cynical expression.

"I'm going up to see Miss Arrington."

"Don't think she's in, sir."

"That's all right. I have a key."

"Sorry, sir. Building regs, you know."

Kelley took out his wallet and fanned it open to the FBI ID. The doorman's expression changed. "Yes, sir. Go right up."

The stairs were quicker, and Kelley reached Eileen's floor out of breath. The door to the unit was locked. He took out his lockpick set and messed around for two or three minutes, sweat stinging his eyes as he got increasingly frustrated and angry. Then he pocketed the set and kicked the handle off the door.

It was quiet and stuffy inside. Nothing much out of place. A dried coffee cup in the sink, a day-old newspaper. No note, nothing out of place. In the bedroom the bed was rumpled, unmade. Kelly could smell Eileen Arrington's perfume in the air, and it wrenched him. He quickly —fruitlessly—examined the clothes in the closet and the items on the chest of drawers. A glance into the bathroom concluded the search.

Kelley walked back into the living room and stood there opening and closing his fists. There was nowhere left to look, and the cold ball in his gut was formed from an icy certainty: they had her.

She had slipped and they had her.

A slight sound in the doorway caused him to wheel, hand clawing for his shoulder holster. It was his partner, Berg.

"Take it easy, take it easy," Berg said, coming in and looking around casually.

"Why aren't you in the van?" Kelley demanded.

"McTeeg called, said for us to break in."

"What else did he say?"

"He said there's no trace of her at the Secretariat Building. Nobody seems to know where Endidi is, or Matsoon, or that woman. And the tail on Leonard Jenkins reports Jenkins has dropped out of sight, too. Nobody knows nothing. McTeeg is issuing an Agent in Trouble.''

Atravi

General Marcos Arman faced the two officers across the presidential desk. ''Are the arrests complete?''

''Excellency,'' the major replied, ''we have not yet located two on the list. We will have them within the hour.''

''*Every* political enemy must be arrested.''

''Yes, Excellency. Mr. Moloto is at the home of his mother, and we have men on the way to arrest him there. The other enemy is Mr. Mhoas, and we have learned he was taken to the hospital last night after suffering a heart attack. Guards are being dispatched to stand at his door.''

''Stand at his door?'' Arman snapped. ''I want him in prison!''

''Sir, his condition is said to be poor—''

''I don't care about that! Remove him on a stretcher! Order one of the doctors to go with you, and then keep him there also! And there must be no outcry. Do you understand?''

''Yes, Excellency.''

''The radio and television stations are secure?''

''Yes, Excellency. Key personnel are in detention, and the facilities have been padlocked.''

''What about the foreign press?''

''Sir, the reports of the supposed fighting in the Anwami have excited all of them. The buses left one half hour ago to take all the press to the site of the fighting as we have reported it to them.''

Arman permitted himself a smile. It would be a hot, miserable ride, and no answers available when they reached the area and found no sign of fighting. The press buses would not be back until midnight, and by then his control would be complete and they could report—under censorship—as much as he allowed them.

''No reporters remain in Atravi?'' he asked.

"Mr. Hardwick, of the New York *Times*, is ill. He is being watched. Miss Jackson, from CBS Television, missed the bus and is also being watched. We have informed them that satellite link and other forms of communication with the outside world remain out of order."

"Excellent. Dismissed."

The officers marched out of the room.

It was going well, Arman decided. Guy Arata's failure in Paris had been a severe blow, but there was no word that Joseph Obutu might know of anything out of the ordinary taking place here, except for the releases about Anwami and the airport, which could only confuse him. In another few hours, Arman's control would be total.

The general walked to the windows and looked out at the city. It was a blazing-hot day, not a cloud in the sky. The weather would be perfect this evening for the dusk fighter attacks against Gero Paasaad's strongholds.

Tomorrow Arman would make his first overtures to the Soviet Union, explaining to the world how "ties too close to the Western world" had brought about much of the turmoil within his nation. It was understood that Russia would give his new government immediate diplomatic recognition.

Later, Arman thought, after he had further entrenched himself, it would not be difficult to outsmart the Soviets. He would have destroyed the rebels and hanged Paasaad, and he could play East against West for the best financial and military aid. . . .

The telephone started blinking, and he picked it up.

"Excellency," the soldier on the switchboard told him, "the call is from the attaché at the American embassy, Mr. Lawrence."

"I have told you what to say to all callers."

"Excellency, he insists it is a matter of the gravest urgency."

Arman hesitated. Then he decided the call might be amusing. "Very well." He punched the other button, making his voice hearty. "Mr. Lawrence? Good day, sir!"

"General," Lawrence said, his voice tight with tension,

"what the hell is going on?"

"Going on? Going on? Nothing is going on. We have had a rebel attack in the provinces—"

"The radio and TV stations are shut down. The newspaper is closed. I can't get a telegraph or long-distance telephone call in or out."

"Temporary problems, Mr. Lawrence, I assure you. Our technicians are working diligently."

"General, I don't know what game you're playing, but I think you should know that our informants have a small band of rebel commandos reported inside Atravi itself during the night. If you're trying some kind of coup—"

"A coup? Nothing could be farther from my mind, Mr. Lawrence. I hope you will reassure the ambassador and anyone else who might have such a silly notion. As to troops moving in the city, I have moved a great many troops myself during the night. I am sure they are the ones your sources must have reported to you."

"General, God damn it, there may be more afoot here than you know!"

"I will investigate at once," Arman assured him smoothly. "Thank you very much, and good day."

He hung up while the American was still spluttering.

Lawrence, he thought, was utterly confused. Everything was according to schedule, and the elite units around Atravi had reported no untoward incidents of any kind. To imagine that any of Paasaad's forces were in the city was absurd. That could happen only with the help of the army, and this was inconceivable.

The general thought of Joseph Obutu in Paris, still alive, thanks to Arata's stupidity, but helpless nevertheless. It was in a way a shame. Obutu was basically a good man, if weak. The coup was a tragedy for Obutu, a necessity for Marandaya.

Obutu's wife would have to be informed soon. Arman would allow her and a small family retinue to leave the country, as a gesture of his humanitarianism. And then, in the months ahead . . .

He stirred himself. He could not afford the luxury of

looking ahead too far. There was much work to be done. Hearing the sound of a staff car outside the palace windows, he picked up a list from the desk and walked into the outer office, where a sergeant and two soldiers snapped to attention. The list was of college professors to be arrested. The staff car surely was a sign of soldiers returning to report on those arrests.

"You may retire for lunch when you wish," Arman told the sergeant. "Leave one man on telephone duty—"

A great booming sound rattled the walls of the palace. Arman spun, looking back through the office door to the windows on the far wall. He saw a huge plume of smoke and fire rising near the palace yard gate, and soldiers running.

"Call the guards . . . !" he began.

Below his feet, on the first floor of the building, a crashing rapid-fire series of explosions erupted. There were shouts, the sounds of running feet, and another long burst. Automatic-weapons fire.

The sergeant ran toward the door to the outer foyer, ripping loose the flap on his side arm. The two soldiers ran after him, unarmed. More firing racketed outside. The sergeant and his men reached the outer doorway. More shots, dozens of them, and the walls and doorway around the three men seemed to explode in flying plaster and wood chips. They went down as if cut in half.

Arman turned and dashed into his office. There was a locked gun cabinet on the far wall, half hidden by the standard bearing the Marandayan flag of independence. He knelt, his fingers tearing at the lock. Mother of God, he had forgotten the combination!

"General!" a voice barked from the doorway.

Arman spun, rising to his feet. Three men had rushed into the room, automatic weapons at hip level. The leader was one of Arman's most trusted officers. *All wrong*, he thought. *This can't be—a countercoup so soon—*

"Wait!" he cried, starting forward.

All three uniformed men fired at once. The plaster and paint and glass behind Arman blew up in a chaos of violence, and Arman's body jerked repeatedly, violently, under the impact of many bullets. Screaming, he was hurled backward. One of his hands shot out for support and grasped blindly at the flag. He fell with the flag wrapping itself around him like a shroud.

18

Paris

Bastille Day had dawned warm, cloudy, humid. Now it was past midday and only broken clouds floated overhead, a general haze making the gray monuments of the city obscure at a distance. It was very warm and still.

Tens of thousands of tourists and French sightseers had flocked into the city for the traditional observances. From the Louvre at one end of the Tuileries Gardens, across the yawning vastness of the Place de la Concorde, and up the majestic length of the tree-lined Champs Élysées to the Arc de Triomphe, the crowds were everywhere—milling, dense, good-natured, casually creating a ground storm of litter as only French crowds could so thoughtlessly do. Islands of clotted trash floated in the pools of the tuileries. Wrappers and bags were crushed like old snow under foot across the Concorde. The police vehicles cruising down the Champs Élysées, clearing the last of the traffic before the great parade, created little storms of debris with the wind from their wheels. French flags hung limp from a thousand poles. Bunting draped lampposts. The bleachers in front of the Obelisk had begun to fill. A band was playing. Traffic was impossible. Many local merchants had simply closed their doors to join in the festivities. In the grassy park in the shadows of the Eiffel Tower, a young couple made passionate love. Tourists carefully walked around them—except for a few Japanese businessmen, who had their inevitable expensive movie cameras trained on the oblivious couple. A jetliner droned overhead.

Part of the amazing throng in the Concorde was visible from the upper floors of the American embassy. Dugger stood at the broad windows with Charles McCoy and Anita Courtright.

"There's nothing quite like it," McCoy said. "There's no telling how big the crowds would be if they had a real spectacle like the Rose Parade."

"Do you really think the Rose Parade would fit the setting?" Anita asked.

"Probably not. Does anything fit this setting?"

They watched the crowds for another few minutes.

"Obutu just about ought to be signing," McCoy said.

"I don't suppose we can hope for them to hit a snag," Dugger said.

"Not likely."

"They're still going to try to kill him today."

Anita frowned. "You're sure it couldn't have been Crouex firing that rifle on the range?"

"If it had been, where's the rifle? And no. I can't believe Crouex had that kind of expertise. Hell, he would have killed us at that old castle instead of missing!"

"The security is as tight as we can make it," McCoy said. "If they sign the pact in time, Obutu insists on laying a wreath at the Tomb of the Unknown Soldier and appearing on the reviewing stand at two o'clock. He says the trouble in Atravi makes it mandatory that he show he isn't afraid."

"He always was a crazy bastard," Dugger said half to himself.

"We're especially watching African nationals," McCoy said, lighting another cigarette and tossing the match at the ashtray. "The shutdown in Atravi may be a coup by General Arman, and it may be something by Gero Paasaad's people. Until somebody can get through, we don't know how to proceed . . . or whether to proceed in any way at all."

"Are we flying photo missions?"

"Yes. I understand two just got back to base. But as good as those pictures are these days, they won't show us the faces of whoever is in charge at the palace."

"It might not even be a black national with that rifle," Dugger said. "We don't even know who we're looking for, and old Joe will be a sitting duck on that platform."

McCoy slumped to the chair behind the desk and stirred his hands in some of the paperwork on the top. There were several newspapers mixed in with the correspondence and reports. "I hope to hell it isn't Paasaad. It still burns my gallbladder to think about that speech he made at the UN. And did you see those pictures of him being escorted in and out like royalty? Jesus."

"I haven't seen a paper for days," Dugger said absently.

McCoy rummaged around and found the paper he wanted. He waved it, the front page of *Le Monde*. "Look at the bastard. God!"

Dugger glanced at the page, started to turn back toward the window, and felt a chill that went all the way down his backbone. He turned back. "Let me see that!"

"Joe?" Anita Courtright said softly. "What is it?"

Dugger stared at the dot pattern of the photo. It was not a very clear shot, depicting Paasaad with five other men, high UN officials, at some distance. He could not be quite sure, although his pulse was already coming faster.

He pointed to the photo. "This is Paasaad in the middle?"

"Yes. What about it, Joe?" McCoy was frowning.

"Do you have another shot of him? Maybe a better one?"

McCoy rummaged again. "There are several shots in the *Times*. Wait a minute . . . you can never find what you want . . . here it is." He handed over another newspaper. "Page three, I think."

Dugger turned the paper open. There were three large photos, and the quality of both the print and the reproduction appeared far superior. He studied them in a glance. There was no doubt.

"Christ, I know why they wanted us dead!"

"What are you talking about?" McCoy demanded,

rising to his feet.

Dugger slapped the paper with the back of his hand. "Paasaad! It's Paasaad! They knew some of the people in my group might remember his face and identify him!"

"Identify *Paasaad?*" Anita said sharply.

"His name might be Paasaad now," Dugger said. "In the Geneva days, it was Logan. D. Logan. He was a courier. We ran onto him by accident, and several of us followed him." Dugger paused, smacking his palm to his forehead. "I followed him. So did Heidigger. So did— Wait a minute. Frank Bauer was sick that summer. It might have been at this time. It *must* have been at this time! Frank never saw him, so Frank didn't have to be killed like the rest of us!"

"We don't know what the hell you're talking about," Mccoy said. "Suppose you—"

"Paasaad," Dugger said, slapping the newspaper again. "He's as phony as a three-dollar bill if he's posing as a Marandayan patriot. The son of a bitch is a Puerto Rican, and in the Geneva days, he was a courier for the Russian diplomatic spy system!"

"Christ sake," McCoy said, reaching for the telephone.

"They had to have us dead," Dugger told Anita, "because one of us might spot his picture in the paper when we went public, and spill the beans about his real ID and loyalties. He was working for the Russians then and he's probably working for them now."

"And Crouex could have been working for the Soviets, too," Anita said.

"Yes," Dugger said, thinking about it. McCoy was speaking in low, urgent tones into the telephone. Dugger wrestled with the new information, seeing how well it explained certain things. Then he thought again about Crouex.

"Yes," he repeated, turning to Anita with a feeling of new insight. "And that means we've probably been wasting our time looking for an African assassin. Unless Paasaad has changed sides or become a maverick—and if Crouex was trying to kill me to prevent my possibly identifying Paasaad and his connections, then—"

Anita Courtright spoke, paling, before he could finish. "The man with the rifle out there somewhere is a Russian agent."

Joseph Obutu walked back into the meeting room. The dozen diplomats watched him with grave concern. It was the President of France who walked to his side. A quick friendship had sprung up between the two men, and the Frenchman's concern was more than diplomatic.

"What word, my friend?" he asked.

Obutu shook his head. "Atravi is still cut off. There is no way to learn what is actually happening."

"The Americans?"

"I have just spoken to Washington. Their high-altitude photo planes have just returned. Analysis of the photos will take some time. But photos will not tell us who is in charge!"

"Under the circumstances, Mr. President, if you wish to postpone final decision and signing of the papers—"

"No," Obutu said sharply. He steeled himself. He could not think of his family or friends. A time like this required leadership. "I will sign the papers at once, in order to allow time for the announcement and the ceremonies."

"Of course," the Frenchman said. "We have only the wording of paragraph six—"

"I accept the wording in the draft document."

The French president blinked in surprise. "If it is not satisfactory—"

"It is close enough. Our alliance must be sealed at once, and it must be announced for all the world to know. This evening I must return to Atravi."

"But you do not know the situation there, Mr. President! To return at this time could be suicide!"

"My place is in Atravi."

The diplomats in the room exchanged grim looks. One of them said, "The ceremonies at the tomb, and on the platform, can of course be canceled—"

"No," Obutu said firmly. "The world must see these ceremonies. I will place the wreath as we had discussed, as a symbol of our new alliance, and to show that I am healthy and unafraid. I *must* do that."

The French president drew a deep breath. "As you say, Mr. President. The final document can be drawn in a very few minutes. I will notify the press."

Obutu nodded.

One of the other diplomats asked solicitously, "Your family, Mr. President? Is there any word of your wife and son?"

"None," Obutu said. "I can only—wait."

He turned quickly from them. They pretended not to have seen the sudden tears in his eyes.

Above the motion picture theater on the Champs Élysées quite close to the Arc de Triomphe, Alexi Crognoi, traveling in France under the assumed name of Franz Bertell, carried a small bag of groceries to his dingy little room. He unlocked the door to the place where he had been camping for the past hours, went in, and locked the door behind him.

Taking the grocery sack to the rickety table, he began unloading items. Only the top few were groceries. Below were several packages wrapped in oily paper. Crognoi arranged these items on the table, unwrapped them one by one, and assembled them. He placed the Skorpion in his special armpit holster. Then, after checking the rifle carefully, he loaded each special bullet. Then he repeatedly threw the rifle to his shoulder, testing weight and balance.

Everything was right, as he had known it would be when he retrieved the rifle from the floor of the other hotel room. But the movements did not dispel his tension.

The assignment was turning sour. He could see far more policemen and security people out along the street, and around the arch, than he had anticipated. Possibly the Marandayan diplomat's failure in his assassination attempt had caused it. Possibly more was wrong. Crognoi knew he could still carry out the killing. But escape now worried him. The timing would have to be exquisite, and there was a chance he would have to revert to the alternate plan . . . one he liked even less.

His superiors had assured him things would work out.

They could afford to be confident. They did not have to be here.

Crognoi sighed. One day, he promised himself, he would retire. His stomach had been hurting. He was not as young as he had been.

Leaving the rifle on the table, he went to the window, which was already raised four inches. He knelt. The field of view was excellent. When his prey left the car—or when he returned—the shot could be made. The light was good and the lack of wind would help.

Escape would be a different matter. . . .

Scattered clouds had begun to thicken quickly over the city, shadowing the sun. The seemingly endless parade had been moving down the Champs Élysées for some time, blocking all traffic.

The police car carrying Dugger and Anita Courtright to the arch was forced to take another route.

In the back seat of the Citroën, Dugger tried to brace himself as the pedestrians darted in front of the windshield from behind double-parked vans on the side street. He was not quite quick enough and was thrown against Anita as the police driver whipped the wheel sharply left, then right again, to shoot by within inches of the startled pedestrians' faces.

"The French people," the police inspector in the right-front seat sighed. "Ah, they believe they are immortal!"

"How much longer?" Dugger asked anxiously.

"If the traffic is not entirely blocked, only another two or three minutes, monsieur."

"And the motorcade is on the way to the arch?"

"*Oui, monsieur*. The press conference is concluded, they are in the automobiles, and proceeding."

Ahead, an intersection looked hopelessly jammed.

Dugger saw a dozen small cars piled up in all directions, a bus in the middle of it, and two trucks sideways, end to end. Everything was stopped. The driver of the Citroën, instead of slowing, seemed to increase his speed as he veered around a parked police van and bore down on the melee. He pressed a button, and the siren began to wail up and down with an urgent note. Up ahead, two *gendarmes* in the middle of things began to wave frantically at various cars. The pileup moved, but only seemed to stir like a thickly boiling mass. The driver touched the brakes and cut a bit to the left, swung the wheel sharply to the right as he scraped past the front of a Volkswagen, cut between a Porsche and a Renault, veered back left around the front of a truck, and accelerated hard through a crack between a series of cars that looked just wide enough to walk through. There was the slightest *chink* of metal on metal, and they were through and barreling out the other side of the jam.

"All will be well," the inspector said, turning with a wide grin. He pointed ahead, and Dugger saw, down a long line of close-packed apartment and business buildings, the distant outline of the side of the arch.

Nearly an hour had passed since Dugger had recognized the picture of Gero Paasaad in the newspapers at the embassy. The recognition had plunged McCoy into a flurry of frantic telephone calls: to London, then Washington, then to French officials where the pact signing was even then being concluded. Word was relayed to Joseph Obutu; he first sent a message through an intermediary, then postponed entry into the news conference on the pact long enough to take the line himself.

"That's right, Mr. President," McCoy said over the telephone while Dugger and Anita Courtright stood by. "We don't think there is any question. . . . Yes, it means the chances are awfully good that there's at least one more would-be assassin out there. . . . I can't advise you, sir, but extra caution in view of this new information—" McCoy stopped, frowning as he listened.

After a moment he put his hand over the mouthpiece.

"He says he's going ahead with the wreath-laying and the appearance on the reviewing stand."

"Let me to talk to him," Dugger suggested.

McCoy hesitated.

"Ask him if he'll speak to Colonel Davis."

McCoy spoke into the telephone. "Mr. President, I have another man here. You knew him once. A Colonel Davis?" There was only the slightest pause, and he handed the phone to Dugger.

"Mr. President, hello again," Dugger said.

Joseph Obutu's voice was deeper than he remembered it, but clearly pleased and surprised. "Colonel, I salute you! It has been such a long time!"

"Much too long, Mr. President."

"Colonel, I was always 'Joe' to you in the old days. Let it be that way now." Obutu paused, and his voice hardened. "I only wish circumstance was not so upset at the moment. It would be grand to see you."

"Joe, you heard what McCoy told you about Paasaad."

"Yes. I am shocked. I never suspected *that* circumstance."

"I'm sure Washington didn't, either. They've been informed. But the real problem now is that we have every reason to believe someone is planning to take another shot at you this afternoon. He's very, very good, whoever he is."

There was silence on the other end of the line.

Dugger went on, "We're advising you to stay out of public view, Joe. I'm urging you to do that as a friend. We don't want to lose you."

Obutu's sigh was heavy and audible. "Colonel, my country may be in chaos. Communications are out. I must show the world that I am well, in control, and unafraid. I cannot hide like a rat!"

It was Dugger's turn to take a deep breath. "I understand, Joe. But the risk—"

"Is one I have to accept, Colonel. I wish I could talk to you longer, or see you. The press is waiting. My schedule is falling behind. Another time . . ." Obutu's voice trailed off with regret.

The call was terminated.

"There's no way to stop him appearing at the arch and on the stand," Dugger told McCoy and Anita Courtright. "Hell, I understand what he's saying. He's got to take the chance or it looks like he's already abdicated."

"I'm going to call for some extra security if we can find any," McCoy said.

"I want to go down there to the arch," Dugger said.

McCoy hesitated, telephone in hand. "You can't accomplish anything."

"You forget one of my specialties for a time was Russian assassins. What if it's an old-timer, someone I could recognize?"

"That's a slim chance."

"I want to go there anyway."

"I can't blame you," McCoy said wearily.

"I'm going with you," Anita said, taking Dugger's arm.

McCoy punched a button. "Let's see if we can't get a fast ride for you."

The ride had not come very fast. By the time the Citroën arrived in the dense traffic, word had already come that the press conference announcements were over and Joseph Obutu, along with a dozen other dignitaries, was preparing to start the motorcade to the arch. It would be a brief drive from where they had signed the documents.

As the Citroën now skidded to a halt on the side of the arch facing the Avenue de Wagram, Dugger saw that the parade had cleared the Place Charles de Gaulle surrounding it, no traffic flowing from any of the packed dozen avenues feeding into the huge circle. Litter covered the pavement, and sightseers darted everywhere across the streets, milling densely around the base of the colossal, 165-foot monument. There were police cars, scooters, and vans everywhere, clusters of *gendarmes* every few paces.

The police inspector got out of the front seat, allowing Dugger and Anita to climb out after him. They were met by several sharply uniformed officers and a thin, pinched-faced man in a gray business suit.

"M. Dugger?" the man in the suit said. He extended a soft hand. "Tornay. Security in charge."

"How far away are they?" Dugger asked.

"Five minutes."

"You know we fear an attack from long range here."

"Yes. As you can see, we have men—both uniformed and non-uniformed—entirely around the circle. Many have small radios, for constant communication. We also have men in many doorways, on some roofs, atop the arch, and on the streets adjacent. On the Victor Hugo side we have two squads of the, ah—what do you call it?— SWAT."

"Where will the motorcade come and park?"

"Zey are to enter from the far side and come around to the Champs Élysées side, over there. When the cars enter the area, tourists will be moved back away from the eternal flame and the floor of the monument. We have sufficient men to encircle the party entirely."

Dugger looked across the street to the most familiar face of the arch. He saw that dark gray police vans framed the area where the cars would pull in. The vans might cut off the view from a few of the hundreds of windows looking down at a range of a hundred yards or so. But hundreds of other windows had an unrestricted view. Many of the apartment windows had small balconies; Dugger saw most of them were crowded with spectators.

Tornay saw his gaze. "We have men on many of the balconies, monsieur. If an assassin makes an attempt here, he cannot escape, I assure you."

"I would prefer to stop him *before* he shoots."

"Of course . . . yes, but of course!"

In a nearby van, radios crackled. Tornay turned. "Excuse me." He bustled to the van.

Dugger exchanged worried looks with Anita Courtright and again swept his gaze around the Place. People streamed back and forth from curbs to the monument in all directions. The top platform of the great arch was vacant except for the few silhouettes of uniformed officers, most with high-power binoculars. That was a plus. But the throng around the base looked denser than before, hopelessly so. The police would have trouble moving them aside. And all around the circle, under poles festooned with flags and banners, people jammed shoulder to shoulder: walking, talking, jostling, smiling or frowning, carrying sandwiches, pennants, bottles of wine or beer. There were children scurrying everywhere. Even in the tiny grassy islands between streets the humanity was packed.

Raising his eyes from the crowd close in, Dugger became aware of the gritty, oppressive heat. He was soaked with sweat and had not even realized it. He mopped his face and looked at buildings all around the central area. He revised his estimate of the number of windows; there were not hundreds but thousands.

Tornay hurried back. "They are approaching, monsieur." Numbers of officers were striding into the Place, turning people back. Others had begun. Dugger saw, to sift into the throng around the arch, pressing them back out of the central area.

A *gendarme* near Anita had binoculars on a strap on his chest. She spoke to him and he handed them over. Seeing Dugger's look, she passed them on to him. "You can use them better than I can."

Dugger adjusted the glasses, which were quite bright and powerful, with an extraordinarily wide field of view. After sweeping the balconies on his side, he turned partially to his right and looked at other buildings on down the Champs Élysées, the tops of the trees along the boulevard forming a fuzzy green blur in the lower part of the viewing field. The crowds were just as dense on down the street, in front of the bank . . . the department store . . . the cafe . . . the motion picture theater.

Behind him, a police car gave a short blip on its siren. He turned back to see motorcycles wheeling around the arch, lights flashing. The first limousine was close behind, banners flapping on its black fenders. At the front of the arch, two officers opened a van and started removing a large floral wreath.

Dugger turned his attention again to the rows of windows that seemed everywhere. He had a strong sense of claustrophobia, of impending doom.

"They're pulling up," Anita said tensely, close beside him. "One limo, now two . . . and here comes the third one. They're lining up."

Around them in the crowd, people began to exclaim and cheer and applaud. The sound swelled over the entire Place, growing.

"The President of France," Anita said. "It looks like Obutu must be in the second car."

In the nearby van, radios blatted. Tornay ran that way. Dugger put down the glasses and watched, seeing a half dozen officers swing around to shade their eyes in the direction he had just been looking.

Tornay came back out of the van, his face contorted. "Over the theater, monsieur!"

Dugger swung the glasses back around. For an instant he saw nothing as he scanned the windows. A number of large ones were painted white, some were hardly visible behind the rusty steel scaffolding for the huge marquee, a few on the top, or third, floor open, a woman standing in that one, the next open only a few inches and evidently—

Dugger froze, bringing the binoculars back.

The window was open four to six inches. He could make out a pale white splotch beyond the curtains, which seemed to be pulled down to the same height. Something was just protruding from the window—a narrow cylindrical object—

"That's it," Dugger said. "That's got to be him."

Tornay was barking orders into a small hand-held radio. Dugger turned and ran, brushing against people roughly, heading for the theater building more than three hundred yards away.

Crognoi, *alias* Bertell, knelt patiently at the window, only the tip of the rifle protruding. He felt very calm now because the waiting was over. He knew how heavy the security was, but wanted it over with; he would trust to mass confusion to allow his escape. He had the route well scouted and even rehearsed.

Down in front of the arch, the black limousines were virtually surrounded by police and other officials. Nevertheless, Crognoi felt a little spasm of recognition when he saw Joseph Obutu's black kinky head appear out of the second limousine. Obutu was taller than many of his companions, and hatless. That was good.

Crognoi waited, watching.

Obutu was surrounded. There seemed to be some parley under way. Crognoi saw many uniformed police in the group. His excellent vision even saw one of them, a high-ranking officer, gesturing excitedly.

Obutu turned and looked toward Crognoi—almost directly at him over the hundreds of yards. Other heads, too, turned to look. A pair of *gendarmes* pressed Obutu back closer to the car. He hesitated, then ducked down and got back in.

Crognoi pulled the rifle out of the window and let it drop to the floor. He rushed to the locked door, unlocked it, and ran down the dusty hallway toward the back stairs. He had not expected to be spotted. Now he was in trouble. By the time he reached the first landing, he had the Skorpion in hand, the stock folded over the barrel. He threw the door open into the lower hall and saw a pair of uniformed police rushing directly at him. He fired without hesitation, knocking one of them over backward and collapsing the other against a side wall. Vaulting them, he got to the window that led to the fire escape. He swung his legs outside onto the metal platform and went down the steel stairs four at a time, making a tremendous racket.

Dugger ran with a group of *gendarmes* into the arcade beside the theater. Scattering frightened customers, they rushed through a candy shop and into the arcade proper, stringing out in the tiled lobby on the way toward the rear. Three officers took stairs up. Dugger followed two others who kept running down a narrow corridor past private offices toward the alley exit. A man in a pale straw hat started out of an office door in their path, then drew back, startled, as they bowled past him.

One of the officers slammed open the back security door, and they ran out into the alley. It was muggy, dirty, lined with metal trash containers. The pull-down ladder off the back fire escape was partly extended toward the cobbles, as if someone had recently used it and it had failed to retract properly.

At the left, where the street intersected the alley, other *gendarmes* ran into view. Above Dugger, someone started yelling down. He looked up and saw more officers on the top floor, hanging from the window.

"He is not up here!" one of them yelled.

Dugger looked to his right. It was a very long block, the vacant-looking buildings staring down on trash and litter. As he looked, flashing police lights appeared at the far corner and men boiled out of a van, running this way. The police with Dugger started up the alley to meet them.

Dugger stood his ground, breathing heavily from the run. The man had been up there, but now he was gone. It had taken place very, very swiftly. He saw police meet one another in both ends of the alley and begin conversing frantically, pointing this way and that.

Dugger thought of something.

Hurrying back into the theater-arcade building, he returned cautiously to the office door where they had startled the man in the pale straw hat. He found the door standing ajar. He bent to examine the lock and saw it had been broken open.

Gun in hand, he entered the office. Desks sat vacant, tops cleared. File cabinets were neatly closed, and only a lone security light glowed in the interior dimness near a glassed-in cubicle against the far wall. On the floor where it had been tossed was a pale, lightweight nylon jacket. Beside it was a torn-open brown paper bag, the kind shoppers carried regularly from haberdashers.

Or hat stores.

Dugger turned and ran back to the front through the arcade. The crowd was excited and there were police everywhere. But there was no sign of the man in the pale straw hat.

19

Paris

Dugger stepped out of the sidewalk telephone booth after talking at length with McCoy back at the embassy. Although the crowds on the sidewalk had thinned somewhat, it took him a few minutes to locate Anita again. She had managed to find a thin space between two older women, accompanied by a small flock of children, on one of the green benches under the trees.

"What did he say?" she asked, standing with a slight wince of fatigue.

Dugger pointed across the avenue a block from the monument toward a sidewalk cafe with broad red awnings. It appeared crowded but not packed.

"I want a beer," he told her. "Very, very badly."

She nodded, and they started across the street together. "So what did he say?" she repeated.

"Well, you know the ceremony at the arch is off. So is the speechmaking, as far as Obutu is concerned. He's been taken back to his hotel. That's where he is now."

"The killer? Any sign?"

"No. Well, you knew that."

They approached the cafe. Many small plastic-topped tables were arranged outside, with the type of chairs they called ice cream cone chairs in the United States. A burly waiter in a white apron came over and showed them a table at the corner of the building with potted shrubs close by.

"*Bière*," Dugger told the waiter. "*Fraîche*. Large."

"And a hot dog," Anita said.

"Two hot dogs," Dugger corrected her.

The waiter went away.

"I forgot lunch," Dugger admitted.

"So *now* what happens?" Anita asked.

"You tell me."

"I don't think it's over. Not until Obutu is on that plane and headed back for Atravi."

"Is it over then? They still don't have any news out of there. Anything could be happening."

"Then why is he going back?"

"He *has* to go back."

"Still, I might feel better when he's out of Paris."

"He was European," Dugger said.

"Who? . . . Oh."

"The man with the funny hat trick. European. I didn't take a close look. I should have. There was something familiar about him, even, like I may have seen him or his picture somewhere before. But that might be a memory trick. Or I could have seen him before—he could be a Russian and have had plastic surgery, and we might even have met. Damn it, I was stupid!"

"There will be no Monday-morning quarterbacking," Anita told him. "You weren't exactly in an armchair situation."

"But as long as he's loose, he could even try again."

"I know, but aren't we overreacting if we think he'll get another chance? The French will be swarming Obutu now. So will his own security people who came on the plane with him. Did you get a *look* at a couple of those bruisers? Brrr. And I'm sure we have a few people standing by, too."

The waiter came with the tray containing two bottles of beer, beaded glasses, and what the French called a hot dog for each of them. Anita dug in ravenously, and Dugger realized how hungry he was, too.

"Did McCoy say anything about the plans? Is Obutu departing at once?"

"They're going to change hotels. They've probably done that by now; it's been an hour since he left here in the motorcade. A smaller place, easier to keep secure. We've asked him right from the White House to stay overnight, or until we can get a better line on what's happening in Marandaya.''

''What did he say to that? Any word?''

Dugger rubbed aching eyes. ''If you knew Joe Obutu, you could imagine. I'm sure he had a screaming fit. He was always a little theatrical. Since he became president, he's gotten a lot more so. McCoy said he said something about giving us four hours.''

Anita smiled ruefully. ''To what? Get off the world?''

''That, or give him the straight skinny.''

''Does he mean it, you think?''

''I think he'll be back in Atravi before midnight, come hell or high water.''

Anita put down the remains of her hot dog. ''The French must make the worst hot dogs in the world.''

''The bread is excellent.''

''How about the meat?''

Dugger grinned at her. ''Did you ever try to eat a hot dog in London?''

''Bad?''

He drank some beer, not bothering to answer. ''I wonder what all this does to Pete LaFontaine.''

''Blows him out of the water, doesn't it?''

''I don't know. All those meetings with Corbinere, the French ministers, and so on. Pete thought he was going to meet with Obutu. I know it.''

''That was before all the trouble.''

''I suppose.''

They finished their beer. Dugger summoned the waiter and paid him.

''Where now?'' Anita asked.

''I don't know,'' Dugger said. He thought about it. ''Back to the embassy, I guess.''

She stood and looked down at him. ''Is it really over?''

''For us?'' He returned her gaze and saw the look in her eyes. She was tired and wilted but still very beautiful, he thought, and he was aware of the double meaning in her question.

"I don't know," he repeated.

Traffic was impossible for a taxi. They walked down the Champs Élysées to the Concorde, a long walk. It was well past three o'clock when they reached the embassy.

Charles McCoy was not in the usual office. No one was in the office. Anita excused herself for the rest room, and Dugger went looking for someone who might fill them in on any late developments.

A low-level security man directed him to an office outside the one usually occupied by the ambassador.

Dugger walked in and was promptly braced by a uniformed guard with a gun in his hand. In a room across the office where he was confronted by the guard, a dozen men were yelling at one another and talking on every available telephone. Dugger saw a general, an admiral, several high-ranking civilians, a French police officer, and McCoy.

"Outside," the armed guard repeated to Dugger, nudging him in the midsection with the old but decidedly lethal .45 automatic. "*Move* it, mac, or—"

"Charlie!" Dugger shouted.

In the next room, McCoy looked up sharply at the sound. Seeing Dugger, he rushed out.

"Jesus Christ, man, where have you been?" he demanded. "Obutu has vanished from his fucking hotel room!"

Security officers had escorted Joseph Obutu and his entourage to a relatively new but modest hotel near The Opera. Every attempt was made to keep the move as quiet as possible, including transportation in unmarked cars and movement of plainclothesmen into the building from the rear alley only. Obutu himself and his own group of security men entered by the side entry, and went directly up to the suite on the third floor.

Uniformed police stood at distant corners, but only as they might have done on any holiday afternoon. Security was heavy on the first floor of the hotel, but, again, kept mostly out of sight. Obutu went directly into the bedroom of his suite, where he conferred with his own men. They then relayed word to the French officers that their president needed a few minutes' rest, but would first make some crucial telephone calls.

The hotel operator gave the Obutu suite direct access to one of its outside lines, and the calls were not monitored. The operator said she could tell by the blinking of the downstairs instrument light that several calls evidently were made.

Twenty minutes passed. Three American security agents arrived on the scene and conferred with the Frenchmen. A small rear elevator was examined, and a decision made to render it inoperative. The manager was asked about means to accomplish this, and protested that the two-person lift could be rendered useless only by doing it mechanical damage. A compromise was worked out whereby the small car would be run up to the hallway beside Obutu's suite and left parked there with a stick propping the door open. In this way it could be used only from the third floor, where it would be available only to Obutu or his own security detail.

Satisfied that rear access to the third floor was otherwise impossible except via a narrow stairway, the security men locked the door to the stairs and assigned one man inside the door, in the stairwell, as an added measure of precaution.

After the Obutu group had been upstairs another ten minutes, a telephone call came in for him from Washington, priority. It went to the third-floor suite. One of Obutu's aides answered and, on hearing the source of the call, said he would notify the president immediately.

Approximately twenty seconds later, the shouting and commotion started on the third floor.

It had not entirely calmed down by the time Dugger reached the hotel, McCoy and Anita Courtright with him.

Thoughts of "quiet security" had vanished. The lobby was filled with people, most of them law enforcement of one kind or another. Two police vans and a car from the national police stood in front with lights flashing. *Gen-*

darmes milled around all the streets in the area, and two
mobile units from Paris radio/TV outlets were also on the
scene with brilliant flood lamps glaring in the gray afternoon light.

The American agent in the lobby was named Townsend.
His collar was askew and his tie crooked. The tail of his
white shirt had come out over the belt pulled tight and low
on a growing paunch. He had blond hair cut in old-time
military fashion, and could have been anywhere from
thirty to forty, or even older, the weight masking chrono-
logical age.

He faced McCoy, ticking off the points on stubby
fingers, while Dugger and Anita listened. "No one went
upstairs by the back stairs. The fire escape was guarded.
The front stairs were guarded, and he didn't leave that
way, either. The elevator was propped open, and then they
found it on the first floor, the prop removed, the door
working normally. He had to have been taken down that
way."

"How did anybody get *up* there to take him?" McCoy
demanded.

"Sir, if we knew that . . . we would know something."

Dugger asked, "Are all his own security people
accounted for?"

"Yes, sir. They were either in the outside rooms of the
suite or in the hall up front."

"Who else was in the suite?"

"As far as anybody knows—no one."

"Was the suite thoroughly searched before the party
went in?"

"Yes, sir." Townsend hesitated, then added, "Four
times."

"Shit," McCoy said. "I want to see the suite for myself
before I call and report this." He turned to Dugger and
Anita. "Want to go up?"

"We'll wait here," Dugger told him.

Fuming, McCoy walked to the elevator with Townsend.
They went up.

Dugger and Anita looked at each other.

"Are you thinking what I'm thinking?" she asked.

"I don't think anyone took him. I think he went on his own."

"Alone?"

"Yes."

"Despite the danger?"

"I know Joe a little bit . . . at least the way he used to be. It's his style. One of the guys once called him 'the African Errol Flynn.' Hell, maybe he was planning this all along, for all I know."

Anita stamped her foot. "And he's probably going to end up dead for his swashbuckling."

"I know that's not the way *he* saw it. His reasoning would be, 'Hey, I'll go alone, no guards, no police, no commotion. No one will look twice at a lone black man in these crowds.'"

"Where was he going?"

"There's one angle I can speculate about. Pete."

Anita looked across the lobby. "There's a telephone over there, and it's between reporters. Let me make a quick call."

"After yesterday, what can you find out? You're blown. You don't work for him anymore."

She made a wry face. "Maybe word of my disgrace hasn't circulated yet. Let me give it a try."

Dugger nodded, and she walked across the lobby to the booth, narrowly beating a reporter to it. Closing the door sweetly in the man's face, she dug coins from her purse and plugged them into the telephone. Dugger watched her dial.

It was nothing like what he had tried to anticipate, but now that it had happened, he was not as surprised as he felt he should be. It *was* Obutu's style. And the signs had all been there: the meetings between LaFontaine and the officials from Marandaya, the verification of the possible tie-in between the rockets and the buried CBW—even the trouble in Atravi should have been an added indicator. For if Joseph Obutu had had any inclination to dicker with LaFontaine in such a deadly game while Marandava was relatively peaceful, the new uprising might increase his desperation . . . make him even more willing to consider some kind of deal.

Dugger did not like to think of Obutu double-crossing the government of the United States. It was even less pleasant to imagine him actually selling some kind of mad "mining rights" to the old German cache. It was the stuff of nightmares. But the world had been filled with wilder nightmares in recent years . . . and a desperate Joseph Obutu might consider anything.

Possibly, Dugger told himself, he was wrong. Obutu might not have slipped off on his own to meet Pierre LaFontaine.

He smoked half a cigarette, telling himself this.

Then Anita Courtright, who had made two calls, opened the telephone booth door to the impatient reporter and strode with long steps across the lobby, her tension visible in every stride. "He's not there."

"Not at the office?"

"Not at the office, not at home."

"You called the house?" Dugger said, surprised. "Maria might be mad as hell, and lie to you."

"No, I talked to one of the servants, and she knows nothing. She wouldn't lie. She said Pierre left more than two hours ago, and said he might not be back until late this evening. She asked if I wanted to talk to Mrs. LaFontaine. She said she was on the patio deck."

"Did he leave the house alone or with someone?"

"The girl said Wilhelm Dortmund came by and they left together in Dortmund's car."

"Well," Dugger said disgustedly, "that tears it."

"At the office, they said he was there with Dortmund until just a little while ago. Then the two of them left together without saying anything to anyone."

McCoy appeared in the elevator, alone this time, and walked stiffly to join them. His face was tight with anger.

"He's gone, and nobody knows from nothing. I've got to report, but they're probably going to have my balls for this and I'm sure not going to let them do it to me over a telephone line. Do the two of you want to come with me?"

"Back to the embassy?" Anita asked.

"The office building downtown. Then the embassy. If I can still walk at that point."

"What are they doing here?" Dugger asked.

"Running around," McCoy snarled, "with their thumbs up their butts." He took several strides toward the front entrance, then looked back at them. "Well?"

"We'll come later," Dugger told him.

McCoy steamed out by himself, the revolving door going around and around in his wake.

"I don't suppose there's anything we can do," Anita said, "but wait and hope."

Dugger walked her to the front door, which had finally stopped revolving. They started it again, but much more gently than had McCoy, as they went out onto the street. One of Paris's countless tiny parks was just across the street, its north corner marked by a set of stairs leading under the earth to a station of the Paris tube system. Much of the holiday traffic—if there had been much in this area —had faded away. It was a stuffy, lazy afternoon.

Dugger walked Anita Courtright into the park and to a bench. He sat down on it, and she stood watching him. Some pigeons came down and walked around their feet, expecting a handout.

"They probably were going to meet all along," Dugger said. "In private, certainly, in secret if possible. That makes sense. If McCoy thinks he's in for trouble, it's nothing to what old Joe would have run into from Washington if they got wind that he was meeting LaFontaine . . . and somebody put two and two together."

"I can't imagine him doing this after two attempts on his life!"

"He's that kind of guy, I tell you. It would be all the more important to him, in his way of thinking, to go

ahead with any planned meeting *because* of the attempts
on him. To close whatever deal they've cooked up and
strengthen his position. Once he's out of the hotel, away
from the cops, in a crowd—''

"They might meet anywhere," Anita supplied.

Dugger rubbed his eyes again. The headache was growing. "You'd think there would have been some hint . . .
some clue." He looked up at her. "Was anything ever said
that might give you *any* idea where they would meet?''

"No," she said, frowning. "They wouldn't meet here,
or at the offices. Too much chance of their being spotted
together. They would go someplace remote.''

"Or someplace," Dugger argued, "very, very public indeed. Where they could meet in a crowd.''

"In Paris that could be practically anywhere.''

Dugger continued to bend over, elbows on knees, rubbing his eyes. "It wouldn't be the Concorde. Too many
police.''

"That doesn't narrow it down much. Notre Dame. The
Louvre. One of the tour boats on the Seine. The Crystal
Palace.'' She went on naming places.

While the names rolled on, Dugger was thinking.

Then, quite suddenly, he remembered the various
words on the blotter in LaFontaine's office the night he
had crawled through the window. His pulse began to
speed, and he reviewed them one by one.

Winged V.—4.

"Good God," he said softly, raising his head. "What
time do you have?''

Anita glanced at her watch. "Three forty-five.''

"I've got three-fifty," he said, getting to his feet.

"This darned watch has been running a little slow—''
Her words were jerked to a halt as he grabbed her hand
and started pulling her through the park.

"I hope it's your watch that's right and mine wrong,"
he told her as she ran to keep up. "Jesus, do I hope that.
We need every minute.''

"Where are we *going?*" Anita cried.

Dugger did not reply. It was not necessary. A taxi through this traffic would never make it in time. They had one hope, and that was the Paris underground. And he was already dragging her down the marble steps to the station beneath the little park.

20

Atravi

At a little after five o'clock, local time, two gray-clad soldiers marched into the courtyard of the presidential palace and approached the tall mast where the national flag of Marandaya had been torn down hours earlier. They had a cloth bundle that they carried between them. They attached the cloth to the mast halyards and pulled the rope, hoisting the new flag. A slight evening breeze unfurled it, black and red against the gathering clouds.

Some nine hundred yards away, in the upstairs window of the building that sheltered his small import-export business, Geoffrey Harrington watched through high-power binoculars. He recognized the flag as the adopted banner of Gero Paasaad's rebel forces, and experienced a deep chill of dread.

Harrington, forty-seven, was a British subject, originally from Belfast, who had spent a number of years in Mexico and the southwestern United States before coming to Marandaya at the age of forty. A widower and something of an eccentric who dabbled in electronics and paleontology with equal enthusiasm, he had built a steady if unspectacular income through the collection, purchase, and resale of African art objects, some of them even authentic. Living on the far western side of Atravi in a rambling old house that had once been the center of a plantation, he amused himself with his hobbies, occasional social outings with other whites in the area, and the periodic seduction of a young black woman hired as office or domestic help. He liked to putter around on a very old Honda 305 Superhawk motorcycle, to which he had bolted a homemade sidecar that no one had ever been known to ride in. He was considered harmless by everyone, with the possible exception of some of the black female help.

Harrington had been watching the palace almost continuously since early morning.

He had no doubt now that there had been a coup and Gero Paasaad's forces were in control. He had not seen more than a few dozen soldiers whose garb indicated revolutionary status, and this puzzled him; he had always imagined that a take-over would require large forces and heavy fighting.

He could only assume that some members of the loyal army had collaborated.

However it had gone, Harrington knew now, watching the flag whip in the breeze, that Atravi—and all of Marandaya—was in deep trouble. He knew Joseph Obutu was in Paris and Paasaad had spoken at the United Nations. He knew the radio, television, and newspaper outlets had been shut down. It seemed that every reliable method of communication with the outside world had been cut off except his amateur radio station.

This both confused and frightened him, as if the oversight were part of some sinister plan. There was nothing at all secret about the station. It had been duly licensed by the Marandayan government for six years, and the post office did a brisk business every week in QSL cards— postal verifications of radio contacts—between him and practically all parts of the world where other radio amateurs were licensed to operate. The dirt road past his isolated home was not heavily trafficked, but anyone who did pass could hardly fail to note his eighty-foot steel tower topped by the big Hy-Gain TH6DXX triband Yagi beam and the long inverted V antenna wires for 40 and 75 meters.

And yet, as all other modes of communication were shut off, he had been left entirely alone.

This placed Harrington in an uncomfortable position. He imagined that the rebels had shut down all communications to keep the outside world in the dark while the coup was completed. He had the ability to pierce the curtain of silence and communicate with dozens or even hundreds of other countries, depending on ionospheric conditions, around the globe.

Part of him said to get home and start operating the radio; the world had to know: the rebels might still be headed off.

Part of him said to forget the radio and maintain the lowest possible profile, to save his own skin.

Harrington continued to watch the palace at his extreme long range for a little while longer. He saw nothing further of interest. The city was amazingly quiet. He decided the normal thing to do at this hour was to go home, so he would go home.

Locking up carefully, he went into the alley and unlocked the old Superhawk. It kicked right over and he puttered west, staying to side streets. Traffic was almost nonexistent, and while it was never very heavy in the suburbs of Atravi, the extreme lightness was ominous. He saw very few soldiers.

The street took him within a few blocks of the center of the city, and past a large municipal park. Here, contrary to what was usual, the area was deserted . . . spooky. The only sound was the old motorcycle puttering along about 30 mph.

As he passed the northwest corner of the park, where the largest trees were, Harrington glanced that way. He very nearly ran the cycle into the curb, then. The trees were full of people.

People who had been hanged.

There were a dozen or more black soldiers, in army uniforms. There were a number of women, and some of them were not black. There were twenty or more white men, some of them elderly, some young businessmen, two wearing the black suits of clergymen.

Off somewhere in the distance there was a brief burst of

hollow, rapid sounds. Harrington had never heard automatic-weapons fire, but he knew instantly that it could not be anything else. Glancing fearfully behind him, he rolled on the throttle of the Superhawk and sped out of the square onto an empty side street, headed west.

Less than thirty minutes later, Harrington was home. To his intense relief, nothing had been disturbed and no one was in sight. Evening was starting to come on. Harrington fired up an old pipe and paced the floor, debating the pros and cons. He saw finally that he probably had very little chance of surviving either way it went, and he could take a chance now and have a faint hope for rescue . . . or cower in a corner and wait for the hangman to add his body to the Caucasian collection in the square.

Harrington's hands trembled as he went into the back bedroom, which also served as his ham radio "shack." Turning on the green-shaded lamp that hung down over the long equipment table, he sat down and faced the radios, flipping on the Kenwood TS-820S transceiver, the home-brew kilowatt linear, the antenna rotator control head. The Yagi had been switched to ground as protection against sudden thunderstorms, and for a moment he forgot this. Then, seeing the coaxial switch pointing down, he turned it to the line that fed the beam. Immediately the white noise from the solid-state receiver section changed to the Donald Duck muttering of single sideband voice signals tuned slightly off frequency.

Still shaking, and perhaps more so, Harrington turned the dial of the transceiver. He was tuned up on 10 meters, and the band was open to the United States. He heard voices with southern accents bombing in 10 over 9, more northern American voices only slightly lower. There were plenty of holes in the band, but it was solidly open.

Finding a vacant frequency, Harrington checked his tuning on the transceiver and the linear amplifier. Pulling the microphone over in front of himself, he hesitated. He had never made a call of this import in his life, nor had he ever imagined a contingency when he might have to do so. But he thought he knew the procedure well enough. Details were not really important anyway; the world had to be told everything he knew about what was happening in Atravi.

Clearing his throat, Harrington pressed the transmit bar on the microphone. "Mayday," he said, watching the power needles jump in response. "Mayday, Mayday, Mayday, Mayday. This is a Mayday call for any Stateside station. CQ Stateside with a Mayday message from Marandaya . . . Marandaya, Africa . . . Mayday. C23CE. Charlie twenty-three Carlie echo, in Atravi, Marandaya, calling Mayday Stateside and standing by."

New York City

In the basement of the house on Staten Island, Eileen Arrington lay unmoving on the mildew-flecked old couch against the wall. Leonard Jenkins and Tella Rhonta sat somber and unmoving at the table, which contained the syringe kit and now discarded rubber tubing. Clarence Endidi paced back and forth like a man on fire.

"How much longer do we *wait?*" he cried out finally.

"We wait until we get word," Jenkins said, raising hooded eyes full of impatience and anger.

"I have to be seen in public this afternoon," Endidi fretted, still pacing fast. "That's imperative! It's almost ten o'clock already!"

"Patience, Clary," Tella Rhonta said with quiet exasperation. She exchanged a look with Jenkins that Endidi did not notice. "All will be well."

"I must be by my telephone, too," Endidi said. "When Joseph Obutu falls, mine will be one of the first telephones in New York to ring! I must be there to provide comment. And then there is so much else to do."

"It won't be long now," Jenkins said.

"But so many things could still go wrong. Even after we hear Obutu is finally dead—assuming our friends don't botch the job just as Guy Arata botched it—"

"Our friends do not botch such jobs," Tella Rhonta said.

"Even so! What if General Arman encounters difficulty

with the army? We all know there are dissident elements. And what if Paasaad and his cutthroats surprise us by trying some fast countermove? I need to be in communication as soon as possible, to be sure all is going according to the plan!''

"Relax," Jenkins said wearily, with another meaningful look at Tella Rhonta. "We will await word from our friends."

Endidi threw up his hands in despair, stopped pacing, and walked jerkily to the couch where Eileen Arrington lay unmoving, her eyes closed. He knelt beside her and took her limp wrist in his hands, probing for a pulse. He looked at the others, horror filling his eyes. "The pulse is almost gone. She is dying!"

Neither Jenkins nor Tella Rhonta replied or looked at him.

"He gave her far too much!" Endidi rasped, getting back to his feet. "I told you that! I told you he knew nothing about administering such a drug! Even *I* know this drug does not operate like ordinary truth serums. The victim does not pass into deep sleep. You saw how she remained conscious, struggling against it and *struggling* against it, and then talking in that hideous, disjointed, mechanical way just before he completed the injection and she went into coma—"

"We were here, Clary!" Tella Rhonta said, her voice cracking. "We don't need your commentary!"

"He killed her! She's dying!"

"My God, man," Jenkins said, getting to his feet. "What difference does it make how she dies? We know what we had to know. She was FBI. She knew about the last set of papers on Obutu we managed to get out. They're going to pick *all* of us up—even you and Tella, with your supposed diplomatic immunity—sooner or later. We have to have our stories solidly constructed, and that woman could never be allowed to live to testify against us. Instead of crying, you should be thinking about how we're going to dispose of her body so it can never be found."

Endidi stared, then began pacing again. Then, flinging his arms about, he went to the old radio that had drawn his attention several times earlier. As he had done every time before, he flicked it on. The dial lighted a dull orange. The radio was silent.

Endidi slammed his palm hard on the top of the wood box in his frustration. "We have no way of knowing anything!" Then he seemed to remember what Jenkins had just said to him. "*I* do not have to hide her body! *I* did no killing! I never countenanced any killing except for the necessary elimination of Joseph—"

"What about the man who was following me the night I left your apartment with the laser-device specifications?" Jenkins cut in. "You were quite willing for our friends to help us that night, to get me away safely and save your own skin."

"I didn't know they would kill him," Endidi said weakly.

"We kill those we must," Tella Rhonta said, her handsome black face as cold as a remote planet.

Over their heads, a sharp thumping sound rocked the ceiling.

"What was that?" Endidi asked sharply, eyes wide.

"What does it matter?" Jenkins asked. "Get hold of yourself, Clary! Grover is up there, with the other one. They know how to handle themselves."

Endidi went back to Eileen Arrington. His face was fearful, and he again picked up her hand and probed her wrist as if knowing he would only verify the worst. He moved his fingers around on her wrist as if making sure he was feeling the right spot for any remaining heartbeat. He let the hand drop.

As he did so, almost as if by cause and effect, the old radio in the corner made a sputtering noise. Then some whistling started.

"It's working!" Endidi cried, rushing to kneel in front of it. "It needed to warm up—something—and now—" He twirled the dial and several stations blatted in, some music, some voices. He looked at Jenkins and Tella Rhonta with mounting excitement. "It's ten o'clock—we can find news!"

"Let it go," Jenkins said sharply.

"No! There may be news from Atravi—or Paris!"

Jenkins squared his shoulders and, with another look to Tella Rhonta, put his hands deep in his coat pockets. Tella Rhonta saw that she was seated between the standing Jenkins and the kneeling Endidi, and she quickly left the chair to go stand near the stairs.

Endidi, turning, brought in the voice of a news announcer.

"*. . . record heat wave throughout the Midwest,*" the voice boomed from the speaker. "*Forecasters see no letup until the weekend is over, at the earliest.*"

"Is that news, fool?" Endidi muttered, staring at the dial of the radio.

"*In other top news stories at this hour, there is still no official response from the White House on the latest Russian proposal to set new limits on nuclear weapons. And in Tokyo, demonstrations continue as a result of the latest round of protective tariff regulations endorsed by the United States. The latest protective measures are the most stringent since the import law of 1980, which even its authors have since admitted as a complete failure in stemming the trade deficit.*"

Endidi waited, a kneeling statue, as did Jenkins and Tella Rhonta. The radio was silent for what seemed a long time.

"*And now this bulletin just in from United Press International,*" the announcer resumed in sharper tones. "*Quoting a source it will not identify, the State Department only moments ago said that it believes the interim government in the African nation of Marandaya has been overthrown.*"

Clarence Endidi gasped and jumped to his feet. "What?"

"*Only late this morning, the State Department issued a release stating that it believed General Marcos Arman, second-in-command to President Joseph Obutu, had*

*assumed all control of the Marandayan government. This
while President Obutu was in Paris, France, to conclude a
mutual-aid treaty.*

"*Now the latest word from State is that General Arman
himself has been deposed, and is presumed dead. The
liberation flag of Gero Paasaad's revolutionary army is
reliably reported to be flying over the palace in Atravi.*

"*Repeating this bulletin just in—*"

The rest was lost as Endidi let out a shriek. "What is he
saying?"

"It's a mistake," Jenkins said. "Obviously—"

"Betrayal! My God, how could this happen except by
betrayal—by *design?*"

"Clary," Jenkins said, his hands still jammed in his coat
pockets, "sit down."

Endidi whirled on Tella Rhonta. "You don't even act
surprised! My God! You *knew!* General Arman *has* been
betrayed!"

"Clary," Jenkins repeated, his right hand coming out
of the coat pocket with an ugly little revolver in it, "sit
down."

"I trusted you! I thought we were in this together—to
bring Marandaya a new, strong leader who would rout
Paasaad! But all the time you were plotting to give Paasaad
actual control—to ruin my country—"

"The take-over is by now complete," Jenkins said
coldly. "Will you accept the inevitable, or join the FBI
whore at the bottom of a lake?"

Clarence Endidi stared, eyes bulging. Then something
seemed to break inside him. With a guttural scream, he
charged Jenkins.

Jenkins fired twice, the shots shockingly loud, close together. The first bullet drove Endidi backward, staggering,
and the second blew most of his face off. He plunged
against the railing of the steps and flopped to the floor,
twitching before he became utterly still.

"Oh, Jesus," Tella Rhonta choked. "Clary . . . !"

Heavy footsteps sounded above, running. The door was
jerked open and the big man who looked like a dock

worker rushed down. He took in everything at a glance.

"Why?" he demanded.

Trembling, Leonard Jenkins put the revolver down on the corner of the table and stared at it as if it were a snake. "The radio—it started working and he heard Arman had been deposed—"

"How did *that* get out?" the dock worker asked with angry shock.

"I don't know. What do we do now?"

The dock worker's chest heaved as he stepped forward casually and picked up Jenkins' revolver, pocketing it. "People must have heard those shots all up and down the street. I was supposed to wait for another man. Now you've ruined that. I can't wait at all."

He reached inside his jacket and took out an automatic weapon with a long, ugly silencer fitted to the barrel.

"What?" Jenkins rasped, his jaw dropping.

"You spoiled everything," the dock worker said calmly. "The FBI woman. The papers she saw. Now Endidi. Even your man in Paris failed. You must know we cannot allow witnesses to live now."

"But," Tella Rhonta said shrilly, "we trusted you! We did everything you asked! Just because our man in Paris failed—"

"We did not expect your man in Paris to succeed. We have our own man in Paris. But you must be blamed. If you examine the logic, you will see the inevitable."

"No!" Leonard Jenkins said.

The dock worker's right hand tightened slightly around the gun. It made a hollow, spitting noise and Jenkins was blown backward as if by a mammoth hand. Even as he spun back to the wall, the gun swung to Tella Rhonta and again made its curious, nasty spitting noise. She was thrown against the stairs very near Clarence Endidi.

The dock worker, gun still in hand, bent first to examine Jenkins. It took only a few seconds. He then bent over Tella Rhonta. Satisfied, he walked to the couch and looked down at Eileen Arrington. He holstered the automatic and expertly probed her throat for the carotid.

He was very tired of killing. He had never liked it, as some of his companions seemed to. Now it was clear to him that Eileen might live. Duty, he thought, required that he make sure of her death.

But he was so tired of it. And really she knew so little.

He decided. Turning, he walked to the stairs and went up.

Twelve minutes later, local police cars raced up to the house. They found Grover Matsoon dead, his throat slashed, in the empty dining room on the ground floor. They went to the basement and looked around and made some calls. They searched the neighborhood, but found no one who knew anything. There was great excitement.

By the time Rick Kelley reached the scene, the forensics people and other technicians had mostly taken over. Kelley, gaunt-eyed, came down the basement stairs in a commotion of anxiety. Then he stopped and stared at the bodies, the lab boys, the photographer.

"A girl," he said, his voice shaking. "A woman, I mean."

A couple of the technicians looked up, eyes hooded, and said nothing.

"Come on!" Kelley screamed at them. "Did you find her?"

"Take it easy, Rick," Berg, standing behind him, said.

A fat sergeant came over from the far side of the basement. "A young black woman? Not that one over there?"

"No, not that one. Another one. She was younger. She was a lot prettier. She—she was my partner."

"Oh," the sergeant said. "They already took her away."

Kelley stared, his face absolutely without color or expression. He was trembling just a little, from head to foot.

"Take it easy, now, Rick," Berg said very softly.

"I think they took her to Memorial," the sergeant said. "She was still unconscious—some kind of drugs, the doc said. But he said he thought he could pull her out of it okay."

"Where did they take her?" Kelley asked.

"Memorial. It's down—"

"I know where it is." Kelley turned and went up the steps very fast, Berg right behind him.

21

Paris

Of all the monuments in Paris, the Louvre museum is among the richest in its history, and the most revered.

Built as a fortress on the Seine in the year 1200, the original Louvre covered less than a fourth of the space now occupied by Cour Carrée, cornerstone area of the present massive edifice. Over the centuries the location has seen destruction and rebuilding, changes in basic design, the birth of kings and their death.

It was in 1793 that the idea of the Louvre as a museum was finally realized with the opening of a section to public view. From Napoleon to the present day, French leaders have dedicated themselves to enrichment of what many consider the world's greatest museum.

Today the visitor is confronted by a massive structure built upon a mammoth block O design a full city block square. From this basic design, two incredibly long, ornately decorated wings extend westward, toward the Tuileries, two city blocks. The grassy, hedged garden area enclosed by the arms of the building forms a kind of park of its own. Closer to the main entrance, in the O configuration, dusty cobbles lie in the deep shadows of the building walls at all times except briefly, when the sun is almost directly overhead.

There are 225 galleries, making the building a fascinating, frustrating, and (for the weary) an even frighteningly complex maze.

French and foreign sightseers, many with children, were

streaming to and from the Louvre when Dugger, with Anita Courtright, emerged from the Paris underground station and hurried toward it. A glance at his watch showed it was ten minutes after four.

"It's a very stupid thing for them to do," Anita panted, running to keep up with Dugger's long strides.

Dugger had one hand in his coat pocket to keep the revolver from banging his thigh. "Let's just hope their timing is as bad as their judgment. We might already be too late."

"How do you know the killer would know about their plan to meet here?"

"Don't forget *I* found out just looking at Pete's desk blotter. 'Winged V.—4.' If *I* got a look at it, Crouex would have gotten the same look, with more time to think about it and make the logical guess. Crouex had to be working with the Russian. That's how he got to sight in his rifle on Pete's range; Crouex must have let him in when no one else was around one day."

"Can President Obutu *really* be planning to sell those things to Pierre?"

"I don't know," Dugger admitted as they rushed across the large, dirty cobblestones toward the entrance. "It looks like it."

"I can't understand why."

"Money," Dugger suggested as they entered the dusty foyer. "Or power. Maybe he sees Marandaya getting the first ultimate weaponry. Come on. Save your breath. You might need it."

Under a high, dirty ceiling, dozens of visitors milled around. Dugger slipped through them as quickly as possible, reaching the half-circle desk under a sign for visitors. He paid quickly and led Anita through a doorway into a deserted-looking space beneath a steel staircase where other outside doors were blocked by sawhorses and chains. On a pedestal was a chart of the building.

Dugger studied it impatiently.

"I think I know the way," Anita said.

"Let's go."

They went around the stairs and up a half flight, through another doorway and into a gallery. Dugger could not immediately identify the area of emphasis, although the glass-enclosed tables and exhibit windows showed obviously ancient basketwork and pottery. The ceiling was not very high, the floor bare marble, the room no longer than a comfortable living room. A few other people were browsing. Anita led him through the next doorway into another gallery containing similar materials, and through still another doorway beyond. The nature of the exhibits changed to the Middle Ages, tapestries and porcelain. Anita hurried ahead, brushing by people going in both directions.

After several more rooms, there was an intersection with another corridor. Anita turned left, to a staircase, and went down a few tiled stairs. Turning right again, she led the way into a huge room with an enormously high ceiling. On the walls, dark with age, were huge oils.

She turned back, frowning. "Wrong turn."

They went back down the steps and turned the other way. Again she led as they plunged through a number of small galleries, this lower level with ceilings close enough that Dugger was aware of claustrophobia. They hurried through the crowds, people gazing, chatting, a few making diligent notes. Dugger looked ahead and had the bizarre feeling that he was looking into a trick with mirrors: inside the doorway ahead, somewhat smaller, was another gilt doorway beyond, and inside that one was another. Dugger could see at least fifteen doorways, one inside the other, marching in a perfectly straight line as far as he had perspective.

He turned and looked back, and had the same eerie view behind. They were all real doors; he and Anita were in the middle of a wing that was unbelievably long and uniform, gallery after gallery marching in both directions.

Anita led him through two more doorways and stopped to say something to a dark-blue-clad attendant. The man looked almost too bored to live. He pointed to his right— the way they had come.

"I missed it," Anita said grimly, heading back.

There was no use complaining. Dugger began to understand what a rat felt like in a training box. Sweat had burst out all over his body. The air was dusty, too warm, with no movement whatsoever. He could not see an exit—even a way to an exit.

Halfway up the wing, Anita turned into a hallway. It led to stairs up. The stairs became broader and then turned again, widening still more. The light that came around the corner was brighter, like daylight, and the qualities of echoing voices promised greater space.

They moved around the corner, and were there.

Just ahead of them, lighted in golden illumination from above, on the two-story landing between floors, stood the Winged Victory of Samothrace. The classic statue, well protected in its own natural pit within the stairs and floors, had attracted dozens of visitors. They sat and stood around it on three sides, on the railings and steps. Small lanterns flickered, adding to the sense of antiquity.

Dugger, however, had time to give the heroic statue only a brief glance. He was already scanning the crowd, looking for Pierre LaFontaine and Joseph Obutu. The corridors fanned out broadly in opposite directions, people everywhere, but he could not see a familiar face or form.

"We're too late," Anita said, breathing hard. "They could have walked on anywhere after meeting here."

Dugger looked down the broad hallways, trying to put himself in their place. It was impossible. He pointed. "You go down that way and I'll go over in this direction. Don't go so far you can't be back right here in five minutes."

Anita nodded and hurried off to the left.

Dugger moved in and through the loose crowd in the other direction. He was again in sculpture and painting. The galleries on this level were so large that they absorbed the considerable crowd and still provided some feeling of spaciousness. He kept swiveling his neck as he moved through two such rooms and into a third.

In this area the crowd was denser, voices rumbling in the

dusty air. A large sign pointed to the left for the Venus de Milo. Dugger glanced in at the milling mob in front of the glassed-in, dark little classic far across the room, then hurried on.

As he approached the next gallery, he slowed suddenly.

Up ahead, perhaps fifty feet away, two very familiar figures stood near a side wall, engaged in earnest conversation. Sweat gleamed visibly on the foreheads of both Joseph Obutu and Pierre LaFontaine. LaFontaine was talking, an unloaded cigarette holder clenched between His teeth, ticking off points on the fingers of his left hand.

Dugger swung his gaze around, looking for the man in the straw hat.

He was standing closer to Dugger, near a tall piece of statuary. He did not have the hat anymore, but his face was unmistakable. He now wore a pale summer suit, the coat very rumpled, and he had his right hand under his jacket on the left side.

Dugger started toward him, taking the revolver out.

The killer turned suddenly and saw him. There was recognition in his eyes, and rapid decision. His own hand came free and he produced a machine pistol with the obvious muzzle shape of a silencer. Raising the gun, he aimed at Obutu and LaFontaine and instantly fired. There was a sharp puffing sound, a great deal of smoke, and the noise of a hammer crashing into a wall. Obutu spun, eyes wide with alarm. LaFontaine was hit.

Dugger rushed toward the killer as heads started turning. There was no alarm, and most people had no idea what was happening. The killer got his gun out of sight, turned, and ran to his right, vanishing momentarily behind a mammoth statue of a mounted horseman. Dugger did not dare fire in the crowd. He glanced back. LaFontaine was on the floor.

"Colonel!" Obutu called sharply.

Guards were coming on the run. Dugger turned and rushed after the killer.

He had gone beyond the statue into the milling throng

beyond, making it into the broad central corridor. Dugger caught glimpses of the bald spot on top of his head as he pushed through as fast as he could. Dugger got tangled up momentarily with a woman pushing a baby in a walker, and lost sight of him for an instant.

It had all happened so fast that any commotion was left behind. As Dugger pushed through a large gallery with medieval paintings on the walls, he realized that the crowd was acting entirely normally. The killer had come this way, hurrying as fast as possible without attracting undue attention. Dugger had to catch him, but could not risk a shot or even a general alarm that might start a panic sure to guarantee the other man's escape. Dugger crossed the next gallery and looked into the hallway beyond. He was almost back to the Winged Victory, and could not see the killer in either direction.

He started to go to the right, and instantly saw Anita Courtright coming toward him.

"They aren't that way," she said. Then she noticed his expression. "What's happened?"

"A man in a light suit, hurrying?"

"No. What *happened*?"

There was no time to explain. Dugger turned and hurried the other way. There was a staircase going down and he took it, footsteps echoing in the still air as he went down.

In the area below the corridors were narrower again, and he had undoubtedly come out somewhere in the Egyptian exhibits. The dimly lighted beige walls contained shadow boxes containing golden jewelry and intricate works in lapis lazuli. A mummy case dominated a tiny gallery room with a ceiling so low Dugger could have reached up and touched it. There were fewer visitors here, some of the tiny rooms entirely vacant as Dugger went through them.

Three steps led downward. As he reached the bottom, in a tomblike series of rooms containing huge stone vessels and relief maps showing a dig, he looked ahead and saw the killer just going up identical stairs on the far side of the series of interconnecting rooms. Dugger ran.

Flanked by circular posts containing glass globes that protected tiny jeweled children's toys, the shallow stairs were empty. Dugger went up them and into another small, low-ceilinged room with many partial partitions to facilitate display of maps and photographs of the ruins of an ancient city of Egypt. Two middle-aged women and a man were standing to the left, studying some section of the photographs.

Dugger started past their area.

Ahead a dozen paces, the other man appeared suddenly from behind a six-foot rock bowl. His gun was in his hand. Dugger started to jump to the side, and the gun winked and something hit him hard in the left side of his chest. One of the women screamed. The killer darted through another doorway. Dugger looked down and saw a bright red hole in his shirt.

Ahead were the sounds of the other man's heels running downstairs.

Dugger moved through the room after him. He was not aware of any pain yet, but there was a buzzing in his ears. He realized he was splattering droplets of blood on the floor as he ran. Several people were coming up the stairs toward him, and they gasped and got back out of his way as he went by.

At the bottom of the stairs was a darkly lighted area with no exhibits. Six corridors went in various directions, into more mazelike series of rooms. Dugger had begun to feel the bright, hot pain. He saw people in all directions, but not the man he wanted. So it was down to a guess.

A guard was standing nearby, his back turned, hands behind his back in the classic French pose of total boredom. Dugger knew it was hopeless to describe the killer to him; the guard had not really looked at anyone in years.

Dugger went to him. *"Sortie?"* he asked, his voice croaking.

The guard did not bother to turn. He wiggled a finger straight ahead.

Dugger brushed by him and plunged down the corridor

in the direction indicated. Evidently the guard noticed the blood at the point.

"Monsieur!"

Ignoring him, Dugger came to a turn. An arrow pointed right. There were some narrow stairs. He went down them, the walls and steps seeming to tilt crazily. He was not seeing at all clearly, and the pain was much worse. He reached a dingy landing. There was another of the endless doorways. He went through it and saw five more steps below, and beyond that, the bright light of the outside. He stumbled down the last stairs and saw a broad, stone-floored reception area, a visitors' booth, doors to the blessed outside.

Ignoring more cries of alarm, he made it to the doors and beyond.

He had come out a main exit on the side of the building facing the Tuileries. An acre of dusty cobblestone court-yard confronted him, with crisscrossing sidewalks and hedges beyond, and even beyond that, the small entry arch and the gardens themselves. Wings of the museum walled in the courtyard, and everywhere families were walking, children running.

Ahead of Dugger about thirty yards, the killer was walking away fast.

Dugger started to run, gun in hand. He was vaguely aware of someone shouting, and a whistle. Ahead of him, the other man stopped abruptly and turned. Seeing Dugger, he leveled the pistol again.

Dugger dived for the pavement, hurting himself badly as he hit the cobbles. The other man's gun made its ugly puffing sound, but the bullet sang off the pavement a foot away. Dugger leveled the revolver with both hands. He hesitated. There were people beyond. A miss could kill an innocent. He wanted the killer very badly, but he was torn.

The killer leveled the gun for another shot. Then suddenly he stopped and whirled. Dugger, with his blurring vision, saw that some of the people beyond him were darkly clad—*gendarmes*. There were at least ten of them in a ragged line, running at the killer from the far side.

He saw them, too. Turning, he raised his weapon. The police went to their knees or flat on the pavement and began firing. Near where Dugger lay, other men ran. They were firing, too. Dugger had the insane thought that the attackers would shoot past their prey—and kill each other off. But the angles were all wrong for that old joke . . . he was not thinking clearly.

The shots hit the lone man. His weapon pinwheeled out of his hands. He stood up very straight, his back arching, and then he tumbled forward. Uniformed and plain-clothes officers rushed up and surrounded him where he lay.

Dugger rested his face on the gritty cobbles and thought he heard Anita Courtright's voice somewhere nearby just as he passed out.

22

Atravi

The parachutes started drifting down three hours before dawn in a rolling savannah several miles east of the city. The troops were black, the elite fighting men of another African nation a thousand miles away. Wearing American-made uniforms and carrying American equipment of the latest design, they moved with the swift efficiency taught by their American combat advisers back home. Squads and platoons formed up, and orders were given. While heavier parachute bundles were opened and made operational, units fanned out along the highway and the river, and into the hills beyond, probing for signs of detection.

There were none.

By dawn the combat team had split into two groups, one moving toward Atravi at top speed, the other taking up prearranged positions on the high ground near the highway.

At 6:14 A.M., forward spotters sent a single alert burst on a radio. Two minutes later, the waiting combat team could hear the sounds of the approaching engines. At 6:19, the first vehicle, a light tank of Russian manufacture, chittered around the bend in the highway and moved into the low stretch below the defilade. Behind the lead tank came an armored personnel carrier flying the dark flag of Gero Paasaad's revolutionary army, and then two jeeps, four heavy trucks with canvas covering, a number of Soviet-made BRDM armored cars, another jeep, finally a second light tank. There were more than six hundred men riding with the convoy, including two hundred Cuban troops and Gero Paasaad.

Paasaad rode in clear view in the lead jeep, two heavily armed soldiers accompanying him. Paasad had clenched in his teeth, but had not yet lighted, the Havana cigar he planned to smoke during the last mile of his triumphant drive to the palace.

The troops in the defilade waited patiently. Their armament included ten bazookas, two recoilless rifles, and four 81 mm mortars. Most of the men had grenade launchers, and ten grenades each.

The lead tank crunched down the rotten pavement toward the far end of the draw. By this time, 6:22, the entire convoy was under the guns of the parachute team.

The attack began. The lead tank blew up, and the tank at the rear of the column was thrown onto its side, treads blown up and its fuel igniting, almost simultaneously. Murderous fire poured down from the ridge and other vehicles exploded—trucks, jeeps, personnel carriers—before many of their riders could try to leap for safety. Automatic-weapons fire formed a deadly latticework across the ground as survivors of the initial strike started to return fire. Then the grenades started raining down, making rose-petal crimson explosions. The big mortars lobbed up their rounds, saturating the killing zone.

Gero Paasaad had one leg out of his jeep when it took a direct hit and blew into a million pieces.

By 6:25 it was over. Smoke rose in dense columns from the shattered hulks littering the road. Mangled bodies were everywhere. The African troops, in their American uniforms, moved cautiously through the wreckage, making sure.

A captain made a brief report by radio.

At 6:29 there was a brief fighting in the courtyard outside the palace in Atravi. A grenade cleared a room on the lower floor, and for the next fifteen minutes or so there was some heavy fighting from room to room and building to building. Then all fell silent.

At 6:52 there was a brief, furious exchange of gunfire in

a street nearby. This coincided almost exactly with the carrying out of a certain number of executions in the court yard.

The flag of Marandaya replaced the revolutionary emblem.

Minutes later, unexpected sounds penetrated the gloomy basement where Tavecki Vi, leader of the Marandayan Assembly, had been hovering between sick, exhausted sleep and miserable consciousness. A door was flung open and bright light stunned his eyes. He thought they were coming to execute him.

The door of the cell was opened. Strong hands helped him to his feet. The soldiers were not wearing Marandayan uniforms, and they were gentle as they took Tavecki Vi up stairs, through a gutted lower room of the palace, and to the presidential office.

Tavecki Vi had never seen the black officer there before.

The officer, a colonel, saluted smartly. "Tavecki Vi, I wish to report that the insurrection has been put down. You are a free man. As senior authority in Marandaya during this grave crisis, you were wise to issue such a prompt plea to my government, through secret channels, seeking our intervention to help you against the rebels."

"I . . . ?" Tavecki Vi said, confused.

"Your action made our intervention legally possible," the officer said.

Tavecki Vi understood. "Yes. We thank you for your quick response."

"It will be well, sir, if you immediately restore normal channels of communication between Atravi and the out side world. My men have moved to start this action for you. It will be well for you to take the air as soon as possible, announcing the end of the revolt and explaining how we responded to your legitimate plea to our govern ment for assistance in this matter."

Tavecki Vi began to smile. "Yes. I see. I agree with you, Colonel."

Only a little after noon, an American jet aircraft flying the colors of Marandaya touched down at the airport. The armed presence around the field was very heavy, although everything had been quiet. The door of the airplane opened, and Joseph Obutu came down the steps to be embraced by Tavecki Vi, three loyal officers from the army, and the mayor of Atravi. A military band played. Then Obutu walked to a waiting Cadillac limousine, where he was greeted by his wife and small son.

It was about this same time that soldiers looking for Geoffrey Harrington found him hiding in a well near his house. When brought to daylight, the ham radio operator was still clutching a plastic bag of sandwiches and a bottle of Beefeater gin. He acted surprised when the soldiers told him he was a hero.

New York City

Dawn had not yet come to the eastern seaboard of the United States. In the quiet hospital room, Rick Kelley, dazed by fatigue and grief, sat beside the bed. Eileen Arrington's face made a dark oval on the pillow. She lay very still, bottles dripping solutions into her body.

Rick Kelley had been waiting for hours now.

Suddenly Eileen Arrington's eyelids fluttered. Her lips parted. Her eyes opened and she looked directly at Kelley.

"Hi," she said almost inaudibly.

"Do you know who I am?" he asked.

She smiled wanly. "Sure. What happened? I guess you saved me, huh?"

"They didn't know if you would be all right or not," Kelley choked. "They thought maybe—your mind—and I've been sitting here—"

"I'm fine. I hurt, but I'm okay. How—" Eileen stopped, then, because Kelley had begun soundlessly to cry with relief.

Eileen watched him. She became aware of a new feeling, one that was very gentle and very nice. She reached a tender hand to his face, touching the wetness on his cheeks.

"Silly," she said softly. "You silly . . . sweet . . . guy. . . ."

Paris

It was three days later when Joe Dugger was ready to walk out of the hospital. The doctors said this was too early. He ignored them.

On the way out, he went by the room where Pierre LaFontaine was recuperating. In the flower-bedecked private area, he found LaFontaine talking with his wife, Maria. Both looked up sharply as he entered.

"They're letting me out," Dugger told them. "I wanted to say good-bye."

LaFontaine, very pale, did not raise his head from the pillow, but his voice was firm. "We'll miss you, Joseph." He twiddled his fingers at his wife, who began loading a cigarette into his holder at the bedside table. "You didn't exactly provide me every assistance I wanted, but . . ." He shrugged.

"You can't expect to win them all," Dugger told him, smiling.

"Ah, but I would have liked to win this one!"

"Your rockets will still make millions for you and your German friends. Unless somebody else gets the idea of blowing you away."

"I believe Joseph Obutu would have sold us the weapons materials if it had not been for all the other turmoil, and then the blackmail from Washington."

"Well," Dugger told him, still smiling, "if he hadn't cooperated, he might not have had any country to go back to. But call it blackmail if you want."

"I suppose," LaFontaine said, letting Maria fit the cigarette holder between his teeth, "I do owe you my life."

"Don't mention it, pal."

LaFontaine, too, grinned as a match was struck and he puffed smoke. "A real pity. So many will believe the myth of Germany rising again—another Reich."

"It's not entirely a myth," Dugger told him. "There are maniacs out there. There are some reasons for the fear."

"You say that? A German apologist?"

"I've never denied the danger. I've only said that the danger is very small at the present time. Right now I can't waste my energy worrying about a Fourth Reich. That's not where the power is today. If the tanks roll across Europe in the rest of this century, it won't be because Nazis started it."

LaFontaine grinned, his cigarette holder at his best FDR angle. "Just remember that, Joseph. The bullets they dug out of both of us were not of German manufacture."

Dugger shook hands, knowing that LaFontaine probably had not been changed at all. Perhaps it no longer mattered. He walked out into the hallway.

"Mr. Dugger?"

He turned. Maria LaFontaine had followed him. She looked drawn from worry, but very lovely in her chic summer dress and heels.

"I wanted to add my private word of thanks," she told him, her eyes warm.

"I won't say it was my pleasure, Maria. But I appreciate it."

"What will happen to Crognoi?"

"He'll go to prison, I'm sure, if he lives. And then one day they'll have some of ours and we'll have more of theirs and we'll swap."

"I heard this man might have been the one you suspected of . . . killing your wife."

"I never knew. I thought it might be Crognoi, yes. But when I saw him, I didn't even recognize him. He had gotten old." Dugger paused. "We're all getting old."

"Do you regret not shooting him when you might have had a chance?"

Dugger thought about it. "No. I'm past that point now."

She hesitated, then asked, "Will you be in Paris long?"

"I don't think so, no."

"Oh, I had thought we might . . . meet."

He looked down at her. The invitation was there again, not blatant or cheap, but very clear. "I really can't," he told her.

"I see." She gave him a little smile.

On impulse, he bent to kiss her cheek. Very quickly she responded with a little catch of breath, clinging to him. Her perfume was lovely. It would have been very nice, the two of them, and he knew that.

That afternoon, Dugger walked out of the American embassy with Charles McCoy and Anita Courtright. It was a brightly hazy day, and he could just make out the shadowy outline of the distant Eiffel Tower. It had rained briefly, and the broad expanse of the Place gleamed under the thrumming tires of a thousand little automobiles. The wood doves were flying near the gate to the Tuileries.

"Well," McCoy said, hitching up his trousers, "don't think it hasn't been fun."

"Anything more from Washington?"

"I told you how our pals in the FBI had infiltrated the spy apparatus around the Marandayan delegation. They've traced back some leads from there and found our leak in the security section. He's in custody."

"How about the writer?"

"A nobody in Manchester. He didn't even really know what he was doing for them."

"What about the agent who was hurt?"

"The lady? I understand she's up and around."

"It's wrapped up, then."

"Well, yes and no. The Russians obviously killed those delegates after everything went sour. We have no leads on that. And they won't have much trouble finding other delegates eager to turn handsprings for them."

Dugger smiled. "I didn't imagine you could retire."

McCoy looked at him, then held out his hand. "Luck, Joe."

"Same to you, buddy."

"Keep in touch."

"Not if I can help it."

McCoy grimaced, turned and walked away. At the corner he went left to walk up the Rue Royale. The buildings blocked further view, and he was gone.

Dugger turned to Anita, who looked pretty in a pale blue dress. She was bare-legged, wearing sandals, and her hair was loose. It made her appear very young. "Well," he said.

"You didn't ask him about the chemicals," she said.

"The CBW weapons?"

"Yes."

"I didn't ask because it isn't my business."

"They're still buried down there in Marandaya, then. They'll stay there, and someone else will try to get them, and it will happen all over again."

"No." Dugger felt more tired. "I think we'll probably move them out now, after this. Eventually. It will cost a lot of money. And we'll never hear about it in the press."

"Where could they put those things?"

"Hell, I don't know. On an island somewhere. Or maybe out in the western United States, where we own millions of acres with fences around them and people don't ask a lot of questions."

"Washington wouldn't do that."

"I imagine we've got a lot worse things buried, Anita."

She looked out over the square, and it was clear that it troubled her still. "It lay buried all those years near Regensburg . . . that legacy of hate. Then even its *potential* caused all this."

"It's all right now," Dugger told her.

"I don't know if I can believe that."

"You can. You will. You're a big girl now. You live with the facts."

She studied his face. Finally she smiled faintly. She was not only a big girl now, Dugger thought, she was a tough one. She would be all right.

He said, "I guess I'll tell you good-bye, then."

"What are you going to do?"

"Well, I'm a little tired. Don't let the doctors know. I think I'll go back to the hotel and lie down an hour. Then there's the matter of buying a car and getting back home."

"To Burghausen?"

"There first. And then I think I might really go home for a while. To the States, I mean. I think it's time I went back. I can now."

She nodded, lighted a cigarette, and faced the square.

"And you?" Dugger asked.

"Well, I have a month off. I don't know."

Dugger hesitated, then said, "You could go with me."

She turned to look at him. "Where?"

"We could drive down into Switzerland, then back through the Alps. Get a Coleman and a frying pan and stop every once in a while to cook some sausage and drink some beer."

She began to smile. "Wine is more romantic."

"Well, wine, then. By all means."

"I suppose we could do that," she told him.

"We could," he said, watching her. There was an un-accustomed stirring in his chest.

Her smile broadened, but she didn't say anything.

"So what do you think?" he asked finally.

She linked her arm with his. "Let's."